THE KELLY SISTERS

Patricia, Tara and Aideen couldn't be more excited about leaving Dublin with their father and heading for a new life in Liverpool. Yet it soon becomes clear that all is not as it seems. The day after they arrive in England, Bernie hastily sweeps the girls onto an ocean liner heading to New York. When their father vanishes, mid-way across the Atlantic, the grieving sisters prepare themselves for a new life in the big city far from home. Whatever their father was running from has every chance of catching up with the girls, unless they can do their best to build new lives in New York.

THE KELLY SISTERS

THE KELLY SISTERS

by

Maureen Lee

Magna Large Print Books
Long Preston, North Yorkshire,
BD23 4ND, England.

British Library Cataloguing in Publication Data.

Lee, Maureen
    The Kelly sisters.

    A catalogue record of this book is
    available from the British Library

    ISBN   978-0-7505-4258-6

First published in Great Britain in 2015 by Orion Books,
an imprint of The Orion Publishing Group Ltd.

Copyright © Maureen Lee 2015

Cover illustration © Joana Kruse by arrangement with
Arcangel Images

Published in Large Print 2016 by arrangement with
The Orion Publishing Group Ltd.

Magna Large Print is an imprint of Library Magna Books Ltd.

Printed and bound in Great Britain by
T.J. (International) Ltd., Cornwall, PL28 8RW

Part 1

Chapter 1

Dublin,
February 1925

Bernie Kelly and his girls were moving to Liverpool on Monday and his friends were throwing a party to see him off.

'Don't make it a big one, lads,' Bernie had pleaded. He'd only given them five days' notice. 'Just half a dozen or so of me best mates, that'll do.'

'Only half a dozen!' Ray Walsh, one of the best mates, chortled, for Bernie, a solicitor, was on best-mate terms with most of the professional men in Dublin – and on slightly different terms with a number of their wives.

'I'd prefer a quiet do,' Bernie had insisted. He winked and squeezed his friend's hand, adding in a low voice, 'I don't want all and sundry knowing I'm taking off, like.' And Ray had understood. Bernie wasn't leaving for the stated reason – that Liverpool would provide more opportunities for himself and his daughters – but for another reason altogether, possibly to do with a woman or an over-insistent bookie.

Hopefully he would only be gone for a while until things blew over, as it were, and he and the girls would be back, his misdeeds, whatever they were, either forgotten or forgiven, though this

11

was more of a hope than a belief. Everyone knew Bernie Kelly sailed pretty close to the wind from time to time. Perhaps this time he had got a bit too close.

It was even rumoured that eight years ago his poor wife, Meriel, had died not because she'd just given birth to Bernie's first legitimate son, Milo, but of a cruelly broken heart. She must have known that every now and again another woman in Dublin was going through the same agony of producing a son or daughter courtesy of her hand-some husband, him of the alluring smile, the dancing eyes and the ever-roving hands.

The party was held on a Saturday night in the Kelly's big, rambling house overlooking Phoenix Park. There were no more than thirty people there, even though Bernie had held parties in the past at which there'd been ten times that many. His girls, the prettiest in Dublin – Patricia, 18, Aideen, 16, and Tara, 14 – went round with the food that had been prepared by old Nora Hogan, who'd done the cooking and cleaning for the family since the beginning of time. Bernie was rumoured to be paying her off with a small fortune in gratitude for all her hard work on behalf of him and his family over the years. Rumours of one thing or another, good and bad, surrounded Bernie like a cloud of noisy bumblebees.

His eight-year-old son, Milo, had already been left with Bernie's sister-in-law, Auntie Kathleen, a widow who'd looked after the girls since his wife had died. They had already moved into a house on the far side of the park and both would be sent for when the time was ready, when Bernie and his girls were settled in their fine new house in Princes Park, one of the grandest areas of Liverpool.

At the party, Bernie handed out cards showing the address and telephone number of his new office in Dale Street, not far from the city's town hall. 'But I won't be properly installed for a month or so,' he told people. 'So don't be calling till then.'

He looked more worried than excited about the big change that was about to happen. Whenever he laughed or smiled, you could tell he was only putting it on. He was rarely seen without a cigarette burning in his mouth. He'd always been fond of cigarettes, but was fast becoming what was known as a chain-smoker. It was the same with drink, his intake of the hard stuff having gone up by a mile.

'Are you sad you're leaving, Bernie Boy?' Ray asked at the party, thinking that was the reason for his miserable gob.

'Of course I am, Ray. I was born and bred in Dublin. The thought of leaving is tearing me guts apart.'

'Well, stay, Bernie. Stay. There's not a single soul here that wants to see the back o' yis. Aren't we all like one big happy family?'

Patrick Adams, Dick O'Neill, Bernie and Ray himself had met at Trinity College in Dublin where they'd been taking their various degrees. They had remained friends ever since. Ray was fonder of Bernie, Patrick and Dick than he was of his own brothers.

'It's not possible,' Bernie sighed. 'Anyway, it's time for a change. Things have to move on, progress, or you just get stuck in a rut for the rest of your life. Like I said, I'm moving for me own and me girls' sakes. We could well end up in London one of these days.'

The party was well over by midnight, a good five hours before Bernie's parties usually came to a riotous end. After everyone had gone, he urged his daughters to go to bed straight away.

'I've changed me mind. We're leaving early tomorrer, 'stead of Monday,' he told them. 'Are yis all packed and ready to go?'

Patricia and Tara agreed they were, but Aideen, always the awkward one, nearly had a fit. 'I'm not nearly ready, Daddy,' she said angrily. With her dark red hair and green eyes, she was the only one to take after her dad, except she didn't possess hardly any of his charismatic ways. The other girls resembled their pale, golden, long-deceased mother.

'Then get your sisters to give you a hand,' Bernie ordered his middle daughter. 'We're leaving promptly at ten o'clock in the morning and that's that.'

Tara gasped in horror. 'But what about Mass?'

'You'll just have to go to the seven o'clock,' her father snapped.

'But, Daddy,' Patricia, the eldest, reminded him, 'all of our friends are coming tomorrow to say goodbye.' They'd been invited to afternoon tea.

'Well, they'll just have to say goodbye to the empty air,' said Bernie. 'Because you'll all be on the boat sailing to Liverpool.'

'Also, Daddy,' Aideen said crossly, glaring at

her father (he didn't scare any one of them the least little bit), 'I really think we should stay up and take the plates and glasses out to Nora for her to wash as well as help her tidy up a bit.' The downstairs rooms were littered with the detritus of the party.

'Go to bed, the lot o' yis,' Bernie yelled. 'Or I'll put you over me knee, one by one, and give you a good spanking.'

Tara laughed. 'Just try it, Daddy, and I promise it'll be you who'll get the spanking.'

Nevertheless, all three went upstairs to bed. They might not be scared of their charming daddy, but they loved him and didn't want him upset. They could tell something was wrong and didn't want to make things worse.

It was February and it was freezing. There were specks of frost in the air being blown to and fro by an icy wind when Bernie Kelly and his shivering girls left the house by Phoenix Park the next morning. A car was parked outside to take them to Dún Laoghaire from where the boat sailed to Liverpool, as well as a van for their luggage. Each girl carried a little valise that contained night-clothes and toiletries – it might be a while before the trunks could be opened, Bernie had explained. A tearful Nora stood on the steps and waved goodbye.

It was warm on the boat in the first-class lounge, though the sea outside was the colour of dirty pea soup, according to Aideen who had a way with words and a vivid imagination. A fierce wind whistled wildly.

15

They were thrilled to finally reach Liverpool, though nearly froze to death when they disembarked from the boat and made their way to another car that was to take them to the Adelphi hotel, where their father had booked a suite on the second floor. Their new house wasn't quite ready to move into, Bernie explained. There were still one or two things that had to be done. Fortunately it only took a jiffy to get to the hotel.

'This is nice!' Tara said as she removed her coat and threw herself onto one of the three single beds, each covered with a voluminous royal blue satin eiderdown.

There was a knock on the hotel suite door and Patricia opened it to a waiter with a tray of coffee. He informed them that dinner would be served from six o'clock onwards.

Bernie emerged from his own room, puffing madly on a cigarette, and announced he could eat a horse. Having reached this far, he was looking more at ease with himself, the girls decided as they tidied their hair, smoothed their frocks and adjusted their stockings ready to go down to dinner.

''Tis a big thing we're doing,' Patricia said while combing her blonde satiny hair and applying powder to her nose and cheeks – she was the only one who used makeup. 'Moving all the way to another country, like. And it's himself who's had to take all the responsibility.'

'Well, none of us wanted to move, so why should we be expected to take any of the responsibility?' Aideen reasoned.

'*I* don't mind moving, not a bit.' Tara adjusted

16

her garters. 'I wish I were old enough to wear a suspender belt.' She sniffed as she attached a white flower to her hair, which was the same colour as Patricia's. 'I didn't want to stay in Dublin for the rest of me life. Liverpool sounds much more interesting.'

Their father knocked on the door. 'Are yis ready in there?'

'Coming, Daddy,' they chorused.

The Kelly sisters created mild consternation in the glittering dining room; one outstandingly attractive young woman was enough to cause eyes to pop, but three arriving all together was a spectacle. Their clothes might not be the latest fashion but they looked smart in their fine woollen frocks decorated variously with buttons, bows and little lacy frills.

Somewhat appropriately, they had Irish stew for dinner, followed by steamed pudding and custard. The meal over, Aideen fancied going for a walk, but her sisters were horrified at the idea.

'It's much too cold,' Tara asserted. 'Me, I'd just like to sit in the lounge and read. We'll have plenty of time to go for walks in Liverpool.'

Patricia claimed to feel the same. 'I might write one or two letters telling people our new address, though I'll need English stamps to send them.'

Bernie looked at her through narrowed eyes, though didn't say anything. 'Get yisselves early to bed,' he advised. 'We'll be having a busy day tomorrer.'

Tara cried herself to sleep that night. She'd been

17

looking forward to the move to Liverpool and was ashamed of such a quick change of heart, but she was already missing her old bedroom in the house by Phoenix Park, her teddy bear, as well as her brother Milo. It had been arranged for Milo to come and stay with them at Easter and during the long summer holiday from school. Auntie Kathleen would bring him.

Aideen didn't cry, but she was furiously angry with her father for bringing an end to the secretly exciting life she had been leading in Dublin for virtually a year. Along with two girls – Frances O'Hara and Bernadette Doyle, who attended the same expensive girls' school as she did – she roamed the streets of the city getting up to all sorts of mischief. Under the pretence of belonging to a mythical Catholic club, as they told their parents, the three girls stole from shops, picked from pockets and smoked cigarettes in the dark corners of the dark streets. Occasionally they would meet up with boys and Frances had once let a boy touch her breasts. Being with the girls had felt terribly daring and enjoyable, and she would miss it.

Patricia was unable to sleep. Daddy had been up to something – well, he was always up to something or other – but this time it was more serious than his usual transgressions. She was worried that Liverpool, being merely a hop, skip and a jump away from Dublin, wasn't distant enough to escape a vengeful husband or a wrathful bookie.

Patricia had attended commercial college and then worked in her father's office, where she was able to keep an eye on him. She had noticed lately the way he jumped whenever the telephone rang and how he insisted on opening the post himself each morning, rather than allowing his secretary, Ruth, to open it, or Patricia herself.

It would only be a few hours before she discovered that her father had a completely different plan in mind that had nothing whatsoever to do with Liverpool.

Bernie hammered on their door long before it was even faintly daylight, came in and switched on the light. He was already fully dressed, including his overcoat.

'C'mon, c'mon,' he growled. 'Rouse yourselves, girls. We've a boat to catch.'

Tara raised her tousled head. 'A boat, Daddy?'

'A boat. I've changed me mind.' His face wore a furtive expression, as if he was aware of the shock and dismay he was about to cause and was embarrassed by it. 'We're going to New York.'

At this, all three girls responded with assorted expressions of astonishment.

'New *York!*' stuttered Patricia, her brain clicking from sleep to very much awake in an instant.

'*What?*' Aideen gasped.

'Oh, no!' Tara began to cry. Having already gone off Liverpool, at that time of the morning she wasn't even sure where New York was.

'It's all arranged. Everything's booked. The boat sails at midday.' He clapped his hands. 'Come on, me darlin' girls, get a move on.'

'What about our luggage?' Patricia asked.

Bernie didn't meet her eyes. 'It's already on the boat,' he rasped. He left the room, banging the door hard and making the girls jump. Patricia and Tara got speedily out of bed, but Aideen just sat there, looking thoughtful.

'He never had any intention of staying here,' she said slowly. 'Our trunks must have gone straight from the Irish boat to the New York one. Those cards he had printed with the Liverpool address didn't mean a thing. He wanted everyone to think it was where we were moving to, when it was New York all the time.'

Patricia was throwing on her clothes. 'We must never write and tell anyone where we are,' she said in a shaky voice. 'Daddy's gone and done something really awful and we have to protect him.' The letters to friends she had written the night before had been a waste of time. 'We are travelling into the unknown,' she announced dramatically.

Aideen nodded and Tara said, 'Does this mean we might never see our Milo again?'

'We *can't* not see our Milo again,' Aideen said passionately.

Patricia agreed. 'I'll be having a word with Daddy later,' she promised. If anyone was after him, they'd know where Milo was – or they'd soon find out – and they'd discover where Daddy was living from the New York postmark. Or any sort of postmark if he decided to move somewhere else. 'We can write to Milo when everything's back to normal.'

If it ever was.

What's he done about passports? Patricia wondered in the car that was taking them to where the New York boat was berthed. It was called the *Queen Maia,* she saw when they arrived. It was a massive white vessel with three black funnels and was at the centre of a hive of activity. Luggage was being taken aboard on one of the many gang-planks, and crates and sacks were being lowered by crane into the hold. A freezing fog had descended on their little part of the world and the busy scene was being acted out in a fuzzy mist.

Bernie paused at the foot of the highest gang-plank and showed what an amazed Patricia saw were four passports to the peak-capped, heavily overcoated man in attendance. He'd actually ac-quired passports without his daughters' know-ledge, using photographs that had been taken when they were at school.

A steward showed them to their cabin, which turned out to be a suite of three bedrooms with an octagonal lounge at the centre. It was even more luxurious than the accommodation at the Adelphi, the in-built furniture glossy white and the beds draped with ivory satin. Thick eau-de-Nil carpets covered the floors and everywhere smelled of expensive perfume.

Aideen disappeared, returning a few minutes later to say, in an awed voice, that the bathroom was actually black and silver. 'And there's a mirror that covers an entire wall, and *two* sinks.'

Neither Patricia nor Tara spoke. They were in the lounge, sitting on the very edge of the white leather chairs, as if they didn't really belong there. Their father had entered the suite with them but had since disappeared.

'I reckon he's gone to look for the bar – or one of them,' Aideen said. 'There's probably half a dozen on this ship. Is this a ship or a boat?' she queried.

'It must be both,' Patricia surmised. She patted Tara's knee. Her sister looked close to tears. 'It'll be all right, darlin',' she promised, hoping it wasn't an empty one.

There was a knock on the door. A lad of no more than thirteen or fourteen was there to ask what time they intended coming to breakfast.

'In half an hour,' Patricia told him. A pot of tea and some bacon and eggs would do them the world of good.

Their father was either deliberately keeping himself out of their way or drinking himself to death in one of the numerous bars. They had been on-board the *Queen Maia* for two days and seen little of him. They met at meals, but he would leave before they'd finished eating and could start a proper conversation. Patricia would hear him return well past midnight, when she wasn't in the mood to get up and interrogate him, which would only wake and upset her sisters. Tara was already forever on the verge of tears.

Under different circumstances they might have enjoyed life on the boat, it being so entirely different to the life they'd always known. They were travelling first class, which was typical of Bernie Kelly. He didn't know what it was like to be careful with money. Patricia felt sure that second or even third class would have been adequate. They were well-off but they weren't rich, not like the other passengers on their deck. The women wore furs made from animals Patricia hadn't known existed.

22

Diamonds sparkled on their ears and around their necks. They dressed for dinner in silk, satin or luscious velvet gowns and had their hair done in the hairdresser's on-board.

Last night in the first-class lounge, an entire orchestra played while people danced and a woman in a gold dress sang 'I'll See You in My Dreams', 'It Had to Be You', 'Tea for Two' and many other songs the girls knew, having heard them before on the wireless back home in Dublin. They had sat in a corner, watching and listening. If it hadn't been for the worry and uncertainty they were facing, it would have been a little bit like heaven. Instead, it felt more than a bit like hell.

It was a moonless night, raining slightly, and the *Queen Maia* looked as if it was sailing into nothingness on an ocean of black ink. The lights from the ship itself illuminated the water around it. Bernie Kelly leant on the rail and watched the reflections ripple and flow in its frothy wake.

Christ, it was cold. It was early morning, two or three o'clock, and he was the only person on deck. An outgoing chap with scores of friends, he wasn't used to being alone and it made him feel utterly wretched.

Until recently he had always been the luckiest of men. But things had changed. The events that had happened in his life, good and bad, had always affected him, but he accepted they were the will of God, so not even the death of his wife, Meriel, had brought him low. Since then, his main concern had been his girls, his son and, of course, himself. But the last three months had been a nightmare. His luck had deserted him and everything that could go wrong had gone wrong, with breathtakingly awful consequences.

He'd been flattered when his very own firm of solicitors had been appointed to manage the estate of the recently deceased Earl of Graniston. Bernie had known his son, Richard Heath, at university, who had since inherited the title. The estate was worth something like ten thousand Irish pounds and Richard wanted it sold and the money transferred to England, where he now lived permanently.

The sale had gone through smoothly without a single hiccup and three months ago a cheque for just over ten thousand pounds had been deposited in Bernie's business account at his bank, from which he was expected to deduct his commission and pass on the rest to his old acquaintance, the new Earl of Graniston.

Except he hadn't.

Bernie threw the butt of his cigarette into the dark ocean and immediately lit another, shielding the lighter's flame from the sharp wind in his cupped hands. Music was coming from somewhere and it accentuated his loneliness, knowing that elsewhere on the boat people were listening to the same music and enjoying it. He couldn't imagine enjoying anything again.

He had seen the money in the bank as an opportunity to make more. An affluent chap and an expert card player, he had never been *this* affluent and visualised himself betting a hundred pounds when he was used to only betting ten. It

24

wasn't that he was greedy, just that it was something he was good at and he enjoyed the thrill of winning.

Right from the start things hadn't worked out as he'd expected, but he knew for sure that if he continued, his luck would turn. It was bound to; it was inevitable.

When it turned out not to be, in desperation Bernie had travelled all the way to London, where he'd heard there was an illicit casino in the basement of the Excelsior hotel in Mayfair. It had always been his dream to go to the South of France and play at a table, throw a dice and make a wish – he felt a surge of excitement now just *thinking* about it – but in London all he did was lose more of the new Earl of Graniston's inheritance, which by now had shrunk to less than half of its original sum. The earl's secretary or some other flunky had already written asking politely for his employer's money.

If you would be so kind as to send a cheque at your earliest convenience the letter had said, or something similar. From now on, Bernie thought with a wry smile, he should expect them to become rather less polite and more demanding.

At some point the reality of his situation had hit him like a giant fist in his solar plexus. He was a solicitor who had embezzled a client out of almost six thousand pounds. Each morning he imagined waking up in an imaginary jail cell. What would happen to his children? The house by Phoenix Park would go – it was only rented, anyway – plus all its contents; his office would close; his car – a three-litre Bentley tourer, now in storage, of which he was hugely proud – would be taken. He would have nothing left and there would still be nothing when he emerged from jail years later. How many years he would spend in prison he guessed would be anything between five and ten.

He let the remains of his second cigarette fall into the ocean just as a voice said, 'Are you all right, sir?' It was a man wearing a black oilskin cape – one of the ship's crew.

'I'm fine, thank you.' Bernie laughed harshly. 'Just contemplating suicide.' The world would no doubt be a better place without the likes of him.

The man clearly thought he was joking and laughed at his words. 'Best to contemplate it from a nice, warm bed, sir. This rain feels as if it's getting heavier.'

'I'll do that in a minute,' Bernie said as he lit another cigarette. 'After I've finished this.'

'Goodnight, sir.'

'Goodnight yourself.'

Bernie glanced at the stars. He didn't know their names, only that his lucky one had disappeared, having somehow managed to float further into outer space and explode.

He sighed. If he were telling this tale to another human being, then he wouldn't have reached the worst part yet. Earlier, a mere few hours ago, he had been wandering around the ship, wetting his whistle in the various watering holes until he was pissed out of his mind. He was at his most pissed when, in one bar, he came across a poker game with four players and half a dozen onlookers. One of the players, a foreigner with close-cut grey hair, beckoned him to join them.

'Why not?' Bernie chuckled, entirely forgetting that his whistle was so wet it had probably drowned. His eyes were glazed, his sight impaired, his brain working at an unnaturally low level.

He threw his business card onto the table. It had his name on – Bernard Casey Kelly, Solicitor – and the address of his office in Dublin. He'd get a new one printed once he'd got settled in his new address, wherever that might be. The man with the short grey hair picked up the card, read it and then nodded at Bernie to sit down.

'Me cash is buried in me luggage,' Bernie explained. 'Will an IOU do for now?' It wasn't as if he could do a runner in the middle of the Atlantic Ocean. 'I'll pay yis tomorrer.'

The man nodded again and Bernie sat down. As usual, he was overwhelmed with a feeling that he was going to win – and this time the winnings would be huge. Nothing would, or could, stop him. Winning was an absolute certainty. He couldn't lose. He had learnt nothing over the past few months.

It was dark in the bar. Music, drums thumping away, was coming from a loudspeaker, and there was a strange smell, pungent, much too sweet, that he reckoned was some sort of foreign aftershave or possibly tobacco. It made his eyes water. The men spoke to each other in a language he didn't understand, but used English to Bernie with an accent he thought might be Eastern European.

And of course Bernie lost. The more he lost, the more sober he became. He realised he didn't even know what currency they were playing in. He examined a note and the figure of 500 stared

27

back at him.

'What is this?' he asked of no one in particular.

'That is a five hundred dollar note,' he was informed.

'But dollars are always green.'

'Not the high currency ones, Mr Kelly.'

Bernie managed to stop himself from gagging. 'Where do I stand?' he mumbled.

The game had paused while everyone waited for the result. 'You have lost six thousand five hundred dollars, Mr Kelly.' The man drummed his fingers on the table. The three other men and the small audience looked amused. 'That is equivalent to about one thousand three hundred British pounds.'

'Thank you,' Bernie said thickly. 'I think that'll do me for tonight.'

The man shoved the IOUs towards him. 'You will see about these tomorrow?'

Bernie nodded. 'I will indeed.'

'What is your cabin number?'

'Twenty-three,' he sighed.

Weeks ago, Bernie had decided that if he was going to be punished, then he'd sooner be punished for a lion as for a lamb. He doubted if he'd get many more years in prison for stealing the Earl of Graniston's entire inheritance than for merely stealing a portion. So, he might as well keep the lot, he decided, take his girls and Milo on a world cruise, stopping off and staying at the best hotels in any place that took their fancy – Venice, for instance, Bombay, somewhere in Australia, or the United States. His late wife's brother, Mick

O'Neill, lived in New York and they'd been best mates as lads.

But, he realised, they wouldn't get far before his crime caught up with him. There was an organisation established only two years before – the International Police Commission – with members all over the world. They would track him down and his children would be left to fend for themselves in a strange, foreign country.

So he decided to pretend to be moving to Liverpool, but move to New York instead, but only with the girls. It would be another few weeks before the alarm was raised, by which time Bernie would be on the other side of the Atlantic where he would change their identities, move house a few times, until all four of them were hidden out of sight. Mick had found them a flat on the lower east side of New York that would do for now. Milo was too young to put up with such an unsettled way of life so he'd leave him with his sister, Kathleen.

By the time Bernie had settled his debts (other than the one to the Earl of Graniston, which was the biggest), paid his staff four weeks' wages so they wouldn't starve before they found new jobs, bought Nora Hogan, who'd been with the Kelly family since she was fourteen, the cottage in Kildare where she was born for her to spend the rest of her days, settled his son with Kathleen, and paid for first-class passages for himself and the girls on the boat, he was left with roughly two and a half thousand pounds – not exactly of his own money, but as good as by now.

Bernie stuffed his knuckles in his mouth to suppress a sob. There wasn't another soul on the planet who would feel an ounce of pity for him, apart from another gambler – he'd just lost more than half that much in less than half a flaming hour.

Jaysus! What was he supposed to do now?

He stared down at the black water and again thought about jumping. It actually looked welcoming. He imagined himself sinking below it, feeling cleansed, all his problems solved. His daughters would manage without him – Patricia had a more or less sensible head on her shoulders and would take care of her sisters. They would get jobs in New York where, unlike in Dublin, no one would know their daddy was a criminal.

Bernie turned away from the water. Before jumping, there was something he had to do.

Patricia was still half awake when she heard Bernie enter the suite. Tara was snoring softly in the other bed and Aideen, who was apt to throw her sleeping self all over the place the whole night long, was by herself in the adjacent cabin.

Bernie went straight into his own cabin and Patricia snuggled her head into the pillow, ready to fall properly asleep now that she knew he was safely back. She was surprised when, minutes later, there was a subdued knock on her door. She got up and opened it to find her father on the verge of collapse.

'Daddy!' she gasped. She closed the door behind her and helped him to a chair. His face was as white as snow, his eyes bloodshot and his best tweed overcoat was soaking wet. This wasn't the result of too much whisky, she realised but something else. 'What's wrong?' She tried to remove his coat but he shrugged her away and instead pushed a brown paper envelope into her trembling hand.

'Hold onto this, darlin'.' His voice was no longer his own, but hoarse and broken. 'Keep it in your suitcase, like, and don't show it to a soul.'

'But what is it?' she croaked.

'It's important, that's all you need to know. You can open it when you need it. Now, get back into bed, me darlin' girl. I'm just about to use the lavvy, then I'll be going to bed meself.'

Patricia clasped the envelope to her breast. Perhaps a good night's sleep was what he needed, though she did wonder if she should call the ship's doctor.

He kissed her forehead, hugged her briefly, then made his unsteady way to the bathroom. She sat for a moment before deciding he probably had a touch of seasickness and would be fine in the morning.

She made her way back to her own bed and climbed in, tucking the brown envelope beneath the pillow. Her father came out of the bathroom and she heard the door to his cabin open and close. It was only then that Patricia slept, unaware that Bernie was back on the deck in the rain and the freezing cold.

Chapter 2

Despite what should have been an exhausting night spent tossing, turning and expending enough energy to have trekked across the Sahara, as usual Aideen was the first to wake up, apparently refreshed. It was she who burst in on her sisters early the following morning to announce one of the ship's officers wanted to see them.

Tara merely turned over and went back to sleep, but Patricia jerked herself into a sitting position, fully alert. 'What about?' she asked.

'I don't know, Sis. He asked for Daddy first, but when I looked he wasn't there. He must have got up at the crack of dawn. I can't think why.'

'Can't he come back when we're properly dressed?' Patricia recalled their father's condition earlier and her heart had started to beat much too fast. She was aware she was foolishly attempting to put off receiving what could well be very bad news. Some sort of a catastrophe might have occurred; Daddy had fallen down a ladder, perhaps, and broken his leg or hurt his head or he was in the ship's hospital terribly sick.

'He said it's urgent, the officer.'

'Oh, all right then.' Patricia reached for her dressing gown, while Aideen yanked the bedclothes off her younger sister, who immediately woke up, complaining bitterly.

The ship's officer was very young. He was standing in the middle of the room, his expression grim. The girls, all in their nightwear, presented themselves in a row and regarded him anxiously.

'Your father,' he stammered. 'Er, I'm afraid there's been an accident.'

'Is he badly hurt?' Patricia asked baldly.

'Nobody is sure.' The man coughed. 'He has disappeared. We think he might have fallen overboard during the night.'

'What on earth makes you think that?' Aideen demanded rudely. 'He might be lost somewhere. This is a very big ship.'

'His watch has been found. We theorised he must have removed it before he jumped,' the officer said. He had gone very red. 'It was discovered in an ashtray in the ballroom – a place where it would very quickly be found.'

'Is it a wristwatch?' Tara enquired. 'Our daddy was one of the first men in Dublin to wear a wristwatch.'

'It is a wristwatch, yes.'

'It could belong to anybody,' Aideen said contemptuously. It was as if she had decided the officer had come purely to upset and annoy them.

Patricia hadn't so far spoken. 'Shush, darlin',' she said quietly to her sister. And then to the officer, 'Does it have his name engraved on the back?'

The man nodded. 'There is a name, yes. It is your father's.'

At this Aideen shrieked and Tara began to cry. Patricia put her arms around both her sisters. 'Thank you,' she said to the poor young man who'd been delegated to bring them such bad news. It must have been terrible for him.

'The captain will come and see you later.' He gave a little bow and left.

He had hardly been gone a minute when a steward arrived with a tray of tea things that he placed on the table in the lounge, saying, 'I'm sorry for your loss, ladies.'

Patricia thanked him and he left. She was as devastated as her sisters at their father's death, but not as surprised – not after witnessing the state he'd been in last night. Not that she had thought him suicidal but, looking back, he had looked pretty much at the end of his tether.

She poured the tea and then, leaving Aideen and Tara to drink it, she went and retrieved the brown envelope Daddy had given her from beneath the pillow and looked inside. There were four passports, a thick wad of money and a letter in her father's big, scrawling handwriting, badly smudged here and there, that she assumed he'd written earlier that morning. It was a sort of joke that he used purple ink in his fountain pen. She began to read it.

My dear, lovely girls,

I have done something devilishly stupid and am about to do something worse – not just break the law but commit a crime against our Lord Himself. Keep this money safe – it belongs to the three of you and no one else. Don't let it be seen by another soul apart from your Uncle Mick, who'll be in New York to meet you when you get off the boat. On no account are you to go back to Dublin. You must make a new life in a new country.

34

May God bless you and love you throughout the years ahead. And may He forgive me.
Your devoted daddy.

As the letter was addressed to all three of them, Patricia took it into the lounge and read it to her sisters, insisting that they sit down first.

'What's he done?' asked Tara, round-eyed.

Patricia shrugged. 'We may never know the truth of it.'

Aideen picked up the envelope and the money fell out. She gasped. 'I wonder if this is stolen?'

Patricia could have sworn that her fast-beating heart missed several beats. 'It might have been,' she ventured.

Tara began to cry again. 'Why on earth would he want to do away with himself, Patricia?'

'I have no idea. It could well be something to do with the money.' Patricia reckoned Daddy had deliberately taken off his watch and left it behind so as to prove he was about to jump overboard. Had he left it on, they could at least have made themselves believe – or tried to – that his death was an accident. He had wanted to convince them – to convince everybody – that there was no chance of him being found alive so it was a waste of time looking for him.

Tara began to moan softly and rock to and fro when the captain of the *Queen Maia* arrived, her face hid in her hands.

He introduced himself as Captain Morgan and gently squeezed their shoulders. A ruggedly built, striking man with a young face and a head of pure silver hair, his blue eyes were kind. In a broad

35

Scots accent, he told them how sorry he was about their father. 'I had so far not had a chance to speak to him, but other passengers have told me what a decent chap he was.'

Once again Aideen began to argue passionately that he must be somewhere on the ship. It was all a big mistake. Despite the watch, despite the letter that Daddy had left, she remained convinced that he was alive.

Captain Morgan didn't speak straight away when Aideen had finished arguing. He seemed to be studying the floor until he looked up and explained to her gently that at about half past two that morning, a member of the crew had spoken to Bernard Kelly, who was leaning on the rail studying the water below and said that he was, '"Just contemplating suicide."'

Patricia gasped. She tried to think of something she might have done to keep him in the cabin when he had returned last night looking so desperately awful. He'd come back to write the suicide letter. She groaned aloud, wishing that she'd kept him there. Instead of going into his cabin to sleep, he'd actually gone outside and thrown himself into the Atlantic Ocean.

She would never forgive herself. Never.

Captain Morgan had stood to leave when there was a tap on the cabin door. Aideen opened it. 'Yes?' she said sharply. She would always be more angry than heartbroken that her father had died the way he had.

A man stood outside, grey-haired, tall, beautifully dressed, wearing a navy blue velour overcoat that was so thick it looked almost like fur. He tipped his matching slouch hat at Aideen. 'I am most sorry to hear about the death of your father,' he said smoothly.

Aideen acknowledged this with a grunt that could have meant anything.

'It so happens,' the man went on in the same smooth voice, 'that he has something that belongs to me and to my friends. Would it be possible for me to take a look in his cabin?'

Before Aideen could reply, Captain Morgan approached and the visitor, who hadn't noticed he was there, took two steps backwards. 'No, it would not be possible, sir,' the captain said coldly. 'Not under any circumstances whatsoever. And I expressly forbid you to approach these three young ladies again. Do you understand?'

Despite his apparent courtesy, it was clearly Captain Morgan who possessed the upper hand. The man went away without another word and the captain said to the girls, 'Do not allow anyone in here who isn't a member of the ship's crew. Later, Mrs Esther Galloway, our chief stewardess, will call to see if you need any help.'

He left and Aideen turned upon her sisters. 'I don't want help from *anyone*,' she hissed.

Patricia rather liked the idea of talking to someone older than herself. 'I'd like her to come and see us,' she said tiredly. 'You can stay in your cabin if you like.'

'Oh, let's all stay together,' Tara pleaded. 'Right now, you two are the only people in the world I want to see, apart from our Milo, that is.'

Patricia sat on the white settee and held out her arms. Her sisters sat on each side, their three pairs of arms entwined. They stayed that way for a long time, talking about their father, sharing memories, laughing one minute, crying the next.

They only stopped when Mrs Galloway, the chief stewardess, arrived to offer sympathy and ask questions about what they would like to do now that their lives had changed so drastically. She was a beautiful fair-haired woman dressed a bit like a nurse in a grey cotton dress and a white overall. One by one she squeezed the girls' hands in her own.

'Captain Morgan will take you back to Liverpool when he returns in a few days' time – if that's what you wish,' she told them. 'He will then make arrangements to have you transported to Dublin.'

'We have an uncle who will meet us in New York,' Patricia told her, thinking about how Daddy had specifically said in his letter not to return to Dublin, but to make a new life in New York. She hadn't mentioned the letter to anyone apart from her sisters.

The woman left after assuring them she was there to help with any problem or worry they might have. 'No matter how big or small,' she emphasised.

Most of the people on-board were aware of the sad end of Bernard Kelly, who had already impressed them with his delightful manner during their few days on the boat. They brought gifts for the girls and their suite became full with flowers, fruit and chocolates. One lady brought a bottle of expensive perfume and advised them to sprinkle it in their cabins when they first woke up and they would find the scent intoxicating.

'It will put you in a good mood for the rest of the day,' she promised.

Patricia was convinced, and she felt sure her sisters felt the same, that she would never be in a good mood again.

For most of the remainder of the voyage, the three Kelly girls stayed in their suite. It was where they ate their meals, only leaving very early in the morning or late at night to get some fresh air by wrapping up warm and going for a stroll on the deck. They witnessed some wonderful sunrises and even more colourful sunsets, as well as avoiding all the kind people who only wanted to say how sorry they were for what had happened, but which the girls found terribly upsetting.

They first glimpsed New York at midnight when it was just a black dot on the dark horizon. The following day there was a great deal of activity outside and the girls imagined everyone watching and commenting as the dot became bigger and bigger.

There were still many people around when they went on deck that evening and the city was a mere few miles away, now brightly lit. Patricia thought it an awesome sight. She'd heard of skyscrapers but had never dreamt they would look so terrifying, such huge monstrosities soaring up into the sky before they disappeared into the black clouds that hung low over the city of New York.

There was a gasp beside her and Tara said in an awed voice, 'Isn't it beautiful, Patricia? Isn't it the most wonderful sight you've ever seen?'

'Well, it'll certainly make a change from Dublin,' Aideen said with a yawn.

Later that day, a customs official, who introduced himself as Mr Adams, came to see them to examine their passports and ask a few questions to save them going through much more formal procedures onshore. It was a kind gesture arranged by Captain Morgan.

Why had they come to New York, Mr Adams wanted to know as he examined the forged documents. He was a bad-tempered individual with an impatient manner. Patricia felt especially annoyed with him because he was Irish and should have been kinder.

'Our father wanted us to start a new life here,' she told him.

'What about your mother?'

'She died eight years ago.' Now they were orphans. Patricia hadn't thought about it that way before. Orphans!

'And where do you intend to live in New York?'

'I don't know. Uncle Mick, our mother's brother, is coming to meet us off the boat and he will know.'

'Do you have sufficient funds to support yourselves?'

'We have enough funds, thank you,' Patricia snapped. 'But we will have to change it into dollars.'

He asked a few more questions before producing a smile that Patricia hadn't thought him capable of and said he hoped they had all the luck in the world in New York.

'May God bless you, girls,' was his final pronouncement.

Captain Morgan's kindness knew no bounds. He had telegraphed the shipping company's harbour office and Mick O'Neill had been identified and informed of the fate of his brother-in-law. He was waiting for them in a small private room where their luggage had already been taken to.

'God, girls, where's St Christopher when he's needed?' Uncle Mick cried when they met. 'He took his eye off our Bernie on the way over, that's for sure.' He was a small, tubby man wearing a flared tweed overcoat with a brown velvet collar. A trilby hat to match the collar was sitting on a bench. Patricia wasn't sure if it was the latest male fashion or terribly old-fashioned.

He was kissing them sloppily, one on each cheek, patting their shoulders, shaking their hands. 'Come on now, girlies, and I'll show you where you'll be living from now on.' He ushered them outside to where crowds of people were still disembarking from the *Queen Maia* and a large black car was parked with *New York Police Department* painted on the side.

'Are you a policeman?' Patricia gasped when he opened the rear door for them to get in.

'Yes, darlin', Captain Mick O'Neill, thirty-fifth precinct,' he said.

Patricia took a deep breath as the police car set off through the long, straight streets lined with the towering buildings of New York. A new life was about to begin, but without the best father in the world, who had also turned out to be one of the least honest.

Since leaving Dublin, life had become as surreal as the strangest dream, but as they drove further and further into the spectacular city, reality set in. This was how things would be from now on and Patricia and her sisters would just have to get used to it.

Chapter 3

They had been in New York for two weeks and, so far, Patricia was the only one who'd been out on her own. Aideen and Tara would sit by the big bay window and wait for her to come back or they would go out together, holding hands defensively as if expecting to be attacked, though the only criminal the girls had come across in their short lives had been their own father.

Their second-floor apartment was on a street of tall terraced houses off Seventh Avenue in Manhattan. The place was old-fashioned with dark cream wallpaper decorated with purple irises in the sitting room, purple curtains, two brown velveteen-covered sofas and two armchairs to match. There were at least a dozen original paintings of flowers on the walls. The two bedrooms – one small where Daddy would have slept, and one large with three single beds – were at the rear. One of these days, Aideen, who slept so tempestuously, would take over Daddy's room, but so far the girls had shared the larger one, preferring to stay together. The beds were covered with beautiful hand-sewn quilts. Patricia would touch hers, thinking of all the hard work and patience that had gone into the making of it.

The place was lovely and warm due to the big iron radiators in all the rooms that were kept hot by a boiler in the basement attended to by a black man called Shakespeare.

The one drawback, which had nothing to do with the apartment itself, was that it was at the end of a busy street and opposite a small row of shops that stayed open until the early hours. Back in Dublin they had lived in a quiet road with only detached houses virtually hidden from each other in their own leafy grounds. But here people lived above and below them and in the adjacent rooms. Even in the middle of the night there were fights, people arguing passionately and loudly, often in a foreign language, so the girls didn't even know what the argument was about. Sometimes the fights went on in the house itself between people either going up or coming down the stairs.

Even so, Tara claimed she liked New York, though she was the only one. 'Or at least I think I'll get used to it, eventually.'

Aideen snorted. 'Liking and getting used to it are two entirely different things. You can get used to something but still not like it. I *hate* it here,' she added furiously. She was angry most of the time.

Patricia had to confess she was in two minds about the place. She'd been in two minds about almost everything throughout her entire life. No matter how much she tried not to, she was nearly always able to see something positive on both sides of an argument or a situation, even if they were basically horrid. New York had an exceptionally nice side as well as one that wasn't very pleasant, like the rudeness of some people who just shoved you out the way when you tried to struggle through the crowded pavements or the man with a long black beard in the international newsagents across the road who appeared most reluctant to sell her an Irish newspaper even though there were some on the rack outside. Perhaps he didn't like the Irish or didn't like women. She would never know because she'd found another newsagent two streets away who was Polish and as nice as pie, with whom she had long conversations about the weather. In fact, most people were nice and friendly with colourful stories to tell about how they'd got to New York in the first place.

'I think we should have a meeting,' Patricia said one day. All three were sitting listlessly around the apartment staring at nothing, thinking about Daddy and worried about the future. It was three o'clock on a dull, depressing day early in March.

Aideen groaned. 'What is it now?' Since arriving in America, all she'd done was moan and groan.

A meeting meant sitting around the long ebony table – they assumed it was ebony because it was black – and discussing things more important than what they should have for dinner that night.

'It's about what Uncle Mick said when he came

yesterday,' Patricia began when they were seated around the table. Their uncle came to see them every other day.

'It's time you decided what to do with yisselves, girls,' he'd said soberly the night before as the smell of his cigar drifted around the room. 'I mean do you want to stay in New York or try another city before you settle down? Do you want to stay *here?*' He waved his hands to indicate the apartment, then nodded in the direction of Tara. 'It's also about time this young lady went to school. I don't know how much dough your daddy's left you with, but however much there is, it won't last forever. So,' he paused for breath, 'unless you want to sit on your little butts waiting for a husband, then it's time you two found yisselves a job of work.' He pointed a little stubby finger at Patricia and Aideen.

Aideen, appalled, had spluttered that she didn't know what a 'butt' was and that the last thing in the world she wanted was to sit on it waiting for a husband. 'It's always been my intention to look for work,' she said. 'I'm not sure what type of work but I'll think of something.'

Patricia covered her sister's hand with her own. For all Aideen's spluttering and bad temper, she felt certain that, just like herself, she was terrified of the future. The quiet, comfortable life they'd led in Dublin had been turned upside down. This life couldn't possibly be more different. What's more, they had lost Daddy and were still grieving; perhaps they might never stop. But maybe the day would come when she would see a positive side to all this. She just wished it would come soon.

'Would you like to go back to school, darlin'?' she had asked Aideen. After all, she had still been at school when they'd left Ireland and she hadn't been trained for anything. 'I mean a commercial college like I went to, or a place where you would be taught something like singing or dancing? Or acting?' she added hopefully.

She wasn't surprised when she saw tears appear in her sister's eyes. 'I don't know what to do with meself since our da died,' she whispered.

'Neither do I,' Tara sniffed.

Uncle Mick, aware he had upset them, looked as if he was about to cry himself. 'Sorry, girls. It's just that I worry about you.' He blew his nose loudly and shortly afterwards went home. He was a bachelor and lived all alone in a house in Brooklyn. He had promised to take them there one day.

That was yesterday, and now Patricia wanted to know, after having had twenty-four hours to think about it, how her sisters felt about Mick's suggestions.

'I know it came as a bit of a shock, what he said, like, but we're going to have to live different sort of lives than we ever imagined we would. For meself, I liked working in Daddy's office in Dublin, so I shall look for an office job.' She turned to Aideen. 'How about you, darlin'?'

'I've thought and thought,' Aideen said hesitantly, 'but absolutely nothing comes to mind.'

'What would you have done had we stayed in Dublin?' Patricia asked.

'I really liked being at school. I had friends there.'

'Well, you can go to school here.'

46

'I know, but it won't be the same school and I won't have the same friends.'

Patricia looked at her sister a touch impatiently. 'But you would have had to leave school eventually.'

'I know.' Aideen leant forward, elbows on the table, and said earnestly, 'Why can't we go back to Dublin, Patricia? It's not like I ever wanted to leave. There's enough money for the fare, and me and Tara can go straight back to school.'

'I don't want to go back to school,' Tara said unexpectedly. 'I'm fourteen and in Dublin I could've got meself a job of work like Uncle Mick said, so I expect I can in New York too. And where would we live if we went back?' she went on. 'There'll be someone else living in our old house by now. And I'd feel silly, turning up only a few weeks after saying goodbye to everyone.'

Aideen dropped her head into her hands and groaned. 'That's true. We didn't *own* that house.'

'Daddy specifically said on no account were we to go back.' Patricia tried to remember his exact words. His letter was in the drawer of her bedroom cabinet but she hadn't felt like reading it again since the first time. 'He said he'd done "something devilishly stupid".'

Aideen lifted her head. 'What on earth could that be?'

'I don't suppose we'll ever know,' Patricia sighed. They'd got nowhere with the discussion so far. 'Is anyone hungry?' she enquired. Both Aideen and Tara announced they were starving. 'Then shall I go and buy something to eat? One of those pizza things we all like?'

Both girls looked pleased about something at last. The other day, Uncle Mick had brought a giant pizza and they had devoured every single little bit. Tara had licked her fingers and said it was the nicest food she had ever eaten. 'I could eat a pizza every day for the rest of me life.'

When Patricia arrived back with the ham and tomato pizza already cut into six slices, Tara had made a pot of tea and Aideen had set the table.

They passed an almost enjoyable half hour eating and drinking until Patricia reminded them that they really should return to the subject they'd been discussing earlier.

'It has to be settled. We *have* to come to a decision about what to do next. We can't just sit here eating pizza for years till we're so fat we won't be able to get up and down the stairs and all our money will have gone. When I was out, I noticed there was something called an employment agency next door to the pizza place. I can't remember its name. Tomorrow morning I shall go there and ask them to get me a job.'

She would wear her new mid-calf-length grey tweed coat, the close-fitting felt hat with a narrow brim that she'd brought to go with it and her black court shoes with curved heels.

A shop selling sheet music was on the other side of the agency. Inside, someone was singing a mournful song while playing the piano. Through the window, Patricia could see it was being sung by a young man with an exaggeratedly wide moustache. He wore a cream and red blazer and straw boater – a quite unsuitable outfit for such cold weather. He looked up, their eyes met and he winked. She felt tempted to wink back but changed her mind and opened the door to the building housing the Roscius Employment Agency on the third floor.

A bell buzzed when she opened the agency door and a woman shouted, 'Come in, whoever you are.'

Patricia headed towards the direction of the voice, passing through an office containing a desk and chair, a typewriter that could well have been the first model ever made, and shelves of dusty files that looked as if they hadn't been touched in years. The walls were full of photographs.

She came to another office holding even more files than the first. Behind a desk, also piled high with papers and magazines, sat an exaggeratedly colourful woman who looked about sixty. Her hair had been dyed a glorious red, though the effect was rather spoilt by a good inch of roots which showed a rather dull grey. Her large blue eyes were exaggerated by the brilliant blue shadow on the lids and the black line drawn around them, and her lips were painted a startling crimson. Patricia had never seen anyone use so much makeup before.

'Hello, darling,' she drawled when Patricia went in.

Patricia frowned. 'This isn't the third floor,' she said. 'It's only the second.'

'Ah! You've given the game away with that,' the woman said, laughing delightedly. 'You're English, aren't you? No, Irish, I recognise the accent.'

'What game have I given away.'

'That you're not American. Americans call the ground floor the first floor. So their second floor is our first, and so on.'

Patricia took it that the woman must be English. She was wondering how to respond when it was suggested she take the weight off her feet and sit down.

'What can I do for you, darling?' Patricia was asked once seated in a rickety chair in front of the desk.

'I'm looking for a job,' she replied.

'What sort of job? Oh, and what is your name, by the way?'

'My name is Patricia Kelly and I want a job in an office,' Patricia said in a rush. 'I can type at sixty words a minute and my shorthand speed is one hundred and twenty.'

'I'm Annabel Jefferies-Squire and I'm very impressed, Miss Kelly. But you see, this is exclusively a theatrical employment agency.'

Patricia felt annoyed that she'd expended quite a lot of mental and physical effort visiting the agency only for it to have been a waste of time. 'Shouldn't you put that outside? I mean that it's a theatrical agency. I wouldn't have bothered you had I known.'

'If you were an actor you would have known.' Patricia was treated to another gay laugh. 'Roscius was a famous Roman tragedian. Any actor worth his salt knows who Roscius is.'

Patricia glanced at the walls full of photographs of people obviously in show business: clowns, ventriloquists with dummies, dancing children, circus performers, all grinning widely or smiling

50

wistfully. Patricia would like to bet that scarcely one had heard of Roscius.

'If I started the Adler employment would you realise it was for office workers?' she asked.

'Why should I?' Annabel Jefferies-Squire replied.

'Because you have an Adler typewriter in the other room.' Patricia got to her feet. 'Every typist worth her salt knows what an Adler is.'

The other woman also stood and went into the outer office. She wore a green georgette blouse with white spots, an elegant black skirt and ankle boots with high heels. 'You can work this thing?'

'The typewriter? Of course. I told you I can type at sixty words a minute.'

'Then would you like to help me out for a couple of weeks? I'll pay you fifty cents an hour. My secretary is off ill at the moment.'

'Well...' Patricia paused.

'I'll let you have time off to go looking for other jobs while you're here,' Annabel Jefferies-Squire said coaxingly. 'I know someone as smart and young as you won't want to work in a place like this forever.'

Suddenly the door opened and a man came in and did a little tap dance on the ragged carpet. 'Morning, Bel,' he sang. 'Have you got anything for me?'

'Yes, I have, Harry.' The other woman turned to Patricia. 'Think about it overnight, darling. If you want the job, then come back in the morning and you can start straight away.'

Today was Thursday. 'I do want the job,' Patricia said hurriedly. 'There's no need to think about it, but can I come back on Monday?'

'Monday's fine, darling. I'll see you then. Oh, and call me Bel. I shall call you Patricia.'

There was a cafe called Joe's Diner opposite the agency. When Patricia came out, she could see Aideen and Tara where she'd left them, seated on stools in the window, drinking milkshakes through straws. They waved and she went inside.

'How did you get on?' Tara asked.

'Well, I've got a job and I'm starting Monday, though it's only temporary.'

She knew her sisters wouldn't want to be left in the apartment without her. Hopefully Aideen would be spurred to make up her mind about what she wanted to do. As for Tara, Patricia had no intention of letting her go to work. She could go back to school and finish her education properly. Uncle Mick had told her there was a Catholic school only a short walk from the apartment.

Once they'd finished their milkshakes, they strolled back to what was now their home, noticing how colourful everywhere was, how fascinating with its pizzerias, patisseries and restaurants offering food from countries all over the world, some shops selling nothing but perfume or soap or gloves or glamorous, somewhat risqué, underwear.

'I'd like some money,' Aideen said suddenly. 'I'd like to buy some new clothes. What I have now is really old-fashioned. It was a waste of time bringing them. And you, Patricia, look overdressed in that outfit, and it's much too long and too old for you. Me, I fancy something more casual. Tomorrow,' she announced grandly, 'I shall go shopping.'

'We'll all go together,' Patricia promised.

'No, we won't,' Aideen said rudely. 'I'd sooner go on me own.'

'Please yourself. Me and Tara will sort out a school together.'

Tara rolled her eyes but didn't say a word.

Chapter 4

Aideen caught a bus the following morning in the direction of 34th Street, which Uncle Mick had told her was a good place to look for clothes. New York was beginning to grow on her. She might not like the people all that much but she enjoyed the way the city seemed to buzz with excitement; there was always a feeling of tension in the air, as if something thrilling could happen at any minute.

'Fifth Avenue would be the best place of all, except everything there costs an arm and a leg,' said Uncle Mick. 'Berry's is a good place to try. They have floor after floor of women's clothes for the working girl – or so it says in the adverts,' he finished.

But despite Aideen scanning acre after acre of women's clothing, she found hardly anything she would have liked to wear. It was all so formal, so neat, so tidy. She eventually settled on a bottle-green jacket (although she would have preferred a brighter colour) with four pockets, a belt and a stand-up collar, a pale pink jumper with a polo neck, a pink beret, a dark red pleated skirt that came to just below her knees, and red shoes with cut-away sides.

She had tried the things on in the various departments where she'd bought them, then she tried them on all together once she had chosen the final item, the jumper.

'Wow!' the girl on the knitwear counter said. She had pretty reddish-brown hair, somewhat similar to Aideen's own, and was roughly the same age. She had glanced in the cubicle to see if her customer needed a hand. 'You look...' She put her head on one side and eyed Aideen critically, then put it on the other side, saying, 'You look a bit unconventional. Are you an actress?'

Aideen was pleased at the idea of being taken for an actress and was tempted to say yes, but it seemed childish to try and impress a mere shop assistant. 'No,' she answered. 'I just don't like looking the same as everyone else.'

'Though you look very nice as well,' the girl added. 'I was worried you might take "unconventional" as an insult.'

'Lord, no. I like being unconventional.' Aideen stared admiringly at her reflection in the mirror. She thought she looked rather jaunty, as if she was about to visit Paris. 'I've never been called it before. Mind you, I've never bought me own clothes before, either. It's nice being able to choose whatever I want.' Patricia had given her the twenty dollars she'd asked for but Aideen had helped herself to another ten just before they went to bed while Patricia was in the bathroom. It was a good job she had, as the clothes had come to just over twenty-three dollars and she wanted to buy a handbag. Although here they called it a purse.

'Are you English?' the girl enquired.

'No, Irish. We only landed here a few weeks ago.'

'My family arrived from Germany a hundred years ago.'

'Miss!' A woman banged her knuckles on the glass counter, looking annoyed.

The assistant twirled around. 'Hope you enjoy wearing those lovely clothes,' she said to Aideen. And then to the other customer, 'Yes, madam?'

Outside Berry's, Aideen decided she wasn't in the mood to go home. She felt quite adventurous, having come all this way on her own, albeit on a bus. Across the road she saw a diner – there seemed to be plenty all over New York. This one was called Dinah's Diner.

She went inside. There were violently coloured paintings of various foods on the wall. She stood in the small queue and when it came to her turn, ordered a hot dog, a doughnut and a cup of coffee. After paying, she found a seat in a corner at the back, where she experimentally took a bite of the hot dog.

Lord, it was *delicious*. The minute it was finished she went back to the counter and bought another. This one she ate more slowly, lingering over each bite until it had gone. She drank some coffee and picked up the doughnut.

'Hi, there,' said a voice.

Aideen looked up and saw the assistant from Berry's looking down at her while holding a tray of food. In the shop, Aideen had hardly noticed what she looked like, apart from the reddish hair.

55

'Can I join you?' she asked.

'Of course.' Aideen wasn't a very sociable person; she avoided people whenever she could. At school she'd had few friends and the ones she had were, like herself, not exactly popular. But perhaps it was New York, the strangeness of the place, her new clothes, the hot dogs, that made her feel more affable than usual.

'My name's Gertie Smith,' the girl said when she sat down.

'I'm Aideen Kelly.'

'That's a lovely name. Is it Irish?'

'Yes. It's a bit old-fashioned nowadays.'

'Gertie's German. It's short for Gertrude. And Smith used to be spelt differently but my parents changed it.'

Aideen was surprised. Not only was Gertie a hideous name but only ten years ago Germany had been at war with virtually every country in the world. Aideen herself would positively refuse to admit she had a German name.

As for Gertie, she was tucking into a bun with a layer of meat inside. 'I'm starving,' she announced.

'What's it like working in that shop?' Aideen enquired. She noticed that as well as Gertie having the same colour hair as she did, she also had green eyes. In fact, she guessed that from afar they looked rather like twins. Except she wore a plain black frock, the same as all the other shop assistants.

'Berry's? Oh, it's a good place to work.' She winked. 'Look, here I am outside having something to eat, yet no one's likely to notice. I won't

56

get into trouble or anything.'

'Honest?' Aideen frowned. 'Aren't you allowed time off for your dinner?' The diner was becoming more and more crowded. The girls were having to shout to each other.

'You mean lunch? Yes, but it's not till after two o'clock. All the office girls come to the shop in their lunch hours, between twelve and two, so the assistants are expected to be there. We eat earlier or later. I would die of hunger if I had to wait till gone two. Next week I'll have lunch at eleven and come in here for a snack in the afternoon.'

'But you're so thin!' They certainly didn't resemble each other in build; Aideen tended to be on the plump side, whereas Gertie didn't possess an ounce of visible spare fat.

'I know,' Gertie said proudly. 'My sisters are really envious of me. I can eat ten times as much as they do without putting on weight.'

'How many sisters do you have?'

'Two – Margaret and Irma.'

'I have two as well – Patricia and Tara.'

'I also have three brothers – Michael, Jack and Robert.'

'I have one brother, Milo, but he's back in Ireland.' Aideen felt unexpected tears come to her eyes. Now that Daddy had gone, she was more fond of Milo than anyone else in the world.

'Why didn't he come with you?' Gertie suddenly ducked her head. 'Jeepers! That's Mr Bergman, the floor manager, waiting in line to order. Where can I hide?' Despite her obvious panic, Gertie's eyes were dancing. 'Lend me your hat, the one you just bought.'

Aideen snatched the pink beret out of the bag and Gertie pulled it on until it covered her head and ears. She crossed her eyes, giggled and said, 'Do I look different?'

'You look unrecognisable,' Aideen assured her. 'Anyway, he's bought food and now he's leaving.'

Gertie removed the beret and tossed back her head. 'I enjoyed that,' she said.

'Enjoyed it?'

'I like taking risks. My heart began to beat extra fast! I was so terrified Mr Bergman would recognise me and I might get into trouble. But at the same time I really loved the feeling.'

Earlier, Gertie had said no one in authority would have minded her leaving the shop, which was clearly an exaggeration. Aideen remembered being back in Dublin, the stealing from shops, buying cigarettes and secretly smoking them. 'I love that sort of feeling too,' she said to Gertie. Their eyes met and they smiled at each other.

'What are you doing tonight, Aideen?' Gertie asked.

In another part of New York, Patricia was in discussion with Sister St Edward, headmistress of Convent of the Holy Name, situated not far from their apartment, at the bottom of Seventh Avenue, close to the river. The convent also served as a school. It was an old building that smelled unpleasantly of damp.

In an adjacent room, Tara was sitting a test to make sure she was clever enough to attend the school, thinking that Americans must be awfully silly because the questions were as easy as pie and you would have to be a complete ignoramus to fail. As she desperately didn't want to go to school, she really should be answering the questions incorrectly, letting them think she was as thick as two short planks and not up to it. But she had too much pride and it would upset Patricia.

'Shall I pay now?' Patricia was saying to Sister St Edward. The fees were two and a half dollars a term. She took for granted Tara would sail through the examination.

The figure of Jesus Christ nailed to the cross hung on the wall behind the nun's head. The sight always upset Patricia, making her feel as if she had played a horrid part in it.

'There are only a few weeks left of this term, Miss Kelly,' Sister St Edward explained. She was immensely tall and very plain, but had a youthfully sweet voice. She wore a huge white headdress shaped like a butterfly. A silver cross hung around her neck and wooden rosary from the cord tied around her waist. 'I think we can forget the fee for now, but you will receive a bill for the summer term before this one ends.'

'Thank you, Sister,' Patricia said gratefully. 'Will Tara need a uniform?'

'Just a navy blue skirt and jacket, a white blouse and grey jersey that can be obtained from any shop.'

The door opened and another nun entered, handing Sister St Edward a sheet of paper, which she glanced at briefly.

'Your sister has passed our entrance examination with nineteen correct answers out of twenty,' Patricia was informed. She wasn't surprised, but would have liked to know what the question was that Tara had failed to answer correctly. She was finding it hard to accept there were nuns with American accents, having only known Irish ones in the past.

Sister St Edward laid her hands on the table as she prepared to stand. 'So I expect to see Tara at nine o'clock on Monday morning,' she said.

Patricia nodded. 'Of course.'

Outside, she gave Tara a hug. 'Clever girl,' she said admiringly. 'Daddy always said you were the brains of the family.'

Tara shrugged nonchalantly as if it didn't matter, but Patricia knew the words meant a lot to her. 'Can I have an ice cream?' she asked. 'A banana split from one of those parlour places?'

'We'll go to the first one we come to,' Patricia promised.

On the way, they passed a shop selling foreign newspapers. They were tucked in the wire hangers outside, including a single copy of *The Irish Record*. Patricia bought it to read later.

When she and Tara arrived home, Aideen was already there with an assortment of clothes that didn't quite match. The skirt was too short, or at least Patricia thought so. She was well aware that last night Aideen had helped herself to more of the money that Daddy had left and which she had since turned into dollars – many thousands of dollars, with it being something like five for each Irish pound. They appeared to be quite rich. Once she had gathered enough courage, Patricia would start a proper bank account – something she had never done before. Sometimes the responsibility of caring for her sisters felt like too much of a burden for her to carry.

When she suggested they go to a pizzeria later, she was taken aback when Aideen informed her she was going to see a movie with a friend.

'A movie?' Her jaw dropped. 'Friend?' It dropped further.

'A movie,' Aideen said, as if Patricia was the most ignorant person in the world for not knowing. She spread her hands and laughed. 'A movie is ... well, a movie.'

'A movie is a film,' Tara explained, glaring at Aideen. The two didn't always get on. 'Remember in Dublin, Patricia, we saw *The White Sister* with Lillian Gish and Ronald Colman? *That* was a movie. At home we call them films or pictures.'

'The movie I'm seeing tonight,' Aideen said boastfully, 'is called *Stella Dallas. That* has Ronald Colman in it too.' She stuck out her tongue at Tara.

'What about the friend?' Patricia asked.

'The friend is Gertie. I met her in Berry's.'

'Berry's?' Patricia wondered if she would use this sad, pathetic, questioning tone for the rest of her life.

'Berry's,' Aideen said with a bored sigh, 'is the shop where I bought the clothes. What's more, I've got a job there. I start on Monday.'

Patricia was astounded. 'A job in a shop?'

'What's wrong with a job in a shop?' Aideen looked cross.

'Nothing.' Patricia shrugged. 'I thought you

61

might want something more adventurous.'

'I've no intention of working there for the rest of me life, Patricia. It'll do for the time being. There's plenty of time to be adventurous.'

Gertie had told her there was actually an office in Berry's basement where people could apply for jobs. Normally, jobs weren't available at the drop of a hat. References had to be supplied from previous jobs and school reports sent for if it was someone's first job. But Aideen turned out to be an exception. It would take forever for a school report to be applied for and sent from Dublin. It was obvious she could join two words together in correct grammatical order. Plus it appeared staff were needed in a hurry for a big Easter pro-motion.

'D'you like Easter eggs?' the man behind the desk enquired. He had a Father Christmas beard and a lisp. 'Do you like Eathter eggth?' was what he actually said.

'Yeth,' Aideen answered. She hadn't meant to say it like that and hoped he didn't think she was making fun of him.

Fed up with Patricia's questioning, she went into the bathroom, using the soap and bath salts she'd got for Christmas back in Dublin. It was her intention to have a long, relaxing soak.

Tara settled down on the couch with a lurid American comic she'd bought that morning, while Patricia opened the *Irish Record* and spread it on the table.

She'd hardly been reading for more than a minute when she screamed, *'Holy Mary, Mother of God!'* and clutched her throat.

Tara almost fell off the couch and Aideen yelled from the bathroom, 'What's the matter?'

'It's Daddy! He's in the paper.' Patricia held up the paper for Tara to see, as well as Aideen, who had emerged from the bathroom wrapped in a towel.

PROMINENT DUBLIN SOLICITOR DISAPPEARS WITH CLIENT'S INHERITANCE

Cash totalling more than ten thousand pounds from the estate of the recently deceased Earl of Graniston has gone missing from the firm of Bernard Kelly, a well-known solicitor based in Dublin. Kelly had told friends he was transferring his office to Liverpool, but it turns out he spent only a single night there and may have moved on to London. His three daughters are also missing.

There was a photograph of Bernie underneath. He was wearing an evening suit and smiling at the camera.

Tara uttered a little cry. 'They've mentioned us!'

Aideen gasped. 'Will people come looking for us?'

Patricia was finding it so hard to breathe she could barely speak. 'I don't know,' she said after a while, almost choking on the words.

'Why would anyone want to do that?' Tara asked in a whisper. 'We haven't done anything wrong.'

'I expect the newspaper would think we were interesting. They would like to put our photographs in their paper too. And the money,' Patricia

63

continued, horrified. 'I took it for granted that it belonged to Daddy, but perhaps it's the money that's missing – or some of it. There was nothing like ten thousand pounds there. We shall have to hand it back.' She recalled, when she'd worked in Daddy's office, there'd been loads of correspondence about the Earl of Graniston and his estate.

'Who shall we give it back to?' Aideen asked sarcastically. 'And if you say the Earl of Graniston's estate, then won't they be wanting the rest of it?'

'I hope Uncle Mick comes tonight,' Tara said. 'We can ask him about it.'

Aideen shrugged. '*You* can ask him,' she said, making for the bathroom before the water cooled. 'Me, I'm going out.'

'But don't you care where we stand about things?' Tara called.

'I know exactly where *I* stand,' Aideen said with another shrug. 'In an apartment in New York. I haven't stolen a penny of anyone's money. By the end of next week I shall have earned an entire week's wages and be able to support meself. It's up to you, Patricia, whether you give the money back or not.' The bathroom door slammed and there was a splashing sound as she got back in the bath.

Aideen had already gone to meet her new friend Gertie by the time Uncle Mick arrived. He usually wore plain clothes but he was in his uniform for a change, having been to the funeral of one of the men in his squad who'd been shot by a man holding up a bank. He already looked grave when he arrived, but was even graver after he'd read the article in the *Irish Record*.

'Bernie Kelly, you blithering idiot,' he groaned when he came to the end of it. 'I suspected he'd been up to no good.'

'Why?' Tara asked.

'Why? Because there's no good reason for anyone to emigrate to another country in such a rush unless they've done something out of order,' he retorted. 'I never said a word about it to youse girls, but people normally take their time about such things and do them in an orderly way. But Bernie was spending a small fortune on phone calls to the United States setting himself up here. And why wasn't he bringing your Milo?' Their uncle raised his bushy grey brows.

Patricia said she had no idea other than he was too young to be involved. 'Will you please find out who I should send the money back to?' she said shakily. There was bound to be an heir that the money belonged to. Patricia began to pace up and down the room. Things had been bad enough before their father had died. She'd known in her heart he'd been up to something daft, but not *this* daft, not something so blatantly criminal involving thousands of pounds. Even if the money he'd given them on the boat was nothing to do with the Earl of Graniston, it would be wrong to keep it.

'If I were you, darlin',' Uncle Mick said, 'I'd hang on to the cash till the fuss dies down. I'd like to bet the new earl won't exactly be down on his uppers. Leave things as they are before deciding what to do about it.' Their uncle shuddered. 'As for me, I'm a cop with a reputation to consider. I don't want anything to do with that damned money, not even to talk about it any more.'

He suggested going out for dinner. 'Let's have something different from pizza,' he said, 'otherwise what's going to happen is you'll get sick to death of 'em to the extent you'll never want to eat another for the rest of your lives. It happened to me with pancakes. Let's try an Indian restaurant this time. What d'you think of curry, the pair o' yis?'

Patricia and Tara confessed they had no idea, having never heard of curry before. Tara said she really would prefer one last pizza before giving them up for ever and Patricia agreed, though neither enjoyed their very last, final pizza all that much at all.

Chapter 5

Patricia arrived at the Roscius Employment Agency at five to nine on Monday morning to find the door locked. For a while she stood in the cold, narrow corridor, before deciding to sit on the stairs outside the office, though she had to get up three times to allow people to climb to the floor above.

'Bel doesn't usually arrive till close to eleven,' all of them told her in one way or another.

A girl of about her own age invited her up for coffee. 'Save waiting on your own, hon. Are you an actress?'

Patricia declined the invitation. 'I'd sooner wait,' she said. 'And I'm afraid I'm only a secretary, not an actress.'

'Oh, hon, don't apologise. A secretary's an honourable occupation. With actresses you never know where they've been.' With that she giggled and tripped lightly up the next flight of stairs.

It wasn't quite ten when Annabel Jefferies-Squire – or Bel, as everyone knew her – came panting up the stairs. Her face looked unnaturally naked, without a speck of makeup on it. Taking deep, hoarse breaths, she produced a key, opened the door, staggered to the nearest chair and threw herself in it.

'Forgot all about you, darling,' she puffed. 'I should've told you I don't open the office till about half ten. I came straight away when I remembered. This is the first time I've been out in daylight without my war paint for years and years. What time did you get here?'

'Just before nine. Oh, and your telephone rang several times.'

Bel groaned. 'Sorry darling. So very, very sorry. I must give you a key. Oh, and I'll pay you double time for waiting.'

'There's no need for that,' Patricia said primly. 'Would you like some coffee?'

'No, darling – tea. There's some in the cupboard behind me.' She sat up straight in the chair and began to breathe deeply while holding her hand dramatically against her chest. As soon as her breath was steady, she produced a packet of cigarettes and lit one with a silver lighter, by which time Patricia had found the tea in a jam jar, a box

67

of grubby sugar lumps, two dirty cups and saucers, and a tin kettle.

'Water's in the powder room,' Bel said, with the suspicion of a grin on her pale face. 'It's on the floor below. There's a gas ring in my office.'

'Powder room' was a flattering description for the tiny alcove housing a lavatory without a seat and a basin barely big enough to wash an adult pair of hands in. A scraggy towel hung behind the door.

Patricia returned with a kettle of water to find Bel in her own office putting makeup on in front of a spotted mirror screwed to the wall and the gas ring already lit. Patricia placed the kettle on it.

'Do you take milk?' Bel enquired.

'Yes.' There was a distinct smell of gas in the room. Hopefully it wasn't dangerous.

'Walt's Market across the road – you can buy milk there, darling. Take the money out of the tin box in the top drawer of your desk. Myself, I don't take milk.'

For some reason Patricia was already feeling exhausted, even though so far she had not done a stroke of work. She collected an assortment of coins out of the drawer and told Bel she wouldn't be a minute. She was longing for a cup of tea.

Walt's Market was only small yet it appeared to stock at least one item of food from all over the world. The seven- or eight-foot high shelves were tightly packed and there was a stool on wheels for when whatever was wanted was too high to reach. A girl of about thirteen was on the stool squeezing yet more goods onto the shelves.

Patricia found the milk in little stubby bottles

on a metal trolley right beside Walt himself – she assumed it was Walt, a huge man with a massive belly that rested on the counter in front of him, almost touching the till.

'Good morning, young lady,' he said in a friendly voice when she put the milk on the small amount of counter that wasn't occupied by his paunch. 'You new around here.'

Patricia wasn't sure if that was a statement or a question. She decided to treat it as a question, so replied, 'Yes, I'm working at the Roscius Employment Agency.'

'Ah, and new to the new world too, I gather. That Irish accent sounds as if you haven't left Ireland all that long ago.' He also had the touch of an accent that she guessed was Italian. 'I've only been here a few weeks,' she replied.

She paid him and left the shop. She had no idea why but her head had begun to ache badly. Once outside, a wave of dizziness passed over her and she dropped the milk on the pavement. The bottle smashed and Patricia swallowed deeply in an effort not to cry.

Walt shouted something from inside the shop and the girl appeared with a broom and began to brush the milk into the gutter while negotiating the bits of glass into a little heap.

Patricia's arm was firmly grasped. 'Are you OK?' someone asked – another man.

'I don't know,' she said. 'I can't see anything.' She could, however, feel a single tear travelling slowly down her left cheek.

'I suggest you open your eyes,' she was advised. When she obeyed, she discovered she was being held erect by a young man in a red and cream striped blazer, though minus the straw hat he'd been wearing when she'd watched him singing last week in the music shop next to the building that housed the Roscius agency. Unfortunately he still had the oversized moustache, but his eyes were brown and twinkly, the colour matching his curly brown hair.

'Come with me.' He led her into the music shop, sat her on a padded bench against the wall and knelt on the floor in front of her. 'Poppa,' he called. 'A glass of water, quickly please.'

In no time at all an old man appeared with the water. Patricia was already feeling better. As soon as she had drunk it, she made to stand up but was gently pushed back onto the bench by the younger man.

'Stay there,' he ordered. Patricia willingly did as she was told. It made a change to have someone telling her what to do after having to make so many decisions herself over the last few weeks. 'I'm Martin Benedek, also known as Marty. This is my grandpop's shop; my pa writes music and I sing it.'

It was a lovely shop, painted white with sheets of music attached with drawing pins to the walls, scattered on top of the grand piano and stuck to the inside of the window.

'I'm Patricia Kelly,' she said. 'I really should go back. Bel will wonder what on earth has happened to me.' She was finding it a bit disconcerting to have a man she hardly knew kneeling in front of her for so long. It was as if he was about to propose marriage.

70

'Are you working for Bel in Roscius?' he asked. When Patricia nodded, he went on. 'I'll run up in a minute and tell her you're indisposed. I suppose you're her new secretary?'

'Only temporarily,' she told him.

'Ah! It looks like Gideon must be coming back. Gideon,' he explained, 'is Bel's brother. He fell all the way down the stairs a few weeks ago and broke his leg.' He turned to the old man who was hovering behind them. 'Poppa, play Patricia a nice tune. Cheer her up a bit.' He grinned at her. 'You look like you need it.'

'With pleasure,' Poppa said. He sat in front of the piano, ran his fingers up and down the scales and began to play 'It Had To Be You'. Marty leapt to his feet, raced upstairs to explain Patricia's whereabouts to Bel, returning in no time to sing the lovely words of the song. Patricia began to feel the tiniest bit happy for the first time since she'd left Dublin.

After about half an hour of entertainment from Marty and Poppa, Patricia thanked them and insisted she go upstairs and start her new job. She found Bel sharing a pot of tea with a woman of about her own age, wearing a jewelled turban and a velvet cloak, both turquoise.

'Darling, darling,' Bel sang when Patricia entered. 'This is my favourite client, Tallulah de Vine. I've left her new contract on your desk for you to type. Do you feel all right now?'

'I feel fine, thank you.' She did, too – light-headed in a pleasant way.

The typewriter was so heavy it made the desk rock and her fingers hurt whenever she struck a

71

note. But Patricia didn't mind. After what had happened that morning, she felt sure that she was going to enjoy New York.

Tara Kelly hid out of sight on the steps of a house further down the street from their apartment until both her sisters had left for work – first Aideen and then Patricia. As soon as both had gone, she went back inside.

Patricia's writing pad was in the drawer of the little chest beside her bed, along with the fountain pen she'd got for her eighteenth birthday. Tara took them both into the living room, where she sat at the table and began very carefully to write a letter.

Dear Sister St Edward,

Due to unexpected circumstances, I regret that my sister, Tara Kelly, will be unable to attend your school. I am sorry if this causes any inconvenience.

Yours truly,
Patricia Kelly (Miss)

Tara read the letter through several times to make sure there weren't any mistakes. Although Patricia would never read it, she felt she owed it to her sister not to misspell a word, leave out a comma or put one in where it wasn't necessary. Satisfied that she had written a letter of which Patricia would have been proud – apart from the actual content, that is – she found an envelope, addressed it, and put it in the satchel that Daddy had insisted she bring with her for when she went to school. She had thought it would be a school

72

in Liverpool, but it turned out to be one in New York. She would have changed out of the navy blue skirt and cardigan that Patricia had insisted she wear and worn something smarter, but you never knew how the day might go and there was always a chance one of her sisters would get home before her and demand to know why she wasn't in uniform.

She wasn't quite sure but Tara had a feeling that she would come to like New York. There was something in the air – she sniffed vigorously as she made her way towards the convent, where she put the letter through the letterbox. Voices and laughter could be heard from within, and somewhere a hymn was being sung: *O Mary we crown thee with blossoms today; Queen of the Angels and Queen of the May.* It was one of Tara's favourites. She felt a moment of regret but shrugged it carelessly away. She hadn't wanted to go to school, and with Patricia having decided to give all Daddy's money back – although they still hadn't worked out who to give it back to – it had made up her mind. She was old enough to work and it didn't seem right, or fair, to be kept by her sisters when she should be paying her share of the rent and the living expenses.

But not just yet. Over the next few days it was her intention to wander about, exploring the city in which they were now living, and think about what she would like to do. She sighed happily. Patricia had given her fifty cents for her lunch and the first thing she would buy was an ice cream.

After she had finished a triple chocolate sundae,

Tara felt as if she could conquer the world. Ice cream was the greatest invention ever made, closely followed by pizza. She absolutely refused to believe Uncle Mick's prediction that the day would come when she would go off them.

Earlier that morning she had noticed the direction Aideen had taken to catch the bus to Berry's department store. Tara followed the same route until she came to a bus stop. The first bus to arrive was stopping at a place called Times Square, so she hopped on, paid the fare and sat down to enjoy the journey, having no idea if it would be a short one or a long one.

It turned out to be neither long nor short, but deeply interesting. She had never seen such an enormous amount of traffic in her life and was wishing she and her sisters hadn't spent so much time more or less cowering in their apartment since they'd arrived. It was all so strange and unexpected – not just ending up here when they'd been expecting Liverpool, but for their darling daddy to die on the way, then to discover he had committed a dreadful crime while back in Ireland. It was almost too much to take in.

But now, this morning, being out on her own, Tara felt if not exactly at home, then almost.

She noticed when the bus passed Berry's department store. Aideen was somewhere inside. Tara wondered what department she was in. Aideen had been worried she might be put on men's clothing, or the department selling paint or boats.

'Boats!' Tara had laughed. Even Patricia, who hadn't smiled once since they arrived in New York, actually looked amused. 'You don't buy boats from a shop,' Tara had assured her sister. 'You get them from a boatyard where they're built.' She knew that much just from living in Dublin.

'Berry's is reputed to sell everything under the sun,' Aideen said, a trifle smugly. She had not only found herself a job but made a friend called Gertie, and was thinking very highly of herself.

The bus had now arrived at Times Square, probably the biggest and grandest bus stop in the world. Tara got off. She stood on the pavement and twisted round several times taking in the tall, vividly lit buildings – a cathedral of light with a sky-blue roof, packed with restless worshippers. This procedure provoked a number of glances from passers-by, some irritated, some amused, but all admiring. Tara was tall for fourteen, taller even than Patricia, who was four years older. Her thick golden hair had been twisted into a single plait and tied with a white ribbon, and her eyes were an unusual dark blue surrounded by gold-brown lashes. Back in Dublin, Auntie Kathleen had told her privately that she would grow up to be the most beautiful of the Kelly sisters.

'Gosh!' she whispered now, though this wasn't a place for whispering, but for shouting your head off. 'Gosh!' she shouted in her loudest voice, but no one seemed to find it the least bit strange.

Aideen had been deployed in the camping and sports department in the basement of Berry's. It was a relief, but only a bit. She would have far pre-ferred clothes, jewellery or handbags, something glamorous, though camping was at least interesting. There were all sorts of tools attached to the walls: knives, hooks, hammers, weird-shaped things with which you climbed mountains, or so she was told by Andy, who was in charge of things. He had a deeply freckled face and a red beard, and appeared to know the first name of virtually every customer who'd been that morning.

There were some clothes too: heavily padded jackets with fur hoods, woolly hats, suede mittens, knitted socks, heavy boots. A few tents had been erected and there was – she couldn't wait to get home and tell Tara – actually a *boat*. It was only a red-painted canoe about six feet long, but nevertheless a boat.

Gertie had come to see her at about eleven o'clock and suggested they sneak out for something to eat at Dinah's Diner, but Aideen had felt bound to refuse. She and Andy were the only assistants in this part of the store. Should she disappear and someone want to buy the canoe, for example, and Andy was busy with another customer, complaints would almost certainly be made and Aideen could be sacked on her very first day. She might not have minded except now it was essential that she and Patricia had jobs and supported themselves. Personally, Aideen wouldn't have returned a penny of the money Daddy had given them, but she knew it was no good arguing with Patricia, who was too honest for her own good and intended giving every penny back.

'It's all right for you,' she said now to Gertie. 'There's loads of assistants on ladies' clothing. If you disappear, you won't be missed.'

'You're not nearly as daring as you pretended to be,' Gertie had laughed.

'Maybe not,' Aideen conceded. 'But I'm not stupid either.'

'What time do you have lunch?'

'Two o'clock.'

'Then we can have it together. Will you call for me or shall I call for you?' Gertie enquired.

'Let's meet in Dinah's Diner. Whoever's there first saves the other a seat.'

Tara had arrived at an enormous park – in fact, she couldn't see the end of it. She was reminded it was spring, or almost spring, by the shadowy green of the trees and bushes that were covered with tiny buds. She could smell spring in the air and the recently cut grass.

'This will look desperately pretty in summer,' she told herself. In fact, she had talked to herself quite a lot that morning. 'I shall come here again,' she promised the park.

She sat on a bench and watched a woman play ball with a tiny boy who could hardly walk. He kept falling on top of the ball and giggling help-lessly. 'I would like to get married and have two children,' Tara said out loud. 'A boy and a girl.'

A dog, a Labrador, came and licked her foot. 'I like your colour, doggie.' It was a lovely shade of apricot.

On a bench opposite, an elderly man was drawing on a large pad. After a while, she realised he was drawing her.

'This is heaven,' Tara informed the world.

She was the first to arrive home, having spent most of the day wandering around Central Park, which she had discovered it was called. Patricia turned up earlier than expected.

'I can't cope with Bel's typewriter,' she said. 'She's ordered a new one to arrive tomorrow. It's coming by train.'

Tara was then obliged to explain every single thing that she'd supposedly done at school that day.

'The first thing was fractions.' She felt uncomfortable lying to Patricia, who was so nice and honest and who she loved deeply. 'I was ahead of everyone else. We'd finished doing fractions before Christmas in Dublin. Of course, their history is different to ours. I did a nice picture in art – we used charcoal. Tomorrow it's cookery for the entire morning.' She was immediately sorry that she'd mentioned cookery as Patricia might expect her to bring home whatever she made.

'Will you need money for the ingredients?' her sister enquired anxiously. 'What are you making?'

'Apple pie. And I don't need money. I'm pretty certain that whatever we make we have for our lunch.'

'That's a nice idea.' Patricia looked pleased. 'Did you find fifty cents enough to buy bits and pieces?'

'Yes, thank you.' Tara stood and hugged her sister. 'I love you, Sis.'

'And I love you, me darlin' girl.' Patricia stroked the younger girl's cheeks. 'Everything's going to turn out fine if we all stick together.'

Aideen arrived back with a catalogue from Berry's camping and sports department. She handed it to Tara. 'Look on page nine,' she demanded.

'A boat!' Tara shouted. 'How many did you sell today?'

'None at all, but they do sell them, see!' She stuck out her tongue.

Patricia watched them, smiling slightly, pleased they were starting to joke with each other again. 'I bought some food on the way home,' she said. 'It needs heating up a bit first.'

Tara licked her lips. 'Oh please, Patricia, say you've bought a pizza and I'll be your slave till the end of time.'

'And so will I,' Aideen promised.

'It's three pizzas, all different flavours. We can all have a third of each. And the sooner someone turns the oven on, the sooner we will eat.' Patricia smiled again as her sisters raced to get to the kitchen first.

Chapter 6

Next morning, Tara made straight for Central Park, walking all the way, which seemed to take forever. She went to the spot where she'd been the day before to find an assortment of young women with their assorted children, as well as some boys playing rounders with a bat that looked like a truncheon. After a while, the old man with the artist's pad arrived and sat on the same bench.

She could have sworn that the scents of the park

79

were stronger than yesterday and everywhere was a touch greener, as if spring was arriving in a rush. She must bring her sisters here. Patricia would love it, though Aideen would probably find it boring.

It was a strange sensation, sitting in what appeared to be the heart of the countryside, yet able to hear the sound of hundreds of cars so close by: engines revving, horns sounding, brakes screeching, as well as the clip clop of horses pulling carts laden with goods.

I'll tell Daddy about it when I get home, she thought, entirely forgetting for the moment that Daddy was dead and she would never see him or tell him anything again.

Her lips quivered and she sniffed loudly, thinking about her father and all he had meant to her and her sisters.

'Good morning, young lady,' a husky voice said, and Tara looked up to see an elderly man standing in front of her. It was the artist, his pad tucked under his arm.

'May we talk?' he enquired, bowing slightly.

'Of course,' Tara said.

'May I sit beside you while we talk?'

'Of course,' she said again. She shuffled along the bench a little to give him plenty of room.

'See!' He held up his large drawing pad and she saw the drawing of herself from yesterday. It had been finished, the background added with the bench she was sitting on, her satchel, the grass and the bushes behind her.

'It's very good.' Tara nodded.

'Can I give you my card?'

'Yes.' She didn't want to say 'of course' again; he'd think she had a very narrow vocabulary. She took the little white card and read it.

Christopher Buchanan, Artist
Apartment D
75 East 65th Street
New York

Classes in Drawing, Painting, Pastels
Mornings 10 a.m. to Midday –
Afternoons 2 p.m. to 4 p.m.

'I'm sorry,' Tara said apologetically, 'I don't know how much you charge, but I couldn't possibly afford it.' She actually liked drawing, but had never considered having lessons.

The man – she assumed he was the Christopher Buchanan on the card – looked shocked. 'I wouldn't dream of handing my cards to strangers in the park, young lady, and inviting them to have lessons. Besides which, there isn't a charge. It's a club of sorts.' He bowed slightly from the waist. 'I merely wondered if you would assist me with it.'

Tara looked at him uneasily. 'Assist you?' She must sound desperately gormless.

'Be my model,' he said. 'I am without one at the moment.'

Until New York, Tara had seen very little of the world. In fact, she had never been far from the environs of Dublin. Even so, she had a strong feeling that being an artist's model was not an acceptable occupation for a fourteen-year-old girl. The expression on her face must have conveyed

81

her feelings to Christopher Buchanan.

She looked at him properly for the first time. Actually, he was very nice with thick silver hair and bright blue eyes, and was still handsome in what Tara could only describe as an elderly aristocratic way. His tweed suit was old and crumpled but looked as if it had been expensive, as did the fluffy checked scarf wrapped twice around his neck and the leather gloves sticking out of his pocket. A green pork pie hat was stuck jauntily on the back of his head.

'You must think I'm a cad,' he said sorrowfully, though with a smile that was as jaunty as his hat. 'An artist's model – a respectable artist's model – is a highly thought of, very well paid occupation. But–' He struck his knee with a long, elegant hand. 'It was foolish of me to approach you out of the blue and ask a question that can so easily be misunderstood. Tell you what,' he said, getting somewhat slowly to his feet, 'come with me and I'll show you where I live. From the outside,' he added after Tara gave him another funny look.

It was at this point he produced a walking stick with a silver knob that she hadn't noticed before. He held out his arm and she felt obliged to link it, otherwise it would have looked rude. They strolled slowly through the park until he stopped and pointed through the trees towards a busy road.

'See that building, the one that looks as if it is made of white marble?'

'Yes, I do,' Tara confirmed.

'Well, my dear, it actually *is* marble. That is where I live, on the fourth floor, which, as you will see, is the very top.' He gestured behind him at the park bursting into bloom. 'That is what we see when we wake up in the morning. It really is a perfect place to live.'

Tara agreed with a little nod, though she preferred the Kellys' apartment, which she imagined was much cosier than one made of white marble.

'I know what I should do.' He gripped his stick. 'Are your mother or father at home? If so, would it be all right for me to call on them to explain why I want their enchanting daughter to be my model?'

'My mother and father are dead,' Tara said. It was the first time she'd said it like that, so matter-of-factly, so unemotionally, to another person.

At this he looked terribly shocked. 'What is your name, dear?' There was almost a crack in his voice.

'Tara Kelly.'

'And you are Irish?'

'I am indeed.'

His eyes glazed over as if he were looking at nothing. 'You never know when you first meet people – no matter how young they are, how beautiful, how successful – what has gone on before in their lives. To have lost both parents – and at such a young age. How old are you, Tara Kelly?'

'Fourteen.' Tara was beginning to wonder if he was just the tiniest bit barmy.

'Who cares for you, my dear orphaned child?'

He was *more* than a tiny bit barmy. 'I care for meself,' Tara said stoutly. 'I live in New York with me sisters, Patricia and Aideen. Our Uncle Mick is a policeman and he comes to see us almost every other day.'

83

'Are your sisters older than you?' he enquired tenderly.

'Yes, Patricia is the eldest and Aideen's a bit younger.'

'Is it possible to contact Patricia?'

'No, she's at work.' There was bound to be a telephone at the agency where Patricia worked but Tara couldn't remember what it was called. Also, it wasn't such a good idea to have Christopher call her and ask if Tara could model for him when she was supposed to be at school.

It occurred to her that Christopher Buchanan was much too old and feeble to attack her if he felt so inclined – she was probably twice as strong as him. 'Look,' she said, 'I'll model for you. Patricia wouldn't mind, honest. Would you like me to come now?'

'I would adore it, my dear.' His blue eyes shone. 'What an astonishing young person you are, Tara.'

Annabel Jefferies-Squire was telling Patricia the story of her life so far. Patricia was seated in front of her employer's desk, a notebook on her knee and a pencil in her hand, waiting to use her excellent shorthand and take down letters. A new Remington typewriter was standing proudly on her own desk in the other room. She was aching to use it.

'Our father brought Gideon and I over in eighteen eighty-five, darling,' Bel proclaimed in her gushy, melodramatic way. 'Most of the males in his family were something or other in the church, a distant uncle was actually a bishop, but father

84

was always an odd sort of cove and was drawn to the stage – vaudeville, in fact. After a while, when we weren't exactly getting on well at home, he fancied his chances across the Atlantic, so we came to New York. By then he had driven our poor mother into an asylum with his funny ways. I often wondered, after he'd gone–' she cocked her head on one side – 'if she emerged from the asylum as right as rain and got on with the rest of her life without him – and us.'

'Did he succeed in New York?' Patricia asked.

'Sort of.' Bel put her chin in her hands and propped her bony elbows on the desk. She sighed. 'He was a comedian, darling, always last on the bill – probably because he wasn't even faintly amusing. But for some strange reason, instead of religion he had show business in his blood, and he made enough to feed us and send us to drama school.'

'That's good,' Patricia said encouragingly.

'Then he had this marvellous idea – to start the Roscius Employment Agency, which he did. It thrived for a bit. But unfortunately no one had ever heard of Roscius and they thought, knowing Father, it was only for vaudeville artistes.'

Patricia recalled being lectured about not knowing who Roscius was only last week, but didn't bother to interrupt.

'Then,' Bel continued, 'vaudeville began to die out. Movies became all the rage and quite a lot of the artistes we knew moved to California. Have you heard of Hollywood?'

'No,' Patricia confessed.

'It's where the movie industry was born.'

'Have you ever thought of moving there?'

Bel threw herself back in the chair in a gesture of despair. 'It's too late now, darling; much too late. I didn't move before because I was doing well on the New York stage. I appeared in quite a few plays by George Bernard Shaw: *Mrs Warren's Profession, Candida, Widowers' Houses,* et cetera, et cetera. He's Irish, is George Bernard Shaw.'

Patricia was pleased to say that not only had she heard of him, but had read one of his plays at school. *'The Devil's Disciple.'*

'Ah, yes!' Bel breathed. 'One of his best, as well as Saint Joan. Oh, how I would have loved to play the starring role in that, but I'm too old now, Patricia,' she added forlornly. 'Too old for the movies, too. Do you know in Hollywood they are planning to produce a talking movie soon? I'm longing to see it.'

At some point Bel remembered she had letters to dictate and eventually Patricia went back into her own office, her notebook full of shorthand, thrilled with the new typewriter that was heaven to use, the keys only needing the slightest pressure to make them work.

There were some visitors around midday: a juggler called Joey, twin acrobats whose names she didn't catch, and a woman called Lulu who played the cello, though she hadn't brought it with her. Later, Patricia became aware that someone was climbing the stairs with the greatest difficulty. Whoever it was reached the top and threw open the door with such force that it swung back and nearly knocked him or her back downstairs.

A red-faced gentleman limped in with the assistance of an old gnarled walking stick. His hair, his little spade-shaped beard and his eyebrows were as black as night, and his expression so angry that Patricia wouldn't have been surprised to see steam puffing out of his ears. She got to her feet to give him a hand but he rudely brushed her away.

'Bel!' he screamed. 'Where are you, you bitch, you damn traitor.'

Bel appeared, leaning casually on the door-jamb. 'Gideon, sweetie pie. What on earth are you doing here? It must have taken hours for you to have climbed the stairs with a broken leg.' She twirled gaily towards Patricia. 'Darling, this is my brother, Gideon.'

Patricia didn't bother saying, 'How do you do?' sensing it wouldn't have been welcome.

'What on earth is *she* doing here?' Gideon screamed. 'I knew you would use my broken leg as an excuse to get rid of me. And what's that infernal machine?' He glared threateningly at the typewriter. Patricia reckoned he would have thrown it out of the window had he been nearer and stronger.

'Patricia is my *temporary* secretary, Gideon. She is here till your leg is better and you can take over your vital role with Roscius again.'

'Don't be so bloody sarcastic, Annabel,' her brother sneered. His face crumpled in a massive sulk. 'Where's my chair? I want to sit down,' he said in a little boy's voice.

Patricia pulled her typist's chair-on-wheels from behind the desk and shoved it towards him. He sat down without a word of thanks.

'Darling,' Bel said to Patricia, 'it's well past

lunchtime. Do go and get yourself something to eat and don't return for at least an hour while I slowly kill my brother. By the time you come back, he will be dead.'

Patricia swallowed nervously. 'All right.'

When Patricia left the building, Marty Benedek came out of the music shop and joined her.

'Can I treat you to a late lunch?' he asked. There was something different about him and she realised he no longer had a moustache. 'It was only stuck on,' he explained when he saw her mystified look. 'I thought it made me look a bit of a daredevil, but I'm not wearing it today in case you thought it was real. You don't look the sort of girl who'd go for a daredevil sort of guy.'

She was flattered that he cared so much about her opinion. 'You look younger,' she told him, and then agreed he could take her to lunch.

'Shall we have a pizza? I bet there aren't any pizzerias in Ireland.'

Patricia agreed she'd never come across a single one, but didn't say she'd eaten virtually nothing but pizzas since coming to New York.

They went to a place with tiled walls and imitation vines hanging from the ceiling, which probably looked terribly romantic in the evenings when the red candles on the tables were lit.

'I heard Gideon make his way upstairs earlier,' Marty said. 'I almost followed him up, in case you needed rescuing. He has a vile temper.'

'He certainly has,' Patricia agreed. 'And he made no secret of not liking me.'

Marty frowned disapprovingly. 'He's terrified of

88

losing his job, that's why. Bel only employs him because he's her brother. He's a hopeless secretary, or whatever it is he's supposed to be. He's also a tosspot, which is why he fell downstairs and broke his leg.'

'What's a tosspot?' Patricia asked.

'A drunkard, an alcoholic. I don't like him because he's rude to Grandpops.' Marty grinned and put his hand on hers. 'Let's talk about you rather than horrible old Gideon. What are you doing here? Were they your sisters I saw you with the day you came for your interview with Bel? I want to know your life story from the day you were born till now.'

Patricia took a deep breath and wondered what sort of reason she could give for the three Kelly sisters being in New York.

Tara was surprised that there were so many people in Christopher Buchanan's large, elegant apartment – about a dozen men and women altogether, mainly very old. The ceiling of the room was at least twenty-feet high and the white walls were full of pictures, both paintings and drawings, and there were items of sculpture on every surface. The furniture was rather odd, made up mainly of settees and giant square pouffes upholstered in plain bright colours. The view of Central Park from the wide, wide window was breathtaking.

Apart from herself, Tara guessed there wasn't a single person there under forty. All were smartly dressed – *over*dressed, even. Back in Dublin, no one went visiting and kept on their hats, coats and gloves once they were *inside* wherever they were supposed to be.

The first person Tara was introduced to was Edwin, a dear little man who was completely bald except for a little fringe of hair on his neck.

'Edwin is my special friend,' Christopher said fondly.

Next she shook hands with a woman who wore a black costume, a hat decorated with a diamond brooch and three-quarter-length gloves. In one hand she waved a cigarette in a silver holder in the manner of someone conducting an orchestra and in the other a half-full glass of red wine. A dead animal with a cute face and a bushy tail was draped over her shoulder.

Yuck! Tara thought.

'This is Olympia,' Christopher said, adding in a loud voice, 'and this is Tara, who has come to model for us.'

'How do you do?' Tara said nicely to Olympia and the room in general, when she saw that every eye had turned upon her.

'She's lovely,' said a male voice.

'And so *young,*' another commented.

'Where did you find her, Christopher?' asked a woman.

'In the park,' Christopher replied, looking kindly upon Tara as if she was a hundred-dollar note that he had managed to spy in one of the bushes.

It turned out that he was a genuine artist, enormously rich, who gave free lessons to his friends. Tara quickly came to realise that the lessons were merely a pretence for the friends to meet regularly without having to admit they were idling away their time socialising and doing absolutely nothing of worth with their lonely lives.

A Chinese waiter in a red embroidered jacket was circling the room with a tray of food – tiny biscuits holding a single prawn, a piece of cheese or a slice of tomato – the sort of delicacies that Nora Hogan had prepared for the Kellys' parties back in Dublin, though hers were considerably bigger.

Music came from somewhere. A man was singing, *'I cried for you, now it's your turn to cry over me'*. Two people were dancing. To Tara's surprise, both were men, which she thought quite touching. She smiled. She was going to like it here.

Christopher suggested she take off her coat and sit down on one of the pouffes. 'Look out of the window, dear girl.'

'I'd sooner she looked at the floor,' a man called.

'No, over her shoulder,' said a woman.

'Out of the window,' Christopher said firmly. It was *his* apartment, *he* had found her, so it was up to *him* which way she posed.

There was a shuffling about as pads and pencils were produced and everyone sat down, their eyes directed at Tara. They began to draw.

Two hours later, her time was up, and she ached all over from sitting still for so long. Christopher paid her two dollars, one for each hour, and a few of the others chipped in when she was about to leave, thanking her for being so pretty and for being so patient for them. She went home, seven dollars in her pocket, after promising to come again tomorrow at the same time.

Seven dollars! Aideen was earning less than that for an entire week's work in Berry's camping department.

Once home, Tara hid the money inside a scarf and put it in the little cupboard beside her bed. One of these days she might make enough to repay all the money that Daddy had stolen from the estate of the Earl of Graniston, and Patricia would be desperately pleased.

Sunday afternoon and Aideen was doing something that would have been totally unimaginable six weeks before. She was travelling by car through a heavily populated area of New York. It was vividly sunny and the streets were crowded. People were seated on the steps of their houses, leaning out of their windows, gathered on corners or just taking it easy as they strolled along the busy pavements – or sidewalks, as they were called over here. It was the strangest sight she had ever seen. The reason for the strangeness was because they were in an area of New York called Harlem and almost every person she could see was black. Up until now, she had thought that black people only lived in Africa and didn't wear clothes.

One of Gertie's brothers, Jack, was driving the car, and another, Michael, was beside him in the front seat. Aideen and Gertie were in the back. Gertie's other brother, Robert, was married and his wife was expecting a baby. They lived in Queens.

Aideen and Gertie had discovered they didn't live far from each other; Aideen lived in the Lower West Side and Gertie in the Lower East Side.

They were in Harlem for two reasons: the search for jazz being the main one, and just driving around having a good time, and stopping frequently for refreshments, the other. This was how she would spend Sunday nowadays, Aideen acknowledged with a happy sigh: full of new experiences.

Everyone was in the best of spirits. They sang, 'California, Here I Come', 'Cover Me Up With the Sunshine of Virginia', and 'All Alone Am I'...

Although she didn't know the words, Aideen sang along with them, la-de-da, la-de-da, at the top of her voice. She felt free and uninhibited, without a single worry in the world.

This sort of music wasn't jazz. Jazz was something to do with black people and came from New Orleans. She was longing to hear some.

Of Gertie's brothers, Aideen liked Michael best. He was eighteen and had sleepy grey eyes and black curly hair. At that moment she would have done anything he asked of her. She had only known Gertie for two weeks, but since then had learnt an awful lot about the private ways of men and women. Until now, she had known how babies were *born*, but not how they were *made*. Now she knew, and she ached to experience it herself, just the actual making of them; the last thing she wanted was a baby, besides which, having a baby and not being married was just about the worst sin in the world. She knew what a John Thomas was, having seen her brother Milo's since he was born, and was aware of it growing bigger and bigger. Gertie said it would eventually become six or seven inches long and grow hairs.

Aideen felt a pleasant wriggle in her stomach at the idea of having Michael's John Thomas inside her. Would it hurt? she wondered. She didn't think she would mind if it did. Hurting would merely be part of the experience.

'Listen!' Michael stuck his head out of the open car window.

Alfred slowed the car down to a crawl. Music could be heard in the distance, loud and exuberant. 'Which way should I go?' he asked.

'Straight ahead,' Michael said. The car went slowly forward for a few minutes. Michael hung even further out of the window before saying, 'Now to the left.'

The streets were becoming more crowded and everyone was hurrying in the direction of the music. Alfred went to turn a corner but had to brake sharply instead. The street was packed with throngs of dancing, clapping, happy, perspiring people, and further along a half dozen black men could be seen on the back of an open truck playing what could only be jazz.

Although she was sitting inside the car, Aideen's feet immediately began to tap. Alfred stopped the car, he and Michael leapt out and, without a word, melted into the crowd.

Gertie laughed. 'They've already forgotten we exist.'

Aideen felt hurt. She had begun to sense that Michael was as much attracted to her as she was to him. 'What are we supposed to do now?' she asked her friend.

'Listen,' Gertie said. 'Don't you think it's the bee's knees, jazz?' She leant back in the seat, fingers twitching, and seemed to go into a trance.

Aideen's feet were still tapping on the car floor. She got out and found that the world had changed. All she could see was exceptionally happy people. There wasn't a miserable face or a still body in sight. Literally every single person was dancing with joy. And what else could she do but give in to the dizzy exuberance of jazz? She began to dance herself.

Chapter 7

The time inevitably came when Gideon's broken leg mended and he was fit enough to return to work at the agency.

'Take all the time you need to find another job, darling,' Bel told Patricia sadly. She would have preferred her temporary secretary to become permanent, rather than have to put up with the bad-tempered Gideon.

Patricia also deeply regretted having to leave. She had really enjoyed her six weeks working with Bel. The job was never boring, fascinating people dropped into the office daily and she had lunch regularly with Marty Benedek, who had promised to write a song and dedicate it to her.

'But I thought it was your father who wrote the songs?' Patricia had said.

'It's about time I started writing them myself,' Marty replied. 'Pop's never had a hit; maybe I will.'

Patricia had already started to buy the *New York Mirror* every day to peruse the jobs column. So far she had been for two interviews. At the first she was rejected for being too young, although she had, naturally, put her age on her letter of application. When she had pointed this out, the woman interviewing her told her sharply that she looked less than eighteen. Her eyes narrowed, as if she suspected Patricia had told a lie. She was asked to return with her birth certificate but didn't bother. The second interview she refused the position because the office was dirty and the windows hadn't been cleaned in months. She dreaded to think what the lavatories must be like – not that they could be much worse than at Roscius.

The third vacancy she wrote after was for an assistant secretary with a firm called The Vanetti Motor Company, attracted by the fact the offices were on the twenty-ninth floor of a building in Times Square. She had been to Times Square a few times with her sisters when it was dark and found the colourful, flickering lights enchanting. And Berry's, where Aideen worked, was close by on the corner of 34th Street.

A reply from the company inviting her for interview arrived three days later.

'We have a very large office and a factory on the other side of the country in California,' the smartly dressed woman conducting the interview told her. Miss Arquette, who Patricia would work for, was French Canadian, in her forties, and had lived in the United States for nearly twenty years. She would have been an attractive woman had she used less makeup. As it was, she looked like a clown with her black eyebrows and scarlet, overdrawn lips. 'Have you heard of the company before? Sometimes it's just known by its initials – VMC.'

'No,' Patricia admitted. 'I've only lived in this country for a couple of months.'

'Of course, I forgot.' She lit a cigarette. 'VMC was started twenty years ago by two young Italian brothers – Leonardo, who was the driving force, and Gianni Vanetti. They built a single car between them and within just a few years they'd had orders for hundreds. Now they sell in their thousands.' She pointed to a colourful poster on the wall showing a bright red car with a low body and large wheels. 'There it is. Under the bonnet it's hardly different from the Ford Model T, but the body design is similar to a genuine racing car. It's only a two-seater, so no good for a family. Men love it, young and old; it makes them feel like a real racing car driver. And they admire the colour when compared to boring old black. Even the odd woman has been known to buy one for herself.'

'I see,' Patricia said politely – privately thinking a car was a car. What did it matter what the colour was, or the shape, as long as it got you from one place to another?

'So,' the woman continued, 'last year the brothers decided to open an office in New York and promote their car here. They've taken a quarter of this floor, which is far too much, but one day this office will cover East Coast sales and world-wide advertising. Gianni, the younger brother, has moved to New York to run it. Back in San Diego,

Leonardo, known as Leo, is in overall charge.'

'I thought you said California,' Patricia queried, and felt a proper eejit when it was pointed out that San Diego was in California. The older Vanettis, she was then told, had all returned triumphantly to Italy, where they lived like millionaires.

She was shown the spacious office that the new secretary would have to herself, though only for now. No one could guess how many people she would share it with one of these days. Looking out of the window, Patricia discovered the twenty-ninth floor was inside a cloud, a real cloud, though she assumed it wouldn't be like that every day. She worked out that if every floor had a ten-foot ceiling, then she was three hundred feet up in the air! If only she could write to her friends in Dublin and tell them.

She looked around her. There was a brightly patterned carpet on the floor and white blinds on the window. The desk was brand new, as was the leather typist's chair tucked underneath, and there was a typewriter, glittering invitingly beside the shiny black telephone.

She was about to say she would take the job when Miss Arquette informed her that she had several other applicants to interview and would let her know in a day or so if she had been successful. 'But before you go,' she said, 'you haven't asked what the salary is.'

'I forgot.' Patricia winced, feeling stupid; it was the first thing she should have queried.

'There's a clothes allowance too.' Miss Arquette glanced critically at the clothes that Patricia had brought with her from Ireland. She had kept meaning to buy more, but was only prepared to touch Daddy's money for essentials since she had learnt it had been dishonestly acquired. She had been attempting to keep the three of them on her own wages and the little bit Aideen gave her. There had never been enough left for new clothes.

The salary at VMC, she learnt, was virtually twice what she was earning at Roscius. She left the building, hoping and praying she would get the job.

A few days later, a letter arrived to say that Miss Arquette would like her to start a week on Monday and she whooped for joy.

When she arrived at Roscius, Bel announced that she had some good news – Gideon had decided to move to Hollywood and have one last try at making it in show business.

'He's heard that an English director has moved there who we knew slightly years ago back home and hopes to get a part in one of his movies, so you can stay here with Roscius, darling.'

Patricia's face fell and Bel noticed immediately. 'You've already found a nice job, haven't you?' She smiled brilliantly and gave Patricia a hug. 'Sit down, darling, and tell me all about it.'

Many times during the years that followed, Patricia would wonder what direction her life might have taken had she stayed with Bel and turned down the job with VMC. Would she have changed her mind had she known what was to happen in the future?

'We can still lunch together,' Marty vowed when Patricia told him she would soon be leaving for a new job. 'It takes no time to get to Times Square on the bus or the subway – and there's more choice of restaurants.'

Patricia was pleased their relationship would continue. Marty was her first boyfriend, though so far he had only kissed her on the cheek. Not only did they see each other every day for lunch, but he'd taken her to the movies twice, first to see *Phantom of the Opera* with Lon Chaney, and then *The Eagle*, starring a desperately handsome actor called Rudolph Valentino. During each movie he had held her hand throughout. And now he had booked tickets for a musical, *No, No, Nanette*, which they were going to see on her birthday in July. Patricia sighed happily; she was really looking forward to it. All in all, life in New York was turning out rather well, she thought on the Sunday before she was due to start work at VMC.

It was now almost June and over the past week rain had fallen every day, only stopping occasionally for a brief respite before starting again even more heavily. Today, though, the city had woken up to vivid sunshine and an increase in temperature. She had been warned that a New York summer could become extremely hot, much hotter than in Ireland.

She was sitting by the window of the apartment with Daddy's leather gloves on her knee, her fingers occasionally touching the creases his fingers had made when he had worn them. He must have forgotten to take them out with him again on his last night on the *Queen Maia* after he'd returned to the cabin to give Patricia the money he had stolen, then left to throw himself over the side.

She could hear the Greek couple who lived upstairs on the third floor having their customary
Sunday afternoon row. The people in the neigh-
bouring apartment had their daughter and her
family over to dinner, and the children were playing football on the landing. Someone must have
had a problem with their plumbing as Shakespeare, who didn't usually work on Sundays, was
in the basement and could be heard singing in his
lovely deep voice.

Patricia had grown used to these routine sounds
and they merely formed a familiar background to
her own thoughts.

Aideen, who was in the bedroom getting ready
to go out and usually so difficult to please, seemed
to be enjoying her job in Berry's department store.
Her friend, Gertie, had visited the apartment a few
times. She came from a big family who lived a
relatively short distance away and Aideen spent
quite a lot of time there. Patricia wasn't too sure if
she liked Gertie all that much, but wouldn't have
dreamt of telling Aideen that.

Tara appeared to have settled down at school
and Patricia was glad she had insisted she continue with her education rather than look for a job.
Although she hadn't brought any friends home,
most Sundays she met them in Central Park,
where she said they just 'lounged about'. She was
there now.

Uncle Mick dropped in at least once a week to
make sure they were all right. Although Patricia
bought an Irish newspaper every week, there'd
been nothing else in them about Daddy.

She became aware that a young man in a

striped blazer was tap-dancing on the pavement opposite. When she looked up, he waved.

It was Marty. He was taking her to a street market in SoHo. Patricia waved back, shouted to Aideen that she was leaving, and ran outside to meet him. It was rather nice to find herself running straight into his arms, and for the first time he kissed her on the lips instead of her cheek.

'One of these days I'll take you to Marcel's and buy you a couple of smart suits,' Miss Arquette remarked when Patricia turned up the following morning. She wore sleek black herself, with black and white high-heeled shoes. 'Today I'm having lunch with Mr Vanetti,' she said boastfully when she caught Patricia's admiring gaze.

'I bought this on Saturday especially for work.' Patricia, feeling offended, looked down at her navy blue linen outfit. It was from Berry's and cost five dollars – it should have been more but Aideen had managed to get it reduced with her staff discount.

Miss Arquette made a face at the costume. 'It looks as if it came out of the ark. Gianni expects his staff to look top drawer.'

Patricia was introduced to the advertising staff, Cain and Abel, two giggly young men who shared an office with drawing tables and a blackboard covering one wall.

They laughed at her confused face. 'We're not really called that,' one said. 'I'm Carl and he's Abner.' He pulled a face. 'Gianni seems to think calling us Cain and Abel is a big joke.'

'It's Mr Vanetti to you,' Miss Arquette snapped.

'Yes, ma'am.' Abner stuck out his tongue as she left.

Outside the office, she said to Patricia, 'You must call him Mr Vanetti, too.'

'Of course.' She wouldn't have dreamt of calling him anything else.

There were only two more members of staff to meet – Mr Stewart, the firm's New York accountant, a harassed, middle-aged man who turned out to be Scottish, and the elderly Miss Goldburg, who spoke five languages fluently and translated English into another language or from another language into English. Her office was a vision of untidiness, her desk a heap of newspapers, magazines and scribbled notes. There were more newspapers in piles on the floor.

'I do wish you would keep your office in order,' Miss Arquette complained after Patricia had been introduced.

'I know where everything is,' the woman answered in a gruff voice. 'You keep your own office in order, Miss Arquetty. You are not my boss. Leave me to look after my own.'

'It's *Arquette*,' the other woman snapped.

'Arquetty, Arquetty,' Miss Goldburg said in a loud stage whisper as the door was closing. She treated Patricia to an exaggerated wink.

'Stupid woman,' Miss Arquette snapped. The door closed and Patricia was asked to come into her office to take dictation.

'Mr Vanetti will only rarely deal with you directly,' she was told. 'Most of the work you do will come through me.'

Patricia nodded. She was dismayed at the

103

unpleasant atmosphere that prevailed within the small group of people in the office. Miss Arquette seemed to be the cause of it.

Gianni Vanetti arrived at about half past nine. Tall and darkly handsome, he was gaudily dressed in a blue silk suit with an embroidered waistcoat, reminding Patricia of the sort of man who modelled things in magazines; cigarettes, for instance, or gold watches. He and his brother Leo were thoroughly Americanised, Miss Arquette said. The family had come from Naples in the last century and the brothers had been born in California.

When Miss Arquette took her into his office to introduce her, Gianni gave her the barest glance, grunted something, and from then on ignored her, which Patricia found a great relief.

She met Marty for lunch – another great relief after what had been a relatively unpleasant morning. Although it was only yesterday that they'd seen each other, it felt like ages. It was nice just staring into his eyes while he held her hand. Neither of them said anything until it was time to go, their meals hardly touched.

Back in the office, Miss Arquette and Mr Vanetti were still at lunch and there was a great deal of giggling coming from Cain and Abel's office. The door was open and Patricia glanced inside. One of the drawing boards had been laid flat and the two young men were playing cards with Miss Goldburg and Mr Stewart.

'Ah, here she is!' Cain, or it might have been Abel, jumped to his feet. 'Poor child. We thought you might not come back having got such a bad impression of us this morning.'

'You were all right,' Patricia protested, only half-heartedly.

'I am not really the horrible person you must have thought me,' Miss Goldburg assured her in a voice that was no longer gruff. 'You must call me Esther. It will drive Madam Arquetty wild if she hears you call me by my first name.'

Patricia wasn't sure if she wanted to drive Miss Arquette wild. She just smiled at everyone and went into her office to type the letters dictated that morning. She was beginning to feel sorry for the woman.

The summer holidays were approaching and Tara realised that pretty soon she would be obliged to tell Patricia the truth about school – in other words, that she hadn't been near the place, and had well over a hundred dollars hidden in her bedroom cabinet that she'd earned from being an artist's model.

From the discussions that took place in Christopher Buchanan's apartment, she had learnt far more from being a model than she would have done as a pupil at the Convent of the Holy Name. She knew about the revolution in Russia in 1917, admittedly only the barest details, though she was determined to study it when she became older and cleverer and had more time. She found it desperately interesting.

It seemed the Russian Emperor, otherwise known as Tsar Nicholas II, had been deposed by a group of Marxists who called themselves Bolsheviks, which was another name for Communists, who were also called Socialists. Vladimir Lenin and Leon Trotsky were two of the main participants but were now dead, and the chap in charge of Russia was called Joseph Stalin, who some people liked, some disliked, and a few actively hated. Karl Marx and Friedrich Engels were another two gentlemen deeply involved in Russian affairs, who were also dead, leaving only their activities behind to be argued over.

Christopher Buchanan claimed to be a Marxist-Leninist, while Olympia was a follower of Trotsky. In fact, everyone argued furiously over just about everything, yet all appeared to have views pretty similar to those of Christopher or Olympia. It was the minor differences that Tara couldn't see mattered that caused the greatest furore, just like in Ireland where everyone believed in the same God, yet for some mysterious reason the Catholics hated the Protestants and the Protestants hated the Catholics.

Speakers with heavy accents came to the drawing club to lecture the members. Not all of these visitors could speak English so would bring their own personal translators to explain what they were saying. On other occasions a new member might appear, often quite young, and the conversation would be solely concerned with art and the different methods of drawing; whether it should be done by pencil, crayon, charcoal or pen and ink or, if it was to be a painting, should it be oil or watercolour? Then the new member would leave and the words 'spy' or 'infiltrator' would float around the room.

'Could he be trusted?' people would ask each

other. 'Was she a spy?'

For Tara, the penny half dropped after she'd been modelling for the group about two months: the drawing classes were a guise for a group of people to meet and discuss the politics they felt passionately about. But why did they need a disguise? Why not meet openly? She could only suppose it wasn't the done thing in America to be a Marxist-Leninist or a Trotskyist.

Perhaps when she grew older she would understand. But she doubted it.

Much to Tara's dismay, Patricia discovered she hadn't been attending school well before Tara got round to telling her herself.

It happened because Marty Benedek was supposed to be selling sheet music, not absenting himself from the shop for at least two hours every day to have lunch with his latest girlfriend, he was told crossly by both his pop and poppa.

'Let's limit it to twice a week, Son,' his pop suggested. He was a mild man but had become fed up with his son falling in love so regularly and committing himself totally to his latest girlfriend. 'Let's say just Monday and Tuesday; there's less business done then than on other days.'

So at lunchtime for three days of the week, Patricia was left to her own devices. The first Friday without Marty happened to be the first Friday in July. She had once done the First Friday Devotions back in Dublin – going to Mass and taking Holy Communion for nine months in a row. But that would be inconvenient in New York. Instead, she decided to go to church in her lunch hour and

107

say the Holy Rosary on her own. St Patrick's Cathedral wasn't far away from Times Square where she worked.

When it was time for Patricia to have lunch, she left the office and headed in the direction of Fifth Avenue and the breathtakingly beautiful Gothic cathedral.

She was walking up the wide steps when a nun on her way down caught her arm. 'Ah, Miss Kelly. How nice to see you.'

It was a recognisably sweet voice and belonged to the tall figure of Sister St Edward, head of the Convent of the Holy Name where Tara seemed to be so happy. Her big, butterfly-shaped headdress waved gently when she bent her head to speak to the much smaller Patricia.

'It's nice to see you too.' She was about to mention Tara, but before she could, the nun went on.

'I have often wondered what the "unexpected circumstances" were that prevented your sister from attending our school. She was such a nice, intelligent girl. I was looking forward to having her as a pupil.'

Patricia chewed her lips. *Unexpected circumstances?* Sister St Edward was waiting for a response and she couldn't think of one. Her first reaction was to insist that Tara had been attending school since March, that she had gone there every single week from Monday to Friday, apart from over Easter, that she did her homework regularly, that she made scones and bread pudding in the cookery lesson, but didn't bring them home because they went towards the midday meal.

108

But something stopped her. She didn't say a word. Tara couldn't possibly have done all of these things – *any* of them, in fact – without being noticed by this nun and all the other nuns at the convent. In other words, Tara had never *been* to school. Her sister, aged only fourteen, had been spending her days wandering the streets of New York for months doing ... *what?*

When Patricia returned to VMC, Miss Arquette and Mr Vanetti were having a fight. This wasn't unusual; they had fights regularly. Their furious, whispered words couldn't be heard properly, but they always sounded vehemently cross with each other. Mr Vanetti was a dark, brooding presence in the office. He rarely spoke to anyone apart from his secretary.

According to Cain and Abel, they were having an 'affair'. In other words, *sleeping with each other.* Patricia tried to imagine them in bed together, but it was impossible. And anyway, Mr Vanetti was married with a child. What's more, both he and Miss Arquette were Catholics. Two such respectable, responsible people couldn't possibly be having an affair, surely! Mind you, back in Ireland, it was said that Daddy had affairs, but Patricia had never believed it. Her mother had been such a dear, delicate woman that she couldn't imagine any man, least of all Daddy, betraying her with another woman.

The angry voices, plus thoughts about her mother and father, as well as wondering what on earth Tara had been up to all this time, gave Patricia a horrible, throbbing headache. She was pleased when there was the sound of heightened voices in Mr Vanetti's office, followed by chairs scraping, before both combatants left the office altogether.

Abel appeared at Patricia's door. 'They've gone to make up in a hotel somewhere,' he said. 'Either that or kill each other.'

Patricia shuddered. 'What do they fight about?' she asked.

'He promised to marry her, but he's no intention of leaving his wife. Every now and then they have a big row about it.'

'That's awful.'

'It might be awful, honey, but it's life. Was life all that pure and innocent back in Ireland?'

She remembered the rumours about Daddy. 'Perhaps it was just like here but I wasn't aware of it,' she said.

'I reckon that's the case, hon. You're too young and innocent.' He came in and sat beside her desk. 'Poor old Arquette, she's as unhappy as sin – not a relative in the world and being strung along by that bastard Vanetti who'll never marry her in a million years. She's too old for him and not nearly good-looking or glamorous enough.'

'If you think that then you shouldn't be so horrible to her,' Patricia chided. They could sometimes be outrageously rude and taunted the woman quite cruelly.

'If she were a nicer person then we would be excessively nice.' Abel gave an exaggerated sigh. 'But I do think she could be just a tiny bit nice to us first. I mean, she's not our boss, we're all equal here. Apart from you, that is,' he remarked with a grin. 'But she keeps telling us off, trying to keep us in order, and creating a truly dire atmosphere all round.'

Patricia couldn't help but concede this was true. Throughout the afternoon she kept wondering what the couple were up to, even though she would sooner not think about them at all.

It was almost five and she was about to leave, not exactly looking forward to the weekend because she had to face Tara and demand an explanation for why she hadn't been to school, when Mr Vanetti returned to the office alone and appeared at her doorway.

'Miss Kelly,' he snapped. He was clearly in a furious temper. 'I have letters to do and my secretary is unavailable. It isn't convenient right now, but tomorrow morning, ten o'clock, I would like you to take some shorthand.'

'All right,' Patricia stammered. Did he realise tomorrow was Saturday? Well, she wasn't going to remind him, not when he looked so cross.

Chapter 8

Patricia had expected Tara to be sorry; really, really sorry. Perhaps even to cry. And Patricia was going to be really sweet to her. Her sister was a gentle girl, still a child, really, and had accepted the drastic events earlier in the year without ever making a scene or complaining in the way Aideen had – and still did if she was in a bad mood.

111

So Patricia was taken aback when Tara didn't appear to be sorry at all when she brought up the subject of school – or the absence of it in her sister's life. Instead, Tara offered all sorts of strange excuses. She was a person in her own right, she claimed. (What exactly did that mean?) She, and only she, had the right to her own body, and she had cast off the yoke of bondage and oppression.

'Where on earth did you get all that from?' demanded her astonished sister. Was it just her imagination or did Tara suddenly appear to have grown taller and look older?

'Nowhere.' Tara disappeared into the bedroom and returned with a fistful of dollars. 'This is my contribution towards the housekeeping. I have become an artist's model,' she explained, tossing her head proudly.

Patricia's answering scream coincided with the entrance of Aideen, who rushed into the room expecting to find at least one of her sisters on the point of being murdered. 'What's wrong?'

'Tara, Tara...' Patricia's head was swimming and she couldn't find the words. 'You tell her, Tara.'

'I am an artist's model,' Tara said slightly less proudly. She was worried about the effect the news was having on her sister.

'Honest?' Instead of being shocked, Aideen was green with envy. What a marvellous way to earn a living. 'How did you manage that?'

'A man approached me in Central Park,' Tara began, at which Patricia screamed again.

By now, Aideen was also concerned about her older sister. She made her sit down and ordered

112

Tara to make a pot of tea.

Minutes later, the three girls were seated around the table and Aideen was pouring tea, as well as demanding that Tara explain what exactly being an artist's model involved. 'I mean, do you have to pose naked?' She put her hand on Patricia's shoulder in the hope of preventing another scream.

'I have never posed naked.' Tara explained that the drawing club was merely an excuse for a group of dilettantes to meet socially and gossip. She thought it best not to mention their political views were possibly unacceptable to the government; it would only upset Patricia more. 'It's like a salon, the sort they used to have in Paris. You can come with me one day,' she offered. 'Both of you. They'd be only too pleased to see you.'

'Would they draw me?' Aideen asked excitedly.

Tara nodded. 'I should imagine so.'

'I don't want them drawing me.' Patricia didn't know what to think. It all sounded highly suspicious and completely innocent at the same time.

Patricia had gone to bed early, the headache that had started in the afternoon having got much worse. When she woke the next morning, she felt pleased that it was Saturday. She could lie in a bit, go shopping with Tara to Berry's, where they had planned to meet Aideen and have lunch. That evening she was meeting Marty and they were going to the cinema to see Greta Garbo in *The Joyless Street*.

Patricia turned over in bed and closed her eyes,

113

then remembered Mr Vanetti had asked her to be in the office at ten o'clock. She sat up, groaning.

'What's the matter, Patricia?' Tara was already sitting up reading a book. She looked worriedly at her sister, wishing she hadn't been so arrogantly defensive the night before. 'Has your headache gone?'

'Yes. But I've just remembered I promised to be in work this morning.'

Tara came over and sat on her sister's bed. 'Shall I make you some tea?'

Patricia sighed. 'That would be a treat, thanks.'

'I do love you, Sis. I'm sorry about school.'

'And I love you, Tara. I don't suppose school matters all that much. You probably learnt far more in that drawing class.'

'I think that's probably true.' Tara kissed her sister on the forehead and went into the kitchen to make the tea.

The normally frantically busy building was virtually empty when Patricia entered just before ten o'clock. She travelled alone in the lift to the twenty-ninth floor and found the entrance to VMC's office unlocked. Gianni Vanetti was already there, his office door wide open. He frowned when she wished him good morning, and told her brusquely to fetch her notebook.

The place was silent, as Patricia had expected it to be. As far as she knew, few offices opened on Saturdays. She wondered whether Mr Vanetti and Miss Arquette had made up. She suspected they hadn't or she wouldn't have been ordered to be there.

114

She was glad she had attended such an excellent commercial college in Dublin where she had been taught shorthand and typing, because Mr Vanetti raced through the letters at such a speed she had a job getting everything down.

At one point he stopped dictating, leant across the desk and said, 'Read back that last sentence.'

Patricia complied. It was complicated wording. Some words, like 'chassis' and 'hubs', she had never heard before, but she managed to read her hurried shorthand back correctly.

When he next spoke, it surprised her. 'You are very good,' he said. 'Much better at this sort of thing than Elaine.'

She presumed Elaine was Miss Arquette. Patricia had no idea how to respond. She looked at him and sort of smiled, then bent her head, pencil poised, waiting for him to continue with the dictation.

When he didn't speak, she looked up again and was surprised at the speculative expression on his face. It was as if he was seeing her for the first time, his eyes narrowed and questioning, his brow furrowed as if with surprise.

'Why are you wearing that?' he demanded.

Because it was such a hot day, Patricia was wearing a pink cotton dress with short sleeves and a frilly neck, and white sandals. Usually she came to work in the sort of clothes that Miss Arquette had selected, but today was Saturday, she was meeting her sisters later, and she hadn't thought it necessary to wear a smart suit to work. On her way there she had noticed the difference in the crowded city, the way men and women were dressed casually in their summer clothes. Most were out to enjoy themselves, not go to work.

'I'm sorry,' she stammered now. 'I didn't realize...'

Her employer didn't wait for her to finish. 'Are you wearing it especially for me?' he said huskily. 'You knew there would be no one else in today.'

Patricia gasped. 'Why, no! Of course not.'

'I think you are, Miss Kelly.'

To Patricia's horror, he rose from the desk and came round to her side, where he bent slightly and put his hands on her small, firm breasts. She could feel his thumbs fondling her nipples.

'Stop it!' She tried to push him away but her strength was nothing compared to his. His hands slid to her waist and he lifted her out of the chair, laying her backwards on the desk with a movement that was as seamless as it was effortless.

Now he was touching her underneath, pulling away her clothes, and she was screaming, screaming even louder when he pushed himself inside her with a deeply satisfied groan.

Patricia didn't know how long the agony lasted – she might have fainted, she wasn't sure – before he lifted himself from on top of her and left the room. She half fell off the desk and was attempting to sort herself out when she heard the main door close with a bang.

Gianni Vanetti had gone. It was over.

She was on her knees on the floor, but managed to sit down and lean back against the desk, pulling on her underclothes, straightening her stockings. She noticed there was an ugly, tattered ladder in the left one and one of her sandals had fallen off.

According to the clock it wasn't quite half past ten. It had all happened so very quickly. One minute everything was ordinary; the next, it had changed and would never be ordinary again. She wanted to cry, but inside she felt numb and emotionless and somehow felt she would stay that way for ever.

After a while, she managed to struggle to her feet. The toilets – the Americans called them restrooms – were outside the office and were for the use of all the women on the twenty-ninth floor. Like everywhere else in the building today, the room was empty. Patricia stared at herself in the mirror, surprised to find that she looked exactly the same as she had done that morning in the mirror back home. There was nothing about her face to show that she had been raped. It took a while before she could even *think* the word: *raped*.

Since coming to New York she had never before longed so much to be back in Dublin. She imagined a Saturday afternoon with her friends, having tea in French's, their favourite restaurant. Tomorrow morning there'd be Mass, followed by a walk in Phoenix Park, back home for a roast dinner, then cards at someone's house in the afternoon, feeling rather daring, because Sunday was supposed to be a day of rest interrupted only by prayers, not sinful card games. But as it was Sunday, they never played for money.

She smoothed down her clothes, returned to the office, collected her handbag, and then remembered her notebook and pencil were in Mr Vanetti's office. When she went to get them, she

117

discovered Miss Arquette there, standing in the middle of the floor looking bewildered. She jumped when Patricia appeared.

'What's happened here?' she asked. 'There's blood on the desk and on the carpet. Has there been an accident? Where's Gianni?'

Patricia stood as still as a statue. She was partially in shock and had no idea how to reply.

'Are you all right, Miss Kelly?'

'Yes.' Patricia turned so quickly that she felt dizzy. She grasped the doorjamb in support. It didn't matter about her notebook or the pencil. She would never return to this office again.

'Miss Kelly – Patricia!' Miss Arquette's voice was as thin and sharp as a razor blade. 'There's blood on the back of your dress. Is Gianni – Mr Vanetti – is he responsible for that?'

Patricia nodded, ever so slightly. Any more would have been too much of an effort.

Miss Arquette burst into tears. 'Oh my God! You poor girl. You are – were – a virgin. Why did I let it happen? I'm so sorry, so very, very sorry.' The tears, combined with her mascara, ran like little dark rivulets down her heavily rouged cheeks.

Patricia was mystified. 'How can it be your fault?'

'I made him so mad. I refused to come in today... Oh, it doesn't matter.' She ran her fingers through her dark hair. 'Where is he now?'

Where was Mr Vanetti? Patricia recalled having heard him leave the office but couldn't remember how long ago that was. 'Gone,' she said.

'Let's get you home.' The other woman took

hold of her arm and led her out of the office as if Patricia could no longer see. 'We'll catch a cab to your apartment.'

In the taxi, Miss Arquette rambled on hysterically about the row she and her boss had had the day before. 'He promised we would get married one day. He *had* to marry Katerina, but they've never got on. They have a child, Annette – she's the reason they got married – but Katerina has never let him touch her since. He's as frustrated as hell, poor guy.'

She reached for Patricia's hand. 'Oh God! That's a terrible thing to say. I'm sorry. I don't feel an ounce of sympathy for him, not after what he did to you.' She squeezed her hand until it hurt. 'I don't suppose you'll be in on Monday morning?'

Patricia shook her head, astonished at the idea that she would return to the place where something so nightmarish had happened. 'Should I tell the gardai – I mean the police?' she asked the woman, whose hysteria then took on a different form.

'Oh no, you can't do that!' she cried. 'Gianni's not a criminal. Anyway, the police wouldn't believe you – there's no proof. They could say you were lying.'

Patricia remembered Uncle Mick. 'I have an uncle in the New York police force,' she said. '*He* would believe me.' She had no intention of telling her sisters what had happened, let alone Uncle Mick, but had recovered enough to resent Miss Arquette's unexpected defence of her assailant – and the idea that she could be regarded as a liar.

119

The taxi drew up outside her apartment. Patricia resisted Miss Arquette's offer to come inside.

'I want to have a bath and lie down for a while,' she said, which was the God's honest truth.

The woman clung onto her after Patricia had climbed out of the taxi and was standing on the pavement. 'I'll keep in touch,' she promised. 'Make sure you're all right.'

Patricia was about to say there was no need, but it seemed rude. Anyway, when she applied for another job she would need Miss Arquette as a reference.

'That's kind of you.' She managed to wriggle out of the woman's grasp and went indoors.

Patricia didn't leave the apartment for the rest of the day. When Tara came home, she sent her round to Benedek's Music Shop to apologise to Marty. 'Tell him I'm not in the mood for a movie tonight.'

To her surprise, she slept well and woke up wondering if she was making too much of the situation. Thousands, perhaps millions, of women must have been raped since the dawn of time. She hadn't been permanently damaged. It still hurt, but only a bit, and she hadn't liked the job all that much anyway, though she would miss Cain and Abel.

She told her sisters she had left VMC. 'The job just didn't suit me,' she said casually. 'I'd prefer to work somewhere with a more friendly atmosphere.'

Neither Aideen nor Tara seemed to find anything remarkable about this and merely wished her luck in finding a new job.

She allowed herself to have Monday off, then bought the *New York Mirror* on Tuesday and scanned the office vacancies. There was a call box in the hall downstairs. She got together a few dimes and rang a company called Epoch Insurance, who wanted a shorthand typist for their typing pool. It was situated in the business centre of New York, just off Wall Street.

A cheery female voice invited her for an interview the same day. Before the afternoon was out, Patricia had taken a short test – the owner of the cheery voice had dictated a letter, which she typed back without a single error. She was promptly offered the job starting the next day. There was no mention of a reference being required.

There were eighteen women and seven men in the vast expanse that consisted of the typing pool, as well as a large number of other staff writing quotations or on the telephone. The noise was horrendous. Staff came and went by the minute, she was told, unable to stand the chaos. But beyond the chaos, there was a feeling of camaraderie. Patricia was taken to lunch by the girl who worked on the desk next to hers. After work she was invited for a coffee by the girl who worked on the desk on her other side. 'There's a crowd of us going,' she was told. And did she fancy playing tennis on Sunday or joining the chess club or the dramatic society?

Lunch apart, Patricia refused everything else, but said she would like to take part some other time. Today she preferred to go home and have tea with her sisters, who were anxious to know how she had got on. But that wouldn't always be the case – Aideen frequently went to tea at Gertie's anyway, and although she wasn't sure if Tara had made any real friends at the drawing class, Patricia suspected she wouldn't feel lonely on her own.

She felt that the incident – 'incident' was too mild a word, really – with Gianni Vanetti had been a defining moment in her life. It was strange, but after it had happened, life in New York seemed to improve out of all proportion for the better, though in reality it was the change of job that had done it. Working for Epoch Insurance was hard, but it was fun. She made numerous friends and led a busy social life.

And she no longer worried about her sisters so much. As it turned out, *she,* not Tara, was the one who'd got into trouble. And as for Marty Benedek, they just seemed to ... not exactly go off each other, but fall out of love. That's if they had been properly in love in the first place. They saw each other less, until they didn't see each other at all. The last time they saw each other was on her nineteenth birthday, when Marty took her to the theatre to see *No, No, Nanette.* Her first love affair had been nice while it lasted, but now it was over and she didn't really mind.

Patricia didn't worry too much when August came and she missed her period. She'd never been regular and it had happened before. Anyway, women didn't become pregnant after going with a man, albeit unwillingly, a single time. But when there was no sign of a period in September either, she was possessed with a feeling of mounting terror.

Then one morning she had to race to the lavatory to vomit, and was forced to acknowledge that a truly shocking thing had happened: she was expecting Gianni Vanetti's child.

Elaine Arquette had been in touch twice over the last two months. It was a kind gesture, but Patricia kept hoping that the woman would forget about her. She was part of a past that she would prefer not to be reminded of, yet her name was the first that came to mind once she realised the seriousness of the situation she was in. She telephoned VMC from a call box in her lunch hour and they arranged to meet after work in a cafe in Madison Square, which was halfway between VMC and Epoch Insurance.

The weather in Manhattan that September was perfect – the temperature at exactly the right level, the sun constantly shining, the trees in Central Park and the pretty squares dripping with golden leaves. Patricia, knowing she was being selfish, wished the weather were the opposite, that it was cold and dank and dark to suit her mood.

Miss Arquette, wearing one of her smart costumes and a little straw hat, was already seated at a table outside the cafe when she arrived. The sound of an accordion and a man singing in a language that might have been Spanish or Italian was coming from inside.

'What's the matter?' she asked when Patricia sat down. 'I could tell by your voice on the telephone that something has happened. I have a horrible suspicion what it might be, but do hope

123

I'm wrong.'

'I think I'm pregnant,' Patricia said. Her voice was ugly and cracked.

'Oh, dear God! I wasn't wrong. What are we going to do?'

Patricia was glad she sounded so concerned, grateful for the 'we', having worried that the woman would regard it as none of her business. Who could she turn to then? There was no one.

'So you want to get rid of it?'

She was confused. 'Rid of it?'

'An abortion, Patricia.' The other woman looked slightly impatient at her naivety. 'It would cost a fortune to get it done decently, but there's no need to worry about money.'

'You mean murder it?' Patricia shuddered. 'I couldn't possibly do that.' She imagined a tiny baby, a boy or a girl, absolutely perfect, curled up in her womb. 'It would be a mortal sin. God would never forgive me.'

'Then your only choice is to have it, then decide whether to keep it or have it adopted.'

'You mean give him or her away?'

'They are your only solutions, dear.' Miss Arquette's expression had softened. 'Have your baby aborted, adopted, or keep it. Can you think of any other way?'

'No.' Patricia fought to keep back the tears. She didn't want the baby – who she'd only just thought of as real – but she didn't want it killed or given away either. 'I don't know what to do,' she whispered.

The other woman suddenly jumped to her feet. 'I have an idea,' she said. 'What day is it?'

'Tuesday,' Patricia told her.

'Meet me here again next Monday. I might have a solution for you.' She patted Patricia on the shoulder and marched away, just as a waitress appeared to ask what they wanted to drink.

'Tea, please,' Patricia said miserably, and was left to drink it all by herself.

She had never known days pass as slowly as they did between Tuesday and the following Monday. She was on edge the whole time and barely slept. Every minute felt like an hour. And the weather changed, bringing frequent heavy showers. She felt a bedraggled mess when she turned up on Monday after work, as promised, at the same cafe. She wasn't surprised to find there was no one sitting outside in the rain. There was no sign of Miss Arquette inside, either, so Patricia sat at one of the empty tables to wait. Once again she was overwhelmed with the wish to be back in Ireland, where things were familiar. This cafe, for instance – she'd never seen anything like it before. It had a Spanish theme, with pictures of bullfights and toreadors painted on the wall, and the black wrought-iron tables didn't have cloths but red tiles instead. The waitresses wore casual clothes instead of a uniform and could hardly speak English.

There was a man sitting alone in a corner and a couple of elderly ladies giggling hysterically over a photograph that one was showing the other.

'This is when I fell in the pool that time in Long Island and the bathing suit Ma had knitted me fell down to my knees. I was so embarrassed.'

'Yes, but Lois, you were only five. Imagine if

125

you'd been ten years older!'

'And Willy had been there!'

They shrieked with laughter.

After a while, the man in the corner rose and began to make his way through the tables towards Patricia, who felt herself turning very hot and very cold at the same time. She was absolutely convinced that Miss Arquette had sent him. But for what reason?

She was right. The man sat at her table on the chair opposite and said, 'Miss Kelly?'

Patricia nodded wildly, unable to speak. Rain was still dripping off her hair and off the hem of her frock. She wiped her nose with the back of her hand and shivered. She must look a sight.

'My name is Leo Vanetti and I am Gianni Vanetti's brother. I am truly sorry about what has happened.'

He was nothing like his brother; smaller, darker, not nearly so handsome, but he had a strong face, there was fire in his dark eyes and his hair was as black as soot and slightly wavy. He wore a charcoal grey suit, a plain green tie, and carried a black fedora hat. She remembered Miss Arquette saying he was older than Gianni. Patricia guessed he was about thirty-seven or eight. His thin lips twisted in the suggestion of a smile as he leant forward in the chair.

She found her voice. 'What do you want?'

The smile, what there had been of it, disappeared. 'Right now, what I want is to buy you something to eat and drink,' he said crisply.

'I only want a cup of tea, please.'

He signalled for the waitress and ordered tea

and coffee for himself. Patricia was glad that he didn't insist she have something grander.

He shrugged. 'What do I want? To help you, Miss Kelly. What do *you* want to do about the baby you are expecting? Is there somewhere you would like to move to? California, say, where the climate is a big improvement on New York?'

Patricia was puzzled. 'What difference would it make where I lived?' Her situation would remain exactly the same.

'I'll buy you a house, anywhere you like, as well as a wedding ring. It's the least I can do. You can move there as a married woman.'

'You mean pretend to be married?' She was shocked.

'I should imagine it's been done before when an unmarried woman has a baby.'

'But I would be living a lie,' she protested. 'People would ask about my husband and I would have to say he was dead, or away somewhere.'

'And would that bother you?'

'Well, yes. *I* would know I was a fallen woman, even if no one else did.'

'But,' he said, more gently than she would have expected, 'you are *not* a fallen woman, Miss Kelly, not by any means. My brother attacked you. Rape is a criminal act. He should, in reality, go to prison.'

'Then why isn't he there?' She couldn't help but sound indignant.

'Because he is my brother,' he said simply. 'He has behaved disgracefully, but we are joined by blood. I understand you have sisters. Wouldn't you do your utmost to protect them?'

This time she allowed herself a slight smile. 'Of course, but neither are likely to get another woman pregnant. Oh, and another thing, I couldn't possibly go to California, or anywhere, without Aideen and Tara. We have sworn to stick together.' That wasn't exactly true, they hadn't sworn any such thing, but Patricia was confident her sisters would feel the same as she did.

'Are they all the family you have?' he asked her.

'We have a brother, Milo, back in Ireland. One day we hope to meet up again, but I have no idea when.'

'What prompted the three of you to come to New York?' He frowned. 'According to Elaine, you are the eldest and only eighteen. Were you looking for a better life?'

'I was nineteen in July,' she corrected him. She paused, realising she had to be cautious with her answers, not let anything slip out about Daddy's criminal behaviour. 'My mother died when Milo was born,' she explained. 'Our father was a lawyer with his own practice but yearned for adventure. He also drank, far too much–' she didn't mind him knowing that – 'and on the way to New York on the boat, he fell over the side and drowned. He was as drunk as a piper.'

He looked puzzled. 'Then why on earth didn't you go straight back home?'

Why hadn't they? Because Daddy had turned out to be a wanted criminal and his daughters hadn't fancied being in all the Irish newspapers. How could she tell him that?

'Because,' she said, licking her lips nervously, 'Daddy had wanted so much to come to New

128

York, we thought we'd give it year, see how we got on, like. If we didn't like it, *then* we would go home.' She shuddered. 'The state I'm in, I couldn't *possibly* go back to Ireland now.'

He nodded. 'I understand.'

The tea and the coffee arrived. Patricia had forgotten that the cafe used tea bags, which she hated. No matter how hard she pressed the bag against the cup with a spoon, the liquid barely tasted like tea. Back home, Nora Hogan had made tea that you could almost stand a spoon in. If someone made it weak, she called it 'gnat's piss'.

Leo Vanetti was slowly drinking his coffee while staring into space, as if he'd forgotten where he was and who he was with. Suddenly he put the cup back in the saucer with a bang, turned to Patricia and said, 'Miss Kelly, today is Monday. I would like to meet you again, say on Wednesday in the same place, and I might have a solution for you – an acceptable solution, hopefully.'

'No!' Patricia said loudly. The two elderly women and the handful of new customers who had arrived looked at her with surprise. She felt herself blushing and lowered her voice. 'No,' she repeated firmly. 'Miss Arquette asked me to wait, so I did, and you turned up. And now *you* are asking me to wait. What for?'

'What for,' he murmured, and then seemed to lose interest in her again, staring at his coffee as if it was a crystal ball about to send him an urgent message. Patricia, not normally a rude person, considered storming out of the cafe in a rage. There was no way out of her situation apart from doing something that she absolutely didn't want to do. She wouldn't have the thing called an 'abortion' under any circumstances, and she felt just as strongly about giving her baby to some strange woman and never seeing him or her again. The least objectionable solution was attempting to raise the baby on her own using the money Daddy had stolen; a baby who would have 'Father Unknown' on his birth certificate. Back in Dublin, Catholic nuns provided homes for unmarried mothers – grim places, full of sadness, where the women and their babies were treated with contempt and cruelty.

Leo Vanetti finally remembered she was there. He placed his arm on the back of her chair, leant across and whispered in her ear, 'Miss Kelly, will you marry me?'

She looked at him blankly. 'What?'

'Will you marry me? It's a simple enough question.'

'*Marry* you?'

'Marry me,' he confirmed. 'I am a single man, although I was once engaged to be married. I met her in France during the Great War, having volunteered to fight. Her name was Antoinette, she was a French nurse, but was killed just before the bloodbath ended. I think the time has come for me to have a wife, even if she is much too young for me and I am too old for her,' he finished with one of his rare smiles.

Patricia wanted to cry, yet at the same time felt furiously angry. 'Are you joking with me, making fun?' she asked.

He looked surprised at the accusation. 'Of

course not,' he replied. 'A person would have to have a pretty odd sense of humour to make a joke like that. I am, quite seriously, proposing marriage.'

'But why?' she persisted.

He looked at her curiously. She noticed his eyes were in fact a very dark green with little flecks of gold, the lashes enviously long.

'Can't you guess?' he said. 'Firstly, the child you're carrying will be part of my family: my niece or nephew. Like you, I don't want it destroyed, or brought up by strangers. It is your intention – and to your credit – that you are determined to have the child. I thoroughly approve even though, as you say, bringing him or her up alone could be wrought with problems. So, let's get married.' He lifted his hands and spread them, as if he was offering the only possible solution and he couldn't understand why she wasn't thrilled with the idea.

'But we might not like each other,' she pointed out.

'That's why I didn't want to see you for another couple of days, so I could sort things out in my head and explain them to you clearly.' He ran his fingers through his black hair as if he was ever so slightly unsure of himself, which Patricia reckoned rarely happened. 'For one thing, I think you should be examined by a doctor, make sure you are genuinely having a baby. There is always the chance that you're not.'

Patricia didn't think there was any chance at all; she was totally convinced that she was pregnant. Nevertheless, she understood his need to have the position confirmed and welcomed the idea for herself.

'I wish with all my heart that I am wrong,' she said. She wasn't prepared to discuss her symptoms with someone who was a total stranger, even if he had offered to marry her, something she was finding hard to accept.

He asked when the baby, if there was one, was due and Patricia said about the middle of April.

'Also,' he went on, 'I need to find out how long it would take to obtain a licence. Should we have a honeymoon or should we not?' He raised his eyebrows questioningly as if he expected her to provide an answer there and then. She didn't even attempt to think of one. 'Oh, and another thing – I know we are both Catholics, but I'd prefer we didn't get married in a Catholic church. A civil ceremony should do us fine. It would mean if, in time, we decide we didn't like each other, it would be a simple matter to get divorced, whereas the church would have no truck with divorce. Do you agree?'

Patricia felt she had no other course but to murmur 'yes'. Getting divorced was a reprehensible thing to do and she had never met anyone who had done it, but it was easier to accept than the idea of bringing up an illegitimate baby on her own with no sign of the father.

She swallowed hard, sighed, and then said, 'Oh, all right.' She realised she sounded terribly rude and said hurriedly, 'Thank you, Mr Vanetti. It's very kind of you to offer to marry me.' It had taken a heavy load off her mind, even though it had been replaced by another load. She had never given much thought to marriage, just taking for granted it would happen one day in the distant future.

He laughed. 'Leo, if you don't mind, since we are about to become husband and wife. And you – do I call you Patricia? Or do you prefer something shorter?'

'Most people call me Patricia.' She remembered Bel had called her Patsy.

'Then Patricia it is. Have you finished your tea?' When she nodded, he suggested they go outside and he would call a cab. 'Is it possible for me to meet your sisters?' he asked.

They would both be home by now. Patricia pressed her hands over her heart as it began to beat at a rapid rate. She felt quite faint. 'Do you have to?' She could hardly hear her own voice.

'No, I don't have to. But I will soon. We shall probably be married before the week is out. Would you sooner not tell them?'

'I don't know,' she said piteously, tears filling her eyes. She felt quite helpless and hopeless. It was bad enough Daddy dying by his own hand and leaving them stranded in a foreign country, but now she was expecting a child and about to marry a man she'd only known for about half an hour.

Leo Vanetti pulled her to her feet and led her outside. He hailed a cab with a penetrating whistle and then helped her in the back when the vehicle arrived within half a minute.

'Your address?' he enquired.

Patricia told the driver where she lived and they were there within ten minutes.

He didn't stay in the apartment for long – just enough time to have more coffee, for Patricia to

133

have more tea, and for him to cast a happy spell on her sisters by being utterly charming to them both. He admired the view from the front window, asked what sort of jobs they had, was particularly enamoured with Tara being an artist's model, enquired what movies they'd seen and had they yet been to the theatre?

'Only our Patricia has,' Aideen said. 'She went to see *No, No, Nanette* with Marty on her birthday.'

He virtually blinded Patricia with a dazzling smile and said, 'What did you think of the show? And did Marty like it?'

'We both liked it,' Patricia said. It didn't cross her mind he might think Marty was the father of her baby.

'I would never have thought that,' Leo said a long time afterwards. 'You have too honest a face.'

Patricia knew that if he had asked Aideen or Tara to marry him, they would have accepted like a shot... Where as she didn't really know how she felt. Leo Vanetti was an actor, putting on a show, this man completely different to the rather taciturn one she'd met in the cafe. But which man was she about to marry?

She decided it didn't matter much. In about six months' time her baby would be born and they could get divorced.

When he left, she went downstairs with him to the front door.

'I'll take you to see a doctor tomorrow,' he told her. 'And in this country we both need blood tests before we can get married. I'll pick you up at ten.'

They shook hands. Patricia closed the door and went upstairs to tell her sisters she was about to marry their recent visitor.

Of course, she had to tell them the whole story. Too many lies would be necessary to convince them that she and Leo Vanetti had only just met and fallen in love at first sight.

'His brother *raped* you?' a horrified Tara gasped after Patricia had only just begun to explain the situation. 'Oh, Patricia, you should have told us.' She flung her arms around her sister. 'I would have gone to the office and given him a good talking to.'

'I would have taken Gertie's brothers and they would have beaten him to a pulp,' Aideen said angrily.

'I didn't want to upset you, that's why I didn't say anything,' Patricia explained. 'I expected it would merely become a horrible memory, not that I would get pregnant.'

'Are you sure you'll love the baby?' Aideen frowned. 'I mean, it's being born as a result of a terrible sin.'

'That's a dreadful thing to say,' Tara cried. 'A baby isn't responsible for the way it was conceived. Our Patricia will have a beautiful baby and the handsomest husband in the world.' She gave Patricia another hug. 'I don't suppose you *love* him, Sis, but you do *like* him, don't you? I mean, you'll grow to love him eventually. He's such a nice chap altogether.' Patricia couldn't argue with that.

Patricia Margaret Kelly married Leonardo Filipe Vanetti in City Hall, New York, at two o'clock on the first Friday of October 1925. She refused to let him buy her a wedding dress and also refused to wear white on the grounds that white meant the bride was a virgin and she no longer was. Aideen got her a pale blue crêpe frock and a stiff organdie hat from Berry's, reduced by her twenty per cent staff discount.

It was a blowy autumn day, but the wind was warm and the sun was in and out like a Jack-in-the-box. It was a solemn occasion for the bride, but a happy one for Aideen and Tara – the only guests – who thoroughly approved of the bridegroom, privately thinking that somehow or other, despite the awfulness their sister had suffered, she had managed to land on her feet. Uncle Mick didn't come, claiming to be on duty and unable to get away. He didn't know his niece was pregnant and disapproved of the union. The girls suspected he didn't like Italians. They saw very little of him from then on.

After the brief ceremony, Leo – as they had been told to call him – hailed a taxi and they were taken to the Plaza Hotel, a glorious building opposite Central Park where they had afternoon tea while watching the leaves fall crazily from the trees in the brisk wind.

Due to Prohibition, Leo said sadly, he was unable to buy champagne as he would have wished to, so they would have to do with lemonade, which duly arrived half buried in ice in a golden bucket decorated with giant diamonds. 'Perhaps another day,' he said cheerfully.

'It's not real gold on the bucket and they're not real diamonds either, but it's nice to pretend,' Tara cried gaily. 'Like we're doing with the lemonade.'

Prohibition was a law that banned alcohol throughout the whole of America. It was a stupid law, broken daily, providing criminals with the opportunity to manufacture drink illicitly. Huge fortunes had been made that way, allowing crime to rise to epic proportions throughout the country.

Her sisters were enjoying her wedding day more than she was, Patricia thought enviously. It was a day for pretending. She pretended to smile and sipped the lemonade slowly, as if it really were champagne.

Later, they all went to the theatre to see *Sunny*, a show with wonderful music written by someone called Jerome Kern. By this time, Patricia was feeling glad that she had sisters. In a way, it was as if he'd married all three of them. They all shared his attention right until the very last minute when the cab dropped them off at their apartment and he said goodnight, shaking their hands vigorously and promising to see them all again soon.

And so it was that Mrs Patricia Vanetti spent her first night as a married woman entirely alone in her bed, for which she was truly grateful.

Leo continued to act as if he had married all three Kelly sisters. He turned up the day after the wedding with the suggestion that they move to a new apartment. 'Somewhere with more modern heating would be nice,' he said encouragingly. 'And with a nice view – of the river, maybe, or Central Park. I'll buy it, it will be an investment.'

Aideen and Tara were all for it, although Patricia

137

had got used to the place and was sad to leave Shakespeare, the superintendent. Nevertheless, three weeks later, they moved to an apartment twice as big on the tenth floor of a block on Fifth Avenue that looked down on St Patrick's Cathedral. It had a spacious living room that the girls referred to as the 'parlour', a big, modern kitchen, five bedrooms, and a long balcony with wrought-iron furniture and potted plants.

Patricia was over three months' pregnant when they moved and finding her skirts too tight to fasten. She was obliged to leave Epoch Insurance, feeling sad because she had made many friends there. She hadn't worn her wedding ring to work and had told no one about Leo Vanetti. It would have meant more lies and she was sick of them. She just said she had found a job with higher pay and left it at that. It was still a lie, but at least a simple one.

A fortnightly appointment was made for her to see Doctor Christopher Barry at his surgery in West 57th Street. The doctor was from Brighton, England, and his surgery had pale green carpets and velvet furniture. His receptionist told Patricia she would 'send the bill to your husband, Mrs Vanetti.'

Leo spent a lot of his time in San Diego, California, where the cars his company sold so successfully were manufactured. He turned up every three or four weeks looking very pleased with himself, travelling there and back on a post office plane along with the mail. They would all go to dinner and see a show, usually a musical. He slept in the smallest bedroom, where he kept a wardrobe of clothes.

To Patricia, it seemed her sisters were more pleased to see him than she was herself. But as time passed, she felt just a tiny bit jealous that she wasn't getting special treatment. She was, after all, his wife. When he brought flowers, they should be just for her, not for Aideen and Tara as well. She'd not long had this thought before it began to worry her. Why on earth should she care? She'd only married him for the convenience of having a father for her child, so his name would be on the birth certificate.

When he bought them all gold bracelets for Christmas, each with five charms, she studied the charms on her sisters'. Were they bigger and more attractive than hers? She came to the conclusion that her own charms were the nicest, the most intricate, as if more care had been taken choosing them than the others. This fact gave her more satisfaction than it deserved and she felt ashamed. What was happening? And how small-minded could a person get?

In January it snowed. The apartment was warm and cosy. Because of the snow and the ice, Patricia, five and a half months' pregnant and already as big as a house, only left to attend morning Mass in the cathedral. Earlier in the month, Leo had taken her to a shop called Bloomingdale's, much posher than Berry's, and bought her an ankle-length fur coat and insisted she wear boots.

'Apart from the baby, you've got hardly any fat on you,' he said, looking at her sternly. Neither the look nor his words were exactly flattering.

139

'You need to keep warm in this weather.'

One day she was picking her way home across slippery Fifth Avenue when she thought she heard her name being called, but she felt too unsteady on her feet to turn around and look. In the lobby of their building, the porter, Jerry, welcomed her back with a grin. He crossed to the lifts and pressed the button for the tenth floor.

'You go on up and make yourself a nice cup of tea, Mrs V,' he advised as she stepped inside. Somehow or other, she'd become famous throughout the building for her pregnancy and preference for tea instead of coffee.

Patricia couldn't wait. She unlocked the door of the apartment, noticing briefly how warm it felt and how cheerful it looked with its cream walls and sturdy oak furniture, and made straight for the kitchen, where she poured water into the kettle. She was surprised when the doorbell rang. She tut-tutted, irritated at being disturbed, and went to answer it.

A scowling Elaine Arquette was standing outside. 'So, this is where you're hiding,' she said unpleasantly. 'I shouted to you outside but you took no notice.' She walked into the apartment without being invited and, still scowling, examined her surroundings.

'I wasn't sure if I heard or not.' Patricia frowned. 'What do mean, "hiding"? We moved here, that's all, because it's bigger.'

'Why didn't you let me know? I went back to your old place twice to look for you but was told you'd gone. I was worried about you. Not that I needed to,' she said grudgingly. 'You're looking

140

extremely well. Obviously Leo was able to help – not that I've heard from him either.'

'I assumed he would have told you.'

'Told me what?'

'That we're married.'

The woman took a step backwards. Patricia didn't think she had ever seen anyone look so surprised, as if inside she had totally collapsed. *'Married?'*

'We were married a few days after I met him in that cafe where I'd met you the week before.' Patricia felt embarrassed at the woman's total astonishment. 'I expected him to have told you.'

'Married.' She said the word again, still with a note of disbelief. 'I thought he would help, give you money, find you somewhere to live, not *marry* you.' Her eyes flared angrily. 'Did you insist on him marrying you?'

'Of course not.' Patricia was beginning to feel angry herself. What grounds would she have had to insist on marriage with Leo? 'It was entirely his idea.'

'Leo,' Miss Arquette whispered, and a number of emotions seemed to pass over her face, so fast that Patricia couldn't put a name to them. 'You have married Leo Vanetti! Do you know how many women have longed to do that over the years? Dozens, possibly more. He has been one of the most eligible, desirable bachelors in America – and *you* have caught him. A nineteen-year-old girl from the back of beyond has captured one of the country's most desirable men. Have you any idea how rich he is? I would give *anything* to be in your shoes,' she hissed. Nodding at the coat that

141

Patricia had thrown over a chair on her way in, she said, 'Do you know what sort of fur that is?'

'Leo said it's ocelet.' Patricia had never heard of it before.

'It will have cost a small fortune, and you have no idea how much it's worth, have you?' She began to laugh hysterically.

By this time the kettle was noisily boiling. Patricia made tea and gave Miss Arquette a cup. After watching her drink it, she sent her packing – actually took her by the arm and manoeuvred her out of the door, somehow managing to do it politely, saying she urgently needed to lie down.

Closing the door, she leant against it with a thankful sigh. 'Please don't ever come back,' she said, but only quietly because she didn't want the poor woman outside to hear, 'Please, please don't ever come back.'

She spent the remainder of the day trying to get used to the idea of having married a man that so many other women had had their eyes on for so long. She was convinced that he hadn't come to the cafe all those months ago with the thought of marriage in his head, and had only decided to propose after they had met. It meant something that she was finding it very hard to understand and accept. He had actually *wanted* to marry her.

By the end of February the sisters had been in America for a year. One snowy evening, they sat in front of the electric fire in the apartment and relived the day on the boat when they'd heard that Daddy had died, going over it bit by bit, recalling the young officer who'd come to their cabin to tell them that their father had drowned.

'I was very rude to him,' Aideen said in a rare moment of self-awareness. 'But I couldn't accept he was telling the truth.'

'The captain was awfully nice,' Tara commented. 'I can't remember his name.'

'It was Morgan,' Patricia told her. 'Captain Morgan. He was ever so kind.'

'I've often wondered,' Tara went on, 'if Daddy's body was ever washed up on a strange foreign shore.'

'Oh, don't say that, darlin'.' Patricia shuddered.

'It had to end up somewhere, Sis,' Tara said bluntly, 'even if it's at the bottom of the ocean.'

After that, Patricia determined to change the subject from their dead father and the where-abouts of his body, to the present. All three were knitting baby clothes and she pretended to drop a stitch so her sisters would stop knitting – and talking – while she pretended to catch it. Once she had, she said, 'I still haven't thought of a name for the baby.' This was something that had occupied them for hours. She wanted an Irish name, Aideen thought it should be Italian, and Tara preferred it be American.

'Like Sinclair or Grant, if it's a boy. Or Abraham, after Abraham Lincoln – there's someone in the drawing group who has Lincoln for his first name,' Tara said.

But Patricia was convinced she would have a girl and preferred something like Maeve, Caitlin or Fionnoula, and wasn't going to be influenced by anyone. 'I wish I'd been called something more Irish than Patricia,' she said, 'like Aideen or Tara.'

'Really, Sis, it's impossible to have a more Irish name than Patricia.' Tara rolled her eyes impatiently as if her sister was the biggest eejit in the world. 'It's the feminine form of Patrick, the patron saint of Ireland. If you have a boy, you should call him Patrick.'

'It's too similar to my own name.' Patricia was certain her daughter would have fair hair and blue eyes like herself and Tara.

She was beginning to feel uncomfortably big and desperately awkward and unsteady. Going out alone, she was scared she might fall or someone would knock her over, so her sisters would come with her, she in the middle linking their arms. She had never loved them so much.

In April, when the baby was due, Leo arrived from San Diego and it seemed he intended staying until after the baby came. Mornings, they had breakfast together, then he went to the office overlooking Times Square where his brother worked. Patricia wondered if Gianni knew she was expecting his child? Had Miss Arquette told him? Or had Leo himself? How did the brothers get on? Would she ever know?

Since he'd been back, Leo had arranged for Patricia to have a live-in nurse-companion called Joyce, who was of Irish descent and had married a Pole with an unpronounceable surname with whom she didn't get on. Leo had insisted Patricia have company during the day.

'Just call me Joyce,' the nurse said when he had introduced them. A tall, strong woman in her forties, she had a nice, friendly nature. Having

144

never been to Ireland, she spoke with a twangy New York accent – at least, that's what she said it was. Most people in New York had accents and Patricia found it hard to tell where they came from except if the accent was Irish or English.

Mornings and afternoons, Joyce took her for little walks in the balmy April sunshine, calling in at the cathedral on the way back to say a quick prayer. The rest of the time Patricia sat with her feet up, reading a book or knitting while Joyce made tea or read the *New York Times* from cover to cover, reading little interesting bits out loud from time to time.

She was a Democrat, she told Patricia. There were only two main parties in America and the Democrats were sort of left wing and the Republicans sort of right wing. The current president, Calvin Coolidge, was a Republican. He was a 'do nothing' president, according to Joyce.

'He doesn't believe in helping people, like the farmers, for instance,' Joyce said gloomily. The country was very slowly getting in a bad state, while all the time the rich got richer and the poor got poorer. 'One of these days it's all going to explode and there'll be a revolution like there was in Russia.'

Patricia wondered if Leo was a Democrat or a Republican. It seemed wrong that she didn't know, but they'd never talked about politics. She hoped he was the first rather than the latter. In fact, they never talked about anything much except things like the weather or what to have for dinner. And, of course, the forthcoming baby.

The baby began its arrival in the middle of the night, long after the clocks in various parts of the city could have been heard chiming midnight in a variety of different tones.

It was the beginning of the strangest, most agonising, most glorious, and occasionally funny day of Patricia's life. She was sound asleep when she was woken by a sharp pain in the pit of her pelvis. It passed over her entire body like a shaft of lightning. In no time at all there was another pain, and she sat up sharply and groaned. She knew all about the pains: they were called contractions.

Joyce, in the next room, was the first to come in and predict the baby was on its way after Patricia told her she'd just had two contractions only minutes apart. Joyce was closely followed by Leo in a navy blue chenille dressing gown, then Aideen in her nightie. Tara, always a deep sleeper, didn't wake up for ages.

'It's a sign of a quick birth,' Joyce announced, 'the labour pains being so close together.' She changed her mind soon afterwards when it turned out that Patricia's pelvis wasn't aligned with the baby's head – or something like that. Joyce's predictions, observations and opinions were going in one ear and quickly out the other.

Four hours later, Joyce ordered everyone back to bed. During that time the contractions had faded and disappeared altogether. Patricia had cried a bit, laughed a bit, and then eaten a boiled egg with soldiers. It was the arrival of the soldiers with the egg that made her cry because it was what Milo had called them back in Dublin. She hardly thought about her brother these days.

Would she ever see him again, she wondered?

Aideen returned to bed, as well as Tara, who had only just got up anyway, but Leo insisted he stayed where he was. As he was Joyce's employer, she couldn't very well insist he too went back to bed. He sat in the room with Patricia and they talked, though she could never remember what they'd talked about. Every now and again he would go into another room and she would smell the cigar he was smoking. She had never known him smoke before.

The contractions returned not long after seven o'clock when Aideen and Tara reappeared. Leo was found fast asleep in the kitchen with a lighted cigar in his hand.

Annoyed, Joyce emptied a jug of water over the cigar, soaking his arm so he was obliged to get dressed. He announced he wasn't going to the office that day, and Aideen and Tara declared they too intended to stay at home.

Just then, Patricia wasn't having the suggestion of a pain and wished everyone would go away, including Joyce, who was getting on her nerves. 'Why don't you have a bit of a lie-down?' she said when the woman began making the bed for the umpteenth time.

'I think I might.' Joyce yawned and disappeared into her bedroom.

Aideen and Tara went to early Mass at St Patrick's across the road. The front door closed and Patricia gave a sigh of relief as she relaxed back on the pillow. She had closed her eyes and didn't open them when someone came into the room and sat in the chair beside her. She knew it was

Leo because there was the slight smell of his cigar.

He tenderly laid his hand on her forehead and murmured, 'How are you, my darling girl?'

'All right,' she whispered. There was a sensation in her stomach that had nothing to do with childbirth.

'I love you.' Her hand was gently lifted and warmly kissed.

Patricia's eyes were still closed. 'I think I love you.'

His lips were still pressed against her hand and he kissed her fingers, one by one. 'Just one look, that day in the cafe, and I knew that you were for me. Ever since I have hoped and prayed that you would feel the same.'

'I do.' The words came out faintly, but with conviction.

His hand left her forehead and stroked her cheek. He kissed the corner of her lips and Patricia turned her head slightly so that he could kiss her properly, just as the front door of the apartment opened and her sisters came in.

'We said loads of prayers for you and the baby, Sis,' Tara called.

'And lit a dozen candles,' Aideen added. 'Six red and six white.'

Patricia listened, half asleep in some dreamy heaven where Leo Vanetti was madly in love with her and she with him.

Not long afterwards, the baby arrived. Patricia remained in her dreamy, preoccupied state. Contractions came and went. It would be a lie to say she hardly noticed them, but she didn't scream once, not even when the baby shot out to be caught in Joyce's large, capable hands.

'It's a boy,' she announced. 'A fine, bonny boy. But he's not a bit like you, Mr Vanetti,' she added with an outrageous lack of tact when Leo entered the room.

Please, God, please don't let him be like Gianni! Patricia had woken out of her semi-stupor. Her sisters were helping her to sit upright, and then Joyce was putting a dark-haired, gurgling baby in her arms.

'He's the image of our Milo,' Tara said delightedly.

'Milo is our little brother back in Ireland,' Aideen told the nurse.

Patricia's relief was so great that before she'd even had time to think about it, she blurted, 'That's what we'll call him: Milo.'

She smiled at Leo, who smiled back, his dark eyes filled with love. He chucked the baby under his tiny chin, saying, 'Welcome to the world, Milo Vanetti.'

Chapter 9

1928

'When will everything be delivered?' the customer asked.

'By Friday,' Aideen assured her. 'Are you on the telephone?'

The woman reeled off her number and Aideen wrote it on the order form. 'You'll be contacted tomorrow morning and be told when the goods will arrive,' she said. The order was for a tent, a groundsheet and various cooking utensils for use on a camp fire. 'I hope you enjoy your holiday,' she added politely.

'It's the first time we've gone camping,' the woman said, making a face. 'Eugene, that's my husband, wants to teach the boys to fish.'

The boys had come with her. They were smartly dressed and about fourteen and fifteen. They also made faces at their mother's words. Aideen reckoned Eugene had a job on his hands. His kids looked the sort who'd prefer to go see a movie or do something vastly more interesting than wait for fish to bite, or whatever it was fish did.

The customer and her sons left. Aideen twiddled her thumbs for a while. Sports equipment wasn't one of the busiest departments in Berry's, particularly on a Monday morning. Andy, the senior assistant and Aideen's immediate boss, had returned from his weekend with a stomach upset and had spent most of the morning in the men's toilet.

Aideen sat on the stool that was used to get clothes out of the six-foot-high glass-fronted drawers. She really must start looking for another job. Last week she'd turned nineteen. Another year and she would be twenty, and there was no future for a woman in Berry's unless they were prepared to stay their entire lifetime and never get married. Apart from women's clothing and cosmetics, the heads of every single department were male, some of them quite young.

Anyway, Aideen didn't want to work forever in a boring old shop. Trouble was, she didn't know what she wanted and was fed up with herself for feeling envious of Patricia for being a married woman with a child – now expecting another. Patricia wouldn't have dreamt of getting married if Leo's revolting brother hadn't made her pregnant. There would have been no need for his desperately handsome brother to have come to the rescue and married her. Aideen secretly had a really big crush on Leo.

I'm not *exactly* envious, she told herself – more resentful that she was being left behind when compared to Patricia and Tara.

She was a bit young at just nineteen to feel that way, but she was still working in the same job, in the same department, at Berry's since they had arrived in America three years ago. Tara, two years younger, led a terrifically interesting life, going to art shows and previews and cocktail parties. Her photograph had twice been in a glossy magazine called *Art in the City*. Beneath one of the photos, she'd been described as the 'muse' of the artist, Christopher Buchanan. Aideen had met Christopher Buchanan and he looked about a hundred years old, so she assumed there was nothing romantic going on. Even so, it was ten times more exciting than selling hiking boots, fishing rods and guns for a living.

'You're late again,' a voice said brightly.

Aideen looked up and came face to face with Gertie, her best friend. 'Late for what?' she asked.

'Lunch, hon. You usually call for me, but I've had

151

to call for you loads of times lately. I hope you're not becoming too involved with your work.' She glanced with amusement at the various items of sporting equipment with which Aideen was surrounded.

I bet the people who buy it are far more interesting than the ones who buy your clothes, Aideen wanted to say. But Gertie would take offence and they'd have an argument, which was maddening as neither was prepared to lose and the argument could go on for days until it petered out. Anyway, it was through Aideen buying clothes in Gertie's department that they'd met. In those days, she *had* been more concerned with fashion than anything else, but she had changed with age.

'I don't know when I'll be able to have lunch,' she told Gertie. 'Andy's sick and I can't leave the department.' She was glad to have an excuse. For months now Gertie had been getting on her nerves. It was another reason for finding a different job where they wouldn't come face to face on a daily basis.

'Of course you can leave the department,' Gertie said scathingly. 'Just call staff and they'll send a replacement for Andy. You can't go without lunch. In fact, I'll do it for you.' She reached for the internal telephone attached to the wall, but Aideen stopped her.

'Don't,' she said. 'Andy doesn't want anyone to know he's sick. I promised to cover for him.' He was married with two young children and was scared of losing his job. He was often sick and Aideen wouldn't have been surprised if there was something seriously wrong with him. When she had shared this information with Tara, her sister had lectured her on loyalty to your fellow workers being far more important than to your employer.

'You're a dork, Aideen.' Gertie shrugged disgustedly. She had no time for Andy – or for most people, come to that.

Aideen shrugged back. 'OK, so I'm a dork, but I'd sooner be a friend of Andy's than of management.' Tara would have been delighted to hear her say that.

'Please yourself.' Gertie turned on her heel and went to lunch, presumably alone, leaving Aideen to think it really was about time she did something drastic about her life.

A year ago, a young man had come into the shop to buy all sorts of gear and said he was about to climb Everest. He was tall, well built, with bright blue eyes and fair curly hair. He bore the confident expression of someone who found the world a jolly good place in which to live.

'Is Everest in America?' Aideen had asked.

The young man had looked at her kindly. 'No,' he said slowly, as if he was speaking to a small child, 'it's in the Himalayas; one side is in Tibet and the other in Nepal. It's said to be the highest mountain in the world.'

'And you're about to climb it?' She was impressed.

He had the grace to look a bit sheepish. 'Well, I'm going to take a look at it. No one has ever managed to climb to the top before.'

'And you'll be the first!' She was even more impressed.

He looked even more sheepish. 'I was perhaps exaggerating,' he conceded. 'After I've had a look, I might just climb halfway.'

'Won't it cost a lot of money, going to those places you mentioned?' She couldn't remember their names.

'I'm taking time off my normal job. I'm a professional ice hockey player,' he said proudly. 'I've plenty of cash saved.'

He bought boots, thick jumpers, knitted socks, a heavy waxed jacket and a woolly hat. He then examined the ice picks and hammers used for climbing. 'I'm not sure which to get,' he said doubtfully.

Aideen had called Andy over to help. When the young man paid, he gave Aideen his card and said he'd bought too much to carry and would collect everything the next day.

'I'll borrow Pop's car,' he said cheerfully.

Aideen looked at the card. His name was Humphrey Noble Grant and he lived in Brooklyn.

She wished him good luck with climbing Everest.

'I'll come and see you when I get back,' he promised. 'You're the only person I've told who hasn't laughed.'

It just so happened that the day Andy was sick and Aideen had upset Gertie was the day that Humphrey Noble Grant returned to Berry's to tell Aideen how he'd got on with Everest. He was browner than when she'd last seen him, perhaps a bit thinner, and his curly hair a bit longer, but he looked even more ruggedly handsome than she remembered. She recognised him straight away.

'Did you climb all the way to the top?' she asked, genuinely interested.

'Well, no, I only managed about a quarter of the way,' he conceded. 'But that's considered quite good for a rookie. I need to get more practice in with climbing, but,' his face fell, 'I promised to work in Pop's office when I reached twenty-five.'

'And are you twenty-five now?'

'Nearly. My birthday's in July.'

'And where is your pop's office?'

'Here, in New York. He's a lawyer.' He sniffed gloomily. 'I did a law degree at college.'

'My daddy was a lawyer back in Ireland,' Aideen told him. 'Though he was called a solicitor. My sister went to work in his office, not that *she* was a solicitor, mind. She was a shorthand-typist.'

'Where is he now, your pop – your daddy, that is?'

'Dead, I'm afraid.' She sighed.

'Jeez, I'm sorry.' He actually looked quite mortified.

Two more customers came in, a man and woman, and they stood waiting to be served. Aideen was about to excuse herself to attend to the pair, hoping this customer wouldn't go away, when a green-faced Andy appeared and approached the couple himself.

Five minutes later, the pair had gone, and Andy suggested to Aideen that she go and have something to eat.

'I'll deal with this customer.' He attempted a sickly smile at the tall figure of Humphrey Noble

Grant, who said courteously, 'I would very much like to buy lunch for this lady?' He turned to Aideen. 'If that is all right, Miss...?' He left the question hanging in the air.

'Miss Aideen Kelly.' Aideen replied. 'And it's absolutely all right, thank you.'

'I've thought about you a lot over the last year,' he confided over lunch in a Chinese restaurant on 38th Street. He regarded her over a forkful of chicken chow mein before putting it in his mouth. There was nothing calculating about the look, nothing to suggest he was imagining, like most men who looked at her, what she would be like without any clothes on and if she would be good in bed. It was just a look of genuine admiration. 'You're very pretty and you have the nicest red hair I've ever seen.'

Aideen blushed for the first time in her life. 'Thank you, Humphrey.' They had agreed to be on first-name terms.

'You're the only person who believed I could climb Everest. Apart from my mom, everyone else laughed.' His brow furrowed. 'Mom was worried. At least eleven people are known to have died trying to climb it.'

'Gosh, that's awful.'

'The thing is,' he said miserably, 'I wouldn't have minded – dying, that is. I shall probably die being a lawyer. I only just scraped through the exams. The only thing I was good at was hockey.'

Aideen was shocked. 'You're a bit young to think about dying.'

'I can't stand the idea of being stuck in an

office. I like wide open spaces, adventure, seeing the sun and the sky.' He lifted his head, spread his arms and yodelled loudly, as if he had just reached the top of a mountain. Everyone in the restaurant turned to look at him. 'I like to feel free,' he said in a deep voice.

Instead of being embarrassed, Aideen laughed in appreciation of his call to nature while sitting in a crowded restaurant in the middle of heavily populated New York.

He caught her hand and said emotionally, 'How can you stand working in the basement of that shop all day without any sign of daylight? It's like a beautiful animal being trapped in a cage.'

Aideen had already gone off Berry's as a place of work, but hadn't given a fig about the lack of daylight. Suddenly, she felt she couldn't stand it another day. 'I shall leave,' she announced grandly.

'Leave now, this minute,' he urged, squeezing her hand so hard it hurt. 'Don't go back after we've finished lunch. We could go for a ride on the ferry.'

'Oh, I couldn't possibly do that,' she said. It was the second time that day it had been suggested she abandon poor Andy. She explained the position. 'But I really will give in my notice soon, once I've found another job.'

Aideen and Humphrey hadn't been going out together for many weeks when she realised that, in a very nice way, he wasn't quite all there. For a man approaching twenty-five, he was extraordinarily naïve, as trusting as a child, and inclined to

157

think the best of everyone apart from his father.

They had been seeing each other for two months when Aideen met both his parents, who came to Manhattan to take them to dinner. She liked his mother straight away, but not his father, which wasn't all that surprising. Mary Grant was an attractive woman in her fifties with a permanently harassed expression, no doubt due to the unpleasant attitude of her husband. Theodore Grant was a bully whose bushy eyebrows met on his forehead in a permanent scowl. He was rude to his wife, openly contemptuous of his son, and not all that nice to Aideen.

'I can't for the life of me imagine why any young woman in her right mind would want to marry him,' he said bluntly to her face. The meal was over and they were waiting for coffee.

'Oh, Theo,' his wife exclaimed. 'That is a terribly offensive thing to say about Aideen.'

'I'm sorry,' the man mumbled, not very convincingly.

Aideen didn't bother to inform him that his son hadn't asked her to marry him, and if he did, she wasn't sure if she would accept. She wasn't in love with Humphrey Noble Grant, but liked him better than most men she'd met – apart from Leo Vanetti, who was already married to her sister.

When she and Mary Grant went to the powder room, the woman apologised for her husband's behaviour. 'None of our sons have lived up to his expectations,' she said mournfully. Aideen knew Humphrey had two elder brothers he hardly saw. 'Charles has become a minister in the Baptist church,' Mary went on, 'and Ludovic seems determined to become a poet. He's written quite a few poems, but none have been published.' She sighed as she patted powder on her face in a lacklustre way; the poor woman must have sighed at least a dozen times since they'd met. 'He supports himself by washing dishes in restaurants. Theo had put all his faith in Humphrey to do something with himself, but yet again he feels let down.' She looked anxiously at the younger woman. 'You do realise, don't you, dear, that Humphrey hasn't quite grown up?'

Aideen ignored the question. 'Being a professional ice hockey player and climbing Everest, even a quarter of the way, are things that most fathers would be proud of,' she said. 'He ought to boast about Humphrey's achievements to the members of his club – if he has one.'

Daddy had belonged to a club in Dublin, where he claimed he never ceased to brag about his girls and his little son, none of whom had so much as set eyes on a mountain, let alone attempted to climb one.

'Theo does have a club he goes to frequently, but I'm afraid he would only find Humphrey reaching the very top of Everest worth mentioning to his friends.'

'Do you still want to marry me after meeting pop?' Humphrey asked after his parents had returned to Brooklyn. The young couple were still in the restaurant where they'd had dinner.

Aideen choked on her coffee. '*Marry* you? You haven't asked me yet.'

'I didn't think there was any need to.' He

159

looked slightly indignant. 'I assumed you felt the same as I did right from the start.'

'You mean since you first came to Berry's last year.'

'Well, no,' he conceded in his slow, patient way. 'But since I came back.' He reached across the table and stroked her hair. 'I love you, Aideen.'

Aideen leant back in her chair. She'd never smoked but there times when she wished she did, and this was one. It would be useful to have something to do with her hands while she thought.

Marry him! He *loved* her. And he'd thought she felt the same about him. But Aideen wasn't sure if she was capable of loving anyone, not properly and thoroughly, apart from her family.

A few years ago she'd thought she was in love with Michael Smith, Gertie's brother, and they'd been a kind of couple for a while. But when he'd tried to touch her intimately, Aideen wouldn't let him. Yet she'd been dying to experience the ultimate way of making love for so long. But look what had happened to Patricia, getting pregnant after just one time! She didn't want to *have* to marry Michael and end up with Gertie for a sister-in-law.

All this while, Humphrey had been watching her intently. 'What are you thinking about?' he asked

She visualised herself elegantly holding a cigarette and blowing out the smoke. 'About marrying you.'

'Haven't you thought about it before?'

She shook her head, then nodded vigorously. 'I have and I haven't,' she said.

At that he grinned, eyes sparkling, showing loads

of white teeth, and Aideen thought what a lovely person he was inside and out. She was never likely to meet anyone nicer or so good-looking who would want to marry her, she realised.

'Oh, all right, I'll marry you,' she said with an answering grin.

'When shall we do it?'

'On your birthday in July.'

'Honest? Really?' He looked childishly pleased.

'Honest and really,' she assured him.

'But what about on *your* birthday?'

'It won't be for nearly another year. Tomorrow, will you come with me to meet my elder sister?' She would introduce him to Patricia first and Tara at the weekend.

'I shall be a perfect gentleman,' he promised.

'Humphrey, me darlin', you couldn't be anything else.'

Leo Vanetti, being the senior brother in The Vanetti Motor Company, had taken charge of the New York office after despatching his disgraced brother, Gianni, to run the factory in San Diego. This was due not only to the fact that his wife didn't want to leave her sisters in New York, but that Leo didn't want her anywhere near his brother.

So it was a blissfully happy Leo who now worked on the twenty-ninth floor of the building overlooking Times Square, and he and an equally happy Patricia still lived in the apartment opposite St Patrick's Cathedral, along with their little boy, Milo.

Patricia was expecting her second child in two

months and, once again, was as big as a house when Aideen and Humphrey went to see her. Joyce, the nurse who'd cared for her when she was expecting Milo, was living there to oversee the birth of her second child and look after her in the meanwhile.

'He's lovely,' Patricia whispered to her sister the following day as she observed Humphrey pretending to be chased from room to room by little Milo in his red pedal racing car, a miniature version of the full-sized cars that had made VMC such a success. They were making a terrible commotion; Humphrey seemed to be enjoying himself as much as Milo, Aideen noted. 'Where did you meet him?' her sister asked.

'In Berry's; he was a customer.'

Aideen had now left Berry's and worked in an antique shop called Bygones, not far from the apartment in Bleecker Street where she and Tara now lived.

'And what does he do for a living?'

'He was a professional ice hockey player who tried to climb a mountain, but once we're married in July he will work as a lawyer for his father in Brooklyn.'

Patricia laughed. 'He sounds interesting.'

'Oh, he is, really interesting.' She watched Humphrey pretend to be terrified as he was chased into the room where she and Patricia were sitting. He collapsed onto the carpet, so Milo got out of his car and sat on him.

In turn, Patricia was watching her sister. 'I never thought you would fall in love,' she said quietly. 'You won't hurt him, will you?'

'Oh, I'm not in love, Patricia,' Aideen assured her. 'But I do like him very much and I wouldn't dream of hurting him. And he's what you would call a good proposition as well as being desperately good-looking.'

'I think he's rather more than those two things, Sis.' Patricia patted Aideen's arm. 'You might well find that out one of these days.'

Later in the week, Aideen invited Humphrey to dinner at the apartment to meet Tara. They turned out to be equally impressed with each other.

'I can hardly believe she's your *younger* sister, Aid,' he said after Tara had left for a party in the French Embassy. 'She's only seventeen but I'd've taken her for twenty-one. She even talks like a much older woman.'

And she dressed like one, too. Tara, who'd grown to be the tallest of the sisters, had gone out wearing an incredibly smart black dress and a dark blue velvet bolero with shoes to match, her lovely blonde hair coiled in a bun at the nape of her neck.

'At times, she hardly feels like me sister any more,' Aideen said sadly. They had so little in common these days.

Humphrey pulled her down onto his knee. She longed for him to touch her breasts and even more secret places but, like the gentlemen he was, he always kept his hands decorously on her waist and never allowed them to roam. She knew she would cheapen herself in his eyes if she encouraged him to go further. Very soon they would be married

163

and he would have a licence to touch her as often as he – and Aideen – wanted. She couldn't wait.

Perhaps Theodore Grant was pleased that at least one of his sons was doing something normal, like getting married, because he made no objection to the wedding being in a Catholic church – Mary, Our Lady of Perpetual Help, a beautiful terracotta building on 59th Street in Brooklyn.

The bridegroom's father may also have been impressed by the bride's family. He hadn't realised that her elder sister was married to Leonardo Vanetti, manager and owner of the massively successful car company, who brought their little boy and baby girl with them; or that her beautiful younger sister would turn up with Christopher Buchanan on her arm. Though not exactly a famous artist, Buchanan was an esteemed figure in the New York art world. He was also reputed to be an outrageous poofter, so it must be a celibate relationship.

Aideen finally met Humphrey's brothers at the wedding. She found Ludovic, with his long, stringy hair and hangdog expression, rather pathetic, and Charles, the minister, oozing holiness and faintly wild-eyed bathetic.

'Pathetic and bathetic,' she said to Tara, considering herself rather clever, but Tara merely smiled coolly. She mixed with people far cleverer than Aideen would ever be. Not that Aideen cared, not on her wedding day. She had never imagined such a day, or meeting a man like Humphrey. On that day she was the happiest woman alive – at least she thought so.

After the honeymoon – a week in a guest house in Oyster Bay, Long Island – the newly married couple returned to Brooklyn to live in a small house built between two large ones, linking all three together. It had been given to Humphrey's father years ago in settlement of an unpaid fee. The place was half furnished and Ludovic had lived there for a while, until taking himself off to Florida where the weather was warmer.

Aideen continued to work in Bygones, crossing the bridge by car from Brooklyn to Manhattan each morning with Humphrey and his father. They sat in the front while Aideen, in the back, longed to lean forward and put her arms around her husband and kiss the back of his neck. But Theodore Grant disliked any show of physical affection. It was easy to restrain herself, thinking about their nights in bed – or long before they went to bed – when they would make love, quite uninhibitedly, not caring if Humphrey's shouts and Aideen's squeals of delight could be heard by the people living on both sides of their funny little house.

Chapter 10

1929

The economy had been a worry for months, though not to Aideen, who only half listened when, during the drive across Brooklyn Bridge and back again, her father-in-law ranted on about consumer debt being too high and too many badly regulated markets. Bankers and businessmen weren't to be trusted, according to Theodore Grant. The agriculture, mining and shipping industries were at an all-time low. The world had become a dreadfully risky place in which to live.

'But where else can we live?' Aideen would say to Humphrey when they were safely at home under their own roof. 'If not the world?'

'Nowhere,' he would shout, sometimes tossing her over his shoulder, racing upstairs and throwing her on the bed. They were young and this was the only thing that mattered.

In October, the banks ran out of money.

'But how can they?' Aideen and Humphrey asked each other. Neither of them knew – most people didn't. One day the money was in the bank, thousands and thousands of dollars, millions and millions of them. The next day, the dollars had all gone. Vanished.

Tara knew the answer. 'It's capitalism, darling,'

she told Aideen. 'As Karl Marx predicted, capitalism is the process of self-destruction. It is evil. One of these days, it will destroy life the way we know it on our planet.'

On a personal level, Theodore Grant's bank had run out of *his* money. His life savings had disappeared overnight and his business account was empty, but he was fortunate that he didn't owe money on his house. And people would always require lawyers. Humphrey was forced to admit that, for the first time he could remember, his pop was looking on the bright side. He would start again, he announced boldly, with less staff. One of those who would have to go was Humphrey. As he said, sarcastically, 'My secretary, Norma, hasn't got a degree in anything, but she knows more about the law than my son ever will.'

Humphrey didn't mind. 'I'll go back to ice hockey,' he announced, but was shocked to discover his team, the Rustlers, had disbanded. It hadn't been one of the top sides and wasn't thought likely to survive what was now referred to as 'the Depression'.

Among the many thousands of shops, offices and businesses that were also considered unlikely to survive was Bygones, which closed in November, leaving both Aideen and Humphrey out of work and without any savings. There'd been nothing to save so they had nothing to lose. They counted what small amount of money they had between them and it came to twenty-six dollars and sixty-five cents.

As loans were called in, mortgages cancelled, bank vaults emptied, some people were left without any desire to survive and suicides became more and more frequent, with some poor souls flinging themselves out of windows; the higher, the better.

America had become a broken country. 'See, what did I tell you!' Tara said to her sister.

Men wearing expensive suits, badly in need of a shave and a haircut wandered the streets of New York with notices hanging around their necks announcing they were available for work – any sort of work for any sort of money. Expensive cars, their owners sitting disconsolately behind the wheel, were offered for sale at knockdown prices. Long queues of hungry people stretched around buildings where soup kitchens had been established.

A shantytown sprang up in Central Park. Known as 'Hooverville', after President Hoover, who most people no longer had faith in, these shacks housed entire families that had lost everything, including their homes.

Patricia offered to help her sister. Good, old, generous-hearted Patricia. Leo had come through the recent troubles with a factory in San Diego full of unsold cars, but otherwise relatively undamaged having recently invested a large chunk of VMC's profits in a drug company. There was likely to be a run on painkillers considering all the headaches that had recently been caused in America and other parts of the world as the Depression spread.

'You can move in with us,' Patricia wrote to Aideen. 'We've plenty of room.'

168

But Aideen wouldn't hear of it. She didn't bother to tell Humphrey because she knew he wouldn't even consider the idea. He didn't realise that while he was, like so many other men in New York, walking the streets in search of work, his mother brought homemade pies, stews and casseroles to the little house in Brooklyn where Aideen sat applying after jobs all over the country.

'Theo knows I'm doing this,' Mary Grant told her daughter-in-law one day just after Christmas when she arrived with a meatloaf and took it into the kitchen. 'He would never let you and Humphrey starve.'

Aideen had already realised that. And she knew she could always rely on Patricia in the direst of emergencies. There was no need to worry that she and Humphrey would starve or be homeless, unlike a lot of poor, hopeless people.

Early in February, they had a visitor. Eric 'Rusty' Steel had been goalkeeper – or 'goalie', as he described himself – for the Rustlers ice hockey team that Humphrey had played for.

'Nobby,' Eric said tearfully when the two men embraced.

'Rusty,' Humphrey responded in kind. 'I thought you lived in Atlantic City?'

'I do ... did.' Rusty sank into a chair. Aideen wondered if he'd always been so thin and looked so ill. 'I've just left – case of having to, I'm afraid. There's something wrong with my heart. Ain't working properly, according to the quack – the doctor,' he explained to a mystified Aideen. 'If it's not beating too fast, then it's beating too slow.'

He sniffed pathetically. 'Sometimes it feels as if it's not beating at all, though I expect it must be, otherwise I'd be dead. Even so, any minute now I could die at the drop of a hat.'

'Great God, man,' Humphrey thundered. 'Are you drunk or are you telling the honest truth?'

'The truth, I'm afraid, Nobby.' He laid his hand on his chest. 'You can listen to it, if you like. Just put your ear here.'

'Have you come to wish farewell to your old friend?'

'Indeed I have, Nobs.'

Aideen presumed all this was some sort of joke that she was incapable of understanding, but it turned out to be true. Rusty had indeed been discovered to have a dangerously weak heart and had been forced to leave his job as sports coach to the senior year at St Joseph's College in Atlantic City, New Jersey, adjacent to New York State.

'And I've recommended you for the job, Nobs, old chap. The principal, Doctor Matthews, was a champion boxer at college. Didn't you win a cup for that yourself in your younger days?' He sighed woefully. 'If you're interested, I should get yourself there straight away, otherwise some lousy Democrat will get it before you.'

'But *I'm* a lousy Democrat, Rusty. You know I am and always have been.'

'Sorry, Nobs. I meant some lousy Republican. It's the heart. These days I don't know my left from my right – physically and politically.'

'Where did the "Nobby" come from?' Aideen asked after Eric had gone – he refused to stay the night – and Humphrey had been bawling his eyes out for almost an hour.

'They called me Humphrey Nobby Grant instead of Noble,' he explained. Aideen fetched another handkerchief when he began to cry again.

Two days later, after Humphrey had made an appointment for an interview with Doctor Matthews, the college principal, he and Aideen went by train to Atlantic City; Mary Grant had loaned them the money for the fare.

After booking into a cheap hotel, Humphrey caught a taxi to St Joseph's college while Aideen went for a stroll around the centre of the city. She found Atlantic City particularly smart and impressive. Some of the hotels were the biggest she'd ever seen and the clothes in the shops were cheaper than in New York, yet just as elegant. It was also a holiday resort, she noted, as she passed a shooting gallery as well as several casinos mostly closed for the winter.

She'd like to live here, she decided, as she strolled along the boardwalk, which was like a promenade except it was made of wood. The Atlantic Ocean lapped busily on her left and there was a row of interesting little shops to her right.

It was a brilliantly sunny February day, though bitterly cold. The air felt fresh and clean, and it must have been the salt in the ocean that made everywhere shimmer. She wandered into an empty cafe, sat in the window, and ordered tea and a doughnut. She'd wanted Humphrey to get the job as coach if only because it meant that at least one of them would be working, but now she wanted it because there would be a big, wonderful change in their lives – a change very much for the better.

'I think I've found paradise,' she said out loud.

As Humphrey had no idea what time he would be back, Aideen continued to explore the city, returning to the hotel from time to time to see if he had returned. It wasn't until four in the afternoon that she found him sitting in the lobby.

'Here she is,' the woman behind the desk exclaimed when Aideen went in. 'She's been looking for you all day.'

Humphrey stood, a look of desperate misery on his face. Aideen's heart fell; he hadn't got the job. But, being Humphrey, he couldn't keep up the pretence for long; the miserable look was swiftly replaced with one of his enormous grins.

'I got it,' he said. 'Now let's find somewhere to live.'

They moved to Atlantic City two weeks later. They rented a one-bedroomed wooden house, fully furnished, within sight of the beach, but only until May, when holidaymakers would hire the place for five times what they were now paying. As soon as they had sorted themselves out, they would look for somewhere more permanent.

They sent colourful postcards of the city to Humphrey's parents, Rusty, Aideen's sisters, Uncle Mick and Gertie Smith. In the case of Gertie, Aideen was merely showing off.

Humphrey worked long hours at St Joseph's,

staying after lessons were over to work with the most enthusiastic of the budding athletes – and promising boxers, if some could be found. The principal, Doctor Matthews, was particularly keen on St Joseph's competing with other colleges in that particular sport, having been a successful amateur boxer himself, way back in the mists of time as he described it.

'You never told me you were good at it yourself,' Aideen remarked. His mother had unearthed the cup he'd won at eighteen and it was now displayed in a showcase in St Joseph's gymnasium, along with other trophies won by old pupils and ex-masters.

'I was good at most sports,' Humphrey boasted. Then he wrinkled his nose. 'The only thing I was hopeless at was law.'

'Yes, but law isn't a sport, is it?'

'It is in the courtroom, Aideen. It's a bit like bat and ball.'

After a week of being left on her own for ten hours a day in a place even smaller than the house in Brooklyn, Aideen knew she would have to get a job. Even had the current place been much bigger, she still had no interest in keeping it clean or preparing food in the minute kitchen. She needed to mix with people, talk to them, have fun.

So she took a job as a waitress.

'You've what?' Humphrey looked aghast when she told him.

Aideen glared at him.

He shrugged his shoulders uneasily. 'It looks bad,' he mumbled.

173

'In what way does it look bad?'

'Well, I'm a member of staff at St Joseph's – the teaching staff – and I don't think it's on for my wife to be a waitress.'

Aideen burst out laughing. 'Not on! You married a shop assistant, Humph. What sort of job do you expect me to have? I haven't got a single qualification in anything.' She kissed his chin. 'You should have married a girl with a degree.' Sliding her arms around his neck, she whispered, 'Would you have preferred a blue stocking for a wife, darling?'

He was so easy to seduce. He picked her up, threw her over his shoulder and virtually ran into the bedroom.

Aideen never told him that there'd been two eating establishments with signs in their windows advertising for staff. The first had lace cloths on the tables and the waitress inside wore a black dress with a little white pinafore and cap. The clientele were mainly elderly and female. There were similar places in Dublin, usually called something like The Copper Kettle. This one was Katy's Kitchen.

Aideen far preferred the busy diner filled at lunchtime with working men and woman. A black man behind the counter yelled, 'Grub's up!' when a meal was ready, the customer would identify him or herself, and a woman in a red dress would deliver the food to the table. With a complete lack of pretence, it was called Jim's Dump.

That's for me, Aideen decided. She waited until lunchtime was virtually over before going in and asking the black man if she could have the job. 'Are you Jim?' she enquired first.

He wore a short-sleeved vest that left most of his heavily muscled arms bare. He looked down upon her from his approximate height of six foot, six inches and asserted that he was Jim. 'And this is my dump,' he added.

Aideen could tell from the twinkle in his eyes that he had a sense of humour. 'It's a very nice dump,' she conceded, 'and I'd like to apply for the post of lunchtime waitress.'

He motioned her towards a table and they both sat down. 'Post!' he said mockingly. 'Post! It's a job, girl, not a post.'

'Well, I'd like to apply for the job, then.'

'Have you ever done it before: posting, waitressing, whatever?'

'Never. I worked in the sports section of Berry's department store in New York for three years and a few months in an antique shop. They're the only jobs I've ever had.'

He didn't appear impressed with her work record up to now. 'What's brought you to Atlantic City?' he asked, but she could tell he was only being polite.

She told him her husband (she just loved saying, 'my husband'!) was the new senior year coach at St Joseph's and his interest suddenly perked up, not so much in her but in Humphrey. 'Does he have a speciality?' he enquired.

'He used to play professional ice hockey, but the team folded due to the Depression.'

'They don't have a hockey team at St Joseph's,' Jim said.

The woman in the red dress came and plonked a cup of black coffee in front of her employer.

'D'you want one, honey?' she asked Aideen, who shook her head.

'Humphrey's good at most sports,' she said to Jim. 'He won a cup for boxing.'

'Professional or amateur?'

'Amateur. He was at college.'

'And is boxing on the curri... Whatever you call it these days?'

'Curriculum. Yes, it is. Doctor Matthews, the principal, used to box at college. He's really keen.'

Jim threw back his shoulders and stiffened his neck, making him look even bigger than he already was. 'Well, when you tell that husband of yours you got a job in a diner, inform him it belongs to Jimbo Collins, who, twenty-five years ago, almost became heavyweight champion of the world.' His lips twisted cynically. 'And it wasn't exactly my own fault that I didn't make it.'

'Whose fault was it, then?'

'That's an awful long story, girl. If I ever have the time, I'll tell it to you. Oh, and if you're going to work here, then it might be a good idea to let us know your name and where you come from. The hours are eleven till three.'

'It's Aideen Grant and I'm from Ireland – Dublin, to be exact. And the hours suit me perfectly.'

In no time at all it was April, it was 1930, and Aideen was about to turn twenty. Easter was just around the corner.

Patricia had written to say she was coming to see her, along with Leo, Milo and their pretty baby girl, Rosie.

We can't let your birthday pass without a party of some sort. Let's have dinner – Joyce will look after the children.

Joyce had left her Polish husband and become a permanent employee who acted as both nanny and nurse now Patricia was expecting her third child.

When they came, the Vanettis stayed in the Paramount hotel, which was built entirely out of green marble imported from Connemara on the west of Ireland. It was reputed to be the most expensively built hotel in the city and charged the highest rates.

'Every time I see you you're having a baby,' Aideen remarked.

It was Sunday afternoon and Jim's Dump was closed. It wasn't her birthday until tomorrow. Leo would have to be back in New York then, so the celebratory dinner was being held that night.

She and Patricia were in the sitting room of the hotel suite, where the walls were lined with pale green suede. It was like being underwater. Joyce had taken the children for a walk along the sands and Leo had gone to do 'a bit of business', whatever that meant. Humphrey was absent but would be at the dinner later.

'We don't see enough of each other, that's why.' Patricia appeared to be unhappy with Aideen's comment about the baby she was expecting.

'Is everything all right, Sis?' Aideen knew what was wrong. Whenever she was pregnant, Patricia

177

liked to have her sisters close by.

'Everything's fine.' Despite the words, she nevertheless sighed. 'It's just that I desperately miss you and Tara. I love Leo and I adore the children, but I had visions of us all living near to each other, seeing each other most days, just like everybody did in Dublin. Remember how all the aunts and uncles and cousins used to come on Sundays, even if it was only for a cup of tea?'

Although Aideen loved both her sisters dearly, she'd had no such visions. All she wanted was to know they were all right. 'Perhaps it's because you're the eldest that you care about such things,' she suggested. 'Along with Daddy and Auntie Kathleen, you've looked after us since Ma died. Then Auntie Kathleen was left behind in Ireland, Daddy died and you were the only one left.'

'I worry about you both all the time,' Patricia said pathetically. 'And Milo.'

'Surely you see lots of our Tara in New York?' After all, they lived less than a mile apart, Aideen recalled.

'I haven't seen her since Christmas – when I last saw you, in fact. She's moved in with that artist chap, Christopher, and looks after him and his friends.'

'Honest?' Aideen couldn't help but be amused at the idea of Tara taking care of a group of old people.

'I don't know why you should find it funny,' Patricia said crossly, having noticed her sister's slight smile.

'I don't know either,' Aideen confessed. 'I just do.'

Leo came in then, followed by two men who put several large packages wrapped in sacking in one of the bedrooms. Aideen noticed that he'd put on a little bit of weight – he wasn't nearly as attractive as Humphrey, when you came right down to it.

The 'bit of business' he'd been doing was buying a crate of wine and a selection of spirits to take back to New York, he announced after the men had gone.

Aideen was amazed. 'But what about Prohibition?' Surely alcohol was banned throughout the entire country?

Leo laughed. 'There's no such thing as Prohibition in Atlantic City.'

Now she was even more amazed. 'Why ever not?'

'This place is totally corrupt. Hadn't you noticed?'

'No.' She was vaguely offended. 'It's always seemed particularly law-abiding to me.'

He was opening a bottle of champagne. The cork came out with an enormous *pop*, making her and Patricia jump. He poured two glasses and handed them one each, then poured a much larger one for himself. *'Bon santé!'* he said.

"What does that mean?' Aideen wasn't sure why she felt so annoyed.

'Good health.'

'Good health.' She grimaced as she tasted champagne for the very first time.

'Don't you like it?' Leo poured the entire contents of his glass down his throat.

'Where did it come from, the champagne?'

'Canada, maybe, possibly Mexico. Who knows?'

He refilled his glass and winked. 'It's even been known for the whiskey to come all the way from Ireland.'

'I had champagne this afternoon,' she told Humphrey later in the day. They were getting ready for dinner at the Paramount. 'It was the first time.'

She thought he would be surprised. Instead, he mumbled something like, 'Did you enjoy it?'

She was so cross, she stamped her foot.

He looked at her, his expression puzzled. 'What's the matter?'

'Don't you care that I broke the law?' she snapped. 'I mean, it's supposed to be banned but not, it would seem, in Atlantic City.'

'But everyone knows that, Aid,' he said, as if she was the biggest fool in the world for *not* knowing. '*I* didn't.'

He disappeared into the bathroom and Aideen sat on the bed, thinking about the way a couple of policemen came regularly to Jim's Dump and made no attempt to pay for their food, just getting up and leaving when they'd finished. Jim would scowl but not say a word. And what about the two men who came in every Saturday morning, just standing inside the door, not saying a word? Jim would open the till and give them some of the contents with another scowl. Thinking about it now, she realised it must be protection money. She'd read about it somewhere, or someone had told her about it happening in Ireland, mainly in the pubs. And who was she to be shocked at people breaking the law when her very own father was responsible for a really big crime in Dublin?

Aideen went over to the window. It was growing dark and the sun was setting somewhere in the sky behind, but it was shining on the ocean, making the rippling waves look like little silver frills. There were more people on the shore than usual – the summer season was approaching and everywhere was becoming more and more crowded.

She and Humphrey had found an apartment above a florist's and were moving in on Friday. They'd even talked about renting something more substantial, like a proper house with a garden – for some reason Americans called a garden a 'yard' – settling down, buying a car, starting a family. They both liked Atlantic City.

Humphrey came out of the bathroom and put his arm around her. 'Are you upset?'

He must be the slowest witted man in the world. It had taken him a good ten minutes to notice. She rested her head on his shoulder. Through the window a dog chased a ball and small children chased each other on the sand. All that was visible was water, sand, people and the dog – they could be anywhere in the world.

'I thought Atlantic City was paradise,' she whispered. 'I thought it was perfect.'

'Nowhere's perfect, Aid.' He kissed the top of her head. 'Paradise is from a poem, that's all. I did it at college: *Paradise Lost*.' She could almost feel his face twisting into a grin. 'I couldn't understand a word of it. There were all sorts of double meanings. I'm no good at double meanings, Aid,' he added with a sigh.

'I know, darling.'

It was at that very moment that she realised she was in love with Humphrey Noble Grant. It came over her in a rush, like one of Nora Hogan's funny little turns back in Dublin. She was so lucky. Despite not being a terribly nice person, she was so very, very lucky.

Chapter 11

Humphrey turned out to be an excellent coach. The boys liked him – they called him 'Humph'. He didn't yell and he didn't bully, but spoke to them as equals, which, in Humphrey's eyes, they were. Under his tuition and encouragement, St Joseph's baseball and football teams were winning more matches than they lost and he'd discovered a sixteen-year-old boy, Rodrigo Martinez, the son of a USA senator, who would move into the top form in September and was a talented boxer.

'He's a natural,' he enthused. 'A light heavy-weight. He could grow an inch or two taller, but not get any heavier. I don't think he's got the strength for an all-out heavyweight.'

Aideen was thrilled for him. Life couldn't be any happier or more fun. She loved Humphrey and her job in Jim's Dump, where she'd got to know most of the customers. On Monday afternoons she and another waitress, Betty, went to see a movie together.

Some of the college wives met every other Wednesday afternoon to chat and knit and do embroidery. Aideen left the restaurant early to attend. She found the wives boring but likeable, and hoped her presence helped boost Humphrey's image in the eyes of the principal, Doctor Matthews, whose wife, Imogen, reigned queen-like over the meetings.

Some weekends they took the time to look around houses for sale or peered in the windows of car salerooms, eventually putting down a deposit on a Ford Model T. It was known as the 'Tin Lizzie', and the cheapest and most economical car to buy. Humphrey had learnt to drive and they drove it home there and then.

The Depression was hardly noticeable in Atlantic City. There was no sign of the shacks, the sort that had sprung up in Central Park to house the homeless; no men had been reduced to begging for work; there were no soup kitchens. It might not be the paradise Aideen first thought, but it was something close to it.

At some point in the midst of everything, Patricia gave birth to another little girl called Kathleen. And it seemed that she was determined that the sisters spend more time together. She and Leo booked the same suite in the Paramount for the entire month of August, including a room for Tara, who came for a few days each week.

'Who's looking after your charges?' Aideen asked when they first met on the Vanettis' own private terrace. Everyone was there, including both husbands, as well as Joyce and the children.

'They are not my charges, Aideen,' Tara said firmly, though with a glint of amusement in her lovely blue eyes. 'They are my friends. I just make sure that they are properly fed, their laundry is done, and their mail is attended to, that's all.'

Aideen giggled. 'They sound like charges to me.'

Her sister was far too beautiful and glamorous to be reduced to looking after a crowd of geriatrics. When they ate in the hotel dining room, or went for a stroll, she was subjected to scores of admiring glances. One of the other residents of the hotel had sent an invitation to a nightclub. Tara had merely torn it up.

'Didn't you want to know who it was from?' Patricia asked.

'What's the point? I had no intention of going.'

'I really fancy going to a nightclub,' Aideen said.

'We'll all go tonight,' Leo called from his deckchair, but Humphrey shouted that a teacher couldn't possibly be seen in a nightclub where illegal alcohol was likely to be served.

To Aideen's intense astonishment, she found she didn't even mind.

The holiday over, life returned to normal. At St Joseph's college, Doctor Matthews invited Humphrey into his study to discuss the career of Rodrigo, their talented young boxer.

Humphrey told Aideen about it when he got home. 'He wants me to arrange fights for him with other kids – other boxers – not just from St Joe's but from other schools and from gymnasiums in the city. I told him it's not the way I would go about it.'

184

'And what did he say?'

'He said that's the way he wanted it done.' Humphrey sighed and looked glum. 'My opinion isn't relevant. He didn't *say* that but that's the impression I got.'

'How would you go about it if it was done your way?' Aideen enquired, stroking his hand. It was rare he looked so down.

'I wouldn't go about it in a different way than I'm doing now. The kid's only just seventeen; he's at college to learn, not to box. But Doctor Matthews has got the bit between his teeth. He wants St Joseph's to become famous for producing fine boxers – champions – and place less emphasis on other sports.' He ran his fingers through his hair so that it stood on end. 'All I want to do is coach the kids – all the kids and all the sports – and I want it to be fun.'

Humphrey continued to complain as the months passed. Every three or four weeks there would be a fight between Rodrigo Martinez and another fighter the same age and weight. Aideen went, although she didn't enjoy watching two young men, merely boys, battering each other. It was a savage sport.

At one match, Rodrigo's parents were present. Humphrey had hoped they might object to their son being subjected to Doctor Matthew's ruthless regime, but both were cheering him on as if it was the world championship he was fighting for.

Poor Humphrey! Aideen's heart bled for him. Normally so easy-going, he couldn't sleep and couldn't eat. He was concerned he was neglecting the other boys by giving too much attention to Rodrigo, who was in turn neglecting his lessons for boxing.

'Clay Morrison complained the other day that I was responsible for the Rodrigo kid missing so much history. He threatened to complain to Doctor Matthews. I urged him to go ahead, said I would be pleased if he complained. We both agreed that Doctor Matthews must be a frustrated boxer at heart.'

One day towards the end of November, Jim approached Aideen after the really busy period was over and asked what the odds were on that week's fight. The fight was only three days away.

She had no idea what he was talking about. 'What do you mean, the odds?'

'The stakes, girl. I mean, they're bringing in this kid from New York for the Martinez kid to fight. Up till now, Martinez has always been the favourite, but I gather the New York kid's shit hot, if you'll forgive my language.'

'And people are *betting* on the result?' She could hardly believe it.

Jim laughed at her ignorance. 'People have been betting on the results of your husband's fights right from when they began, girl. This city is addicted to gambling in one form or another – haven't you noticed all the casinos around?'

'Yes, but that's different; gambling on slot machines, I mean.' Betting directly on a particular thing was something else altogether. She had thought it was against the law.

'"They're bringing in a kid from New York,"

you said. Who's "they"?'

Jim bit his lip and regarded her worriedly. 'The mob, girl,' he said. 'The Mafia.'

'Are they here, in Atlantic City?'

'They're everywhere where there's money to be made, Aideen.'

She didn't say any more to Jim, but brought up the matter with Humphrey that night. To her astonishment, he became agitated and refused to talk about it. This caused Aideen to also become agitated, and they ended up having a heated argument.

'*Why* won't you talk about it?' Aideen demanded.

Humphrey collapsed into tears – he easily cried. Aideen wouldn't have thought it possible for her to fall in love with a man who cried, but somehow she had and it hurt terribly.

'I don't want to talk about it,' he repeated hoarsely. 'Leave me alone.'

So she did, though with a great deal of reluctance.

The fight was two days away and this time when she approached Humphrey, he assured her he wasn't worried about anything. Doctor Matthews was getting on his nerves, that was all. Some of the other teachers were being unpleasant.

'They don't think it's right that one kid, Rodrigo, is getting so much attention and they're blaming me. We've had sports reporters approach from all over the country. There's a photo of Rodrigo in a New York paper and Friday's match will be on the radio.'

187

'I think you should look for another job,' Aideen said. Humphrey wasn't cut out for this sort of thing.

He seemed grateful for the suggestion. 'I might well do that after Christmas,' he agreed.

'Can I come to watch the fight?' Aideen asked.

'All the tickets have been sold,' he told her. 'Not only that, I'm worried it might be an ugly affair. You won't like it. The kid from New York is rumoured to be a different type of boxer altogether than we're used to. He was raised on the streets. I'm concerned what he'll get up to in the ring. It sounds silly, but Rodrigo is a gentleman; he hardly ever draws blood.'

'Won't the referee be able to stop the other guy?'

'Only if he's quick enough.'

Shortly afterwards, he drove to work. Aideen sat and thought for a while before tidying up the house in her usual careless way and going to work herself.

It was Friday 13th and the strangest day. It started off blindingly sunny, but as time progressed it began to rain, lightly at first, then more heavily, until it was a downpour. With the downpour came thunder, rumbling ominously towards the city, cracking furiously, staying overhead much longer than it normally did.

Humphrey always stayed at the college on fight days, eating in the school canteen. Aideen switched the radio on but couldn't find the New York station that was covering the boxing match. She listened to music instead. 'Happy Days Are

Here Again', 'My Sin', 'I Can't Give You Anything But Love, Baby', which made her think of Humphrey. She could hardly hold back the tears. What a pair of crybabies they were. She cried even more when a velvet-voiced crooner sang 'Leaving Dear Old Ireland', in a real Irish accent. Life had been so peaceful in those days, if a bit dull.

It was eight o'clock when the storm returned. The fight should be over by now. Aideen looked out of the window and saw everywhere was black, with lightning angrily criss-crossing the sky. The noise was horrendous and she barely heard the banging downstairs on the front door.

She went down, her heart beating crazily, and opened the door. A strange man was standing outside, wearing a mackintosh that reached his ankles. A hat, dripping water, was tipped over his eyes. Behind him a large car was parked, the engine running.

'You have five minutes,' he said, 'to get your possessions together and come with me.'

'Where to?' she asked dazedly.

'Never mind that, you're wasting time. Fetch your things and we'll be on our way.'

Aideen stamped her foot. 'I'll do no such thing. Where's Humphrey?'

'Waiting for you. If you don't come in two and a half minutes, I shall go and you'll never see your husband again.'

She'd heard his voice before but couldn't remember where. She decided to obey and rushed back up the stairs, pulled on her best coat, put her purse in her bag, including the money from the blue striped jug in the kitchen that they'd been saving, though had no idea what for. She didn't possess any jewellery apart from her wedding ring, a pair of gold stud earrings and her watch, all of which she was wearing. She hurried downstairs. The man was sitting behind the wheel of the car, the passenger door was open and the seat was getting wet.

Aideen climbed in and the car sped away, so swiftly that she was thrown back in the seat.

'Who are you?' she demanded angrily. 'And where is my husband?'

The man didn't answer. The car slowed at a corner while he waited to join the traffic on a busy road. Cars sped by, spraying water on the windscreen so it was hard to see. There was a lamppost on the corner and she glimpsed the driver's face properly for the first time.

'Daddy!' she screamed.

Chapter 12

The car turned into the parking area in front of a brightly lit single storey building called Enoch's, which was a restaurant as well as a casino. Inside was noisy and crowded, and the sound of thunder and torrential rain had been stifled beneath the sound of music and voices. A woman on a tiny stage wearing an emerald green crinoline and matching bonnet was singing a song that Aideen could have sworn was part of a well-known opera.

Bernie Kelly pushed his daughter onto a wooden

bench at the first table with empty spaces that they came to.

'Be quiet, Aideen,' he hissed. 'Don't make a scene.'

It was why they had come to the roadhouse, to calm her down, stop her from screaming.

'Quiet!' she spluttered. 'Quiet! What do you take me for? Who wouldn't make a scene when the father they thought had been dead for five whole years turns out to be alive?'

'I'd've thought me own sweet girls would have had enough sense to realise that Bernie Kelly would never, ever have taken his own life. What sort of fella did you think I was? Did you have no faith in me at all?'

He sat on the bench as if he was riding a horse, one leg on each side. He looked so inelegant, so odd, that Aideen became upset again.

'You monster,' she spat. 'You're the biggest criminal in the world. I hate you. We all hate you, Patricia and Tara, too. At least they will once they know you're still alive, that you only pretended to take your own life.'

His eyebrows joined together in a frown. Aideen remembered they used to laugh at his frowns. 'You're not to tell them,' he said sternly, though it was more of a shout. The sound of people enjoying themselves made shouting a necessity.

'I *will* tell them, of course I will. You have no right to be alive, then expect me to keep it a secret. Me sisters – your *daughters* – have the right to know. Anyway, I'm not capable of keeping it a secret, even if I wanted to.' It was while she was pausing

191

for breath that she remembered Humphrey. 'Where is my husband?' she demanded. 'What have you done with him?'

'Only rescued him from a bloody maniacal Italian; at least, me friend has. He would have had half his face ripped off by now if Willy hadn't got there in time.'

Aideen screamed, so piercingly, that the other people on the table stopped to stare.

'It's all right,' Bernie explained. 'She's had a really bad shock.'

Everyone continued with their conversation as if the scream and the short pause had never taken place.

A waitress approached, dressed like a little girl with a pink bow in her hair, and asked what they would like to drink.

'Two sodas, honey,' Bernie said.

'What happened at the boxing match?' Aideen asked when the girl had gone. She felt almost sensible again, as well as desperately worried about Humphrey.

Her father lit a cigarette before answering – he hadn't stopped smoking, then – and said, 'The mob wanted the school kid to lose – what's his name?'

'Rodrigo Martinez.'

'That's right. And they wanted *their* kid to win. They gave your hubby his orders, and the money – the bets – went on that way.' His face twisted in a rueful smile, reminding her strongly of the daddy of old, and reinforcing her astonishment at finding him still alive and kicking. 'I don't know whether it was Rodrigo who ignored the order or your dear husband – what's his silly name?'

'Humphrey, and it's not a silly name.'

He ignored her comment. 'One or the other, Humphrey or Rodrigo, ignored the order. Rodrigo won the fight, knocking the Italian kid senseless in the fifth round. I wasn't there; I don't know what the reaction was at the scene. Willy rang to tell me what had happened. I came and collected you; Willy and other people are looking after your hubby.'

'Looking after?' She squeezed her forehead in the hope it would help her to understand. 'Why does he need looking after?'

'Do you no longer have your wits about you, Aideen?' her father asked impatiently. 'Because the wrong man won the fight, that's why. It wasn't the one the bad men wanted. A lot of very important people, very dangerous people, very angry people, have lost an awful lot of money and it's almost certainly the fault of Humphrey Grant, who ignored their instructions.'

The drinks arrived. Daddy produced a small bottle of whiskey out of his breast pocket and, glancing both ways, surreptitiously poured a decent amount in each glass. Aideen threw hers down her throat the way she'd once seen Leo do with champagne. She waited, sitting stock still for something to happen, but nothing did.

Daddy did the same with his whiskey. Then he took her arm and half dragged her out of the building, pushing her back into the car.

'Why did I have to be collected?' she queried when they were on their way.

'Jaysus!' her father groaned. 'Were you always

so bloody thick? The nasty Italian people, they might have decided to punish you as well as your hubby. I understand they were very, very angry. Very!' he finished with a sort of flurry.

The journey continued in silence for almost an hour. Aideen wondered where they were going, but wouldn't deign to ask. She kept praying, over and over, that Humphrey was all right. She sent mental messages to cheer him up and tell him that she was on her way.

'What happened all those years ago on the boat?' she eventually asked her father.

He paused before answering, as if wondering how to put it. 'I threw me coat over the side,' he said eventually, 'put my watch in the dining room, where it was bound to be found, then hid in the bowels of the ship with the crew. I grew a bit of a beard, borrowed a passport, and then disembarked in New York without raising suspicion. It was as easy as pie,' he said boastfully. 'And it wasn't as if I'd planned it beforehand, but something happened on-board that meant I had to change me plans.'

'Oh, what a clever daddy I have,' Aideen said sarcastically in the voice of a small child.

'You always were a nasty piece of work, Aideen. Don't I get a word of thanks for rescuing you and this Humphrey guy from the clutches of the bloody Mafia? I didn't *have* to. I could have left the pair o' yis to your fate.'

Aideen uttered a huge sigh and laid her head on his shoulder. 'Thank you, Daddy. Thank you very, very much.' She really meant it. Mind you, it was *his* fault they were in America in the first place.

A few minutes later, she raised her head and asked, 'Have you been keeping an eye on us ever since we arrived in New York?'

'Yeah.' He nodded.

'Was it with the help of Uncle Mick?'

He shook his head. 'It was a private detective. They call them private eyes over here. Had to hire another guy when you and hubby moved to Atlantic City.'

'Our Patricia and Tara are fine,' she informed him.

'I know, but it's a pretty weird crowd Tara hangs out with.'

'They're incredibly old.' She looked out of the window. 'Where are we going?'

'Washington DC. There's an apartment that I share with a couple of other guys. It's empty at the moment. You and hubby can stay a while till I've sorted things out, found out what the repercussions are from last night's match.'

So it was already tomorrow. 'What do you do in America, Daddy?' she asked idly. She didn't really care.

'What do you think I do, Aideen? I'm a solicitor, always have been – in American jargon that means I'm a lawyer. It's a very highly paid profession, particularly on this side of the Atlantic where I specialise in politics.'

'Huh! I would have thought you'd been struck off over the entire world from practising again.'

He reached into his breast pocket for a business card and handed it to her. 'Read that some time.'

'I will indeed, Daddy, dear.' It was too dark to read it now.

The car stopped outside a tall building with a well-lit lobby; it looked like a hotel. It was still raining outside. Her father jumped out of the car, ran round the front and opened the passenger door.

'This is it,' he said. Apparently it was an apartment building, not a hotel.

'Why, hello, Mr Davis,' a woman seated behind a desk said in surprise when they were inside. She stood. 'We weren't expecting you. It's a terrible night to be driving. I'll get Ralph to put your car away in a minute.' She went over to a row of three lifts and opened the middle one. 'I'm afraid you'll have to manage this yourself,' she said. 'Ralph's the only porter on duty and he's busy mending a leaking window.'

Her father smiled. The woman was young and pretty, and Aideen recognised the smile that had been bestowed upon her friends when they'd visited the Kelly house in Dublin. He hadn't changed a bit.

'I was expecting some friends,' he said to the woman. 'Do you know if they have arrived yet?'

'Sorry, Mr Davis, I only came on duty at midnight. I don't know if anyone's upstairs.'

'Might Humphrey be there?' Aideen asked when the lift doors had closed.

'He should be by now,' he confirmed. 'Willy left Atlantic City with him before us and they won't have stopped for a drink.'

Aideen's heart twisted pleasurably at the thought of being reunited with her husband. Inside the lift, her father pressed the button for the eighth floor and it ascended quickly and smoothly. They stepped out into a corridor with dark blue carpet and had turned two corners before her father produced a key and opened a door. A man was standing by the window, looking out at the rain, and turned to greet them.

'Where's Humphrey?' she cried.

The man came over and whispered something in her father's ear, something that caused his expression to become as serious as she had ever seen it.

He turned and took her in his arms. 'I'm sorry, Aideen, darlin', but your hubby's in hospital. Those flamin' Italians cut him up a bit rough, like. We'd better get over there straight away.'

The George Washington University Hospital was quiet and dimly lit. Daddy knew exactly where Humphrey was and made straight for a row of lifts just inside the entrance. They were taken to the fourth floor. The man who'd been in the apartment had come with them. His name was Frank and Daddy's friend, Willy, had stayed in the hospital with Humphrey.

They were in a room where a red light burned and where a body lay as still as a dead man's on an iron-framed bed. Apart from one eye, which was closed, the body's face was thickly covered with bandages. Willy was sitting beside the bed.

'Humphrey,' Aideen called desperately.

'What's the prognosis?' Daddy asked.

'Well, as you can see–' Willy got up and pointed towards the patient – 'he was beaten up pretty bad. The doctors say his face will heal with time, but there's nothing they can do about his eye.'

'What's wrong with his eye?' Aideen was already sitting in Willy's chair and holding her husband's hand.

'He's lost it, miss. He's lost his right eye.'

Aideen had never expected to fall in love. She hadn't thought herself capable of it. But she loved Humphrey Noble Grant so much that she would have willingly offered her own right eye in place of his.

Mary and Theo Grant came from New York to see their son and cried at his bedside – Theo the most. By the time they arrived, the bandages had been removed from Humphrey's black, blue and swollen face, apart from the one over the socket of his right eye.

'There's hardly another man who would have stood up to the mob the way Humphrey did,' Theo wept.

'He's admirable,' Mary echoed. 'You can't possibly go back to Atlantic City, Aideen. Where will you live now? There's room for you in our house in Brooklyn.'

'Later, perhaps,' Aideen said gratefully, though she didn't think Humphrey would agree. 'As soon as Humphrey's up to it, we're going to California. A friend is arranging it for us. The sun will be out there and he thinks it will help Humphrey's face heal faster than here.' The 'friend', of course, was Daddy. So far she hadn't let on to her sisters that he was very much alive. She'd let them know when this horrible period in her and Humphrey's lives was finally over.

The white-painted clapboard house was the last one in the road that wound through the tiny fishing village of Bray. It was barely fifty feet from the blue Pacific Ocean and roughly halfway between Santa Barbara and Los Angeles. Aideen and Humphrey swam together most mornings. The water was surprisingly cold that early in the day but warmed up as the sun rose.

It wasn't long before the skin on Humphrey's face was as smooth as it had always been. There were a couple of scars that might never go away and some broken teeth that the father-in-law he hadn't known he had was paying to have fixed. He wore a black patch over his lost eye, which Aideen thought made him look dashing, like a pirate.

He'd never been the smartest of men, but something had happened to Humphrey's brain when he was beaten up; his thinking was much slower and his memory poor.

Aideen would soon be twenty-two and had always thought that one day she and Humphrey would have children. But from now on she decided she would make sure she never became pregnant; Humphrey was the only child she would have and she would dedicate herself to him.

Patricia and Leo were planning to move soon to San Diego, where the VMC factory was, and her sister was pleading with her to live in the same place so they could see each other every day. But Aideen thought every day would become too much after a time; once a week would be enough. She and Humphrey were happy in Bray. Aideen went to work in the students' records office at

Santa Barbara City College – she had a feeling it was her father who'd managed to get her the job. They gave up the house, rented a smallholding and Humphrey worked hard growing all the fruit and vegetables they would ever need. Best of all, there was a mountain in the distance that one day he might climb.

It wasn't until March, when it was time for them to move in, that she wrote and told Patricia and Tara about Daddy.

Part 2

Chapter 13

The homeless hostel provided for forty-three men and twenty women. The number of children differed from week to week; Tara had no idea where some of them came from or where they disappeared to. It was a shabby place, a former school, built a century ago, mainly of stone. Tara looked upon it as a failure of a building. Dust seemed to ooze out of the stone, making it impossible to keep clean. It was also impossible to keep warm in winter, or cool in the summer months. It used to be called St Benedict's School; now it was St Benedict's House. It reminded Tara of the Convent of the Holy Name, the school Patricia had registered her for when they'd first come to New York.

Most of the food was donated, as well as the money that kept the place going. Between them, Christopher Buchanan and his friends contributed a decent sum, meaning Tara was able to order staple food such as bread, potatoes and tinned beans to be delivered daily. Quite a few shops sent meat and vegetables that were on their last legs (she supposed such a term could be applied to food).

She was in charge of the kitchen, Lydia Friedman, the laundry, Peter Lewis worked in the office, and Carl Hoedemaker kept the place clean, along with a small army of voluntary workers who came in every day for a matter of hours – it might be just one hour, or could be half a dozen. The residents were also expected to give a hand with the cooking and cleaning if they were up to it.

The person in overall charge was Edward Van Dalen, who Tara, Lydia, Peter and Carl loathed. Edward, a councilman, had a marvellous talent for doing absolutely nothing but lending his name to the venture and getting all the publicity. His photo was frequently in the New York newspapers alongside glowing articles describing him as virtually a living saint. This was all in the personal hope of Edward raising his role of minor politician to a major one. It was his intention to stand for mayor of the city at the next election.

In the depressing kitchen, Tara gave the stone slabs, which acted as draining boards, a final wipe. She sighed. Another breakfast over; another ninety-something people fed and now about to wander the streets of New York until five o'clock, when they were allowed to return for the evening meal and to sleep.

She'd never liked the idea of not letting the hostel residents remain indoors during the day. People who were more sensible and less soft-hearted than she was argued that they would never get a job, never look for a place of their own to live if they were allowed to stay in the building day after day.

'All they'd do is lie on their bunks and play cards,' the sensible people would say, adding in a threatening tone, 'and have fights.' Tara supposed they were right. The population of St Benedict's

House would never change if things were done her way. Life would be too comfortable.

'Hello, dear,' someone said, interrupting Tara's thoughts. 'Are you off now?'

The woman who spoke was a millionairess. Abigail Hawthorne's fortune was in diamonds, which hadn't lost their value during the Depression. She was almost ninety and completely hairless, but came in most days to peel and chop vegetables in preparation for that night's meal. It was what she was about to do now and why she wore an ankle-length, coarse cotton apron that belonged to one of her servants. She also wore an elaborate feathered hat and a blonde wig.

'I'm longing for some fresh air,' Tara replied.

It had been dark when she'd left home early that morning. By now the March sun, which had no warmth, was a vivid yellow in a powder-blue sky. She wrapped the pieces of untouched bread left over from breakfast to give to Mrs Yesikov, a widow with six children, who lived in one of the Hoovervilles – the hundreds of little patchwork buildings that had been erected in the park out of scraps of wood, metal, carpet and asbestos. Tara passed the family on her way back to Christopher Buchanan's apartment in Central Park, where she now lived. Mrs Yesikov would fry the bread, adding a sprinkling of salt to make it tastier. The family had lived on little else for over a year.

After delivering the bread, she made her way across the park, her footsteps becoming faster, her grave expression lighter. Oh, it was wrong, horribly wrong, to feel so much happier the further she got away from the poverty and misery that was still so obvious in New York.

'One of these days it's bound to get better,' she told herself. Then she would be able to feel happy, without feeling guilty at the same time.

There was often a little group of tenants airing their grievances or exchanging gossip in the lobby of Christopher's building. They were there now, on their way out or on their way in, draped in furs and wearing the latest fashions, discussing President Hoover and if the country would get rid of him at the next election. And what about this Franklin Delano Roosevelt chap who was standing for the Democrats? Was he any good? What did people know about him?

Tara was greeted with an assortment of 'darlings', 'sweethearts', and 'dears', when she entered the building. She had become a well-known and popular tenant over the years she had lived there, which was since Aideen had married Humphrey and moved to Atlantic City and they had given up the apartment they had rented together on Bleecker Street. She was admired mainly for working at St Benedict's House and for being so beautiful.

'You look tired, darling,' a woman in a cream astrakhan coat remarked. 'You must have a little lay-down once you get in.'

'I shall do my best,' Tara promised. She would sooner sit down with a newspaper and a cup of coffee. Her main interest was current affairs.

There was a flurry of movement, the discussion group broke up and either summoned the lifts or left the building. The only ones remaining were

Tara and the handsomest man she had ever set eyes on – not just in New York but back in Ireland too. He was tall, slim, olive-skinned, fine-featured and the owner of a pair of brown velvet eyes, the intensity of which were visible from where Tara stood about twenty feet away. His hair was straight, black and shiny, and he was holding a black fedora, twisting it nervously in his long, slender hands.

His suit wasn't the sort normally seen in this lobby full of immensely rich people – black with white chalk stripes, a white shirt with an over-large collar and a black and white checked tie. He looked as if he were playing the part of a criminal in a Broadway play.

He was staring at her, but after a brief glance on her part, Tara ignored him and went to collect what mail there was from the row of boxes on the wall. There was actually a letter addressed to her for a change; as usual, most of the mail was for Christopher and his partner, Edwin. Her letter was from Aideen, and Tara tucked it in her purse to read later when she was alone. She hoped Humphrey had completely recovered from his horrible experience in Atlantic City, though he would never recover his lost eye.

'Miss Tara Kelly?' It was the handsome guy, looking directly at her, rather sternly, in fact, as if she were a fellow criminal. She gave no hint that she found him enormously attractive.

'Yes,' she confirmed with a brief nod.

He produced a badge. 'I'm Agent Green from the Bureau of Investigation. I'd like a word with you.' He spoke with a broad East Coast accent.

She nodded again. 'Yes, go on.'

'Can't we go somewhere more private?' he said with a frown.

'No. I live in the penthouse apartment with three other people. None of them would approve of me being left alone with a member of the Bureau of Investigation.'

'Why not?' he asked indignantly.

'Because they don't trust you. Come to that, neither do I. Your organisation has far too many powers.'

His indignation was now accompanied by a glare. 'Could we sit over there?' He pointed to a cream satin upholstered settee against the wall. There was a painting of a largely unrecognisable sunset hanging above, which had been done by one of the tenants and gifted to the building. It had 'Sunset' written on a little white plaque underneath so that people wouldn't have to wonder what it was meant to be.

'If you wish.' Tara strolled across to the settee, where she obediently seated herself. Agent Green sat next to her and produced a black leather notebook and the stub of a pencil.

'How old are you, Miss Kelly?' he enquired a trifle pompously.

'Nineteen; almost twenty.'

'And what are the names of the people living with you in the apartment upstairs?'

'You already know their names.' Agents of the government, the police and the Bureau of Intelligence knew everything there was to know about Christopher Buchanan, Edwin Goddard, their servant, Chang Li, and Tara Kelly, their secretary and right-hand woman. They were on numerous lists and numerous files – or, in the case of Christopher, had files all to themselves.

Her calmness was clearly getting on Agent Green's nerves. Perhaps he expected her to stammer nervously, be afraid, or even burst into tears.

He produced a photograph from his breast pocket. 'Have you seen this man before?' It was of a dark-haired man with a wild beard and totally mad eyes.

Tara shook her head. 'Never.'

In fact, the man had been living upstairs for the past two weeks, coming and going using the back entrance when it was dark, and his name was Sebastian Moreau. He was an anarchist and guilty of a few minor crimes in France, where he was born. He had travelled to the United States using a fake passport.

'What's he done?' Tara asked.

'In this country, nothing – yet,' he added, ominously.

'Then why are you looking for him?'

'It's what he might do that matters.' A bead of moisture had appeared on Agent Green's brow. Tara wondered if he found her as attractive as she did him or did he merely find the lobby too warm?

'Will you be much longer? I've been on my feet since six o'clock this morning and I'm longing for a coffee,' she said, adding, 'I work at St Benedict's House.'

'The homeless place across the park?'

'That's right, yes. I do the breakfasts.'

'Well, I do have a few more questions, Miss Kelly. Isn't there a place not far from here that serves coffee? I'd like to buy you one.' He stood and held out his hand, making it difficult for her to refuse. Or so she told herself when she promptly took it.

It was almost two o'clock by the time Tara got home. Borodin's 'Polovtsian Dances' from *Prince Igor* was being played on the gramophone and Christopher smiled at her from across the big room. He was rearranging his books, which he did often. Edwin lay on a sofa that had been placed in front of the window since he'd become ill about four months ago. He spent his days fast asleep or looking down on Central Park. Despite Christopher's constant nagging, he refused to see a doctor. 'They might want to cut me open to take bits out,' was his excuse.

Pink, bald eighty-year-old Edwin was presently asleep. He used to be chubby but was now rapidly losing weight as he grew more frail and Christopher grew more worried. They had slept in the same bed for more than half a century, he'd told Tara, and had no idea how he would live without his long-time lover and friend.

Homosexuality – men loving men and women loving women – was something Tara had been totally ignorant of when she first came across it in Christopher Buchanan's apartment six years before. He and Edwin were a couple, and what they did in bed together was a crime, though it was no one else's business but their own – at least, Tara thought so.

Now Christopher abandoned his books and came and kissed her on both cheeks. 'Have you

210

been working all this time, darling?' he enquired.

'No.' Tara lowered her voice. 'Where is Mr Moreau?'

'In his room, writing angry letters. Why?'

'There was an agent from the Bureau of Investigation in the lobby when I came in at about half eleven. He showed me Mr Moreau's photo and asked if I'd seen him. I denied it, naturally.'

'Good girl.' She was in receipt of an approving pat on her shoulder.

'I let him take me for coffee. I thought it would be a good idea to find out what the Bureau knew about him – Mr Moreau, that is.' She had thought no such thing; she had just wanted to spend a few hours with the exceptionally handsome agent. Tomorrow night he was taking her to see a movie: *Svengali* with John Barrymore.

'And what do they know about him?'

'Hardly anything,' Tara assured him. 'He seems to have an undeserved reputation as a successful anarchist.'

Christopher laughed. 'And you, my dear, have a far too cynical view of the world for someone who has not yet reached the age of twenty-one, though you are without doubt the sweetest and kindest girl who ever lived.'

Tara laughed with him and headed towards her bedroom-cum-sitting room. The wallpaper was white and decorated with giant pink cabbage roses. When she'd moved in, she'd been despatched to Bloomingdale's to choose it herself, along with the pink satin curtains and white furniture. It was similar to the bedroom she would like to have in heaven and she loved it desperately. On the way, she helped herself to a cup of coffee, a chicken sandwich and a blueberry muffin from the kitchen.

'Good morning, miss,' Chang Li said when she went in. He was attacking pastry with a wooden rolling pin and never had any idea of the right time. He was a small, neat, middle-aged man addicted to crimson satin shirts.

'Good afternoon, Chang. What's that for?' She eyed the pastry.

'Apple pie, miss.' His eyes twinkled. 'Very nice, very delicious.'

'I'm sure it will be.'

Tara closed the door of her room and sat on the bed, propping a pillow behind her. She opened that morning's letter from Aideen, which she'd been longing to read. A matter of minutes later, she leapt off the bed with a cry. *'You bastard!'*

The music outside must have been loud enough to make her cry go unheard. Breathing hard, she sank back on the bed and re-read the letter.

Prepare yourself for a really big shock. Just before Christmas, I discovered our father is still alive. That it was all a big act on the boat. Ever since, he has been living in New York 'keeping an eye' on the three of us. He knew Humphrey and I were in danger from 'the mob', would you believe! Had it not been for Daddy, who knows what might have happened to us. I find myself feeling really angry with him, yet terribly grateful... Oh, and he calls himself Malcolm Davis – he gave me his card.

Aideen went on about what she and Humphrey

212

might do next with the rest of their lives.

We have bought a small farm, sort of in Santa Barbara and will be moving soon. There is a mountain in the distance that Humphrey can climb – something he has always wanted to do. Our Patricia will be moving this way soon and we shall become neighbours – well, almost. With love, Aideen.

Tara forgot all about the coffee, the sandwich and the muffin, and went charging round to Patricia's apartment on Fifth Avenue, arriving out of breath and in a terrible temper, though she was normally a very calm person.

The place smelled of baby milk, baby vomit and talcum powder. Her sister was expecting a baby in three months and was resting with her legs on a stool. Joyce was feeding Kathleen with a spoon, while Milo and Rosie were squealing with delight as they attempted to feed each other.

'When are you going to stop having children?' she enquired of her sister. Without waiting for a reply, she went on. 'Remember Auntie Minnie, Ma's sister?'

'Of course I remember Auntie Minnie,' Patricia answered. 'She used to come and see us every Sunday. She had loads of children.'

'She had ten,' Tara continued. 'Her last baby, Colleen, was born when Aunt Minnie was forty-seven. It meant, on average, she'd had a baby every three years. You, however, are only twenty-four and already have three and a half children – if you continue at this rate, by the time you're forty-seven, you will have had twenty-seven.'

213

Joyce looked up. 'Twenty-eight,' she said.

Tara made a face. '*Twenty-eight* children. What do you say to that, Mrs Vanetti?'

Patricia made a face back. 'I'll think about it seriously when I have ten.'

'I don't suppose we'll have long to wait.' Tara was aching to discuss the magical reappearance of their father, though not in front of Joyce. 'Did you get a letter from our Aideen this morning?' she asked.

Patricia agreed that she had. She nodded slightly towards Joyce, a sign that she felt the same. Tara nodded and Patricia said, 'I'm really pleased that she and Humphrey have moved to Santa Barbara, though I wish they'd gone to San Diego and we could have seen each other every day.' She looked tearfully at her youngest sister. 'And what's going to happen to you, eh? Stay here and you'll be thousands of miles away from us. How often are we going to see you?'

Tara hadn't really thought about it, but felt unexpectedly bereft at the idea of living so far from her sisters.

'More and more people are travelling to the West Coast by plane,' Joyce said. 'It takes no time.' She considered herself as much a member of the family as the sisters and at liberty to take part in their conversations.

'Yes, but flying costs the earth,' Tara pointed out, wishing Joyce would go away. 'It's all right for Patricia, but not all of us are married to millionaires.'

Patricia looked at her indignantly. 'You know very well you only have to say the word and Leo would buy you a ticket whenever you wanted to come and see us.' She raised her voice. 'Joyce, darling, would you mind very much taking Milo for a walk to the park and let him run around a bit?' She turned to Tara. 'He needs loads of exercise, otherwise it's impossible to get him to sleep at night. In fact, that's the main reason we're moving to San Diego. It's healthier and it's about time the children had a garden to play in. But you won't be able to pop round the corner for a chat then.'

Tara's heart fell. Patricia was right. She would be left all by herself in New York. Now it was a bit late to try and talk her out of it. Some of their possessions had already been sent ahead.

'Leo's house in San Diego is lovely; I've seen photographs, though I've never been,' her sister went on. 'It has a swimming pool and a tennis court. I've always wanted to play tennis.'

'You'll never get to play tennis if you continue to have babies at the rate you do,' Tara argued.

'I think we should go,' Joyce commented. 'I'm sure I'll love California.' Having left her husband, she was dedicating herself to the Vanettis from thereon. She laid Kathleen on a mattress in the middle of the floor and urged Milo to get his coat. Five minutes later, both had left and were on their way to Central Park.

'Daddy!' Patricia expostulated after the door had closed and they were free to talk about him to their hearts' content. 'Our deplorable trickster of a daddy. Poor Aideen, she must have got a really horrible surprise when he announced who he was. I wonder if he's grown a beard or something?'

215

'Yet he more or less saved her life, so she says. And Humphrey's. I wonder whereabouts he lives in New York.'

'She doesn't say.' Patricia shrugged. 'Maybe he didn't tell her.'

'She says he gave her his card. And he calls himself Malcolm Davis.'

'Perhaps it didn't have an address on it.'

It was Tara's turn to shrug. 'It's not much use having a business card without an address.'

'Even if it did have an address, it would probably be a false one – and Malcolm Davis is a false name. Knowing Daddy, if there was a telephone number, that would be false too.'

They both giggled, already close to forgiving their outrageously untrustworthy father. They hadn't expected him to appear from the dead, but they weren't exactly surprised.

That evening, Tara was accompanying Christopher to a poetry reading in Greenwich Village. He was frequently invited to attend various artistic events; the premiere of a B-movie or an off-Broadway play, the launch of a book by an unknown author, the opening of an out-of-the-way gallery, for which he would provide a review for publication in a minor magazine. His name was well known enough in artistic circles for his opinion to be of value to the cultured citizens of New York. Particularly when it was provided for free.

Tara wore her blue velvet dress that had long tight sleeves and ended at her knees, and what she called her 'Charleston' hat – a cloche made out of the same material as the dress and decorated with a silver lamé flower. At first, Christopher used to advise her what to say if she was asked for her opinion, but as time passed she had acquired enough taste to provide her own, as well as enough knowledge to take part in the conversation.

'I simply adore his [or her] suggestive brushwork,' she would opine. Or 'I find her [or his] poetry has so many underlying meanings'. She wouldn't have dreamt of being cruel – like some critics – and say exactly how she felt about the grotesque paintings or the poetry that made no pretence of rhyming – she only liked poetry that rhymed, and plays, movies and novels that had an actual plot, and paintings that *meant* something. Christopher claimed she was the nicest critic in the world.

'Though totally useless, darling, if people wanted a genuine opinion.'

Tara enjoyed the poetry reading. The poet was only twenty-one and recited his work in a loud, passionate voice that was lovely to listen to, even if his poems didn't make much sense. He invited her to another reading the following week.

When they got back to the apartment, Chang Li had put Edwin to bed. Several friends of Christopher's had arrived and Sebastian Moreau, the would-be anarchist, had been to a meeting and brought back three people he'd met of like mind.

As happened most nights, there were still a few souls present when Tara rose at half five to make breakfast at St Benedict's House on the other side of the park.

She tramped through the wet grass, from which a faint mist rose like tiny smoke signals, mentally hugging herself. Despite there being some awful things happening in the world, it was a wonderful place in which to live. And to cap it all, tonight she was being taken to the movies by the handsomest man on earth.

Agent Green was enthralled by the plot of *Svengali*, whose main character was a hypnotist played by John Barrymore. It was the story of a young girl, Trilby, who had been hypnotised to sing in concert halls all over the world.

'It's an adaptation of a novel by a writer called George du Maurier and is based on fact,' Tara told him afterwards over a strawberry milkshake. 'There really was such a person and it was a harpist who hypnotised her to sing.'

'It could be used by the forces of good to obtain confessions from criminals,' Agent Green said enthusiastically and with the air of a man who'd just discovered the Holy Grail. 'You're very knowledgeable for a woman.'

Tara nearly choked on the milkshake, but didn't say anything. She couldn't be bothered saying how much she disagreed with both those statements.

'I wonder if a person could be hypnotised into committing a crime?' he ruminated further.

'It's possible you already have,' Tara suggested.

'Me?' He raised his fine black eyebrows. 'Already have been what?'

'You and all the members of the Bureau of Investigation have been hypnotised into committing crimes.'

'Are you having me on, Miss Kelly?'

Tara gasped. 'As if I would, Agent Green!'

'You can call me Pete.'

'You can call me Miss Kelly.'

She was glad to see him smile. Until then, she'd thought him incapable of it.

'Would you like to go a club?' he asked.

'What sort of club?'

'A nightclub. We could dance.'

'Sorry, but I have to be up at five to go to St Benedict's House.' Although she rather liked the idea of them dancing together in a dark, smoky club.

'Oh, yes, I forgot.' His mouth turned down. 'You make breakfast for the homeless.'

'Is that criminal?' she teased.

'No, of course not.'

'I bet you could be hypnotised into thinking it was. If I'm not careful, I could end up in prison.'

'You *are* having me on.'

'It wasn't my intention, Agent Green.'

'You're an exceptionally clever dame.'

Dame! Was this man real? He must be, because sitting next to him, their bodies touching, was causing her an acute physical, but also extremely pleasurable, pain. 'Not as clever as you, surely.' She gulped.

Without warning, he put his hand on the back of her head and twisted her towards him, then leant over and kissed her full on the lips. After that, nothing seemed to matter any more.

The next day, Tara emerged from St Benedict's into a cold, wet morning that hardly seemed lighter than when she'd arrived five hours before.

She wasn't all that surprised to find Agent Green waiting outside. He linked her arm and they went together to deliver the bread to Mrs Yesikov and her children in their Hooverville, then to have coffee in the stall in the park where they'd gone the other day.

Somehow, without a word being spoken, both knew what the future had in store for them and were quite happy with it.

At least, so Tara thought.

Chapter 14

Having spent the last six years of her life in New York, possibly the most modern and forward-looking city in the world, Tara Kelly was now a curious mixture of naivety and sophistication. There was very little concerned with sex that could shock her, as long as it didn't involve herself.

So when Agent Pete Green made known his urgent desire that they make love, she surprised him by turning him down. He was even more surprised when he learnt she was a virgin – *still* a virgin.

'A dame like you!' he spluttered, as if he considered her the type of woman who had slept with every man in the city.

'Yes, a dame like me,' she said haughtily. 'Irish dames don't sleep with men before they're married.' She hoped by saying that, he didn't get the idea that she was hinting he propose.

He laughed sarcastically, grabbed her arm and pulled her towards him. 'I can show you a place where Irish girls sleep with men for a dollar a time.'

She pushed him away. 'Then you'd better go there.'

They enjoyed taunting each other; it gave Tara a thrill, and she guessed Pete felt the same. Conversation had become difficult as she continued to refer to him as Agent Green, refusing to use his first name out of sheer cussedness. And it wasn't just a question of morality that put her off making love while she was still single, but practicality too. Look at the mess her sister, Patricia, had very nearly got herself into with that horrible Gianni chap, Leo's brother! If it could happen to one sister, then it could happen to another. If she gave in to Pete Green, she could be on her way to being a mother, but possibly not a wife.

Although no words had been spoken, Tara had managed to hint that she would sleep with him as soon as they found somewhere suitably romantic, a sweetly scented place lined with swansdown and filled with the sound of heavenly music.

'You're asking a lot,' Pete said, rolling his eyes.

Tara emerged from St Benedict's House one pretty May morning to find Pete waiting – always a welcome sight – but the spring-like atmosphere was totally ruined by the smell of frying food coming from the Hoovervilles and, later, after saying goodbye to Pete, who she would see again that night, there was the sickly scent of lilies in the apartment that a friend had sent to Edwin, who

221

was becoming frailer as the days passed.

Tara bent over him, kissed the fingertips of her right hand and laid them gently on his forehead. 'How do you feel today, darling?' she asked tenderly.

'As if an angel has just breathed upon me,' Edwin whispered without opening his eyes.

Chang Li entered the room from the kitchen. 'Christopher gone shopping,' he announced. 'Gone to buy silk PJs for Edwin; black and gold PJs for him to wear in coffin.'

Tara stamped her foot angrily as she left the room. She positively refused to appreciate Christopher and Edwin's bizarre sense of humour.

She changed into fresh clothes and went to see her sister. Patricia, Leo, their children and Joyce were moving from Fifth Avenue, New York, to San Diego in a fortnight and their apartment was an unholy mess. Toys had been packed, unpacked, and repacked again. No one knew where anything was.

Patricia was nursing Milo, who'd just had his ears boxed by Rosie, who was a tough little thing. 'You're not to hit your brother like that again,' Patricia was saying, tenderly kissing her little boy better while casting stern glances at her little girl.

'It was him who hit her first,' Joyce pointed out, rolling her eyes at Tara, as if to say, 'She's showing favouritism again.'

Patricia never hesitated to treat Milo as her favourite child. 'Yes, but look at what he went through before he was even born,' she would protest when this was pointed out. 'People wanted to give him away, even kill him. If it hadn't been for

222

Leo, he might never have been born.'

'That's nonsense,' Tara always argued. 'That Arquette woman was the only person to suggest an abortion or having him adopted. Neither me or our Aideen would have let you do either of those things.'

'I should think not,' Joyce agreed, as if it was any of her business. She hadn't been around at the time, anyway.

The telephone rang and Patricia answered. She waved it at her sister. 'It's for you. It sounds like that nice Chinese gentleman from Christopher's apartment.'

Chang would never telephone if there wasn't something badly wrong. Tara just knew it. She seized the telephone and said cautiously, 'Hello, Chang.'

'You come home, please.' The man's voice was thin and shaky. 'Edwin just die and Christopher been taken to hospital.'

By the time Tara had alighted from the taxi that had returned her to the apartment, the two men who had loved each other for more than fifty years were dead; Edwin had suffered a heart attack at home and Christopher the same thing in the ambulance that was taking his lover to hospital.

From that moment on, everything changed, a heartbroken Tara wailed to her sister later the same week.

'But things never stop changing,' Patricia pointed out. She made the comment in an argumentative way, as if Tara was denying that things

223

changed. 'They changed when Daddy pretended to die on the *Queen Maia*, then changed for me when Leo's desperately horrible brother attacked me in his office.' Patricia refused to use the word 'rape'. 'Now they've changed for you, Tara.'

Tara wished she hadn't said anything. What she badly wanted to know was – what had happened to Pete Green, who had apparently disappeared off the face of the earth since Christopher and Edwin had gone to meet their maker? He was, after all, an agent of the Bureau of Investigation and, Tara had deduced, been using her to find out what he could about Christopher and Edwin's friends. In other words, she had been double-crossed. She would never trust a man again.

Two letters arrived on the same day in early June, both typewritten – one addressed to Mr Chang Li and the other to Miss Tara Kelly. Both letters politely requested that they quit the apartment in which they lived before the end of the month so that the new owner could take possession.

The name of the new owner wasn't revealed in the letter, and neither Tara nor Chang Li ever discovered who had inherited Christopher Buchanan's charming apartment. Chang Li had been left $1000 in Christopher's will and Tara the same sum, but the money was to be held in a trust until she reached the age of twenty-five.

As a result, Chang moved to New Jersey to help his brother run his laundry. 'We are going to expand,' he told Tara excitedly the day before he left. He followed this by bursting into tears. 'I never stop missing Christopher and Edwin,' he

224

gulped. 'What will you do, Tara?'

'I'll never stop missing them either.' Other than that, Tara had no idea. Soon she would feel obliged to give up St Benedict's, as it was a voluntary job that didn't pay a nickel and she would now need actual money to live on.

Daddy turned up at the apartment the following day.

'Hi, honey!' he said when Tara opened the door, and there he was, grinning from ear to ear, looking at her as if it was only the day before since they'd last faced each other on the boat bringing them to New York, not almost seven years.

'Hi, Daddy.' She left the door open and turned back into the apartment to continue packing her last few possessions while pretending to look nonchalant.

'Ah, so Aideen must have told you I was still around,' he said. 'Otherwise you'd've looked surprised.' He strolled in after her.

'Still around and still alive.' She threw the words over her shoulder.

He stood in the middle of the room. 'Nice place you've got here,' he said admiringly.

'Except it's not mine. I'll be moving out soon; later today, in fact.' The place looked and felt different now that she was the only person living there.

'And where will you be moving to, darlin'?'

Oh, that 'darlin'' – it reminded her vividly of their lovely life back in Dublin.

'I'm not sure,' she said airily. 'I'm in the throes of making up me mind.' She shrugged. 'There's not

225

much I can do. I wasn't at school long enough to have had a proper education. The person in charge of me wasn't around when he was needed,' she said accusingly.

He had the decency to blush. 'Well, he's around now,' he said.

'A bit late in the day,' she pointed out. He could disappear at the drop of a hat if he got up to his old nonsense again, like spending other people's money, then allowing one of his girls to be picked up in Central Park by a gentleman of dubious morals and even more dubious politics, yet who she had grown to love over the years.

'You're too grown-up for education,' her father claimed now. 'One day soon you'll be married like your sisters, and there'll be nothing left to learn except for a bit of cooking, like. I mean, I bet you don't even know the name of the president. Being a woman – what's the need?'

'Of course I do,' Tara assured him, outraged. Christopher had always admired her intelligence. 'His name is Herbert Hoover – those perfectly horrible Hoovervilles are named after him. He's a Republican. Hopefully, in November, Franklyn D. Roosevelt, a Democrat, will be elected in his place; he's a much nicer person. In fact, I'm a member of the committee to elect him. Christopher and Edwin were too, though they were Communists, not Democrats, and people daren't vote Communist in America because it's much too left wing and no one would stand for it. It's possible someone could get away with it if they called themselves a socialist, but even then it'd be like declaring you were the devil incarnate.'

Daddy swallowed hard, looking amazed, and decided he would never mention politics in front of his youngest child again. 'Anyway, girl, what are you going to do with yourself now?' he asked.

Tara said she needed to think about it and that Patricia, who was in the course of moving to San Diego, had invited her to think about it while staying with them, which Tara intended to do, transferring from a damp, dark city to a luxuriously furnished bungalow on the edge of the Pacific Ocean. Plus Aideen and Humphrey lived not all that far away.

Daddy looked thoughtful, saying he wouldn't mind moving that far himself. 'Then I'll be close to all my girls,' he said, leaving Tara wanting to crown him with the nearest brick.

San Diego was lovely. Patricia and Leo's single-storey house was elegant and beautifully furnished, and the sparkling blue pool was a delightful and welcome feature in the warm weather. Tara loved the children but neither they, nor their parents, were capable of an intelligent conversation about politics and the state of the world in general. She quickly grew bored and was eagerly looking for something to do, something other than a coffee morning, a fashion show, a matinée, or parties for this and that. What she wanted was a charity or organisation that she could join or help with.

She was relieved when she was approached by an agent from the Federal Bureau of Investigation (they had just added the word 'Federal' to the title), who came up with the perfect job for her.

Sydney Hamilton, a senior operative with the FBI, arrived at the Vanettis' house in San Diego at the end of September 1932 to ask Tara a few questions. She told Leo she felt perfectly capable of coping on her own when he offered to be present during the interview, even though she was slightly worried she might be arrested on a trumped-up charge, given that the Bureau had tried on numerous occasions to get Christopher and Edwin behind bars.

'How do you feel about our country, Miss Kelly?' was the agent's first question when he was settled in one of the property's numerous rooms. It had cream walls and peach-coloured curtains that drifted in and out of the full-length windows in the warm breeze. The children could be heard playing in the pool.

'Why, I think it's a wonderful country, Mr Hamilton,' Tara replied with genuine warmth.

Sydney Hamilton had been expecting a curt reply, so was surprised that Tara sounded as if she really meant what she said, despite being hand-in-glove with that pair of aging, pansy, degenerate anti-Americans for years.

'Have you been happy living here?' he further enquired. 'I mean, since you arrived in America.' He had her file on his knee.

'Extremely!' Tara nodded. 'Till my friends passed away, that is. I've been unhappy ever since; though it's lovely living here.' She glanced through the filmy curtains at the flower-filled garden.

'You worked for a charity in New York?'

'Yes, St Benedict's House. I was a volunteer but

had to leave when my friends died because I needed proper wages.'

He knew how hard she'd worked for more than two years in that St Benedict's place. He knew too that she was a thoroughly decent young woman, as well as a real looker, who'd been led astray by a crowd of lousy Reds. 'Does that mean you'll soon be looking for another job?'

She smiled and it took his breath away. 'I already am looking, Mr Hamilton.' She'd written after a few jobs advertised in the papers, which she wasn't really qualified for, and hadn't even received a reply.

'Well, Miss Kelly, we have a vacancy that might suit you. How do you fancy the idea of living in London for a while?'

Tara's eyes sparkled. 'It sounds a lovely idea, Mr Hamilton. And for what reason would I live in London?'

'Have you heard of Sir Oswald Mosley?'

'He used to be a member of the British parliament and is now the leader of the British Union of Fascists.' Tara spoke in the manner of a child answering a question at school.

'And what about Adolf Hitler? Are you familiar with him?'

Tara treated him to another thrilling smile. 'I'm familiar with his name and have seen his photo in the press, but not with the gentleman in person.' She coughed briefly. 'Adolf Hitler was recently appointed chancellor in the German government. He leads the National Socialist Party, also known as the Nazi Party.' Christopher and Edwin had hated both men. 'He is also a Fascist.'

'Well done, Miss Kelly.' The agent leant forward and continued in a slightly hushed tone. 'We in the Federal Bureau of Investigation do not normally tinker with matters outside our own country, but this would be an exception. We would like you to go to London, live there for a few months – six months would probably do – and find out all you can about the British Union of Fascists. If Hitler's name should come up for any reason, we in the Bureau would like to know what that reason is.' He smiled as if he and Tara were the best of friends. 'Can you do that for us, do you think?'

'I shall do my very best,' Tara answered solemnly. 'It might be a good idea if I joined the Fascists.'

'No, no,' the man said hastily. 'That could be dangerous. Just attend a few meetings, that will do.'

Part 3

Chapter 15

Patricia and Aideen were distraught to see their little sister leave San Diego for another country altogether.

'I mean,' Patricia said tearfully, 'I know New York is miles and miles away from here, but at least we're on the same landmass. We could find each other eventually, even if we walked there.' It was a ludicrous exaggeration, but it was true. 'And it's right at the beginning of winter too. London's reputed to be a terribly damp and foggy place.' September was coming to its end.

'I know.' Aideen sighed. She had enjoyed having Tara with them in California, who had turned out to be smarter and more knowledgeable than her sisters had ever imagined. And now this American bureau or agency or whatever it was, wanted to send her to London on such an important mission that Tara had been forbidden to say what exactly it was about.

Was she to be a spy? The sisters were appalled at the idea. After all, Tara was only twenty-two.

'It's all Daddy's fault,' Aideen said bitterly. 'If it weren't for him, we'd still be in Dublin and Tara would be married to one of those nice lads from St Kentigern's Sunday school.'

Patricia made a face. 'They were a sanctimonious lot. I'd sooner she went to London than do that. Anyway, darlin', if it weren't for Daddy,

233

I wouldn't have met Leo and you wouldn't have met Humphrey.'

Aideen made a face of her own, but didn't say anything.

An apartment had been reserved for Tara in an area of London called St John's Wood. From outside, the building looked like a large modern house. Inside there were six apartments on three floors – she must remember to start referring to them as 'flats' again. A mid-brown carpet covered the floors and stairs, and the walls were a slightly lighter brown. The only splash of colour was a bowl of faded wax fruit on the table where the post was left.

Tara only stayed six weeks. During that time, she had glimpsed just one other tenant, a middle-aged woman who replied with great reluctance when Tara had wished her 'Good morning'.

There were four other people living there – they could be heard returning home in the evenings and leaving early the next day. The only voices audible were on different wirelesses that had been switched on at their lowest level.

Tara couldn't help it – she felt lonely and depressed, and wished she'd remained in San Diego with her sisters and ever-increasing collection of nephews and nieces.

She had no idea how the rent was being paid, but on her sixth Friday there, worried she might die of boredom, she put an envelope marked 'Landlord' on the table in the hall, giving a month's notice. She had already written to a gentleman in Washington, whose address had been provided by Mr Hamilton (he described this person as her 'contact'), and told him she had moved to an area called Camden, where she had found another apartment herself.

I hope you don't mind, she wrote. *But the St John's Wood flat was deathly miserable. The new house is much more cheerful.*

While Tara didn't expect investigating the British Union of Fascists to be an enjoyable venture, she had decided it was also time she did something that involved other young people, even if it was nothing to do with politics. She would never regret living with Christopher and Edwin, but now she was looking forward to making friends, going dancing, playing tennis and joining something like a dramatic society or a theatre club.

The room she'd moved into had been advertised in the window of a tobacconists on the corner of Madeira Road off Camden High Street. It was actually in the road itself, one of a long terrace of once-elegant four-storey houses, most of which needed their doors painted, the windows cleaned and the gardens weeded. The Depression, although it had begun in America, had spread throughout the world, decimating the banks and the financial institutions. Those unlucky enough to have been wiped out yet still own their own homes had turned them into apartments or bedsitting rooms for the people who had lost their jobs in other British cities and had now poured into the capital looking for work. Some had been lucky, some not.

Tara was one of the lucky ones – the extremely lucky ones. Not only had the Federal Bureau of Intelligence organised her somewhere to live – which she had rejected for somewhere more acceptable and rather more disreputable – but it had found her a job that was interesting, even though it added nothing to the betterment of the human race.

She was now the author of the 'Voice of London', a column aimed at people who enjoyed reading about scandal, crime, and the comings and goings of the still-wealthy members of British society – usually people with titles. Members of parliament, for instance, or minor members of the aristocracy, who were frequently up to no good. The column appeared weekly in the *Worldwide Voice*, a New York-based paper aimed at readers who enjoyed what was mainly considered idle gossip. Who had been seen in a nightclub in Soho with someone of the opposite sex when they should have been at home with their wife or husband, for example? Or who had been glimpsed at the theatre with a partner or friend – news that appeared to be of interest to some people only because the theatregoers were slightly famous. Or young women who were presented at court, their coming-out dresses described in detail as well as the great balls attended afterwards by upper-class young men on the lookout for a suitably rich bride, their own family money having disappeared in the Depression. Edward, the Prince of Wales, played a notable part in all the papers' gossip columns, his dissolute lifestyle being of global interest.

Tara worked three mornings a week in a small office on Fleet Street, otherwise dedicated to the production of the British paper, the *News of the World*. She was ashamed of how much she enjoyed the job because she thoroughly disapproved of the people she wrote about. She despised gossip as well as the people who wanted to read about it week after week. Her job had actually been 'invented' by someone in the Bureau and she mainly gathered her information from other newspapers. Nor was she interested in royalty. Christopher Buchanan, a Republican to the core (although not the American political sort) had actually written a book about it – *Why Does the World Need People with Titles???* it asked, using three question marks. She must see if she could buy a copy in an English bookshop.

Tara made friends with the residents of the house in Madeira Street on her first Saturday there due to the fact a chap called Roman, who lived on the second floor, was throwing a party and the whole house had been invited.

The landlady, Mrs Shawcross-Brown, who lived in the basement, was the original occupant of the house, though she didn't own it. Her husband had been a stockbroker until the time all the money in the world appeared to have lost its value. He had disappeared 'into the wide blue yonder', as his wife put it, and she had been reduced to letting out the house, room by room. She managed to cope by being horribly rude to everyone, even Tara when she came to see about the vacant room, which used to be the parlour and was the biggest in the house.

'Why on earth should someone like you want to live in a dump like this?' Mrs Shawcross-Brown had demanded when she had opened the door and found Tara outside in her expensive red boucle coat and little feathered hat.

Tara explained that where she lived was too quiet. 'And nobody's friendly. I had to move before I went mad.'

'Well, dear, you'll find living here is never quiet and the other tenants are much *too* friendly. A few weeks here and you'll be even madder.' She flicked her cigarette and the ash landed on Tara's black suede court shoes and the surrounding carpet.

'I think I'll risk it.' Tara had smiled, stamping on the ash before it burnt the pathetically ragged carpet.

The party didn't start until after the pubs had closed, so those whose intention it was to get drunk were already inebriated when it began – including Mrs Shawcross-Brown, who wandered around clad in black chiffon, a bottle of gin in her hand, insisting people call her 'Jean'. Different sorts of music was coming from almost every room. Upstairs someone was playing a concertina; a piano was being beaten to death where the Shawcross-Browns had once eaten breakfast; the strains of a violin came from somewhere un-known; and a man on the stairs was getting quite a tune out of a comb covered with tissue paper.

Tara, who until then had only partaken of the finest wines throughout her life, was astounded

238

to discover that some wines tasted of vinegar and other noxious substances.

'Ugh!' she gagged over a mouthful of liquid that was a beautiful rich red. 'What's this?' she asked of no one in particular.

'It's Roman's cough mixture, I expect,' a girl said, 'mixed with lemonade. He claims to get quite a kick out of it.'

Tara put the glass on the mantelpiece. 'It's not the sort of kick that appeals to me,' she said. 'I'm Tara, by the way. I live in what was once the parlour.'

'I'm Pamela. The parlour is the biggest and most expensive room in the house.' She looked Tara – who was wearing a just-below-the-knee silver georgette frock – up and down. 'Yes, you look like you can afford the parlour. Are you slumming it or something?'

Tara could only guess what 'slumming it' meant. 'I like it here,' she said.

They were standing on the landing on the first floor. Two men shoved past. The second man, tall and blond, turned back, grabbed Tara's hand and pulled her through the door of a room containing a large bed, on which at least half a dozen people lay kissing each other. The blond man pushed Tara onto the bed and began to do the same to her.

Tara, outraged, lifted her knees and kicked him away. He sprawled backwards onto the floor, his head hitting the wall with a loud thump. When he tried to get up, she stamped on his ankle and left the room.

'Gosh!' Pamela was still on the landing. She

looked worried. 'Do you know him?'

'No, and I don't want to.' Tara shrugged as she closed the door.

'Shall we go to your room, case he comes storming out – or limping out – and attacks you?'

'Is he likely to?' Tara felt slightly worried.

'I don't know. I've never seen that chap before.'

'Neither have I.' She was accustomed to attending cocktail parties in an apartment overlooking the very nicest part of Central Park, surrounded by exquisitely attired guests listening to a speaker wanted by half a dozen governments for his or her ultra left-wing beliefs. 'Perhaps we should go in my room and just talk. If I leave the door open, people might come in and join us.'

Which was exactly what happened. In no time, half a dozen people were sitting or laying on Tara's bed, while more sat on chairs and the floor, discussing the surprising decision taken by Spain the year before to become a republic. And again last year, another political earthquake when the city of London refused to support the Labour government's decision to cut back on public spending. A general election followed and the Conservatives and Liberal parties formed a coalition government with Labour.

Tara listened avidly. She loved politics and listened even more closely when the name Oswald Mosley was mentioned along with the British Union of Fascists, which he had founded. Everybody there was opposed to him, some even booed at the mention of his name. Tara realised she would have to be extremely careful when the time came for her to investigate the union to

240

make sure no one in the house found out. She might even join, despite what Mr Hamilton had said. However, it turned out that at least one of the residents of the house would approve of her action.

Mrs Shawcross-Brown staggered into the room and accused them all of defiling the name of a fine man. 'Sir Oswald has the interests of our country close to his heart,' she shouted. 'And get out of my sitting room, you monsters. If anyone has dared to stub out their cigarette on my best furniture, the whole lot of you will be out on your ear in the morning. And you–,' she turned to Tara '–I thought you were a cut above this lot.'

'I'm not a cut above anyone,' Tara said. She felt sorry for the woman. 'Not only that but I don't smoke.'

Mrs Shawcross-Brown left the parlour in tears, followed by a dozen or more disappointed debaters.

'Would you like me to go too?' Pamela asked when she and Tara were the only ones left.

'No, stay,' Tara assured her. 'I'll make coffee – or would you prefer tea?'

'I've never drunk coffee before, only tea.'

'Well, have some now. I've got cream. I can't abide coffee without cream.'

'Cream! I've never had cream either, least not in a drink. At home we only have it with jelly or tinned fruit on high days and holidays.'

Tara was tired. She looked at her new friend properly for the first time. Pamela was about her own age, but much smaller, no more than five feet tall. Her eyes were grey and her face unhealthily pale, without even the trace of pink on her cheeks. But Tara would never turn down what appeared to be an offer of friendship by telling the girl she'd like her to leave.

'I'll just put the kettle on,' she said.

The next day was Sunday. Tara went to ten o'clock Mass at Westminster Cathedral and then to Speakers' Corner in Hyde Park. This, she had been told, was proof that Britain was one of the best in the world when it came to freedom of speech. In many other countries, the crowds would have been mercilessly broken up or even shot by the military or the police if they dared make a fuss.

The morning's fog had disappeared by the time Tara reached the park and a watery sun was struggling to make its way through the clouds. It was November and shockingly cold. A handful of policemen were scattered about – not to prevent anyone from speaking but to break up any fights that might erupt.

All but one of the speakers were men. The first she listened to was loudly proclaiming that the earth was flat and providing all sorts of facts and statistics to prove it. The next wanted rid of the monarchy. 'They're not even British; the whole bloody crowd are German. Why else did they have to change their name from Battenberg to Windsor?' He was being loudly booed.

The female speaker – a tall, angular woman with a bent nose – demanded equal rights for women when a couple divorced. 'Why should only the male have full rights to the property when a man and woman want to end their marriage?' she wanted to know, and was treated to roars of un-flattering abuse, most of it heaped upon her nose. Tara, who agreed with everything the woman had said, clapped loudly and shouted, 'Hear! Hear!'

Her heart twisted slightly when a leaflet was thrust into her hand and she realised that she had arrived at the stand of the British Union of Fascists. There was something sinister about the loud, hectoring voice of the man standing behind a black-painted lectern. His eyes were dark and penetrating, his hands clutched rigidly behind him. Had he not been speaking, it would have been easy to think he was a statue, he stood so still, as did the unsmiling men poised on each side of him bearing large flags; one was a Union Jack and the other black with a white design that Tara never seen before.

The man speaking had an accent that she couldn't recognise, He was addressing the small crowd spread in front of him, lighting upon their faces one by one, pausing there for a matter of seconds, as if he wanted his words to penetrate their souls and their images to impress them-selves upon his brain for all time. When his gaze fell directly upon Tara, she quickly looked away.

'...So that is why the white man is superior to the negro; his brain is larger. A black man's brain is barely half the size of the whites. There is no room in it for imagination to spread or thoughts to flourish. A black man will never write a poem or a novel. He will never invent a single useful thing. He will–'

A voice erupted from the back of the crowd.

'What about Sojourner Truth?' a man shouted. The fact that he was well educated and confident was obvious from the tone of his voice. 'And Phillis Wheatley, the first Afro-American woman to be published way back in the eighteenth century?'

More names were called. Tara, to her shame, had never heard of any of them. She would look them up as soon as she found a library.

There was another shout. 'And what about–'

Before the man could finish, the flag bearers plunged into the crowd, flags held like spears, causing a couple of policemen to approach, truncheons drawn.

Tara hurried away until the sound of heads being cracked and punches being exchanged could no longer be heard. She walked in the direction of Oxford Street, hoping to find somewhere open where she could buy a late breakfast or an early lunch. She spotted a restaurant called Lyons on the corner of the next street and hurried towards it. Within five minutes she was seated by a window overlooking Oxford Street, waiting to be served.

She read the leaflet, still clutched in her hand, and saw the Fascists were holding a meeting in a hall in Bermondsey next Wednesday evening, which would be addressed by Sir Oswald Mosley himself, and on Saturday the following week there would be a march along Whitechapel. Tara felt elated. She would go to both.

A waitress came and Tara ordered a pot of coffee with cream, Welsh rarebit – she hadn't had Welsh rarebit since leaving Ireland – and a bowl of trifle.

When the coffee arrived, Tara sipped it while gazing admiringly at the restaurant and its clientele. She could well have been in New York, perhaps around ten years ago. In those days, the clothes the customers were wearing here had been the height of fashion across the Atlantic. Nowadays frocks were shorter, heels a fraction higher and hats a trifle cheekier. But the conversation was just as animated.

The setting was glossy and expensive. This wasn't a place where poor people came. Neither was it for the overly rich, but for the comfortable middle classes who had survived the Depression intact.

Tara was so involved in her observations that, for a moment, she didn't notice the young man hovering over her table until he'd sat down in the chair opposite.

'Hello,' he said when she blinked her awareness that he was there.

'Hello,' Tara said crossly. How dare he sit down without her permission?

Her feelings had obviously got through to him because he leapt to his feet and said politely, 'May I join you?'

'Why?' she asked. She didn't want to appear rude but she was quite enjoying being left to think in peace.

'I saw you in Hyde Park – and you have a BUF leaflet.' He pointed to the pamphlet in her hand. 'I was there at the meeting and saw you leave.'

'Have you been following me?'

He blushed. 'Yes.'

She respected his honesty. After all, he didn't

have to agree. 'Oh, all right, sit down,' she said. 'Did the fight last long?'

'Hardly any time at all. When the police joined in, everyone dispersed. As I was leaving, I saw the Fascists back in place with a fresh audience.'

Tara's Welsh rarebit arrived. The waitress transferred her gaze to the customer who had invaded her table. 'Would you like to order, sir?'

He, in turn, looked at Tara, eyebrows raised. 'Do you mind?'

'Not at all,' she assured him, though she did.

'I'll have rarebit too,' he told the waitress, 'and a glass of dandelion and burdock.'

'I really should introduce myself,' he said when they were alone. 'My name is Hugh Furnival. I work for the BBC – that's the British Broadcasting Corporation if you've never heard of it.'

'Of course I've heard of the BBC,' Tara said crisply. What sort of ignoramus did he take her for? Her two old friends in New York had admired it greatly. 'What do you do there?'

'They call me a sound engineer. I look after the microphones, make sure they are adjusted to the correct pitch, that sort of thing.'

'That sounds very interesting,' Tara said politely.

'It's absolutely fascinating,' he told her. 'You must come to the studio one day and watch – and listen, of course.'

Tara thought it a rather good idea. 'Is that allowed?'

'Well, yes. We quite often have an audience present when there's a discussion. The programmes are taken more seriously if our listeners out there are aware of there being an audience, albeit

246

small, and hear them reacting to the views expressed – applauding when a speaker says something that they like, or hissing if they disapprove,' he added with a grin. 'At times that can be very satisfying if it's someone I disapprove of myself.'

'Such as?'

'Well, Sir Oswald Mosley is a prime example.'

'Him! Has he actually been in your building?' Tara was impressed.

'It's called a studio. He's been interviewed a few times. Not by me,' he hastened to add. 'I'm not important enough.'

His food and drink had arrived and he consumed half the dandelion and burdock straight away. 'Phew,' he said with a happy sigh as he tucked into the rarebit.

Tara was barely halfway through her own meal. She watched him eat, having not seriously taken him in since he had so rudely sat at her table without an invitation. He was, she now realised, a rather nice young man with excessively curly hair, brown eyes and a mischievous expression. He wore round spectacles with metal frames that made him look studious and extremely clever. Although they hadn't so far stood side by side, she guessed he wasn't very tall – about the same height as herself. His clothes – flannels, a checked shirt, with a tie that didn't match – looked old but expensive.

'What did you say your name was?' she enquired.

He waited until the food in his mouth had been swallowed before answering. 'Hugh Furnival. I'm from Wales,' he told her.

247

'I'm Tara Kelly, from Ireland.' She smiled, feeling sure they would be meeting each other again quite soon.

In fact, it so happened that they stayed together for the rest of the day. After the meals had been eaten, he invited her to a party in Essex.

Tara announced that she had never been to Essex – indeed to any part of England other than Liverpool – and had no idea where it was. 'And what sort of party is on a Sunday afternoon?' From what she'd gathered so far, London on Sundays appeared to be rather depressingly empty.

'It's a delayed wedding reception,' she was told. 'Two friends of mine from the BBC got married last weekend on the furthest bit of coast in Scotland. Hardly anyone was able to go, only family, so they are having the reception this weekend, having spent the intervening week in Paris on honeymoon.' He looked at her soulfully. 'Would you like to come with me?'

'I think I would, yes.' She looked down at her clothes. 'But I'll need to go home and change.' She was wearing a fawn mackintosh and a knitted hat that covered her hair, as well as a very ordinary blouse and skirt.

Mr Hamilton had advised her to be as inconspicuous as possible when she went to meetings of the BUF. 'Don't become familiar. They're a suspicious lot. You'll soon be noticed if you attend their gatherings frequently. They'll wonder who you are and why you're there.'

'Do you live far?' Hugh Furnival was asking.

'Camden, off the High Street.'

'Oh, we'll be there in five minutes,' he said in an offhand manner.

'Are you sure?' Tara doubted that. 'It took me ages to get here this morning on the bus.'

'I've got a car parked nearby. You sit here, and I'll stop across the road and sound the horn. I'll be back in a mo.' He leapt to his feet and was gone.

It was nice to be pretty, Tara reflected as she sipped an extra half cup of coffee that she'd manage to squeeze out of the pot. And she wasn't just ordinarily pretty, but exceptionally so. She wasn't conceited about it. It was something to do with her mother's looks and her father's, as well as a contribution from God Himself. It made life easier, though could sometimes be a nuisance. Men were inclined to follow you, as Hugh Furnival had done from Hyde Park, but not all were as nice as him, nor as useful. Some were hard to get rid of and were inclined to take offence if their advances were turned down. Nevertheless, it made life easier. She had never had to look in the mirror and wish her nose was a different shape or her hair a different colour. And she liked being tall.

All in all, Tara was perfectly satisfied with herself. Yet, she thought ruefully, despite the good looks, she had only been in love once, and that was with Pete Green, the government agent, who had disappeared out of her life without even saying goodbye.

The horn had sounded several times across the road before it actually registered on her brain. When it finally did, she saw Hugh Furnival sitting behind the steering wheel, frantically waving his arms.

'Oh, so there you are,' a voice said crossly when Tara went into the house in Madeira Road. Pamela, wearing a hat and coat, was sitting on the bottom stair glaring at her.

'I'm sorry,' Tara stammered. Had she promised Pamela she would be back earlier? If so, she couldn't remember. They hadn't spoken that morning.

'You said you would be home before lunch. I thought we could go for a walk or something.'

'I think I said I *might* be home; I didn't say for certain. I had lunch out.'

The young woman looked even crosser. 'I wish I'd known. I'd've had lunch out myself.' She got to her feet. 'Never mind, I'll have something while we're out. I'll just get my gloves.' She ran upstairs where she lived at the top of the house in the smallest room.

Oh lord! What had she got herself into?

'I'm sorry,' Tara called after the retreating figure. 'Right now I'm off to a wedding.' Hugh was waiting for us in his car outside. 'Well, not exactly a wedding, but a wedding reception. I was just about to get changed.'

Pamela ignored her and continued up the stairs.

'I'm sorry,' Tara called again, though conscious she had done nothing wrong and unsure whether to pretend to be cross herself or terribly sympathetic. She felt uncomfortable. 'I'm sorry,' she said for the third time, but Pamela had disappeared and she was speaking to the empty air.

Jean Shawcross-Brown stepped into the hall — she appeared to have been eavesdropping on the basement stairs. 'Don't worry,' she said. 'The poor kid imagines what she would like to happen, then believes it to be true. She's had a frightful life at home. I'll take her out for a cup of tea when she comes down,' she continued with unexpected kindness, 'and then go for a walk to cheer her up a bit. So where's this wedding reception being held?'

At first, Tara thought she intended to invite herself and Pamela along, but it turned out she was merely interested in where it was.

'Don't worry,' she said a second time, laughing at Tara's worried face. 'I've no intention of forcing myself upon you, it's just that I used to lead such a busy social life and nowadays I go absolutely nowhere at all — apart from walks with Pamela. You can tell me about the wedding when you get back.'

The trunk full of clothes that Tara had brought with her from America was as big as a moderately sized wardrobe and designed as such with a metal rod inside for the hangers. Most of her outfits were still hanging in the trunk, while a few had been transferred to the proper wardrobe where they now hung loosely in the hope the creases would soon come out.

It was from there that Tara chose a rust-coloured tweed costume with a fur collar and cuffs, and a hat shaped like a tam-o'-shanter with a fur bobble. She completed the outfit with a pair of dark brown suede shoes and matching gloves. She wore her

251

hair loose.

She wasn't surprised when she left her room to find Pamela and Mrs Shawcross-Brown in the hall, apparently waiting for her to appear.

'We were wondering what you would be wearing,' the older woman explained. 'Doesn't she look smart?' she remarked to Pamela, who nodded shyly. 'I didn't realise Dublin had such exclusive clothes shops. That suit is surely a Jean Patou. It must have cost the earth.'

Tara had left the apartment in St John's Wood because the tenants were so unfriendly. In Madeira Road she was beginning to suspect they were the opposite. If the landlady continued to be so nosy and Pamela was determined they become bosom friends, then she would just have to find somewhere else to live.

Oh, but that was a horrible thing to do – to even *think*. She silently apologised to all the people who were able to listen to her thoughts. She was so lucky when compared to Jean Shawcross-Brown and Pamela.

After she had closed the front door behind her, it was immediately opened again. 'I'm sorry to be so curious,' Jean Shawcross-Brown said in a stage whisper, 'it's just that I can't stop wondering what the hell someone like you is doing here.'

The reception was made up of young people, friends of the newly wed couple, who were in their twenties and thirties. It seemed parents, aunts, uncles and children had enjoyed a more conventional affair in the Ritz Hotel in London the day before.

Today's location was found at the end of a long, winding country lane and comprised an old manor house set in a couple of acres of grounds, which included a tennis court full of soaking wet leaves, a long series of stables, and a swimming pool that badly needed cleaning – more leaves floated thickly on the dirty water.

Tara and Hugh, along with another dozen or so guests, didn't join in the party games that were pretty energetic – Tara had had little sleep the night before, so was too exhausted, plus she was wearing high heels. Compared with last night, today's party guests were more interested in winning games than connecting with a member of the opposite sex or consuming alcohol. They formed themselves into teams and raced up and down the stairs while playing hide-and-seek, shouting, 'tally-ho'. They played musical chairs with terrifying vigour, pausing for charades when they felt like a rest, did the conga, going out to kick leaves that were a foot deep through the orchard while singing so loudly it must have been heard miles away on an otherwise sleepy Sunday afternoon.

Tara had never come across anything like this in New York, but then she was usually the only young person at Christopher and Edwin's parties. And instead of sex and playing exhaustive games, there were literary quizzes and poems narrated in Latin or Greek, a couple of acts from a Shakespearean play performed by a group of genuine Broadway actors, while everyone sipped champagne or rare wine.

'Would you like to leave?' Hugh Furnival said

253

in her ear.

'Yes, please,' she said eagerly, 'if you don't mind.'

'I don't mind a bit. This isn't really my cup of tea.'

She wondered if it would have been his cup of tea if he was with a woman willing to join in the games, rather than someone like herself who was old before her time, at least where parties were concerned.

'Am I spoiling things for you?' she asked.

'No, no, of course not. Absolutely not,' he added, shaking his head so furiously that she laughed. 'Oh, all right,' he conceded. 'You're not spoiling things. But if you were willing to let me kiss you non-stop for the next few hours, I certainly wouldn't refuse, but I can tell you're not willing, so have no intention of trying and so would just prefer we went somewhere else.'

'Are you two off?' the man sitting beside them enquired. Hugh nodded. 'Well, in that case, do you fancy meeting up with me and my girlfriend back in London? We could have a bite to eat, by which time the drinking holes will be open and we can finish the evening off with a cosy drink.'

Hugh looked at Tara. 'What do you think?'

'That would be very nice,' she said politely, though she didn't like the man's rawboned face and ginger moustache. She was being awfully picky today.

'I'm Bunny Holt,' he told them, 'and my girlfriend is Lucy Fielding. See you in The Liszt Cafe in Frith Street, Soho, in an hour or so. Shall we race back?'

Hugh shrugged. 'Why not?'

But once in the car, Hugh announced he had no intention of racing all the way back to London. 'I wish I hadn't agreed to meet that chap and his girlfriend. I just wanted to get away. This afternoon has been more like a children's party than a grown-up do.' At that precise moment, Bunny Holt roared past, sounding his horn. 'Oh, dear,' Hugh groaned. 'I'm not even going to try to keep up.'

Tara laughed. 'It's been an interesting afternoon,' she said. 'And now you've promised to meet that couple, it would be rude for us not to turn up.'

After an early dinner at The Liszt Cafe – where they served delicious Hungarian food – the day turned out to be even more interesting. When it was suggested they transfer to a basement bar in Oxford Street, Tara pleaded total exhaustion. 'I really must go home,' she said. Any minute now, she'd fall asleep sitting up.

At this, Bunny suggested they give the bar a miss and return to his flat for 'a bit of fun'.

'What sort of fun?' Tara enquired. She noticed Hugh was frowning. He threw a couple of pound notes onto the table and pulled her to her feet. 'Let's go,' he said crisply.

'But where?' She was bewildered.

'Home. *Your* home.'

'But–' Bunny began.

'Tara, get in the car,' Hugh snapped.

Slowly the penny was beginning to drop as she realised what Bunny meant by 'a bit of fun'.

255

Hugh's car stopped outside the house in Madeira Road and Tara got out.

'See you tomorrow,' he called.

'Tomorrow,' Tara agreed. They were going to the cinema to see *The Front Page,* which was on in the West End.

It was unnaturally quiet in the house and Tara felt lonely when she went into her room and closed the door.

'How did I do today?' she whispered, imagining her two old friends in heaven seated like angels on white satin chairs, nodding to each other when she spoke.

'You did very well, Tara, dear,' Christopher murmured.

'I miss you.' She began to weep.

'And we miss you, darling.'

When Tara woke up, the clocks in the house were chiming midnight and she couldn't remember which part of the day was real and how much of it had been a dream.

Chapter 16

1934

It was November and raining slightly the day she arrived back in New York. The taxi drew up outside the apartment on Fifth Avenue where Aideen and Tara had lived with Patricia and Leo when they were first married. The foyer had been done up since she'd last been there, the old tasteful green carpet replaced with a black one scattered with giant gold leaves – a bit too garish, Aideen thought – and the soothing Impressionist prints on the walls were now replaced with cold, clinical creations that she imagined being classed as 'abstract'.

Through the stout glass doors she could see Jerry, the little tubby porter that Patricia had become so fond of that she'd actually cried when the family had moved to San Diego. He saw Aideen struggling to enter with her luggage and shot across to open the door, a smile almost splitting his face in two.

'Miss Kelly! I didn't know you were expected back. Will you be staying for long?'

'Two or three weeks – I'm not sure.' It might be two or three months or even years. Aideen patted his shoulder and offered him an answering smile. 'And we made an agreement when we used to live here – if you let me call you *Jerry*, I'll let you call me *Aideen*. Otherwise it's Mrs Grant to you, Mr Phillips, as I'm no longer Miss Kelly.'

His smile widened. 'It's real good to see you again, Aideen,' he said cheerfully.

'You too, Jerry.'

And it was just as good to see New York. She'd been brought up in a city and preferred it to a stretch of empty sand and a million gallons of water that comprised some ocean or other. The sound of traffic was far preferable to the lonely screech of a thousand hungry birds. She hadn't realised how much she'd missed it.

'I'll go down and turn the boiler on in your

place,' Jerry said as he shuffled back towards the lift. He's getting old, she thought, like us all.

When she entered the apartment, Jerry must have already reached their boiler because the pipes were making clicking and gulping noises. *That* was the sort of water she liked best: in a basement, heated, invisible. It was probably only her imagination that everywhere already felt a touch warm. For the first time in years, she felt properly at home.

She'd only made up her mind to come to New York at the very last minute when, back in the seaside village of Bray, the post arrived with a letter from Gertie to say Andy, her boss in the sports department at Berry's, had died, it would be his funeral on Friday, and why didn't she come?

You and he were good friends, weren't you? Me, I always thought he was a bit of a dork. It would make a break for you though, if not a particularly jolly one.

Yes, looking back, she had liked Andy and they had been friends, of sorts. He'd been the only man in her life at the time, though there was nothing faintly sexual about it. She just never let on to management when he wasn't well and came in late, and he'd kept quiet the times when she'd disappeared with Gertie for a coffee. Now it was Humphrey, her husband, who had disappeared, though there was nothing secretive about it. Aideen knew where he had gone and why.

'I won't stay away for ever,' he had promised. 'For a year, say. I've just got to go and have

258

another try at that mountain.'

'But no one has ever managed to climb Everest,' she had reminded him. What else was there to say? Anyway, looking at it one way, *trying* could only do some good, give Humphrey a purpose, though what purpose he would find to stay alive once he was back, who knew? As it was, he had given up growing fruit and vegetables, and instead used all his energy on climbing silly American excuses for mountains – hardly more than a hill when he'd already had a go at the biggest mountain in the world. People took their children for walks on the nearby American mountains on Sunday afternoons. Boy Scouts and Girl Guides camped on them overnight; sat on the grass and lit fires; flew kites from them. Humphrey had lived on them for days without coming home, and without any sense of adventure. If he stayed away for long, Aideen would go and look for him, shouting his name.

The time came when he was desperate for one more try at a real mountain and it had to be *the* one. 'I'll be perfectly safe, honey,' he promised. 'Whatever happens, I'll come home and grow things for the rest of my life.'

'But what about me?' she exclaimed. 'What shall I do?'

'Why don't *you* climb your own mountain, hon?' he suggested. 'I don't mean a real one. I mean do something, like go see Tara in London. Or go back to Ireland. Have an adventure.'

But women aren't supposed to have adventures, she wanted to tell him. Women stay at home and look after the children.

Aideen had finally reached the stage of wanting

children. But not like Patricia, who now had eight – three boys and five girls, the latest being twin girls, Siobhan and Deirdre. Twins would be perfect for Aideen; she didn't care what sex they were.

She told Humphrey that now wasn't the time to go to Ireland or London, but that she quite fancied going to New York for a while, even getting a job, having a proper break away from Bray, like Gertie said. But at the back of Aideen's mind was the hope that she would never see Bray again.

'Then go,' Humphrey said in a regal voice, like a king.

So Aideen did. First of all, she gave in her notice at the college where she'd worked, then she recklessly rented out their smallholding in Bray for five whole years. It was the first move in the hope that she would never see the place again.

Humphrey's parents had sent a hundred and fifty dollars for his 'holiday'. Aideen was about to leave the smallholding when a cheque for the same sum arrived for her.

'You deserve it,' Mary, her mother-in-law, wrote. 'A lot of women wouldn't have stuck by her husband the way you have our son.'

Aideen toured the increasingly warm apartment, looking in drawers and opening cupboards. Some of her and her sisters' clothes were still hanging in the wardrobes and folded in the drawers, along with loads of children's stuff, some of Leo's belongings, plenty of bedding in the airing cupboard, plus tinned food on the kitchen shelves.

Aideen made up a bed in a room that looked out

on the cathedral and imagined sleeping there, listening to the bells. She shivered with pleasure, already looking forward to it.

After unpacking, she made a cup of Horlicks and then decided to eat out, feeling almost dizzy with joy at the idea of dining in a New York restaurant; perhaps somewhere Italian with candles on the tables. *Pasta!* She was desperate for pasta.

When Aideen went outside, the rain had formed little pools on the sidewalk in which the streetlights were reflected like giant blinking eyes. People were pouring out of their offices. Tara had called Times Square a 'monument to Mammon' and now her sister blinked at its brilliance. She identified the twenty-ninth floor where Vanetti's New York offices were situated and where Patricia had worked. Before Aideen had left Bray, Leo had said she could have a job there if she wanted.

'Does your brother, Gianni, still work there?' she asked.

Leo nodded. 'Yes.'

'Then I don't think I'd be interested in a job, but thank you for the offer,' she said politely.

'I understand,' he'd said. Leo was the kindest brother-in-law in the world.

Gianni Vanetti had played no further part in their lives after making Patricia pregnant. Aideen could understand Leo not wanting him anywhere near his wife and the son that most people assumed was his.

She passed through Times Square and came to 42nd Street, the street of song, where the theatres were situated. She must go and see a show at the very first opportunity – a musical.

There was a huge display on one theatre advertising something called *Hullabaloo* starring Marty Moore that she quite fancied.

She carried further on until she neared Berry's, where she'd spent so many happy years. She smiled, recalling that in fact they'd been rather boring years and she'd thought so at the time. She'd spent her years in Berry's wanting to leave for a more interesting job.

She pushed her way through the main entrance – the store had always been busy – and there was a doorman she'd never seen before, quite old, easily in his sixties. A salesman was selling umbrellas on a temporary stall just inside the door, which usually appeared when it was raining. She glimpsed a face she recognised on the glove counter. The woman saw her and waved frantically. Aideen waved back.

Downstairs, in the sports department, where for some reason she went first, a remarkable thing had happened. There was a photo of a grinning Andy – about a foot square, pinned onto a sheet of red crêpe paper. Written underneath, it said: *In memory of our employee and friend, Andy Januk, who sadly died 14th November 1934, and will be missed by us all.*

Holy Mary, Mother of God! To her horror, Aideen discovered she was crying. She was bawling, in fact, because she had never been all that nice to Andy during the time they'd worked together, even though she'd been on his side rather than Berry's. And she hadn't known his name was Januk, and was genuinely sorry he was dead.

'Aideen!' Someone grabbed her arm – it was Gertie. 'Aideen, you bitch, I bet you wouldn't cry like that if it was me who was dead.'

'Would you?' Gertie's voice persisted minutes later when they were seated in a decently furnished office – not one of the shabby rooms where the staff had gone for their coffee breaks, but much superior. She'd been dragged through a couple of sets of swing doors and in and out of a lift to get there.

'If you died, I wouldn't cry at all,' Aideen conceded, knowing it would make Gertie laugh.

At some point after she had left, a miracle had occurred and Gertie had started to behave responsibly. She'd been promoted more than once and was now a buyer. She was wearing an incredibly smart black dress with a black and white polka dot collar. Their relationship had reached the stage where they could be hideously offensive to each other, mainly by letter, and treat it as a joke.

'You didn't like me, did you? Not towards the end, not before you married your lovely Humphrey.' Gertie managed to sniff disapprovingly and laugh at the same time. It produced a strange barking sound.

Aideen had stopped crying. 'Not a bit. I felt superior to all the women on earth when I married Humphrey.'

'Where is he? How is he since he lost his eye? You never tell me anything in your letters.' She produced a pack of Strand cigarettes, shook one out and sort of threw it in her mouth. She smoked it like a train in separate puffs.

'He's gone to climb Everest,' Aideen informed her.

'Jaysus, Mary and Joseph, to borrow one of your favourite curses.' She hadn't known about Humphrey's attachment to Everest. 'What's all that about?'

'It's how we met,' Aideen said fondly, 'in Sports Equipment. Andy was ill, but he let me go to lunch with Humph while he looked after the next customers.' She blinked, wanting to cry again.

Gertie leapt to her feet. 'Shall *we* go to lunch, calm you down? Somewhere classier than Dinah's Diner where we went the first time.'

'That'd be great, except it's time for tea – or dinner.'

'Then we'll go to tea or dinner, push the boat out – say the Plaza? My treat. Have you ever been there?'

'It's where we went after our Patricia got married, but I haven't been since.'

'Then we'll go now, but not before I show you some of the clothes I've ordered for our spring collection. D'you fancy a new coat or suit?' She winked suggestively. 'I have samples. The catch is you have to sleep with every member of the board of directors before I'm permitted to give you one – though it'll have to be let out to accommodate your big ass.'

'I agree,' Aideen said, hand on heart.

'I have a couple of Chanel suits.'

'I'll sleep with them twice.'

In fact, Aideen had lost pounds in weight and the skirt of the Chanel suit had fitted perfectly when she tried it on. Now the suit was in a carrier bag in the cloakroom of the Plaza, where she and

264

Gertie were having dinner – a rather belated Thanksgiving Day dinner of turkey, roast potatoes and all the other bits and pieces, because Aideen couldn't be bothered making it back in Bray at the time. She had never enjoyed a meal so much and couldn't help but have the feeling she'd just got out of prison.

'Oh, dear,' Gertie said when Aideen described the feeling.

'And there's something else...' Aideen paused.

'What's that, Aid?' Gertie was about to pour gravy over her meal and also paused.

'I've got the most awful feeling I'll never see Humphrey again.' Gertie, who was as hard as nails, looked as if she was about to cry. 'Jaysus, Aideen. What makes you say that?'

'It's been that way ever since he was beaten up, when he lost his eye. He only seems to remember me when we're together. If I disappear, or he goes away, even if it's only for a little while, he forgets he has a wife. The police have brought him home a couple of times. I regularly have to go and look for him. I bought a St Christopher medal for him to wear when he's away and it has his name and address engraved on it, and of course he'll be carrying a passport.' She swallowed painfully, wanting to cry again. 'I thought long and painfully about leaving Bray, about not being around if he gets lost and is brought back and I'm not there, but I left our Patricia's telephone number in the house, and told our neighbours and the local police. I've told them where I'll be living in New York, and where our Patricia lives in San Diego. I mean, they'd be bound to find me, track me down, don't you think?' She looked worriedly at her friend.

'Jeez, Aid, I reckon so.' Gertie leant across the table and squeezed her hand.

'Have I spoiled the atmosphere?'

'Yes, but then you always did. But I know a way of mending it.' Gertie signalled a waiter and ordered a bottle of champagne.

Lord, I look so much older than you, Aideen wanted to say, but it would only spoil the atmosphere further, despite the champagne. She recalled how alike they'd been when they'd first met almost ten years ago at sixteen, but now she looked considerably more than ten years older, whereas Gertie had merely become sophisticated. With Aideen, it wasn't so much wrinkles as a worn-down look, an expression of sadness, perhaps too much sun making her hair look like straw. It was already too short and badly cut, whereas Gertie's was richly red, long and in a healthily plump French roll.

'Does Berry's still have a hairdresser's?' she asked.

'Berry's will always have a hairdresser's,' Gertie replied. 'And it's still on the fifth floor. I'll book you an appointment for ten o'clock tomorrow morning. A trim, a henna rinse and a set. We'll soon have you looking human again.'

Now Aideen was back in the apartment, which was full of memories – sad ones and happy ones. She longed to call someone and tell them about her day, about the Chanel suit and the scrumptious meal. She'd drunk too much champagne to know what time it was in San Diego, where Patricia lived, and if she might have already gone to bed. In London, Tara didn't have a telephone; least she'd never given anyone a number. She had no idea where Humphrey was apart from on his way to Everest. And even if it should cross his mind to contact his wife, he didn't know she was in New York. She longed, literally yearned, for someone to talk to. And as if this was a magical night when wishes came true, the front door of the apartment suddenly opened and someone came in.

It might be a miracle, but Aideen was still a bit worried. 'Who is it?' she called, aware of the tremor in her voice.

A man opened the door but didn't enter the room. He remained in the hall, holding the door handle. He was slim, dark-haired, in his late forties and obviously nervous.

'I'm Gianni Vanetti,' he said. 'Leo's brother. You must be one of Patricia's sisters.' His mouth twitched into an unwilling smile. 'We meet at last.'

'Leo's not very sociable,' Gianni Vanetti said minutes later, when he was sitting down – which he had done of his own accord without being invited. 'But I've never been able to understand why we have lived on opposite sides of the country all this time. Even the occasions when we've all been in the same place, we have never met for some reason.' He frowned. 'Do you know?'

Aideen understood he was being deadly serious. He was hurt that he'd been excluded

267

from his brother's family without knowing the reason why. She shook her head and mumbled 'no', then coughed and repeated 'no' in a clearer voice. This was the man who had raped her sister and had fathered Milo. Yet he seemed unaware of it. Had he done it in his sleep? Or had he been drunk at the time or in a trance?

She found her voice. 'Do you live here?' she asked. Surely not. It was Leo who had suggested she stay in the apartment.

'No, but there are files here; hidden. We have some pretty oddball employees in the office, so Leo moved the important stuff here – plans of new models, that sort of thing. He gave me a key when he moved out. I've never used it before. The papers are in one of the wardrobes. We have this woman, Miss Goldburg. She can speak about a hundred languages and I'm convinced she's a spy.' He gave her another reluctant smile. 'It would appear that other companies are interested in getting their hands on our future designs.'

Aideen smiled weakly back. 'Oh, dear,' she murmured, not very convincingly.

'Which sister are you?' he asked. 'The middle one or the youngest?'

'I'm Aideen, the middle one. Tara is the youngest. She's living in London at the moment. We miss her awfully.'

'Doesn't she miss you?'

'Apparently not. She's always been the most independent of us.'

'So you're married and Tara is single?'

He must have been keeping a check on them. 'That's right,' she agreed.

'Is your husband here with you?' He sort of nodded towards the rest of the apartment as if Humphrey might be present.

Aideen contemplated saying that he was, in case Gianni Vanetti pounced upon her if she said he wasn't there, but it might prove awfully embarrassing if he asked to meet him. It already seemed a bit odd that, if her husband was there, he hadn't come to see who was calling at this time of night.

'He's travelling in Europe,' she said. She had no idea which continent Everest was in. 'It's business. Cigarettes. Strand,' she gulped.

'You must feel lonely here,' he remarked.

'I know plenty of people in New York. I used to work in Berry's and tonight I've been out with an old friend from there. And my in-laws live in Brooklyn – I'll be meeting them soon.' And Gertie was going to arrange lunch with a group of women from Berry's she'd been friendly with.

'Would you let me take you to dinner one night?'

Would she? She neither liked nor disliked him, but was intrigued by how such a seemingly mild-mannered man could have brought himself to rape her sister.

She spent the next day buying underclothes, having thrown away her old stuff when she left Bray. It really was *old*, having been bought in Berry's when she'd worked there. She'd never felt like renewing it because Humphrey didn't even look at her any more. Their sex life was nothing like it had been in Atlantic City. Only on the last

269

night, before they were due to separate for an unknown length of time, had there been any passion.

Today she bought prettier garments, embroidered and trimmed with lace, despite the fact that when Humphrey came back – *if* he came back – there was no reason to expect he would start looking at her in her underwear again. There might *never* be a reason to look pretty again for the rest of her life.

She was wearing a new bra, pants and petticoat set when she met Gianni Vanetti for dinner the following night, even though there wasn't a chance in hell of *him* seeing them. She was also wearing the new Chanel suit, which was a flattering blue and an equally flattering figure-hugging shape. Her hair had been hennaed a lovely cheery red and was virtually the same colour as Gertie's.

'You know, I must have met your sister – Patricia,' he said when they were seated in a very smart silver and black restaurant. 'I remembered today that she worked in the office but left suddenly. I wonder if I was rude to her, but can't even remember what she looks like.'

'Patricia never mentioned why she left,' Aideen lied.

'Then I can't have had much of an effect on her,' he mused.

Oh, if only he knew! The effect was eight years old and called Milo, who lived happily in Gianni's brother's house in San Diego.

He continued to reminisce. 'My secretary at the time told me I was a bit of a mess in those days.'

'In what way?' she enquired. He wore a wedding ring but hadn't mentioned a wife.

He made a face, sighed, shrugged and spread his hands, palms upwards in a typical Italian way. 'I drank too much, swore too much, was unfaithful to my wife, Katerina, and ignored my one and only child, my daughter Audrey. In the end, my wife threw me out and refused to let me see Audrey.' He went through the same dramatic procedure again. 'And, for all I know, I may have alienated my brother's wife. I would appear,' he said disconsolately, 'to be a complete failure as a human being.'

'Not as far as I'm concerned,' Aideen said comfortingly. Well, not yet, she thought.

Her in-laws took her to see *Hullabaloo*, the show Aideen had noticed when passing 42nd Street the other day. It turned out to be a happy, riotous performance, full of tunes that she would never forget. The leading man, Marty Moore, was a star made in heaven; he had an appealing singing voice and was a brilliant dancer. Aideen could have sworn she'd seen him somewhere before.

'I could watch that again every day for the rest of me life,' she sighed happily afterwards when they were strolling along 42nd Street looking for a place to have a drink. She stopped suddenly and clapped her hands. 'Marty Moore,' she gasped. 'I was sure his face was familiar. His real name is Marty Benedek and he went out with our Patricia when we first came to New York. Oh, I must write and tell her. She'll be thrilled to bits.'

'You should take it up yourself, the stage,' Mary

271

said. She cast an admiring glance at her daughter-in-law. 'She'd make a perfect showgirl, wouldn't she, Theo, with that gorgeous red hair.'

'Perfect,' Theo grunted. He was much nicer now than he'd used to be, but still didn't have the sunniest of natures.

'I always wanted dancing lessons when I was a girl,' Mary went on, 'but my mother wouldn't hear of it. All she wanted was for me to get married and give her some grandchildren. Me, I would love a daughter-in-law who danced professionally – she could get us tickets for the latest shows.' She nudged Aideen. 'It would be good for your health and your stature.'

'Leave the girl alone,' her husband growled.

'No, it's a good idea.' Aideen was always on Mary's side when her in-laws had an argument. She was too old to become a chorus girl, but she wouldn't mind training for a career of some sort.

She was still thinking about Mary's words when she arrived home and came down to earth with a bump when, from behind the desk in the reception area, Jerry called, 'Your pop's upstairs, Aideen. He arrived a couple hours ago. It's a good job I recognised him – he didn't have a key.'

'What!' It was the last thing Aideen expected to hear and wasn't the least bit welcome.

'There you are!' Daddy said when she burst into the apartment. He looked uncomfortable, as if he hadn't expected her to be there, though Jerry would have mentioned she was staying. And he must have stayed there before otherwise Jerry wouldn't have recognised him.

'Does Leo know you're using his apartment?' Aideen demanded. Leo and Daddy had only met the once.

'Well, no, but he invited me to stay here next time I was in New York.'

It was just the sort of thing big-hearted Leo would have said. And Daddy was the sort of person who wouldn't hesitate to take him up on it if it suited his purposes and even if it meant not letting him know. She presumed he didn't have the cash for a hotel if the state he was in was anything to go by. His shabby tweed overcoat looked as if it came from a thrift shop and his shoes were scuffed and down-at-heel. He was definitely down on his luck.

'What have you been up to?' she asked.

'Just got meself in a bit of a hole,' he muttered.

'And how do you intend getting out of it?'

'Dunno.' His shoulders slumped.

'Can I help?'

'Only if you can lend us a couple of thousand dollars.'

Aideen yelped. 'Of course not.'

'How about ten?'

'Ten dollars? I can let you have that.'

'Thanks, darlin'. It means I can have something to eat at last.'

'Oh, Daddy!' She grabbed his shoulders and gave him an affectionate shake. 'Shall we go out now and have a pizza?'

He managed a thin smile. 'I can't stand pizzas, but I'm so hungry I could eat two.'

'There's no need for that, Daddy; we can buy something else.'

'What have you done?' she asked when they were in the Indian restaurant across the road and he was attempting to eat his curried prawns and rice politely, even though she could tell he wanted to throw the meal down his throat. He looked reluctantly at his plate when he'd finished as if he would love to have licked it.

It was only then that he answered his daughter's question. 'Got in with a couple of guys who turned out to be crooks,' he complained in an injured tone, as if he'd never come across a crook before and hadn't noticed he was one himself. 'I thought I was buying a share in a racehorse but it turned out to have died last year.'

'Poor Daddy.' She squeezed his hand, only half sorry for him. It served him right. This was the man who'd stolen the entire fortune of the Earl of somewhere or other back in Ireland. 'Would you like a pudding?'

'These Indian places don't serve proper puddings,' he pouted.

'Shall we go somewhere else and have pancakes?'

'Please, darlin'. Till tonight, I hadn't eaten in days.'

Next morning she woke up early. The clanging of the cathedral bells was making the furniture buzz. Her father was asleep, snoring his head off in the adjacent room. Knowing him, once he was awake, he would expect her to fetch him tea in bed, then make his breakfast. Looking back, she couldn't remember him lifting a finger when

274

they'd lived in Dublin.

Her rather nice, lazy, peaceful and so far very enjoyable stay in New York had ended. Last night, Daddy had claimed to have no idea when he planned to leave – that was after he'd asked where Leo kept the wine.

'In the wine cellar in San Diego,' she'd told him.

She buried her face in the pillow and gave in to an unexpected fit of giggles. After a while she slid out of bed, got dressed in perfect silence, then went out and bought half a dozen eggs for breakfast. She'd make him pancakes. Back in Dublin, he used to claim Pancake Tuesday was his favourite day of the year.

Chapter 17

'This,' Tara said, stroking the skirt of the blue velvet, knee-length dress she was wearing, 'I first wore at a poetry reading I went to in SoHo with Christopher.'

'Soho in London?' queried Pamela.

'No, dear,' Tara said patiently. The girl had already been told the history of the blue dress but loved hearing it again. 'The one in New York. It stands for South of Houston Street. It had a hat to match, but I can't find it.'

'What a pity,' slurred Jean Shawcross-Brown, waving her glass that was never empty. She must spend a good part of the rent from the property on gin. 'Did you leave many of your clothes in New York?'

'No, the ones I have left are in San Diego at my sister's house. Patricia will look after them for me.' Though by the time she and her clothes were reunited, they could well be out of fashion.

'Is Patricia the sister with the swimming pool and eight children?' Pamela asked.

'That's right.' Sometimes Tara felt like a very old lady who was telling tales of her younger life to her grandchildren. The three women were in Tara's room, where they often gathered, and Pamela was literally sitting at Tara's feet while Jean lounged on the bed nursing her gin.

'How is your other sister getting on, the one who used to live in Atlantic City and moved to California?' she asked.

'Aideen? Oh, she's no longer in California. I had a letter from her only the other day. Her husband is on his way to Nepal to have another go at climbing Everest – or at least as high as he can reach – and she's back in New York. She'd only been there a couple of days.'

Jean fanned herself with her hand as if she was about to faint. '*Everest,*' she gasped. 'Christ Almighty, Tara, your life is like a book, not to mention that fantastic job you have.'

'It didn't feel like a book while I was living it,' Tara said. Though it had been interesting.

'What's the name of that paper you write for?'

'The *Worldwide Voice*. I have a regular column.' Tara preferred not to talk about her column.

Looking back, it all seemed quite fascinating, the way her life had turned out. She was immensely lucky to have known Christopher and Edwin, and get such an interesting job working for the FBI. And not many people could admit to having an outrageous crook for a father – not that she was going to tell Jean and Pamela that or about the FBI. But one thing had led to another and who knew what the future might hold?

And now things were fascinating in a completely different way. She was going out with Hugh Furnival, an extremely nice young man who appeared to expect nothing of her apart from her company and a polite kiss at the end of the evening. They sometimes went to the British Society of Fascists together or Tara might well go on her own when they were held in daylight with the police present. When she arrived home, she would write to Mr Hamilton in America with anything noteworthy that had been said, such as the loudly expressed, loudly supported craving of the members for Great Britain to become a Fascist state. Nobody seemed to have any idea how this could be achieved. None of the members had yet called for violence, which was dangerous with so many police around.

The task she had of writing the 'Voice of London' had suddenly become totally enthralling. She had discovered that no one seemed to mind if she slipped in comments about Adolf Hitler, who was stirring things up in Germany, or if she mentioned the death of Anna Pavlova, the ballerina who Tara had once very nearly met, her being an acquaintance of Christopher. She also wrote about the hunger marches in Britain held by the National Unemployed Workers Movement, their latest march ending in violence in Hyde Park, where the police were there to meet them and far more willing to knock the heads together of people who wanted nothing but food than they were the Fascists. She also mentioned books such as *I, Claudius* by Robert Graves and the movie *King Kong,* which had terrified her.

This activity proved a success because, in America, people began to write to the paper arguing with or supporting her views and the letters were sent to her in England suggesting that she respond. Prior to that, Tara had wondered if her contributions had merely been thrown in the wastepaper bin, the job merely being a sop thought up to keep her happy. Now she took great pleasure in writing back to her readers in America.

It was approaching Christmas when, one Sunday, she and Hugh went to a BUF meeting held in Trafalgar Square. The occasion was special in that it was to be addressed by Sir Oswald Mosley, founder of the Fascist party in Britain.

It was a cold, bright day. Tara and Hugh stamped their feet and blew on their hands while they waited for the leader to arrive. The men who usually attended with him were already there: stern, hard-faced, dressed in black, though the pair who were seated behind a trestle table with a place in the centre for Sir Oswald Mosley to sit or stand were of a different type. Elegantly dressed in boots and full-length overcoats made of leather that shone like silk, they were of a different class, their features more refined than the bodyguards who stood, arms folded, legs apart, keeping the crowd well at bay from their master.

Tara was struck by one of the men at the table wearing a leather overcoat. He was infinitely more handsome than the other, with white-blond hair and penetrating blue eyes. She was convinced she had seen him before.

Sir Oswald Mosely arrived to a chorus of cheers and boos in equal measure, but Tara was too immersed in trying to remember where she'd seen the leather-coated man to concentrate on what was more or less the same thing that was said at most meetings, the tone always getting more and more strident as time progressed.

'I know where I've seen him!' she gasped. Not in person, but in photographs, loads of photographs, some of which had been featured in the 'Voice of London' over the few short months she'd been producing it. He was a minor prince, a member of the British Royal Family, though not close to the throne. He was also very much a man about town, seen regularly at nightclubs, theatres and virtually every fashionable event that occurred in London. His name was Prince Arthur.

'What did you say, Tara?' Hugh turned to her.

'Nothing,' she murmured.

She very much enjoyed writing the Christmas edition of the 'Voice of London' the following week. Most of the news she published was mundane, the same people attending various social events with slightly different people who she had mentioned before, going to places with other people. It was, she thought, numbingly boring, like a game of musical chairs, except no one ever got left out.

But then she finished with:

Sunday was a special day for the deliciously handsome Prince Arthur, who attended a meeting of the British Fascist Party in Trafalgar Square – this is the party whose ambition is to turn Great Britain into a Fascist state. He was to be seen seated next to the Fascist leader, the saintly Sir Oswald Mosley, who entertained the crowd with cheery speeches, winding up with the song, 'It Don't Mean a Thing if It Ain't Got That Swing'.

Tara rubbed her hands together. It was brilliant. Christopher and Edwin would have thoroughly approved.

Christmas was unexpectedly enjoyable. She was invited to the *News of the World* staff party, while back in Madeira Street, Jean Shawcross-Brown held a party virtually every night. People brought their own food and the house was even more awash with gin. Hugh took her to dinner in Soho, which was seeped in crime when compared with the SoHo in Manhattan, which comprised nothing but innocent market stalls – if Tara remembered rightly.

'Sorry, but at home it's nothing but family over Christmas,' Hugh said, explaining the reason for not inviting her to meet his family. 'It's not that strangers aren't made welcome, but they're inclined to feel a bit out of things.'

'I really don't mind,' Tara said gaily. It meant Hugh didn't have any romantic intentions towards her and, as she didn't have any for him, nothing was left between them but friendship.

She'd been inundated with cards and presents from home over the last few weeks. Even Chang Li had remembered to send her a card – initially to the apartment in Fifth Avenue, which was then forwarded on by Aideen. She felt ashamed she hadn't thought to send one to him too.

Christmas was well over. Two hours ago, the advent of the New Year, 1935, had been celebrated, and by now Tara was fast asleep in bed when there was a crash that instantly woke her. It turned out to be a brick that had been thrown through her window.

'It was a drunk,' she told herself. 'It can't possibly have been deliberate.'

Except it was.

The only way of anyone contacting Tara by phone was telephoning the *News of the World* on the days she worked in their office, which happened to be two days after the incident with the brick.

'Tara, I think you'd better come back home,' said Mr Hamilton of the FBI rather abruptly. He didn't announce who he was, but she recognised his voice.

'Why?' Tara asked, startled. She had hardly been at her desk five minutes.

'Because, dear girl, you are in trouble. You have upset a member of the monarchy over there. This Prince Arthur guy didn't want it known he was a friend of Sir Oswald Moseley, plus the sainted knight didn't want anyone making silly jokes about him. There are people over there who are

281

out to get you. We have had numerous messages in that vein over the last few days. The last one threatened to kill you. Apparently you've annoyed, to put it mildly, a lot of folk on your side of the Atlantic.' He sneezed and apologised for having a cold. 'All over Christmas too,' he complained.

'I'm sorry,' Tara felt obliged to say. Someone had threatened to kill her! What had happened to free speech?

'What shall I do?' Was she to be driven out of the country?

'I've just told you. We'd like you to get out of England *tout de suite* before these bastards find out where you live.'

'Someone threw a brick through my window the other night,' she told him. 'It might not have been an accident. But how would they have known where I lived – even the exact room?'

'Ask your friend Hugh Furnival about that. On second thoughts, don't. We've just found out he's a long-term member of the BUF and has been leading you on for weeks. I think you might be in danger of receiving something more dangerous than a brick,' he said drily. 'In fact, don't go home again, but make your way to a hotel. Buy some nightclothes and go to the Ritz; I'll ring them now and book you a room. We have someone in Paris who'll get to you today or tomorrow to put you on a boat home.'

What was more dangerous than a brick, she wondered after Mr Hamilton had rung off. Well, a bullet, she supposed, or a bomb. Tara was shocked to discover that nice Hugh Furnival had been a Fascist all along. She was clearly much too naive for this type of work. Nevertheless, she grinned, proud that she had managed to invoke the ire of both the British royal family as well as a group of silly Fascists.

She didn't go straight to a hotel; there were things in the house in Camden, such as jewellery, that she had no intention of leaving behind, plus she needed a warmer coat.

Jean Shawcross-Brown came knocking on her door as soon as she realised it was Tara who had entered the house. She walked into her room without waiting for a response.

'Hello, darling.' She waved her glass. 'You're home early.'

'I have to go away for a while,' Tara lied. She didn't want the woman knowing she was going for good. She opened her wardrobe and surveyed the expensive clothes. What should she wear on the voyage to New York? She removed a heavy purple boucle coat with a quilted lining and changed it for the plain navy blue coat that she was wearing, lifted out a couple of light frocks that wouldn't take up much room, as the only suitcase she had wasn't all that big – she wasn't willing to cope with the wardrobe-sized trunk she'd brought with her. She took out her jewellery which was only of sentimental value; she far preferred glass to diamonds.

Impulsively she picked out the blue velvet frock she'd worn when Christopher had taken her to the poetry reading in SoHo. 'Give this to Pamela,' she said. 'And is there anything you fancy?'

Jean snorted. 'Me, I fancy the lot.' She eyed the clothes critically. 'I adore that tan suit you wore

283

on the first day you were here,' she said. 'If I lose a few pounds on my hips, I'm sure it will fit.'

Tara handed it to her. One of these days she'd write and say she could have all the clothes; sell them, if she liked. They'd cost quite a lot of money.

She fastened the suitcase. 'I'll be off,' she said.

'You're going for good, aren't you, Tara? I can just tell.' The woman looked close to tears. 'We'll really miss you, Pamela and I.'

'And I'll miss you.' Tara swallowed hard. She felt she could easily cry herself.

Jean Shawcross-Brown kissed her for the first and last time. 'Oh, and something came for you this morning,' she said. 'Looks like a card. It's on the table in the hall.'

Tara picked up the envelope on her way out. It had an American stamp and had been posted in New York. The handwriting belonged to her sister, Aideen.

'Goodbye, Jean,' she said.

'Goodbye, darling. Look after yourself, won't you? You must let me know your new address and I'll send on the rest of your clothes.'

'Thank you,' Tara said with a sigh.

Chapter 18

I shall never sleep tonight, Tara had thought when she'd climbed into bed several hours ago, and she'd been right.

Her head was throbbing and she had tossed

284

and turned ever since, not sleeping a wink, wondering what had possessed her to be so flippant when she'd written the Christmas edition of the 'Voice of London'?

A prince and the leader of a political party were not to be offended and made fun of. She'd been a fool. Not that she intended to apologise. She'd meant every word. Prince Arthur deserved to be exposed and Sir Oswald Moseley deserved to be made fun of. She couldn't help but smile to herself. In fact, she was glad she had done it; Christopher and Edwin would have approved.

She sat up and switched on the bedside light. Her room in the Ritz was disgustingly luxurious: brocade curtains, thick carpet, lots of gold. She wondered how much a night it was costing Mr Hamilton? Enough to keep a small family for months, a year even, she supposed. She wished he'd booked her into somewhere more ordinary.

There was a card on the table beside the light saying that room service was available twenty-four hours a day. Her indignation that some poor people in the kitchen were probably being paid peanuts for working the whole night through was overcome by her longing for a pot of tea. She picked up the phone and ordered it, along with a turkey sandwich.

After finishing both while sitting on the bed surrounded by pillows, she remembered the card from Aideen she'd picked up when leaving Madeira Road. She fetched it out of her handbag and returned to the comfort of the bed. Three months ago Aideen had moved back to New York while Humphrey had gone to have another go at

Everest. Then Daddy had turned up in some sort of trouble – when was Daddy not in trouble! Anyway, he'd been there ever since.

It was a New Year's card with a long message inside.

Dear Tara,

I have two items of news for you. Firstly, Daddy made a telephone call yesterday – there's an old friend in Dublin he rings from time to time who brings him up to date with the latest news. This time the news was bad – Auntie Kathleen is dead. She died six weeks ago and our Milo has disappeared. Gosh, I do feel horrible for not writing to him more often. It's ages since I last sent a letter. How about you? Over the last few years, we seem to have forgotten we had a little brother. (That smudge is a tear that has just fallen on the card.)

Daddy is going to Ireland to look for him as soon as he feels up to the journey – he's had a really wretched cold for a week.

I hope you are happy in London and have a wonderful 1935.
Your loving sister,
Aideen.
PS. And the second thing – I'm pregnant!

Tara put the letter on the bedside table and slid down the bed. She went asleep almost immediately, having made up her mind that tomorrow, rather than return to New York, she would go to Dublin and look for her brother. America could wait.

Next morning she was having breakfast when a

286

waiter approached.

'Madam,' he said with exquisite politeness, 'a gentleman has asked if he may join you for breakfast. That is him standing by the door.'

Tara remembered Mr Hamilton saying someone was coming from Paris to put her on the boat to New York – not that she wasn't capable of putting herself on a boat, but she fancied being looked after, particularly since the brick had come through her window.

'Tell him to come over,' she told the waiter.

She looked towards the door and saw Agent Pete Green approaching. He looked as astonished to see her as she was him.

'Where did you disappear to?' he demanded. 'That pair of old lefties died and I was suddenly drafted to Seattle, but when I tried to get in touch, you'd vanished.' He had the nerve to bang the table with his fist when he sat down.

'You took your time,' Tara said accusingly. 'I went to live in San Diego with my sister, but that was weeks after Christopher and Edwin died. And how dare you refer to them as "old lefties"?'

'Because that's what they were,' he hissed.

'Is that a crime in America?'

'Of course not, but they didn't have to be so *open* about it.' He let out a breath that sounded like a collapsing balloon. 'Anyway, what are you doing in London?'

Tara smirked. 'Working for the FBI.'

His jaw dropped. 'Honest?'

'Honest.' She nodded. 'But my service has come to an end.'

'So it's *you* I'm expected to take to Southampton! I thought it would be a man. They didn't tell me your name.'

Tara nodded. 'They didn't tell me your name, either.' He was the last person she'd expected to see.

'Gee!' He shook his head in amazement. 'Anyway, there's a ship leaving for the States a week on Friday: the *Queen Maia*. I'll reserve berths on that.' He grinned slyly. 'Shall I book a cabin for two?'

The *Queen Maia* was the boat that had taken them to New York almost exactly ten years ago; the one on which Daddy had pretended to throw himself off. She remembered how devastated she and her sisters had been. Now she was about to take Agent Pete Green down a peg or two.

'I'm not going to the States; I'm going to Ireland,' she told him.

His eyes bulged. 'You can't.'

'Are you going to try and stop me?' she asked lightly.

He looked confused as he tried to think of a way of stopping her. 'I don't suppose I can,' he concluded sadly. 'Can I have a cup of coffee?'

'Why not have breakfast?' The table was laid for two. She beckoned the waiter who sprang forward and brought a fresh cup, promising to refill it and bring another breakfast.

'When are you going to Ireland?' Agent Green asked. There was a hopeful glint in his bright blue eyes that they might have a few days in London together.

Tara contemplated this, but rejected the idea almost immediately. 'There's a train from Euston

Station to Liverpool at ten past eleven this morning, and from there I shall sail on the overnight ferry to Dublin.'

He sighed and clearly couldn't be bothered arguing. 'I'll come with you to Liverpool,' he said tiredly, 'and put you on the Irish boat.'

Despite assuring him there was no need, he insisted on coming, and as she didn't see it would do any harm, she let him. They didn't talk much on the journey and merely shook hands when they parted and she boarded the ferry. She had booked a cabin but was unable to sleep much, this time due to the choppy sea. She was glad to have met Pete Green again, relieved to discover she was no longer enamoured with him – well, only a tiny bit – but she wanted the first man she was to sleep with to be someone else. He wasn't nearly as good-looking as she remembered, and she'd found him rather irritating this time round, as well as just a little bit thick.

She stood staring at the empty house where Auntie Kathleen and Milo had gone to live when the rest of the family had left for America. The windows were dirty and the tiny front garden had clearly been neglected for years. The buildings were tightly crammed together in a narrow street. Tara approached the front door and looked through the letterbox. Inside, the house looked dilapidated. It had never crossed any of the sisters' minds to take a look at where their ten-year-old brother was being sent to live while his father got out of the way of the police. She felt ashamed for not caring and really angry with Daddy.

'What d'you think you're doing?' snapped a voice. The woman from the next house had come out to investigate. Her hair was in curlers and covered with a thick pink net. She had her arms folded aggressively and her rawboned face was screwed into a frown.

Tara was rarely tempted to be rude to people, but she wasn't in the mood to be harangued by someone as unpleasant as this woman for merely looking at a house that may, or may not, belong to her father.

'I'm minding my own business,' she said icily, 'and I suggest you do the same.'

Instead of taking offence at these words, the woman suddenly became quite friendly. 'Kathleen Noonan used to live there,' she offered, 'but she died, poor woman, last October. I understand it was a heart attack.'

'What happened to her nephew, Milo?'

'Oh, *him*.' The words were almost spat out. 'He made poor Kath's life a misery. Never still a minute and too noisy by a mile. He was thrown out of school for smoking, and I think there was a bit of drinking involved too, as well as something to do with a girl – or was it girls?'

'Do you know where he is now?' Tara asked, not at all put off by the description of Milo. She genuinely hoped he hadn't made Auntie Kathleen's life a misery, but apart from that, Milo sounded like someone after her own heart.

The woman shrugged. 'No one knows. I mean, there's no one round here that would take the little devil in, like. But he has been seen singin' and dancin' on the streets of Dublin.'

'Singing?' Tara gasped. 'And dancing?'

'Both,' the woman confirmed with a forceful nod that could have easily snapped off her scrawny head. 'And playing some sort of instrument.' She looked Tara up and down, as if only now aware of her costly purple boucle coat and fine leather boots.

'And who are you when you're at home?' she enquired. Her tone had returned to being un-pleasant.

'Me?' Tara said lightly. 'I'm the little devil's big sister.'

Street performers, they were called – buskers – people who sang and danced in the streets of New York. Some played musical instruments or did acrobatics. She'd seen a couple in London's West End, too, usually outside theatres and in places such as Trafalgar Square and Piccadilly Circus.

Tara returned to the centre of Dublin but didn't see a single soul singing or dancing on the streets, or outside the famous theatres – Smock Alley, the Abbey or the Gate – or French's, where sometimes she, her sisters and their friends used to go for coffee.

The buildings she'd once been so familiar with now seemed strange and shrunken, not nearly as grand as they'd used to be. She arrived at Con-nolly Station, where the taxi from the ferry had dropped her off. She'd booked into a nearby hotel, which she had, somewhat recklessly, vowed to never leave until she'd found Milo.

Three days later and there was still no sign. There

291

were plenty of entertainers but none of them were Milo who, by now, would be eighteen. She found an institution somewhat similar to St Benedict's in Central Park, where she had been a volunteer during the worst of the Depression, but the nuns who ran the place neither knew or had heard of him. An elderly man with a filthy moustache, who was playing the hornpipe outside the Gate Theatre, asked, 'Does he play the ukulele, darlin'?'

'I don't know,' said Tara. She wasn't used to failure. So far in her life she had been blessed with success. The things that had gone wrong, such as the death of her old friends, her father's criminal past – or present, for all she knew – had been things over which she had no control. It was a job not to let her shoulders become more and more hunched as she walked the streets of Dublin for yet another day.

Out of interest, she walked as far as their old house on the far side of Phoenix Park. It made her angry that her family had been torn apart for no other reason than to save Bernie Kelly's yellow skin.

Each night she was going to bed earlier yet sleeping less and less. At the end of the fourth day, she bought tea in a cardboard cup and took it back to her hotel room. It was a clean hotel, respectable, but nothing like as luxurious as the Ritz – not surprising as it cost a fraction of the price.

She was seated on the bed – it was early and she was still fully dressed – listening to the traffic that hardly stopped all night, when there was an infinitesimal pause and she heard what was possibly the sound of a banjo being played. She put on her shoes, raced downstairs and outside onto the pavement.

And there he was, eighteen years old and instantly recognisable, Milo, her brother, playing the banjo and singing: 'There was a wild colonial boy, Jack Duggan was his name. He was born and raised in Ireland, in...'

He was so lively, so full of joy and high spirits, so unbelievably handsome, that she would have fallen in love with him there and then had they not already been related. He wore trousers that were too big, kept up with a piece of rope, and a striped jersey that was too small. A cap sat back to front on his too-long black curly hair, and mischief shone out of his sparkling brown eyes.

She stood in front of him, about four feet away. He grinned at her and danced a few steps, before suddenly stopping, looking at her with wonder.

'Milo,' Tara whispered.

Despite the noise of the traffic, he seemed to hear. 'Tara. Can it possibly be you?'

She threw her arms around his neck. 'It's me, it's me,' she cried, and burst into tears. 'I've found you at last.'

She wanted to buy him decent clothes, but he claimed he already had some. The clothes he wore on the street were like a costume. The next day, when they met, he was in flannels, a checked shirt, an oatmeal-coloured sports jacket and casual shoes. She had booked him a room in her hotel and insisted he have his hair cut. He only agreed to having a little bit cut off.

'I like it long,' he said stubbornly.

'Where have you been living since Auntie Kathleen died?'

'Oh, here and there,' he replied, and then flatly refused to expand any further.

He wanted to know why he'd received so few letters from his sisters in America.

'Because we were so busy,' she told him. 'I mean, our Patricia has eight children and Aideen's husband was a teacher, but now he's a mountaineer. As for me, I was an artists' model and I've been a member of the FBI – though all of it turned out to be a lot more complicated than that.'

He was more impressed with the eight children than anything, though still complained he should have been sent more letters. 'Though I reckon it was up to me corrupt daddy to keep an eye on me and good old Auntie Kath.'

Agent Green had mentioned a boat was sailing from Southampton to New York on Friday the following week. Well, it was Wednesday the following week by now. Using the hotel's telephone, Tara booked adjacent cabins on the third deck of the *Queen Maia*. On the Thursday, she and Milo contrived to reach the city of Southampton by an assortment of different trains and buses.

She showed Milo the very spot from where their father had pretended to throw himself off the boat. His normally sunny face darkened whenever they spoke about Daddy.

'The police scoured Liverpool when it was discovered he was missing,' he said. 'There were rumours he'd been lost at sea, but it all died down after a while. I was never sure what to believe, whether he was alive or dead, until Aideen wrote and told me years later that he'd turned up. A cheque used to arrive monthly from some bank in Dublin, but it stopped after a while. I was still at school and poor Auntie Kath had to go to work even though her hands were twisted with rheumatism.'

Neither of them had the right clothes to attend the various dances held on the voyage – though these mainly took place in the first-class accommodation rather than third class, where they were, so they sat in a bar and sipped wine, played cards or attended quizzes, which Tara usually won. A score of young ladies gave Milo their addresses and he promised to write to every single one.

'Will you?' Tara asked.

'I shall do my best,' he said, winking. She had no idea what that meant.

She was looking forward to turning up at Leo's apartment on Fifth Avenue where Aideen and Daddy were staying. No one had been told she was coming home, or that she had found Milo.

The porter she knew well was hovering in the lobby; she thought his name was Jerry, but didn't like to use it in case she'd got it wrong.

'Good afternoon, young lady,' he said when Milo carried in their suitcases. He must have forgotten her name! 'Your sister's up there, and your pop.'

Tara pressed the button for the lift. Her stomach was twisted with pleasure at the thought of the wonderful surprise she was about to present to her sister and their father.

Aideen opened the door. She stepped back, hands on both cheeks when she saw first Tara and then her companion, who she recognised immediately.

'Milo,' she gasped. 'Oh, I just knew it was you.' She dragged her brother inside the apartment and into the room where their father sat smoking a cheroot and drinking beer out of a can.

'Daddy,' she cried. 'Look who's here!'

Daddy's face went red with delight. He put down the cheroot and the beer and half stood up, only to be met by Milo's fist landing directly on his nose with a really loud thump. The older man fell back in the chair, blood trickling out of his left nostril.

Milo rubbed his right hand, which must have hurt after landing such a tremendous blow. 'I'm glad he's still alive, the bastard,' he chortled, 'otherwise I wouldn't have had the opportunity to give him the punch he deserved. Oh, and can someone kindly make me a cup of tea and hand me one of them weird cigarettes our daddy is smoking? Or was.'

'What's happening next week on Saturday,' Aideen explained that night over steak and chips in a Seventh Avenue restaurant, 'is our Patricia and Leo are coming to stay in the apartment. You see,' she said earnestly, 'when I came back to New York a few months ago, my in-laws took me to see a show in a theatre on forty-second Street. It was called *Hullabaloo* and the star was Marty Moore, who only turned out to be Marty Benedek, who our Patricia went out with for a few months when we first came here. Do you remember him, Tara?'

'Of course I do,' Tara said. 'I had a bit of a crush on him myself.'

'Well, I got in touch with Marty and he's booked a box on Saturday for just our family. We're all going to dinner afterwards, Marty too, so you can both come as well. I'm sure we'd all fit in a box.'

'What about Daddy?' Tara asked. 'Will he be coming too?'

'He expects to.' Aideen turned to Milo. 'How do you feel about Daddy coming?'

Milo shrugged. 'I don't care whether he does or not. I feel quite satisfied with the punch I gave him. I won't do it again.'

'It will be the first time all the Kellys will have been together for more than ten years,' Tara remarked. 'And, Milo, did you know you have a namesake? Patricia's first baby was a boy and she called him Milo.'

'Yes, I do know,' Milo said sarcastically. 'She told me in one of the rare letters you sent after you'd gone away. I trust that Milo receives more attention than this one did.'

The following morning, Tara wrote and told Jean Shawcross-Brown to either sell the clothes that she had left behind or keep them. 'I don't mind what you do, but please make sure everything is shared with Pamela.' Since being in New York, she'd realised that her wardrobe was well out of date and she fancied a new frock to wear at the

297

dinner, a copy of something that had been modelled in Paris as late as the spring of last year.

She then telephoned Mr Hamilton in Washington and told him she was safely back in New York. 'Have you any more jobs for me?' she asked hopefully. She was, after all, currently unemployed and there wasn't all that much left in her bank account. 'I enjoyed spying on the Fascists.'

'We have nothing suitable for young ladies,' she was informed. 'But I'm sure the world is your oyster, Miss Kelly. Someone like you could become a major star of stage and screen, model outrageously expensive clothes, write for an important newspaper. You would be wasted working for the FBI.'

'There's no need to be sarcastic, Mr Hamilton.'

'I'm not being sarcastic, Miss Kelly – well, only a bit. There's truth in most of what I said.' He rang off with a chuckle.

It was only the next day that Tara discovered he was right.

She was perfectly happy to buy a dress off the rack in a chain store producing their own cheap versions of the very latest models by now. There was a small chain of shops she'd noticed years ago called Harper's, and the New York branch was on East 35th Street. Their windows – there were only two – were always tastefully dressed.

Realising that she no longer had the money to hail taxis all over the place, Tara walked to the store. There were only day clothes in the window. She went inside and sought out the evening frocks at the back.

An assistant approached and offered to help.

'I'm looking for something to wear for the theatre followed by dinner on Saturday,' Tara told her. 'Not too showy, and not black; I don't suit black.'

'I'm sure you'd suit any colour, madam,' the woman said respectfully. She was in her fifties and looked tired. 'Would you prefer full-length or calf-length?'

'Calf-length would make a change.' Tara plucked a pale green calf-length silk and velvet dress off the rack. It had a bolero to match, studded with diamonds. 'This is nice.'

'That is a copy of a Norman Hartnell model worn at last year's Paris shows,' she was told. 'The diamonds on the original frock were real.'

Tara tried on three frocks, eventually deciding to buy the green one. The price suited her pocket at the present time. She wrote a cheque and was surprised when the saleswoman returned almost immediately, still holding the cheque, accompanied by a younger woman.

'You're Tara Kelly, aren't you?' the younger woman enquired, and Tara agreed that she was.

'I often used to see you in magazines. Although you were always with some old chap – I think he was a poet or a painter, or something – but you looked so beautiful and everyone used to admire your clothes. I just wondered, if you are willing to accept this frock as a gift, will you please tell people you got it from Harper's? It would be wonderful publicity for us.'

'Yes, but,' Tara protested, 'there's no need to give me the frock for nothing. I can still pay for it.'

'It's the way it's done, Miss Kelly. If your pic-

299

ture gets in one of the papers, it would be mar-vellous. Oh, and do come back to Harper's whenever you want something new to wear.'

'I will,' agreed Tara, dazed. To do so would make her feel greedy. Next time she needed a frock she would get it from Berry's and pay for it herself.

Patricia and Leo arrived on Thursday, Leo armed with a new camera. He delighted in taking snaps of Bernie, who he secretly didn't like all that much and whose nose was still purple and swollen. He took several of Milo to show the other, smaller Milo back in San Diego.

That night, they all headed out to the theatre.

He was my first love, Patricia thought when Marty Moore, who she'd known as Marty Bene-dek, danced onto the stage and began to sing. She recalled when she'd first heard him – the Kelly sisters had only been in New York a few weeks and she was on her way to the Roscius Employment Agency. And now she was a married woman with eight children! She slid her hand into Leo's and he kissed her cheek.

'I love you,' he whispered.

'And I love you,' she whispered back, glad that she and Marty's relationship had come to an end, sweet though it had been.

As Marty Moore danced around the stage, Aideen thought about Humphrey, wondering how he was getting on and if she would ever see him again. He might never discover he had fathered a child – a child who had yet to be born. And the baby would grow up without having known his or her father. Oh, God; she badly wanted to cry. She pretended to blow her nose instead.

Tara felt serenely happy. Already quite a few people had admired her frock and she'd told them it came from Harper's. She wished Daddy had come with them to the theatre and to dinner, but he and Milo just weren't getting on. She felt convinced everything would turn out well in the end; things usually did.

The show over, they transferred to the Stardust restaurant just around the corner, where a table had been reserved. It was an enchanting place with a black ceiling full of blinking stars. The maître d' met them at the door.

'Can we really expect Mr Moore later?' he enquired reverentially.

'Absolutely,' Leo assured him. 'He was once my wife's boyfriend, you know,' he added boastfully.

There was a burst of applause when Marty entered the restaurant. He waved, twirled round a couple of times, apparently well used to the admiration of the crowd. He arrived at the table, hugged everyone extravagantly, even Leo and Milo, who he had never met before. He knelt in front of Patricia and sang one of his old songs, swearing he'd been madly in love with her ever since they'd first met. Close up, he was quite ordinary, but had managed, by the force of his personality, to make himself extraordinarily special.

He paused in front of Tara. 'Is this your little sister?' he gasped. 'You are the most beautiful woman I have ever met. I'm already passionately in love with you.'

'You were passionately in love with me once,' Patricia reminded him. 'But it didn't last long.'

'Ah, but this time it will last for ever.' He kissed Tara's long white fingers and asked when they would meet again.'

Tara shrugged elegantly and said she had no idea, leaving Marty looking downcast, though being an actor, nobody could be certain of that.

The next morning, everyone slept in, worn out by the excitement of the previous night. It wasn't noticed until just after eleven o'clock, by which time everyone had emerged, bleary-eyed from their bedrooms, that Bernie Kelly had once again disappeared from their lives. Not only was there no sign of him, but his meagre belongings had gone too. And he hadn't left a note. All three girls wondered if this time their father had gone for good. As for Milo, he didn't appear to give a damn.

'At least this time I'm old enough to look after meself,' he said darkly. 'I don't have to rely on *him*.'

After lunch, Aideen went to meet Gertie at Berry's to tell her about the previous night; Tara went to an art exhibition in the public library of work done by a good friend of Christopher's; Milo went to explore New York; and Leo went to pay a visit to VMC's offices in Times Square.

Patricia was, rather annoyingly, left behind alone. She would have been willing to take part in either of her sisters' or her brother's plans, but not one had bothered to invite her. She had no wish to accompany her husband to VMC and possibly come face to face with Gianni, something she had managed to avoid for eight whole years.

She missed her children badly. It felt odd not having even one around. It made her feel incomplete. Patricia pulled herself together, put on her coat and went out. She had no intention of allowing herself to sit alone and mope.

It was a miserable January day. There were flecks of snow in the air and the pavements were wet. Patricia stood on the pavement outside St Patrick's Cathedral, snuggling inside her coat. She didn't feel in a holy enough mood for a visit. If she hailed a taxi, where would she ask it to go? For some reason Leo's gentle kiss in the theatre last night came to her mind and she felt drawn to visit the place where they'd first met, the restaurant that Miss Arquette had taken her to when Patricia was at her very lowest, but where she'd subsequently met Leo, who had offered to marry her – no, *proposed*, that sounded better. It had a Spanish theme and hadn't been far from Madison Square; Le Toreador, that was the name. A taxi was crawling through the heavy traffic in her direction. She waved her arm and asked the driver to take her there. After she'd had a drink, she'd call on Bel from Roscius, who Marty had said was still there. She was really looking forward to seeing her old friend again.

The sign, Le Toreador, was flashing on and off as she approached, and Patricia found herself almost longing to see the place again. It was warm inside and about half full. Patricia sat down as a waitress approached and she ordered a pot of tea – she'd just have to put up with the tea bags.

She felt much better with the tea in her hand, surrounded by warmth, music in the background, along with the hum of civilised conversation. It was under this roof that her entire life had changed – and where it was about to change again. Had she not come here that day, she would never have met Leo, never had his children, probably never gone near San Diego. She was in the throes of a cloud of pure happiness when she noticed a man across the room seated at a table with two women, two very beautiful women, one middle-aged, the other considerably younger – mother and daughter perhaps. The man picked up the younger woman's hand and squeezed it, following up with a kiss on her forehead. The recipient laughed prettily and tapped the man affectionately on his nose.

The man was Leo, *her* Leo, her *husband* Leo. He hadn't gone to VMC as he had claimed he was about to do; he'd come to Le Toreador to kiss strange women! Perhaps he had a double, she thought, but a quick glance showed him wearing the grey suit he'd put on that morning. Yet he had a yellow flower in his buttonhole that hadn't been there when he'd left.

The earth was moving! She was going to faint, she couldn't see. Patricia spilled her tea; it went right through her jumper and scalded her breasts. She stumbled outside and caught a taxi back to the apartment. Once there, she ignored the scald and stared into space, thinking that her life with Leo was over. All she had now were her children and it was imperative, for the sake of her sanity,

304

that she see them as soon as humanly possible.

She and Leo had been brought to New York in an airplane that had taken hardly any time at all. Back at the apartment, Patricia went downstairs and asked Jerry, the nice porter, if he knew how she could catch one back. Nowadays there were internal flights all over the States.

'I mean, how on earth do you arrange these things?' she asked pitifully.

'Don't worry, honey. I'll do it for you,' Jerry said, patting her hand in a fatherly fashion.

It turned out that the nearest airport was in Newark, which was eighteen miles from New York. There was a plane leaving for Los Angeles later in the day, at ten past six, to be precise, from where she would have to hire a car and drive to San Diego. 'Can you drive, honey?'

'No.' Leo had been encouraging her to learn for years.

'In that case, you'll need to hire a car and driver. Shall I book it for you, hon? You'll need to pay at the airport.'

'That's fine,' Patricia whispered.

Half an hour later, she presented herself in the lobby. Jerry carried her bag outside and hailed a cab. Patricia slipped him five dollars as she climbed inside.

It was a long time before she was missed. Leo was the first person to arrive at the apartment and he assumed his wife was out with Aideen or Tara or perhaps her brother. But, one by one, all three returned without there being any sign of Patricia. He had the sense to ask Jerry, down in

305

the lobby, who explained she was on her way to San Francisco.

'And I booked a car and driver to take her to San Diego,' he added. 'It's a nice white Buick; she'll enjoy the ride.'

That made Leo worry that there'd been an accident back home and Patricia had gone rushing there to sort it out. In a panic, he telephoned Joyce in San Diego who, annoyed for some reason, told him that nothing of the sort had happened. 'I can see six of your kids right now,' she informed him. 'They're in the games room playing. And I just put the twins to bed.'

Leo had the idea that his wife might have left a message for him somewhere in the apartment, but a thorough search proved unsuccessful. By now he was furious with Patricia, who'd left him with nothing else to do but return to San Diego himself. As Jerry downstairs was so brilliant at it, he thought caustically, he asked him to sort things out. According to Jerry, however, there wasn't another flight from Newark or any other local airport to San Francisco for another three days. But Jerry managed to work out a way of getting to San Diego by train, changing frequently.

Leo accepted this. He'd sooner be sitting on a train than in the apartment. There was something seriously wrong with Patricia and he was desperate to find out what it was.

Neither Aideen nor Tara were worried about their sister. Patricia was far too sensible to do something daft and Leo had just got himself into a state about nothing.

They'd all enjoyed their day out. Aideen and
Gertie had lunched at the Plaza; Tara had met
several people she knew at the library and they'd
all gone to a cocktail party; and Milo decided he
really liked New York, but he'd been talking to a
girl on the subway and she'd said California was
a more exciting place to be – and the weather
there was glorious.

'I thought I'd hitch that way tomorrow,' he said.
'Get a job.' Patricia had given him money, so he
wouldn't starve.

'Can I come with you?' Tara asked. 'I've no
intention of hitchhiking, but I'll pay for us on the
bus. We can get an apartment together – what
about Hollywood? It sounds really interesting.'

There'd been a message for her at the desk
downstairs from Marty Benedek – or Marty
Moore, as he called himself nowadays – but she'd
torn it up.

Chapter 19

There were sleeping carriages on some of the
trains Leo travelled on, but although he lay down
in a bunk a couple of times, he never slept; not a
wink. Whenever they reached a terminus and he
changed to another line, he rang home, but was
increasingly fobbed off in his attempt to speak to
Patricia. 'She's asleep,' he was told. 'Out shopping.' 'Seeing to the children.' 'On another phone
talking to a friend.' The latter was the limpest

excuse of all.

There wasn't a single decent reason offered to prevent a chap from talking to his wife. To add to his miseries, he developed a pain in his chest that he attributed to eating the wrong food over the last few days, or no food at all on one.

By the time Leo reached San Diego, he felt sick, absolutely exhausted and furiously angry.

Joyce let him in, Leo having lost his key. 'She's in the bedroom, asleep,' she said tersely, as if he had no right to bother Patricia until she deigned to get up.

'Huh!' He strode along the corridor and threw open the bedroom door with such force that it sprang back and almost hit him. The drapes were closed and the evening sunlight was visible at the sides – was it evening? He had no idea. A hunched figure under the bedclothes stirred and struggled to a sitting position.

'What the hell's the matter?' He tried to feel sorry for her – her eyes were swollen and she looked utterly wretched – but could only feel resentment at his treatment. She looked at him and didn't speak.

'Why did you leave New York the way you did? What happened?' he demanded.

'Are you pretending not to know?' Her voice was dull and thick.

'I *don't* know,' he shouted. 'I haven't the faintest idea why you are behaving like this. Right now, I feel as if I'm living in a madhouse.'

Joyce opened the door. 'Is everything all right, Patricia?' she asked.

'Fuck off!' Leo slammed the door in her face,

which was enough to spark some life into his wife, who got awkwardly out of bed as if she were an invalid.

'How dare you speak to Joyce like that? You should go and live in a madhouse. It's where you belong.'

Leo gasped when the chest pain he'd been experiencing returned with a vengeance. Fortunately it was only momentary.

'But what on earth have I done?' Leo asked, bewildered.

'You're having an affair – don't deny it! I saw you, in that restaurant.'

So that was it! For some reason he pulled back the curtains, allowing the sunlight to flood in, making him blink. He turned to his wife.

'Her name is Eve,' he said, 'and she *is* my daughter.' He sat down on the chair in front of the dressing table and spoke to Patricia through the mirror. 'Do you remember the day we met I told you I met a girl in France during the war? Her name was Antoinette. She was a nurse, we were going to get married, but she died. Do you remember?' he repeated angrily when Patricia didn't answer.

'Yes,' she said bad-temperedly.

'Well, we, Antoinette and I, had a daughter, Eve. She was raised first in Limoges in France, then in London by her aunt, Laure, who married an English man. Laure was with us yesterday. We meet a few times a year, usually in New York. Yesterday I took them to the restaurant where I'd met you, just to show them, as it were, where I asked you to marry me. I don't know if you noticed, but I was sitting at the same table as we

309

did. But what prompted you to go there?' he asked curiously.

'I wanted to see how it felt, just sitting there with a pot of tea. I was so miserable on my first visit, and so happy on the second.' She frowned. 'Why didn't you tell me about Eve?'

Leo sighed. 'Because I thought you were too young,' he said. 'Eve was illegitimate. I thought you'd be so shocked you'd refuse to marry me.'

'Why haven't you told me since?' she insisted.

He turned and looked at her face to face. 'Because you're still too young,' he snapped. 'You're twenty-six but you behave like a child. I can't have a grown-up conversation with you, not like with Tara. All you ever think about is children.' Christ, that was so cruel and it wasn't true either. 'I'm sorry.' Now he felt horrible and heartless. 'I didn't mean that.'

'If you didn't mean it, you wouldn't have said it.' She climbed back into bed and pulled the clothes over her head. 'I have a headache; I need to sleep,' she said in a muffled voice.

As he was leaving, her head appeared out of the clothes. 'I would never have believed, after being married to you for eight years, you didn't tell me you had a daughter.'

'And I would never believe that after eight years you would have assumed I was having an affair. You mustn't have an ounce of faith in me.'

With that he left the bedroom and made for his den in the basement. It had a comfortable couch where he occasionally snoozed. He didn't expect to sleep, but he dozed off straight away, dizzy with tiredness.

When morning came, the house was quiet and he wondered where everyone was. The kids hadn't come in to see him so presumably they weren't aware he was home – either Patricia or that Joyce woman, who he'd never liked, had deliberately not told them. There was a clock on the wall above his desk shaped like a ship's wheel that told him it was quarter to ten. By now his children would be at their various schools and nursery places. The little ones would be home by twelve.

As Leo couldn't think of a satisfactory way to pass the time at home, he got dressed and went into work at the VMC factory he had started.

He slept at his golf club for a week. It had rooms for neglected husbands like him. He telephoned Patricia twice and she called him just the once. The first time he called, Joyce told him she wasn't in, and the second time she was in, but refused to speak to him.

'I don't believe you,' he snarled.

'She's sitting here, in front of me, and mouthing "no, no, no",' Joyce said, so Leo rang off.

Later that night, Patricia phoned the golf club. The internal phone in his room rang and a male voice informed him his wife was on the line.

'Tell her to buzz off.'

'He said buzz off,' he heard the voice say.

It all seemed like a silly game, he thought sadly, nursing the pain in his chest that had come back. How easily a perfect marriage could be ruined through misconceptions and misunderstandings – or were they the same thing? he wondered. And Patricia, he recalled, had not been all that forthcoming when it came to hiding family secrets. When he had announced to his lawyer, Brook Dyson, that they were getting married, Brook had insisted on looking into her background.

'Whatever you find in her background, we're still getting married,' Leo had informed him. 'But go ahead if you insist.'

He'd found it rather amusing when Brook discovered that his future wife's father had been a major criminal who had fiddled a client out of ten thousand Irish pounds and in all probability thrown himself off the boat bringing himself and his girls to Ireland.

'That's a helluva lot of dollars,' Brook told Leo, with a touch of admiration in his voice.

Leo had urged his lawyer to investigate further. 'Find out if the money's been recovered. If it hasn't, then repay it,' he said. Patricia's late father would still be a criminal, but at least he wouldn't have left any victims behind.

It had come as a shock considerably later to find the guy himself was still around; the suicide had just been an act. It had been an unpleasant surprise to find him living in the New York flat when they'd arrived last week. He felt inclined to punch him in the nose, only to find someone else had done it before him.

The golf club had a small shop selling sports clothes. Leo had bought a pair of chocolate linen trousers and a couple of open-neck shirts. He bought a fresh shirt the next morning to wear for work.

When he entered his office, his secretary, Lily,

was on the telephone. 'It's Patricia,' she said, handing him the receiver.

Leo waited until she had left and closed the door before speaking. 'Yes?' he said politely.

'Oh, Leo,' Patricia said tearfully. 'Please come home, darling. We all miss you. The children are wondering where you are. I'm sorry, really sorry.' Her voice was anguished. She was undoubtedly genuinely sorry. 'I've been horrible as well as an idiot. Can I meet Eve? How long will she be in New York? Could she come and see us?'

Leo's relief was so great that he broke out in a sweat. He could feel the moisture running down his arms. 'Another couple of weeks. I'll give her a ring later, Laure too. Shall I invite them to stay with us?'

Patricia was babbling now. 'I should have known you'd never have an affair, but it was such a shock seeing you in the place that meant so much to us at the time. I should...'

'Darling,' he said quietly. 'I'll come home straight away. Are the kids still there?'

'They'll be leaving soon.'

'Keep them there; I'll take them in later.' He was aching to see his entire family. After the kids had gone, he'd take his wife into the bedroom and make love to her in a way he'd never done before. 'I love you,' he said, but wasn't sure if she heard.

It was a great day; he was in an open-top car, enjoying the warm wind on his face. He sang at the top of his voice, one of the songs from *Hullabaloo*. Was it really only a couple of days since

313

they'd seen it? *The moon and the stars, tonight they are ours...* he sang.

He was still singing when a terrific pain tore through his chest and he lost control of the car. He didn't see the gas tanker he'd crashed into, because by then Leo was already dead.

'It was a heart attack that killed him, not the accident,' the doctor told Patricia when she arrived at the hospital.

'But there was nothing wrong with his heart,' she protested. What had happened hadn't yet sunk in and she was still able to think clearly.

'I know that. I gave him a check-up a couple of months ago and his heart was behaving perfectly.' With his sun-bleached hair and golden tan, Doctor Ted Robbins resembled a tennis coach rather than a member of the medical profession. He was Leo's regular doctor. 'Is there someone who can look after things for you?'

At first, Patricia wondered what he was talking about. She realised he meant the funeral, buying a coffin, finding a grave, that sort of thing. 'Oh, yes,' she said stoutly. 'I'll manage myself.'

'Hasn't Leo got a brother somewhere in New York?'

'Yes, Gianni is his name.'

'Perhaps it would be a good idea to get in touch with him.'

'I'll do that,' Patricia said, 'as soon as I get home.' She wasn't sure whether she would or not.

One of the gardeners had driven her to the hospital when the call had come to say that Leo had

314

been badly injured. But she'd arrived to find him dead. On the way home, at something like halfway, the reality sank in and she froze in horror at the idea that her dearest, darling Leo was no longer part of her life, but had gone for ever. She would never see him again; never touch him. They would never speak. His children would never fully know what a wonderful father they'd missed having.

If it hadn't been for the children, right then she would have willed herself to die.

It was such a fuss, dying. Not for the dead person, but for those who were left. There was so much to do, no time for ordinary things, just seeing undertakers, ordering flowers, making lists of people who should be invited to the funeral, ordering food, choosing music, deciding what to wear, putting notices in papers and magazines, being interviewed, photographed, taking care of visitors...

Joyce couldn't possibly be more upset than Patricia, but seemed to think she was. 'We'd got on so well for all those years,' she wailed, 'but his last words to me were "fuck off".'

'Oh dear,' Patricia sighed. She had considered several times over the last few days giving Joyce her notice, insisting she leave the house immediately because she was driving her employer wild. But it helped, actually helped, having this supremely irritating woman constantly at her side saying how much she missed Leo. But it was Patricia who had heard his final words, 'I love you'.

Then there was Gianni. He seemed mild enough, almost harmless. Leo had kept him out of her

315

way, never wanting them to come face to face. He was handsome, helpful, took over some of the most irksome tasks, like conversing with the priest. There would be a requiem mass and Milo was to be an altar boy for the first time.

Her brother Milo had already arrived, along with Tara. They had managed to make their way to Hollywood by bus and Tara had called to tell her they had arrived safely, only to learn about Leo. Aideen was on her way.

On the day before the funeral, Bernie Kelly arrived, still looking as if he hadn't two ha'pennies to scratch his behind with. He took his eldest daughter in his arms. 'I'm sorry, darlin'', he whispered. 'It was obvious how much you loved each other. It's a crime he's been taken.'

'How did you find out?' Patricia asked.

'I was in a bar and it was on the wireless,' Bernie said. 'I hadn't realised Leo was that well known.'

It was over. Was it over? Had she really sat through that service? Spoken to so many mourners? Actually managed to stay on her feet for the entire day?

It was close to midnight and people were still there: Daddy, her sisters, Milo and Gianni, who had a house nearby. A clock struck the hour and Tara and Aideen came and took their sister to the bedroom where she'd lain for hundreds, if not thousands, of times with her husband, Leo. Her clothes were removed, Aideen slipped her nightdress over her head and Tara tied the bow at the neck. They led her to the bed and lay down each side of her. Aideen held her hand and whispered, 'There, there, darlin'.'

316

'Go to sleep, Sis.' Tara stroked her forehead.

Both sisters had gone when Patricia woke up the next morning to an unnatural silence. There wasn't a sound being made anywhere in the world. But then a bird tweeted, a dog barked, a car revved its engine in the distance.

Patricia got out of bed. This was how it was going to be for the rest of time: silence, sleeping alone in bed. There would be no Leo, never, never again.

It was difficult to mourn properly when you were living with eight children. It wasn't true about sleeping alone. More often than not, Patricia would wake up and find one, two, or even three children in bed with her. The smaller ones missed their pop, but couldn't put it into words. They clung to their mother more tightly, just in case she too should suddenly disappear.

Patricia thought, somewhat cynically, Leo had died when her own father was particularly down on his luck and how he'd quickly taken advantage of it. Her sisters and Milo had returned to their own lives, but there was no suggestion that a time would come for Bernie to leave. Somehow he acquired his own bedroom, inherited some of Leo's clothes, did jobs around the house and watered the garden. He and Joyce got along well and they had a drink together each evening. Despite her cynicism, Patricia was glad his familiar figure was still around.

Somehow they reached summer, which was when the letter came.

Dear Patricia

I was sorry to read the news about Leo – it was in the newspaper. I read it in the library as these days I can't afford to buy a copy for myself.

I suppose this means Gianni will now be in charge of the San Diego end of VMC. You won't know, but I left the firm many years ago. Well, I didn't exactly leave. It would be more correct to say I was pushed – none too gently. My services were no longer required. Gianni had no intention of marrying me. He claimed his bitch of a wife positively refused to give him a divorce, but I know for sure these things can always be resolved if you have enough money. He could have married me if he'd really wanted.

You never know, he might fancy marrying his brother's widow once an acceptable amount of time has passed, particularly if he discovered it was him, not his brother, who was the father of your eldest child. I know Gianni was desperate for a son – it would seem most men are. You wouldn't believe just how far he will go to get his own way. Even if you refused to marry him, he will insist on getting to know his son, playing a part in his life, have some say in his education. He will be totally ruthless.

So, probably best if he didn't know anything about Milo, eh!

To ensure this doesn't happen, a check for around $1000 would be very welcome. You could say it was in appreciation of the help I gave you when you were in trouble. Because if it hadn't been for me, you wouldn't have married Leo.

My address is at the top of this letter.
Your friend,
Elaine Arquette

She was still living in New York, somewhere in the Bronx. Patricia sat back in her chair. She felt curiously calm. She realised Elaine Arquette was attempting to blackmail her and it was like something out of a novel or a film. People didn't do things like this in ordinary life. Nevertheless, it had to be dealt with.

The only people in her own family who knew what had happened at the time were her sisters. Patricia had no wish to pass the secret on to her father, actually tell him she'd been raped. As Aideen was pregnant, living with her in-laws in Brooklyn, and likely to give birth any minute, contacting her was out of the question, but Tara was in Hollywood, a mere few miles away, with Big Milo, as he was now called. She carefully made a copy of the letter and sent it to her.

A reply came within a few days.

Patricia, darling, don't let that awful woman have a dime. If you sent her a thousand dollars, she would have you in her power and only want more. She could blackmail you for the rest of your life – or her life. Would you like me to come and stay with you a while?

Patricia wrote and thanked her sister for her advice, telling her that there was no need for her to visit. She still wasn't sure what to do. Leo was the only person whose opinion she would trust, but Leo was no longer around to talk to. Anyway, if he had been around, Miss Arquette wouldn't have sent the letter and his advice wouldn't have been needed.

At the conclusion of this reasoning, Patricia felt quite dizzy.

She'd had little to do with her brother-in-law since Leo had died and Gianni had taken over the running of the main VMC factory in San Diego. She'd found him to be a quiet, reclusive man, who'd shown no interest in them being friends. Somebody must have given him a list of the children's birthdays because he sent cards and gifts on the correct days. Apparently he was still married, but had been separated from his wife for years. They had a daughter who he never saw.

His personality bore no similarity, none whatsoever, to the man who had raped her all those years ago in VMC's offices in New York, an act he appeared to have no memory of, and who had been having an affair with Miss Arquette. She had no idea if he had a girlfriend now. He hadn't brought anyone to the funeral.

The situation, as it stood, suited Patricia well. As far as she was concerned, everything was fine and she put Elaine Arquette's letter to the back of her mind. She was thrilled when Mary Grant, Aideen's mother-in-law, called to say Aideen's baby had arrived.

'It's a boy and, oh, he's so handsome,' Mary gushed, delighted. 'She's calling him George.'

'Is there any sign of Humphrey?' Patricia asked.

The woman's delight fled. 'I'm afraid not,' she said. 'My husband has hired someone to go to Nepal and look for him, but we've had no news as yet.'

'I'm so sorry. But please tell Aideen I'll come

and see her as soon as I can.' She would fly, Patricia decided. If the planes were at convenient times, she could stay a few days. They really were a wonderful invention, airplanes.

Tara came with her. It was a month later and, the funeral apart, it was the first time the three sisters had been together since they had gone to the theatre to see *Hullabaloo*.

'One husband dead and another one missing,' Aideen said. 'It's not a very good record for the Kelly sisters, is it?'

Patricia sighed. 'Why don't you come and live with us, Sis?' she pleaded. 'Tara's no distance away in Hollywood. We could all meet regularly.' There was real longing in her voice.

Aideen disagreed. 'Mary is a really nice woman and she's my mother-in-law. I love her dearly and we are both waiting for Humphrey to come back. I'm part of her life now, and you and Tara are part of my past.'

Patricia shuddered. 'Don't say things like that! You're shutting me and Tara out.'

Aideen laughed. 'Not at all! The longer we live, the more friends we will make and the more relatives we will collect. We should all be moving forward, not back. By the way, neither of you are admiring my baby nearly as much as you should.'

George was a tough little soul with chubby arms and legs. 'He's too beautiful for words,' Tara announced. 'He's going to be an athlete like his father.' She chucked George under his little wrinkled chin and he made a face at her.

'Mary *is* a nice woman,' Patricia said to her sister on the plane back to San Diego, 'but I can't for the life of me understand our Aideen wanting to live with her when she could live with us. As far as I'm concerned, blood will always be thicker than water.'

When their plane landed at San Diego airport on a beautiful evening in August, it was their father, standing beside Leo's blue Chevrolet, who met them. He had driven a car back in Ireland and had taken a driving test so he could transfer his skill to the USA. He waved and ran towards them.

'Patricia, oh me darlin' girl,' he burst out, 'something terrible has happened – Milo has disappeared.'

Patricia didn't know where her son had gone, but she knew intuitively who was responsible. Elaine Arquette had carried out her threat and told Gianni he was Milo's father. This was his first move in laying a claim to his son.

'Have you told the police?' she asked, trying to stay calm.

'Yes, there's a couple of them back home talking to Joyce. It seems she went to meet him and Rosie off the school bus, but Milo wasn't with her. Apparently he didn't catch the bus; Rosie has no idea why. The poor kid's in tears; thinks it's her fault.'

Two policeman were standing beside their car while four of the Vanetti children crawled all over it, occasionally sounding the horn. Joyce held the frustrated twins in her arms while Tara went indoors to comfort Rosie.

Patricia didn't feel particularly panicky when she got out of the Chevrolet and approached the police.

'I think my son might be with my brother-in-law,' she told them. 'His name is Gianni Vanetti and he lives on Custer Drive.' She made a point to not sound accusing. Best not to start a war with Gianni – yet!

Righteo, Mrs Vanetti.'

The two policemen looked relieved to get the children out of the car. 'Won't be gone long, ma'am,' one of them said.

Joyce was outraged. She knew nothing about any contact the family, particularly Milo, had with Gianni. 'He was only ever here for Leo's funeral.'

'He's been in touch a few times on the telephone,' Patricia lied. 'He was talking about throwing a party for the children.' Joyce glowered, annoyed she hadn't been consulted, and was about to create a scene when Bernie suggested she make them a cup of coffee, if only to get her out of the way.

Patricia was standing in the drive waiting for the police to return with Milo, but it was one of VMC's own small cars that turned up first. Gianni climbed out, looking troubled.

'What's the matter?' he enquired. 'Is Milo really missing?'

'Y ... yes.' Patricia swallowed, unable to think of what to say, but Tara was never one to be short of words.

'We thought we should bring in family to help. You've lived here much longer than us and might know of places children would go.' It was a bit limp, but Gianni seemed to accept it.

'There's always the beach,' he said. 'And there's a fairground and the roller-skating rink – there's a junior one for the under-tens. Would you like me to help with the search?'

Patricia was beginning to panic. If Milo hadn't been with Gianni, then where was he? She looked at her watch – nearly eight o'clock. 'Where are the police?' she asked of no one in particular.

It was Gianni who answered. 'When they left my house, they said they were going to the school to see if anyone saw anything suspicious.'

'It's a bit late for that,' growled Bernie. 'There won't be anyone at the school at this time of night.'

'There's a parents' meeting,' Gianni informed him.

The ensuing silence – no one could think of anything to say – was broken by the entrance of a vehicle built like a small bus into the drive. There were half a dozen children inside. It stopped and Milo stepped out, holding a balloon.

'Hi, Mom, you're back,' he said. A female voice from the bus shouted, 'Goodnight, all,' and the vehicle drove away.

'Where have you been?' Patricia yelped.

'Luke's party.' Aware his arrival had caused a shock to his family, Milo said a trifle belligerently, 'I brought a letter home from Luke's mom the other day inviting me to the party. She said to give it to you.'

'You never gave me a letter,' Patricia pointed out. She wanted to laugh and cry at the same time.

'You weren't here, were you?' Milo pointed out in turn.

'Then why didn't you show it to Joyce?'

'She mightn't have let me go. I just wrote "OK" on the note and gave it back to Mrs Richardson, Luke's mom.' The little boy crossed over to his mother and held her hand. 'That was all right, wasn't it, Mom?'

Patricia knelt down and hugged him. 'It was fine, darlin'. Absolutely fine.'

'Well, I'll be off.' Gianni was about to get into his car.

'Please stay,' Patricia called on impulse. She couldn't help but feel sorry for him; he seemed so alone. 'Have coffee with us.'

'Well, if I'm not intruding.' He looked pleased to be asked.

'I wouldn't ask if you were.'

So everyone went indoors and had coffee. Bernie called the police and told them Milo had been found. Gianni offered to take Milo to the skating rink one day, where he could have skating lessons. Rosie asked if she could go too.

'I suppose I really should start helping to look after the kids for you,' Gianni said later to Patricia. 'As far as I know, I'm the only uncle they have.' She didn't remind him there was Big Milo.

Next day, Patricia wrote a cheque for $1000 and sent it to Elaine Arquette, thanking her for her help all those years ago. She suggested there was no need for a reply and didn't get one.

325

Chapter 20

Easter, 1936

Tara and Milo's apartment in Hollywood overlooked a little theatre where plays written by unknown playwrights were performed by unknown actors. Lines weren't learnt but read from a script. It only cost a quarter to get in. Tara had played parts in a couple of the productions and Milo was in the course of writing a play, having decided to become a writer.

'I shall write film scripts as well,' he informed Tara, without any suggestion of modesty. 'Gosh, Sis, I'm glad you came to Dublin to look for me,' he added, sighing happily. 'I'd forgotten what it was like to be happy.'

Tara patted his cheek fondly, but didn't say anything. Daddy had a lot to answer for after ruining quite a few other lives back in Ireland and in New York. She made a point of not talking about him in front of Milo, who was likely to fly into a rage and say he hadn't punched his father nearly hard enough when they were reunited in Leo's New York apartment.

'I feel inclined to give him another, more powerful thump next time we meet,' he'd said threateningly. 'I might go to the gym and get some practice in.'

His sister advised him to put all his energies into

script-writing, not hitting his father. 'He can't help being the way he is,' she said reasonably.

'Neither can I,' Milo said, just as reasonably.

Like Aideen before her, Tara's days were spent waiting on tables in a diner, though in Tara's case it was called Salome's and was situated on Sunset Strip. It was open from eight in the morning until ten at night. It was a big place with paintings of a scantily clad Salome covering the walls that could well have been sacrilegious, as Tara had a feeling she was mentioned in the bible. The sixteen waitresses worked seven-hour shifts each. The manager/owner was a Russian immigrant called Iggy, whose real name was Igor Dmitriyev. He was a large, impressive individual, somewhere between forty and fifty, with powerful shoulders and pockmarked skin, who was in a permanently bad mood. His days were spent stationed behind the till keeping a sharp eye on staff and customers alike.

Except for Tara all of Iggy's waitresses were desperate to become movie stars, just like virtually every other waitress in Hollywood. It was their sole aim in life. Same with most of the men – if they weren't budding actors, they were musicians or scriptwriters like Milo, or something else to do with movies. But Tara wanted more than to spend her life pretending to be someone else on a celluloid screen, not even a real woman; the creation of a person like Milo who wasn't even all that intelligent and would find it impossible to invent a decent female part.

Most of the people she had met in Hollywood

327

were interested in only one thing: fame. They were greedy for it. No one wanted to become a nurse, say, or a doctor, or do something to help others. Much as Tara was enjoying herself mixing with such happy, determined young people, it was noticeable how disinterested they were in the world outside Hollywood. They appeared to know nothing about what was happening in Germany, for instance, where the Fascist Adolf Hitler had taken control of his country in a number of cynical and illegal ways, no doubt with the support and encouragement of Fascists like Sir Oswald Mosely and others all over Europe.

According to the radio and the newspapers, the continent was in turmoil and a war in the relatively near future involving Great Britain and possibly America was a distinct possibility. That meant the people of the world needed to be warned about it and prepare themselves. On behalf of the world, Tara was only too willing to help. She had applied to several major newspapers for a job as a reporter stationed in Berlin.

Only one paper had bothered to reply and she was turned down because she was too young, too inexperienced, as well as having committed the unforgivable sin of being a woman. Not only that, she didn't possess a single qualification. Tara had left school in Ireland at the age of fourteen knowing hardly anything until she'd met Christopher and Edwin, who'd taught her the sort of things that she was much too young to know. Now she began to study books on grammar and history, geography and art, all borrowed from the library. After all, who had painted the *Mona Lisa?* Who had written *War and Peace?* There were lots of important things she didn't know.

Perhaps the best way would be to *move* to Germany – Berlin, the capital, would be ideal – and send articles to the American newspapers about these awful Fascist people. She would become 'our reporter on the spot'.

The following day, at Salome's, she asked Iggy if she could do extra shifts.

'I could work two shifts a day instead of one,' she offered. She had a little bit of money saved, but not nearly enough to set up home in Berlin. She was a good waitress and earned more in tips than she did in wages so it wouldn't take her long to save up enough.

Iggy scowled – he rarely did anything else – and said it was probably against the employment laws, which he had no intention of breaking.

'One shift a day enough for anyone,' he growled.

Tara had been told he had taken part in the Russian Revolution. 'On whose side?' someone had asked.

'Of the workers, of course,' Iggy had snarled.

It was a baking hot evening in July 1936 when a customer came in the diner and straight away began to attract more than usual attention from the other customers and staff alike. It was a young man who was youthfully handsome, blond-haired, blue-eyed, with a huge grin. Every time Tara looked, he seemed to be staring at her.

'He can't take his eyes off you,' one of the other girls remarked enviously.

329

'I've met him before,' Tara told her. It was Marty Moore, in Hollywood to star in a movie based on the fairy tale *Cinderella*. Milo had read it in *Variety* the other day. 'My sister used to go out with him long before he became famous.'

'Well, it's you he's interested in now, Tara, not your sister. You're the only one he's looked at since he came in.'

Tara remembered about six months ago when they'd all gone to see *Hullabaloo* and Marty Moore – she would always think of him as Marty Benedek – had gone down on one knee and expressed his undying love for her, or some such nonsense. She hadn't taken the slightest bit of notice. He was waving to her now and she supposed she'd better take notice since he was a customer and she was a mere waitress. She went over to his table, aware the other girls were watching.

'Hello, Tara. We meet again at last.' To her surprise, he jumped to his feet and kissed her.

Well, Tara hadn't exactly been longing for them to meet again. 'Hello,' she said politely, pushing him away. 'I understand you're making a film here.'

'That's right. It's a musical, a modern-day version of *Cinderella*.' He sounded boyishly enthusiastic.

'So I understand.' She recalled how nice he'd been to all the Kelly sisters when they'd first arrived in America. There was no need to be rude, though she was finding him irritating now. 'Where are you living?' she asked politely.

'The Hollywood Hills – I've rented a place that's described as a log cabin and has eight bedrooms and an indoor pool.'

'Gosh! I'm impressed.'

'So am I. It's so big, I sometimes get lost in it.'
He reached out and caught her hand. 'Would you
like to come to dinner there tomorrow? I haven't
got a chef, but I can order food in.'

'Sorry, but I'm working late.' She was pleased
to be on the late shift this week and have an excuse to turn him down. The last thing she wanted
was to get involved with a man when she already
had quite different plans of her own.

'How about the next night?'

'I'm working late every night this week, and
when I'm not working, I'm studying,' she said
before he could get as far as the following week.

'Studying?' He gaped.

'Studying,' she confirmed. 'I intend to become
a reporter in Berlin; newspaper or radio, I don't
mind which.' Tara reckoned that would put him
off her for good. But she was to be disappointed.

Instead, he merely looked more surprised. 'Will
you please sit down, Tara. I'd like to talk to you
seriously about something.'

She laughed. 'I can't sit down; I'm a waitress
and have another two hours to go. And by the
way, would you like something to eat or drink?'

'I'll have both, anything will do. Excuse me, sir,'
he shouted to Iggy, who was glaring at him from
his usual perch behind the till. 'Can this young
lady sit down so I can propose to her?'

There was a buzz amongst the guests and the
other waitresses. Tara sat down quickly before
she fell down. Her face felt as if it was flaming
red. 'How dare you?' she said angrily. She had

gone off him completely.

'No, she can't sit down,' Iggy growled. 'She got customers to see to. Attend to your customers, Tara.'

Tara scurried away. Marty Moore shouted, 'I'm never giving up, Tara. I'm only making the movie so I can be near you.' He waved and left the diner, followed by loud applause.

Iggy caught his waitress's arm as she hurried past. 'Go upstairs, girl,' he hissed, 'and stay in my apartment till we close. I'd like to talk to you.'

Tara supposed she was about to be sacked. She went up the narrow wooden staircase and sat in Iggy's surprisingly neat and cosy apartment. There were dark religious paintings heavily decorated with gold on the walls and family photos spread on top of a lace-covered chest, as well as numerous books, mostly Russian, but a few by John Steinbeck, Henry Miller and Nathaniel Hawthorne, who Tara had heard of but never read.

The windows were open and an electric fan whirred noisily in the empty fireplace. As time passed, the sound of conversation in the diner below became fainter and fainter until it ceased altogether. There was silence for a few minutes and then the main door closed and the bolt was drawn. Iggy began to slowly climb the stairs.

It was only then that Tara began to feel concerned. What was this all about? What was Iggy up to? Had she jumped out of the flying pan into the fire?

He came in carrying two cups on a tray. He would have been a handsome man if it hadn't been for his poor skin. 'No sugar, but plenty of cream,' he said to Tara, pushing one of the coffees in her direction.

'That's how I like it,' she said. He must have noticed. She murmured 'thank you' when he put her cup on a tiny table beside her chair and seated himself opposite.

'That thing you say earlier, about going to Berlin to be reporter, is that true?' he enquired. When she nodded, he went on. 'You ever done anything like that before?'

'I spent some months in London reporting on the British Union of Fascists for the FBI.'

He looked impressed. 'Was this for – how you put it – publication?'

'Yes – the *Worldwide Voice*. It didn't have a very big circulation,' she felt bound to add. 'And I haven't got a job as a journalist,' she added further. 'All I can do when I get to Berlin is try.'

'And is it why you ask for extra shifts, to raise money for Berlin?'

'That's why, yes,' Tara agreed. 'I already have a bit of money saved. Another five or six months working here and I will have enough.' She smiled. 'I can always get a job as a waitress in Berlin.' The one thousand dollars that Christopher had left her in his will had already been paid into her account but she was saving it for a vitally important emergency.

Iggy shook his head. 'There is no need to work another six months. I give you money now. Berlin far more important than Iggy's diner. Anyway, if you stay here, in Hollywood, that man, that famous star who bothered you, he going to push and push. He will send flowers every day, buy

333

you diamonds, get you part in movie, take you to expensive restaurants and on expensive holidays. No matter how much you say no, he will never give up. I know the type. One of these days you will marry him just to get him off your back.'

'Absolutely not,' Tara said firmly. "What makes you say that?'

He sighed mournfully. 'Because I did same thing when I was young.'

'Did you succeed?'

'Yes, but she left me within a year. Another week and I would have left her.'

He removed a picture off the wall. Behind was a safe that he unlocked, removing a wad of dollars held together with an elastic band. 'Here five hundred dollars. Let me know if you need more. Oh, and don't come to work tomorrow. Tonight we say goodbye, Miss Tara. Goodbye and good luck in Berlin.' He stood and bowed courteously from the waist down. 'Look after yourself,' he said. 'This will help.' He lifted her hand and a gold cross and chain slithered into her palm. 'St Christopher will keep his eye on you.'

She told Milo of her change of plan that night. He was having a great time in Hollywood and seemed unmoved by her decision to leave.

'Our Patricia's not all that far away,' she reminded him. 'She'd welcome your company any time. And Daddy's there...'

Milo grimaced. 'That's more likely to prevent me from going to see Patricia.'

'You'll have to make friends with him sometime,' Tara said.

Milo shrugged, muttered something about 'death beds', and refused to talk about it any more.

Patricia was just sitting down to tea in the nursery with the twins, Siobhan and Deidre, when the telephone rang. Daddy answered it and came in to ask, 'Do we know anyone in Bray?'

'Not as far as I know,' she answered. Aideen had used to live there. 'Did they give their name?'

'It's Charbonneau, which is French, but the woman sounds Canadian.'

'Did she say what she wants?'

'Only that a young man, a complete stranger, has just turned up at her house insisting he lives there.'

'Did he give his name – oh, it's all right, Daddy. I'll speak to her. Will you please give the twins their eggs?'

'Righteo, girl.' He loved having anything to do with his grandchildren, which is more than could be said about his attitude to their parents.

'I'm sorry to have bothered you,' Mrs Charbonneau said graciously when Patricia took over the phone from her father, 'but he's such a nice young man, somewhat confused. It seems he thought he had relatives living here. Your name and telephone number is written on the back of the kitchen door and I wondered if he was anything to do with you?'

'Has he given you his name?' Patricia asked.

'Yes, it's Humphrey. He doesn't seem to know his surname.'

Patricia gasped. 'Please keep a tight hold of him

335

till I get there. I won't be long.' At last, Humphrey Grant was back on American soil!

In Brooklyn, Aideen burst into tears when her sister telephoned to say Humphrey had come home, albeit to the wrong address.

'Well, I couldn't tell him I'd moved, could I? He left Bray before I did, but I wrote your telephone number all over the place, seeing as you lived nearby. I'll come straight away,' she cried. 'Oh, but I can't. George has a cold and I can't possibly leave him – or take him with me. Humphrey's home,' Patricia heard her shout at the other end of the line – someone must have asked what the commotion was, presumably Mary or Theo – or both. 'Hold on a minute, Sis.' There was a long, loud conversation on the other side of America, until Aideen came on again, saying excitedly, 'Mary's offered to look after George so I'll be on the very first possible plane to San Diego. See you soon, Sis. And Humphrey.'

Humphrey was sitting in the middle of the floor playing with a number of small children when Aideen finally arrived at her sister's house in San Diego forty-eight hours later. She remembered him doing the same thing many years ago when the family had lived in New York and there'd been far fewer children. And Leo had been alive and Humphrey hadn't lost an eye to a couple of gangsters. Life could be so cruel and sad, she thought.

She said softly, 'Humphrey, darling.'

He looked up and when he saw it was her, the

smile he gave her took her breath away. He looked gloriously healthy, tall, thinner and absolutely adorable.

'Darling.' Dodging the children, he came and caught her in his arms, burying his face in her neck. 'I love you.'

'And I love you. Did you manage to climb Everest?' she asked jokingly. His answer took her breath away.

'Oh, yes. I climbed one night when everyone was asleep. It was mighty cold up there.' Aideen looked into his eyes and could tell that he wasn't telling a lie, but was quite serious about it.

'Darling,' she whispered. 'Can you remember my name?' So far he hadn't mentioned it. She felt cold inside.

'Well, no, I can't for the minute. But I know you're the woman I love more than anyone else in the world.'

Aideen thought that would just have to do – for now, at least.

He took to five-month-old George straight away, but it was a while before he grasped that the baby was his.

'You are a father,' Aideen said slowly. 'George is your son.'

She took him to Berry's, where they'd met, and to her pleased surprise he recognised the basement department straight away.

'This is where we met,' he said delightedly. 'There was a guy who worked here too. I remember he let you go early so we could have lunch together.'

'That was Andy,' Aideen told him. 'I'm afraid he died. It happened while you went away and I came to New York for the funeral.'

'Did you really?' he marvelled, as if she too had climbed a great mountain.

'Do you recall where we had lunch?'

'A Chinese place. Can't remember what it was called, I'm afraid.'

'I can't either,' Aideen said.

It was worrying. At times he was like the old Humphrey and they joked and laughed a lot. Other times he seemed to sink into a dark mood during which he hardly spoke. He still appeared convinced he had climbed the mountain and no one contradicted him when he spoke about it, though undoubtedly someone would, one day, and neither Aideen nor his parents knew how they would deal with it.

Aideen took him to see a doctor – a psychiatrist – who didn't think there was anything that could be done.

'Most of the time's he's too happy for drugs,' the doctor said, 'though I can't see him earning a living. What was he before the accident happened?'

'A sports coach,' Aideen said with a sigh. There was no likelihood of Humphrey taking it up again.

'I tell you what – are you able to support yourselves for the next year? In that case,' he went on when Aideen nodded, 'let's have a look at him again then. Just carry on being as happy as you can. Enjoy yourselves, laugh a lot – I can tell he's good at that. The year will fly by and you will have had a better time than most people.'

The psychiatrist was right. Aideen and Humphrey had fun over the next few months. They walked for miles in Brooklyn with George in his pram, or Mary and Theo would look after George while they went to see a movie or a Broadway show. But Humphrey showed no sign of improvement. More often than not he would forget his wife's name, or it would come as a surprise to him to realise he had a son he absolutely adored. And he still claimed to have climbed Everest.

'Did you really, darling?' Aideen would say.

'I think this is as much as we can hope for,' she said to her in-laws after a few months. 'But I'd sooner have this Humphrey than no Humphrey at all.'

'Me too,' Mary agreed, and Theo nodded. 'I wouldn't bother with that psychiatrist if I were you.'

'You're right.' Aideen nodded. Perhaps the best medicine for Humphrey would be if George had a little brother and sister. It would be a pleasure, not a hardship, she thought

Chapter 21

In Hollywood, Tara had been able to cope with life, passing smoothly from one day to the next without incident. Everyone spoke the same language, she had no trouble finding somewhere to live or getting a job. She knew exactly where

339

she was.

It hadn't crossed her mind that in Germany hardly anyone would speak English. After a fortnight, she was still living in the same cheap hotel, The Alfred, hadn't found work, and was feeling rather hopeless and helpless.

As a journalist she had got nowhere. Other journalists had already covered the sinister atmosphere in Berlin; the stars on some people's clothes to indicate they were Jewish; the sign, 'JUDEN', in certain shops meaning the owners weren't pure-blooded German; men being attacked quite brutally, she presumed for the same reason.

There'd only been two other guests at the hotel, a man with a deep, guttural voice, who had left the day before yesterday, and a woman who was leaving today – she was outside now with her luggage waiting for a taxi. The place had been advertised, as were so many of its ilk, on a postcard in the window of a tobacconist, and it was in an out-of-the-way road behind a church. The road comprised one side of five large detached houses that had all seen better days. A row of statuesque trees grew opposite, shutting out much of the traffic noise as well as the light, so her room was always dark. Because it was a cul-de-sac, the road attracted little traffic of its own.

So far, Tara had never gone out at night. There were too many troops about, creating a feeling of danger. She missed having conversations with people. She blamed herself for coming to Germany with such supreme confidence, expecting the country to suit *her*.

I shall give Berlin another two months, then go

340

home if things are no better by then, she decided. She had more than enough money to give Iggy back his five hundred dollars.

But where was home? New York, Hollywood, San Diego? They were places where her sisters and her father lived, where Milo was. She hadn't settled anywhere. In fact, of all the places she had been, London was the one where she'd been the happiest, but it meant living an entire ocean away from her family.

It was early afternoon – various clocks in the area had just tolled half one – when her reverie was disturbed by a commotion outside. She crossed to her first-floor window to see what was going on.

'*Oh, my God!*' She said the words out loud.

On the street outside, a gang of five soldiers were violently beating a middle-aged man with the butts of their rifles. His body was becoming more bloody by the minute. Having been beaten to the ground, he was now hardly moving.

Tara rushed from her room and was halfway down the stairs in a bid to rescue the man from his attackers, when the owner or manageress of the hotel, Frau Henschel, suddenly appeared at the bottom of the stairs, arms outstretched to stop her from going further.

'No, no, no,' she shouted.

'But they're killing him out there!' Tara protested.

The landlady didn't understand. 'No, no, no,' she repeated. She seized Tara's sleeve and dragged her into what looked like a parlour at the front of the house, where the curtains were drawn. Tara was pushed into a barely visible chair. The sound of the man outside being beaten (to death, Tara had to believe) could hardly be heard. She was aware her heart was beating wildly against the back of the chair.

Frau Henschel spoke to her in German, a long, angry tirade that Tara realised wasn't being directed at her but at the soldiers outside, for the woman kept gesturing towards the window, her eyes full of tears. She was about fifty, wearing a shapeless grey dress the same colour as her hair and a string of pearls that Tara had no way of telling were real or not. She had a pleasant grandmotherly face.

'I'm sorry,' Tara said meekly, as the rant continued, 'but I don't understand a word you are saying.'

The woman looked at her despairingly. She jumped to her feet and went into the hallway. Minutes later, she could be heard jabbering away on the telephone.

Tara leant back in her chair. Her eyes had become used to the unlit room with its closed curtains. She had never been in it before – the hotel business was conducted from a desk in an alcove beneath the stairs and the dining room was at the rear of the house. The only meal the hotel provided was breakfast, served by a young woman with waist-length plaits, who so far had not spoken a word to Tara, just fetching the simple breakfast as silently as a ghost.

This room was beautifully furnished in an old-fashioned way. The two armchairs and large settee were upholstered in black velvet, the carpet patterned with rust and black flowers, a grandfather clock ticked away against the wall next to a vast glass-fronted cupboard packed with delicate china dishes and silver ornaments. There was a vase of imitation red flowers and tall black feathers on each side of the black marble fireplace. It reminded Tara of her grandmother's parlour back in Dublin, though that had been much smaller and hadn't had so much black in it. For a brief moment she was carried back to her childhood, which felt part of another life altogether than the one she was living now.

Frau Henschel returned. She said something incomprehensible and then disappeared again. Minutes later she returned with a tray of tea things.

Two cups were poured, the milk jug was tapped with a spoon and Tara received a questioning look – in other words, did she want any? Tara nodded, then shook her head when the sugar was given a similar tap.

The landlady was nodding and making tutting noises. Tara somehow got the message that she wasn't to leave. They were waiting for someone, possibly the person who had been spoken to on the phone.

The doorbell rang, a deep, rusty sound – it needed oiling. The other woman almost shot through the ceiling, though she must have been expecting it to ring.

She left to open the front door and returned with a pretty woman around her own age, dressed more smartly in a navy blue and cream checked costume. She wore a little cocked hat sporting a felt bird. A black star had been sewn to the back of her jacket.

'Greta.' The landlady pointed at the new arrival. She pressed her hands against her chest. 'Katia.'

Tara did the same thing. 'Tara,' she said.

'Pleased to meet you, Tara.' Greta came and shook her hand, and Tara was so relieved at the idea of conversing in English that she almost cried.

'Katia and I are cousins,' Greta went on. 'Apparently you both had a most unpleasant experience this afternoon.'

Tara shuddered. 'It was horrible,' she concurred. Now that it was over, it was hard to believe it had actually happened.

'We know – knew – the gentleman concerned, the victim,' Greta said. 'He was a slight acquaintance. His name was Selinger and he was a Jew, as are myself and Katia.'

'I'm sorry,' Tara said uselessly. Virtually everyone in the world who could read a newspaper was aware of the way Adolf Hitler treated the Jews. Their property, their possessions and increasingly their lives were being taken away, destroyed at the whim of a vicious and dangerous dictator.

Katia said something to her cousin, who left the room with the tray.

'She's gone to make more tea.' Greta sat next to Tara on one of the black armchairs. 'We are widows, Katia and I,' she said. 'Both of us are anxious to leave Berlin and settle in the United States, where we have relatives.'

'When will you go?'

Greta smiled ruefully. 'Not till my cousin feels able to leave this house and everything in it. This is where she was born. This road, with such fine houses, was once considered one of the best places in Berlin to live. See that cabinet?' She pointed to the cupboard full of fine china and ornaments. 'The stuff in there is priceless and irreplaceable: dinner services, tea sets, fine porcelain, some of which is more than a hundred years old, even older. You will have heard of Limoges, Minton, Royal Doulton, Wedgwood. Our grandmother was a collector of figurines. Some of the items were given to Katia and Moritz when they were married. I do believe there is something of mine in there, but I've never been one for collecting. My little apartment in Jordanstraße is sparse compared with here. There is little I would want to take with me to America except for a few clothes.'

Tara remembered the clothes she'd left behind in London. 'Clothes can quickly go out of fashion,' she remarked.

'I would only take the fashionable ones with me.'

'How is it you speak such good English?' Tara asked. The woman had only the slightest of accents.

'My husband, Heinrich, was a diplomat. He served in Canada many years before the war. We returned in 1914 so he could fight for his country. He was killed within a year, as was Katia's husband, Moritz.' She sighed. 'We had been brides at about the same time and now we are both widows.' She dropped her eyes and stared at the carpet. 'Never, never in my whole life did I think

345

things would turn out the way they have; worse than the worst of my nightmares.'

By the next morning, Herr Selinger's body had been removed. As it had rained overnight, there was no sign that anyone had been slain directly outside Frau Henschel's house.

Greta arrived just after breakfast. She wore the same navy blue and cream costume with a different hat – a red beret. 'I do enjoy speaking English for a change,' she told Tara. 'But do you have the time? I mean, have you an occupation to go to? Why are you here, if you don't mind my asking? I don't want to be holding you up.'

'You're not,' Tara told her. 'I am a journalist. I came to Berlin to look for stories.'

'Well, there are plenty of stories to be found these days, mostly horror stories. Have you been sent by a newspaper?'

'No, I am freelance.'

'Are you American? I can't quite catch your accent.'

Tara felt as if she was being subjected to the third degree. 'I've lived in America for ten years, but I am, in fact, Irish,' she said. 'I was sent by a newspaper to London two years ago to write about the BUF – the British Union of Fascists.'

'Ah!' Greta's eyes brightened. 'That's interesting. Look, will you allow me to take you out to lunch? I talked with Katia and another cousin last night and we have a proposal to put to you.'

Half an hour later, Greta and Tara were seated in a dark corner of the Zur Letzten Instanz, the oldest restaurant in Berlin.

'The restaurant doesn't go all the way back to the thirteenth century,' Greta said, 'but bits of the building do.'

'It's very busy,' Tara remarked. 'We were lucky to get the last table.'

'We weren't lucky; I had booked the table early this morning. Now what would you like to eat, Tara?'

'You choose. I don't understand a word on the menu.' It was discomforting to feel so ignorant about everything.

Greta studied the menu and ordered roasted chicken, red cabbage, bread dumplings and potato salad, followed by apple cake and coffee for them both.

'Would you like wine?' she enquired.

'Only if you're having a glass,' Tara replied.

The waiter was requested to bring two glasses of Riesling. They sat back and waited for the meal, talking about casual things such as movies and books. Greta was impressed to learn that Tara had spent the last few months in Hollywood.

'You have led a fascinating life, Tara, for someone so young. I have always wanted to visit Hollywood – I should imagine most people do. But, you never know,' she smiled cheerfully, 'I might well get there one of these days.'

By then Tara was longing to know what the proposal was that Greta had for her. The meal was highly enjoyable, but she was glad when it was over and the woman began to explain.

'I said yesterday that my cousin, Katia, refuses to come with us to America because she is unwilling

347

to leave behind the precious items that our family has been accumulating for more than a century. We have another cousin, Heinrich, who lives not far from here and also wishes to leave the country. We have sworn to stay together – we Jews no longer have the self-belief and confidence that once we had.'

Tara made a little murmuring sound, as if to confirm she was listening.

Greta put her hand on her arm and said earnestly, 'If Katia packed all her treasures in a tea chest – or two or three tea chests – would you very kindly have them sent to New York once we were there? We can't risk taking them with us; it would be dangerous. The Nazis would almost certainly confiscate them and we might be prevented from leaving.'

'When would you go?' Tara enquired.

'There is a ship sailing from Hamburg in eight days' time that has room for us.'

'I would be only too pleased to help,' Tara said without hesitation. 'Will the packing be done before you leave?' The idea of so much as touching all that beautiful, expensive china terrified her.

Greta was nodding her head, smiling a little. 'Katia has already started – the boxes were delivered this morning, as well as tons of straw. She predicted you would agree to help us. She thinks you are a very nice young lady who looks like an angel.'

She took coins out of her purse and put them on the table for the waiter. 'In the meantime, Tara, the house and everything in it is yours. Heinrich and I have no intention of ever returning to Germany, and I suspect Katia will feel the same once we are settled. You can live there as long as you wish. I will give you the name of someone to tell when you decide to leave. It can still be a hotel and you can take on more guests, if you wish – it will provide an income for you. Zillah, the girl with the plaits who makes breakfast, will do the housework, though she would have to be paid.'

Tara wondered what she was letting herself in for, but she liked taking chances. She was only too pleased to agree.

It was almost a month later that a letter with a New York postmark arrived addressed to Tara, saying the boxes would be collected the following Monday.

She was relieved. While she and the boxes had been under the same roof, she had felt uneasy, even though they had been left safely in a down-stairs room and it was hard to imagine how they could have been harmed. She was pleased when Monday came, a van arrived, and the boxes and their precious contents were carefully stowed in the back and the van drove away. She wondered, once they arrived in America, how long would it take for everything to be unpacked and would Katia have a suitable place to put them?

She wrote an article about the three cousins and her role in their departure for the United States, starting with the incident outside The Alfred when Mr Salinger had been murdered. She described the desperation of her new friends, who were un-willing to give up treasures collected over several lifetimes in order to escape their German oppressors.

She submitted it to where she'd used to send her articles on the British Union of Fascists in London – the *Worldwide Voice*.

Then she decided it was time to do something about the hotel. There hadn't been a guest since the woman who'd left weeks ago, which wasn't surprising as there was no longer a card in the tobacconists advertising its existence. Tara wrote another to replace it, this time in English. It would be of mutual advantage to herself and the guests if they both spoke the same language.

She also took the opportunity, having nothing else to do, of writing to her sisters, to Milo and to Iggy, who had made her trip to Berlin possible. It was such a kind gesture, yet she regretted he had made it. She'd sooner be working as a waitress in Salome's diner any day.

It took a week before another guest arrived. He was, in fact, a Frenchman who'd lived in London and whose name was Louis. He was well dressed, exceptionally good-looking, with dark curly hair and lovely brown eyes.

'Whereabouts did you live in London?' Tara asked.

'Fulham,' he replied.

'I lived in Camden.' It was a place that held fond memories. 'Have you got a job here?'

'Yes, in a nightclub.' He raised his particularly fine eyebrows. 'Would you like references?'

'Good heavens, no. This isn't my hotel. I'm just looking after it for someone. Would you like a front room or a back one?'

'Whichever is the cheapest, darling.'

She was a bit put out by the 'darling'. 'All the rooms cost the same,' she told him, after making a quick decision.

'Then I'll have a front one.' He had a very cheeky smile.

At about nine o'clock that night Louis shouted that he was going out and could he please have a front door key?

'Of course,' she called. 'Here you are,' she said cheerfully when she opened the door and found Louis outside wearing a sequin-covered dress and a diamanté tiara on his dark curly hair that had grown an entire foot longer since that morning.

'Have a nice time,' she stuttered.

'Oh, I will, darling.' His smile held a touch of pity and Tara felt conscious of being left home alone while he was off to a nightclub to have a jolly good time. 'Tomorrow night,' he said, 'why don't you come with me? You don't look the sort of girl who should be staying in at night while there's still a nightclub left in the land.'

'OK. I'll come,' Tara said before she closed the door and surveyed the horribly empty room. She suddenly felt desperately lonely.

It was the next night and the club was down a dark narrow staircase, which was hung with a collection of mismatched mirrors that she glimpsed Louis and herself in more than a dozen times (she was wearing the green dress she'd been given by Harper's in New York). They descended into a place that Tara could well have imagined hell was like when she was a child. The walls of the club had been painted a glistening black and the numerous pillars strung with brightly coloured naked bulbs. She determined not to touch anything.

'Sit here, darling.' Louis had escorted her to the back of the room and gestured towards a chair in front of a tiny stage, where a man (or was it a woman?) in yellow satin was playing 'Begin the Beguine' on a white piano.

People were dancing. A man in an ordinary evening suit asked Tara to dance. She wanted to refuse but was too embarrassed. After all, why was she there if not to dance and enjoy herself? She longed to be back in her horribly lonely room. She had been to nightclubs before, but they were never like this.

Louis had put a drink on the table in front of where she'd been sitting. It was blue with a leaf floating on it. The man she was dancing with said, 'I've never seen you here before, sweetheart,' and she realised she was dancing with a woman.

There was an explosion in her head and she fell to the ground. Then all the coloured bulbs made popping noises and the world went black.

When Tara opened her eyes, she was lying on a bed in a small white room that she recognised was part of a hospital. Lots of voices were talking at once, both inside the room and in the corridor outside, and the sound was deafening. Her head was hurting. She touched it gingerly and found a bump. Apart from that, she was pretty sure she was all right.

'How are you feeling?' asked a voice.

Tara turned her head and found Agent Pete Green sitting beside her, wearing one of his flashy suits. There was something odd about the situation that she couldn't quite grasp. When she did, she said in astonishment, 'What on earth are you doing here?' The last time they'd seen each other was in Liverpool when she'd been on her way to Ireland to look for Milo.

His reply astonished her even more. It seemed the FBI had been keeping 'an eye on her' ever since she'd returned to the States. 'When we learnt you were off to Berlin,' Agent Green said, 'I thought we should keep an even closer eye. So I followed you. You're not safe on your own, Tara.' He shook his head sadly. 'You don't seem to have any sense of danger. Berlin's no place for a young woman by herself. Those three friends of yours, the ones planning to go to New York – well, none of them got there. They'll be in a German prison – or even dead – by now, and all those fancy dishes will be in the home of some Nazi bigwig.'

'Oh, no!' she cried, horrified. 'But how could that have happened?' Had she let the three cousins down in some way?

'You have a spy in your midst, Tara,' he said darkly. 'That girl, Zillah, has a brother in the army. She told him everything. I have no idea who sent you the letter from New York to say when the boxes would be collected, but it must have been one of Hitler's crowd.'

'What about Louis?' she asked. She reached for his hand, really glad that someone was there to

353

hold her own.

'I know nothing about Louis, other than that the guy's dead. Got caught in the blast that took out the nightclub – someone tossed a bomb down the stairs. Homosexuals, any sort of deviants, are no longer welcome in this country. You were well out of the way at the back and I was still outside.' He sighed. 'I think it's time you got out of Berlin, Tara, the same way you got out of London – in a rush, leaving your belongings behind. There's a train going from Lehrter Bahnhof station at ten o'clock this morning. If we catch it, we can somehow make our way to Paris – and home.'

Chapter 22

27 December, 1937

It was Bernie Kelly's birthday and a party was being held in his honour at his daughter Patricia's house in San Diego. It was three o'clock in the afternoon and the sun was burning a hole in the sky. So far, only two of the girls were present. Aideen was lying on a blow-up thing at the foot of his deckchair, which had been strategically placed beneath a tree providing plentiful shade. Overhead, the birds were making tiny breathless noises, as if they too had been affected by the suffocating heat.

Inside the big, single-storey house it was quietly busy. The older children had transferred to the indoor pool, where it was considerably cooler, and the younger ones had been put down for their afternoon nap. Patricia was in the kitchen and, aided by Joyce, was preparing either a late lunch or an early dinner – no one was quite sure how to describe it. The smells from the kitchen weren't the sort you would expect on such a summery day. Chicken and potatoes were being roasted, plum pudding was being boiled, custard prepared, as well as gravy and chestnut stuffing.

It was Christmas dinner. There were crackers to pull, paper hats to be worn, and a magician booked to arrive when the meal was over.

'What would you like to eat most in the world at your birthday party, Daddy?' Patricia had asked when she brought up the idea of them having a do.

'I really fancy having a proper Christmas dinner, girl,' Bernie had replied. There was something distinctly unChristian about having salad and nothing but cold food over the Christmas period.

'It'll lie really heavy on your stomach,' Patricia warned, but Bernie didn't care. Nothing would feel right again until he'd eaten a proper dinner, which would hopefully happen in the next hour or so.

Sounds were muffled, as if the world had been covered with a layer of cotton wool. Bernie would have loved to have fallen asleep, but his brain refused to stop thinking. Where am I at now? he wondered. What would happen tomorrow and over the rest of his life? What exactly was it all about?

After he'd been living a full year at Patricia's house in San Diego, Bernie had reckoned it was safe enough to write to three of his old, most trustworthy mates in Dublin telling them he was alive and well, knowing they would never give him away: Patrick Adams, Ray Walsh and Dick O'Neill.

At university, more than once the four young men had solemnly sworn to honour their commitments to each other, occasionally in lousy Latin, mixing blood with blood, going down on one knee, hand on heart, and usually pissed out of their minds.

All three had responded to his letters with letters of their own, saying how thrilled they were to know he was still alive – in fact, they'd never truly believed he was dead – and Jesus himself must have been breathing heavily on him all this time, keeping him alive, and would he be back in Dublin soon for the mother of all parties?

Not yet, lads, Bernie had replied. *Don't forget, I'm still a criminal in the eyes of the police.*

There was still, after all, the matter of the ten thousand Irish pounds owing to the new – well, newish, by now – Earl of Graniston to be resolved. The old friends had been exchanging letters ever since and there'd even been a few phone calls, though they'd cost the earth. Yet Bernie's calls had gone unnoticed on his daughter's phone bills.

A letter from Roy Walsh had arrived just before Christmas. It read:

Dear Bernie,

I went to a Christmas do at our old rugby club the other night and who should be there but Richard Heath, who these days is known more impressively as the Earl of Graniston, the guy whose inheritance you allegedly squandered at various gaming tables back in the mists of time. He's back living in Dublin.

You didn't say, Bernie boy, that you'd repaid him the missing money and he'd instructed the police to get off your back. He was perfectly happy with how things stood. After all, he said, 'Bernie was a mate. He'd helped me out of a few scrapes in the past.' (It's not exactly the sort of thing you expect an earl to say, but getting a title clearly hasn't gone to the chap's head.)

Roy went on to tell Bernie one of the dirtiest jokes he'd ever heard and finished by wishing him a Merry Christmas and a Happy New Year, signing off, *Your old mate, Roy.*

It could only have been Leo, his son-in-law, who'd paid off the sodding earl.

Jaysus! Yet again – it happened every time he thought about it – Bernie felt tears spring to his eyes. He could have cried forever. He'd been a lousy father and an even lousier father-in-law. He'd never considered Leo up to much, but it turned out the guy had really turned up trumps after all – though it would have helped a lot had he bothered to tell Bernie about his astoundingly generous act, rather than leave it for him to find out himself years later.

'Are you all right, Daddy?' Aideen's head appeared at the foot of his lounger. 'You're breath-

357

ing heavily, like you're about to cry.'

'Well, I suppose I might shed a tear or two as the day wears on. After all, love, I'm flamin' sixty,' Bernie said, with a throb in his voice. 'I mean, it's the start of the last stage of me life. From now on I'll be an old bugger. The only thing to look forward to is death.'

'Oh, Daddy!' Aideen was shocked. 'Don't be so silly. You don't look sixty, and you certainly don't act sixty.'

'You're a good girl, Aideen.' He recalled the night he'd rescued her from that gang of crooks in Atlantic City, the ones who'd laid into the sweet guy who was her husband and caused him to lose an eye. He had kept some pretty weird company in those days.

'Are you short of a few bob at the minute?' Bernie asked her now. The sweet guy hadn't had a job since. 'Won't you and Humphrey be wanting a house of your own quite soon?' They already had one kid and Aideen was expecting another in May.

Aideen looked at him with narrowed eyes. She was either surprised or suspicious. 'What have you been up to, Daddy?' She was definitely suspicious.

'Nothing, love,' he replied, his own eyes wide with innocence.

Except that, in the not too distant future, investors in Glendower Island Properties would be expecting their share of the yearly profit, only to be bitterly disappointed to find there were no returns – indeed, there were no properties to boast of either, nor was there an island. Nor was there a chance in hell of the swindle being traced back to him.

'Me and Humphrey don't want to buy a house, Daddy,' Aideen said. 'We'll always live with Humphrey's parents. I get on with Mary as well as I'd get on with me own mother. But thanks all the same. It's really generous of you to offer.'

Bernie reached down and patted her red hair. Now he was feeling all choked up again. Life just wasn't fair, and he was partly the cause of it, taking advantage of their naivety, taking them to live in New York when they were expecting to live in Liverpool. Yet they'd generously welcomed him back into their lives when he'd chosen to reappear.

'Our Tara and Milo should be here soon,' Aideen reminded him. 'They're coming in a car from Hollywood.'

Bernie was looking forward to seeing Tara, but not his son, with whom he still felt distinctly uncomfortable. 'Milo doesn't like me,' he grumbled.

'Who can blame him, Daddy?' Aideen said severely, leaving no room for argument. 'I wouldn't like you if you'd done to me what you did to him.' She recovered her good humour in a flash. 'Would you like a drink?' she asked, smiling.

'I'd like a bottle of Guinness, darlin',' he said. Patricia had ordered a crate of milk of the angels from Boston, a city favoured by the Irish. He couldn't for the life of him understand why his daughters thought as much of him as they did.

Two hours later, a silver limousine glided through the gates and Tara, Milo and two men Bernie had never seen before stepped out. Bernie could never get over the beauty of his youngest daughter. She was wearing white, her golden hair smoothed back into a chignon on her slender neck. She was the image of his late wife, who he never thought about nearly as often as he should.

Milo made a face at him and went indoors. Tara threw her arms around his neck, 'Hello, Daddy.' The other two men stood respectfully in the background, waiting to be introduced.

Bernie felt tearful again. Jaysus, his emotions were all over the place today. 'Hello, me darlin' girl,' he said thickly.

She stepped back, her arms still around him. 'Daddy, I've got a surprise for you,' she cried. 'I'm married. This is my husband, Igor Dmitriyey, better known as Iggy.'

The two men standing behind her were as different to each other as chalk and cheese. The younger man was blond and engagingly handsome. He wore white flannels, a striped blazer and a straw hat at a rakish angle. The other man, huge with bulging muscles, looked as if he was his bodyguard. Also handsome in his own tough way, but vastly different.

Yet it was he who stepped forward, towering over Bernie, as he shook his hand. 'Pleased to meet you, sir,' he said in a respectful tone.

Sir! Bernie felt about a hundred years old. 'Pleased to meet you, too,' he stammered. He wondered if perhaps Tara had introduced the wrong husband.

But apparently not. 'Oh, and Daddy–' she pointed to the other visitor '–that's Marty Moore. He's making a movie in Hollywood. When we first came to America, he went out with our Patricia.'

360

She danced away, holding her giant husband's hand.

'You wouldn't believe just how tender he is,' she wanted to say to her sisters minutes later when she introduced them to Iggy. 'Just how soft and incredibly gentle.' It moved her in a way no man had ever done before and all she wanted was to stay in his arms for ever. And his politics matched her own. Christopher and Edwin would have approved of the marriage.

But she could see on Patricia and Aideen's faces, just as she had on Daddy's, an expression of dismay and a complete lack of understanding as to why she had married her darling Iggy.

They had arrived just in time. The table was already set, there was a Christmas tree in the corner of the room, and the curtains had been closed so the lights could be seen twinkling on the branches.

There was an odd atmosphere. Tara almost felt as if they were back in Ireland, in Dublin; that any minute a choir would start singing Irish songs on the wireless and it would be freezing cold outside. They would sit down to a hearty meal, the same as they'd had every year since she could remember, alongside old aunts and uncles, and there would be heaps of presents beneath the tree.

But then Patricia shouted, 'Sit down, everyone,' and Tara blinked herself back to the present day. Iggy was there and Daddy had become an old man.

The meal was over. The house was mainly silent

361

while the adults slept off the weight of starchy potatoes, suet pudding, creamy trifle and too much wine. The children lay on their beds, dozing off and waking up, wondering if the day was over. Would they be allowed back in the pool?

Patricia couldn't have slept a wink until all the dishes had been washed, dried and put away on the shelves in their various cupboards. In this, she was aided by Marty Moore, star of stage and screen, who had thought he'd left his dish-drying days long behind him.

'You could have got someone in to do all this,' he commented as he picked up a giant metal roasting dish to dry. 'Don't you have servants?'

'Yes, but I prefer to do it meself,' Patricia said. 'Besides which, I enjoy it. And it keeps me in touch with me roots.'

'I must say,' Marty said thoughtfully, 'I think I was happier back in Manhattan with Pop, Poppa and the shop – and you.' He went on. 'Being successful is a bit frantic and you're never sure if people are only pretending to like you and being nice because their job depends on it. I feel as if I'm continually putting on an act. I thought I was in love with your Tara, but *that* was just an act.'

'On your part or hers?'

'Oh, mine,' Marty emphasised. 'I wasn't exactly upset when she turned me down. I think I was only attracted to her because she wasn't attracted to me.'

Patricia smiled. 'Poor Marty.' She agreed with what he'd said about Manhattan. 'I enjoyed us going out together,' she said. 'You were my very first boyfriend. And please don't tell me I was your first girlfriend because I know it's not true.'

He frowned. 'Why did we split up?'

Patricia couldn't remember and neither could he. 'Maybe we just got bored with each other,' she suggested. 'I'm glad we did, else I wouldn't have met Leo, who was the love of my life.'

Marty sighed. 'Maybe we could get together again? If I had a wife, it would stop women throwing themselves at me. They send passionate letters along with items of their underwear.'

'What?' Patricia laughed. 'It wouldn't do your image much good, getting together with a woman with eight children. Do you know,' she went on in a low voice, in case there was an eavesdropper around, 'I planned on having ten. I thought that was a nice round figure. Leo would have approved.' She smiled nostalgically. 'He really loved the children.'

'*We* could have the other two.' Marty put down the jug he was drying and slipped his arms around Patricia's waist – much plumper now than the last time he'd done it. 'Think about it,' he whispered.

Patricia giggled. 'I'm thinking about Clark Gable or Douglas Fairbanks taking on a widow with an extra-large family and it makes me want to laugh.'

'Think about it with me,' Marty urged. 'That's all I ask.'

'All right,' Patricia said meekly. 'I'll think about it.'

Bernie was wandering around the garden looking for someone to talk to that was over the age of twelve. He came across his son, Milo, who was reading a script while perched on a swing, rocking

363

himself slightly to and fro.

'Is that one of your own?' he asked nervously, while keeping well out of reach of Milo's fists.

'Yah,' Mio said tersely.

'Have you got anywhere with your writing, like.'

'No, I haven't got anywhere,' Milo snapped.

'You should come back and write in Ireland, lad. Ireland is the birthplace of some of the world's most famous writers: George Bernard Shaw, for one, Samuel Beckett, William Congreve, Sean O'Casey. There's some say Shakespeare was an Irishman. There's something in the air.' All of a sudden Bernie was hit with a desire to be back home, walking on the green, green grass of Phoenix Park, meeting his mates for a dram and a jangle after Mass on Sundays. 'I miss it, home.' He was close to tears again.

'So do I,' Milo said surprisingly. 'I'd sooner be in Dublin any day than Hollywood.' Though he'd definitely like to come back one day.

'Would you now?' Bernie took an envelope out of his pocket and held it out towards his son. Milo slowed down the swing until it was no longer moving. He opened the envelope and took out the contents – three photographs – and studied them.

'This is our old house in Dublin,' he said in surprise. 'When did you take them?'

'I didn't take them; an old friend did. I only got them the other day. It's up for sale.'

Milo looked at him, smiling slightly. 'Our house? I thought it was only rented.'

'It was, but now it's for sale. I thought I might

buy it. What d'you say, Son, about coming back with me? Doing your writing there like so many other successful Irish writers?'

Milo gave his father the sort of look that Aideen had done, a mixture of surprise and suspicion. 'But where would the money come from, Dad?'

'Don't ask, lad.' Bernie winked and tapped his nose. 'Just don't ask.'

The publishers hope that this book has given you enjoyable reading. Large Print Books are especially designed to be as easy to see and hold as possible. If you wish a complete list of our books please ask at your local library or write directly to:

Magna Large Print Books
Magna House, Long Preston,
Skipton, North Yorkshire.
BD23 4ND

This Large Print Book for the partially sighted, who cannot read normal print, is published under the auspices of

THE ULVERSCROFT FOUNDATION

THE ULVERSCROFT FOUNDATION

... we hope that you have enjoyed this Large Print Book. Please think for a moment about those people who have worse eyesight problems than you ... and are unable to even read or enjoy Large Print, without great difficulty.

You can help them by sending a donation, large or small to:

**The Ulverscroft Foundation,
1, The Green, Bradgate Road,
Anstey, Leicestershire, LE7 7FU,
England.**
or request a copy of our brochure for more details.

The Foundation will use all your help to assist those people who are handicapped by various sight problems and need special attention.

Thank you very much for your help.